THE ACCIDENTAL TURN SERIES
BOOK ONE

The Untold Tale

J.M. Frey

REUTS PUBLICATIONS

Cover design by Ashley Ruggirello
Cover art from ftourini/Riverd-Stock/gd08 on DeviantArt.com
Book design by Ashley Ruggirello
Map by Christopher Winkelaar

Paperback ISBN: 978-1-942111-28-3
Electronic ISBN: 978-1-942111-27-6

REUTS Publications
www.REUTS.com

For Gabrielle Harbowy, who began as my first acquiring editor and grew into a remarkable advocate, cheerleader, and friend. I'm so blessed to have someone so positive, so ambitious, so clever, and so kind on my side in this journey.

Also by J.M. Frey

Novels
Triptych (Dragon Moon Press, 2011)

Novellas
(Back) (SilverThought Press, 2008)
The Dark Side of the Glass (Double Dragon Press, 2012)

Short Stories
"*The Once and Now-ish King*" in *When the Hero Comes Home*
    (Dragon Moon Press, 2011)
"*On His Birthday, Reginald Got*" in *Klien*
    (FutureCon Publications, 2011)
"*Maddening Science*" in *When the Villain Comes Home*
    (Dragon Moon Press, 2012)
The Dark Lord and the Seamstress
    (CS Independent Publishing, 2014)
"*The Twenty Seven Club*" in *Expiration Date*
    (EDGE Publishing, 2015)
"*The Moral of the Story*" in *Tesseracts 18: Wrestling With Gods*
    (EDGE Publishing, 2015)
"*Zmeu*" in *Gods, Memes, and Monsters* (Stone Skin Press, 2015)
"*How Fanfiction Made Me Gay*" in *The Secret Loves of Geek Girls*
    (Bedside Press, 2015)

Anthologies
Hero Is a Four Letter Word (Short Fuse, 2013)

Academic
"*Whose Doctor?*" in *Doctor Who In Time And Space*
    (McFarland Press, 2013)

The Sigil that Never Fades

The Quill that Never Dulls

The Cup that Never Runs Dry

The Parchment that Never Fills

The Blade that Never Fails

The Desk that Never Rots

The Spirit that Never Lies

With these tools our world was born,

And with them can be broken.

Or born again.

One

 am upstairs when I catch sight of the approaching cart and its cargo through the thick glass of my window. I assume the body in the back is a corpse, brought to me for study and then burial.

But no one handles a corpse with such care; the driver is directing the horse to travel slowly, avoiding each hole in the dirt road. They also do not stop to pick up a healer for a corpse. Yet Mother Mouth is in the back, hunched as best she is able over the blanket-wrapped body.

By the time I make it down the grand staircase to the foyer, three of my Men are lifting the bundle from the cart with careful concern. I gesture to the threshold, and they lower it onto my front step. As soon as they set the body down, I can see that my assumption was correct.

It is a young woman.

And she is still alive. But only barely. I contain my shudder of revulsion, clamping my teeth down hard on my tongue to keep from gagging. I think I am only successful because I've seen this sort of thing before.

Bootknife has flayed her very prettily.

Artistic tendrils of bloody ivy are torn into the vellum of the young woman's flesh. I can only see a little of the pattern, however, from between the blanket's folds. Bootknife has written spells and agony into the muscle he's carved, into the wounds left by the strips he filleted from her. It's as detailed as any woodcarving for a stamp—some deep; some wide and shallow; some the merest scrape, only a layer or two of skin absent. Disgustingly beautiful. But it is not art.

It is torture.

She is unconscious. A blessing. I can't imagine how much the young woman must have been screaming before my Men forced poppy milk down her throat. Well, I suppose I *can* imagine it—I have seen quite enough of Bootknife's handiwork to be able to envision her pain. What I mean is that I do not *want* to imagine it. I can't bear the thought of the sounds that must have ripped her throat bloody.

She is as wrapped in rough blankets as she can be with such extensive injuries to her back. The blankets are filthy and crusted with blood and other bodily fluids, which means they were probably the only protection against the chill spring morning that her rescuers could find. I clench my hands into fists and jam them into the pockets of my house robe to keep from rushing forward and helping. *A Chipping Master does not dirty his hands in labor.* I hear the invective in my father's hateful voice in my head, and I take great pleasure in telling it to go drown itself.

All the same, I stay back. I would only be in the way.

Mother Mouth assesses the young woman's injuries, and when she is done, we ensure together that there are no Words of Tracing carved into the victim's skin.

It would not do to give our enemies such advantageous leverage as to lead them here. To the unknowing, my home appears to be no more than the manor of silly, crumpled Forsyth Turn, younger brother to the great hero Kintyre and a man quite stodgily attached to his library. And those on the outside must *remain* unknowing. Even the slightest slip would bring the Viceroy down on my Chipping, and I will not have the people under my care endangered.

I do not bother to ask why my Men brought the woman to me and not to the king; if the king had the security and ability to protect himself and those in his charge from the Viceroy, he would never have secretly employed me as his Shadow Hand.

There is nowhere safer for the injured visitor than Turn Hall. Not even Kingskeep.

Assessment done, they take the woman inside. I catch the attention of my butler and order a wing of my home that I have not entered in years be opened specifically for my surprise guest.

It has been a long time since there's been a need for lady's chambers in Turn Hall. They have remained shut since my mother's death. It has been even longer still since the need for a lady's maid; my staff are nearly all men. This is not out of preference, but because there are no women in my household who require women servants, and it made sense to leave the town's supply of employable young misses for houses where they were more needed.

I am going to have to find a woman. Blast.

We linger in the hallway outside the room long enough for servants to strip the dusty bed linens and replace them with fresh. I dismiss my Men to write up their debriefing reports, and then help Mother Mouth lay the young lady on the bed myself. The only way we figure she will be comfortable is belly-down, her face propped to the side with a feather pillow.

Once she is installed on the bed, I step back into a corner to remain out of the way. Mother Mouth takes a short breather—she is no longer young; her skin is papery thin and scored with laughter lines, but still glows with vitality—and all this rushing and lifting has winded her. She then ties her silver-streaked hair back and begins the careful work of spreading tinctures and ointments, mixing potions meant to neutralize spells and remove pain before she starts cutting away, with gentle knife work, the meat that has rotted from neglect.

My staff moves around them both in an orchestrated dance, fetching lamps and candles and water in an ewer; bringing in, using, and then removing brooms and cleaning supplies; opening windows and laying a fire in the hearth. I do as I always do, what I am best at doing: I observe.

When Mother Mouth finally sits back, a smear of blood on her forehead where she pushed a stray tendril of hair out of her face, I offer her a handkerchief. It is russet, the color associated with House Turn, my family. She takes it graciously, though she wrinkles her nose at the fineness of the fabric.

"We've had this discussion before," she says. "Good silk should be saved for dressing wounds, and rough cotton for wiping faces and noses."

"I agree, Mother," I allow, a smile sitting in the corner of my mouth and trying so very hard to stretch into the rest of it. "However, there *are* expectations at court, and when one's work relies on creating a good impression, the silk must be used for snot."

"And that's why I've no use for court."

Mother Mouth rises and goes to the bag of medicines she left on the bedside table. She pulls out phials and jars, each neatly labeled in her spiky hand. She is leaving behind tinctures and syrups to add to my young visitor's wine when she wakes in pain, along with bandages and ointments enough to cover the whole of the vicious patterns on her back several times over.

"Right, then, my boy," Mother Mouth says, standing and cleaning her bloody hands at the washstand. "Let the lass sleep it through, and I'll return in the morning to assess her healing. I tell you, I wouldn't want to be her right now. Keep her asleep if you're able, lad. And send for me at once should she turn feverish or her wounds begin to fester and reek," she finishes.

"No stitches?" Mother Mouth has sewn each of my Men up at one point or another, myself included. There are none among the Shadow's Men who do not bare the gratefully earned signature of her needle. It seems odd now that she is not doing the same for our guest.

"No," Mother Mouth agrees. "The slices that remain open are shallow. Where they are also narrow, there is no need. Where they are wide . . ." She shrugs. "I could not make the skin meet over the exposed muscle without tearing it. The rest of the deep cuts have begun to scar already. Better to cover it over with the salve, and with Words, and leave it to nature."

I nod, well used to this particular healer's pointed and honest instructions—she is the best within an hour's ride from my keep, and thus my preferred go-to healer. My Men and I call her Mother Mouth because of her bluntness, her willingness to bully us verbally into obeying her commands, and we always do so with a smile, and to her face. She has another name, but has long since gamely resigned herself to this one.

"I will reapply both salve and spells personally when it is t-t-time," I promise.

"Oh now," Mother Mouth scolds playfully. "None of that, my boy. No need to be nervous. It's just a woman and a bit of blood."

"I'm not ne-nervous of her," I say.

She pats my arm. "Of course not. You're a good boy, Master Turn."

I pretend to bristle at the juvenile endearment, but it secretly pleases me. Mother Mouth has known me my entire life. She pulled both my elder brother and I from our mother. She set my broken arm when Kintyre dared me to climb an orchard tree to the top. She put her hands into my brother's guts after his first run-in with a goblin brigade and held them in place until the Words of Healing could take hold. She closed my mother's eyes after a fever took the Lady Turn away. She called my father's corpse a silly shit while she cleaned it the day he drank himself into a tumble down the foyer staircase and into his own grave. She has more than earned the right to call me her "good boy," should she so choose. And I always do my best to live up to it.

Mother Mouth packs her small case and takes her leave. When my staff has finished ferrying ewers of both hot and cool water, wine, a modest bowl of broth, fresh candles, towels, my mother's newly cleaned dressing robe, my mother's slippers, and my portable writing desk into the room, I dismiss them to their suppers.

One last young lady lingers at the door, and she must be freshly arrived for she does not wear russet livery. I do not know her, and she seems eager to be of help, which is extremely encouraging. She is slim, her hands rough and calloused, giving her the appearance of one who looks like she works hard, and her apron is very starched. She resembles Cook—same rigidly marshaled brown hair, same firm lines around her eyes, very competent and very discreet. She waits silently on the threshold, obviously waiting for me to speak first.

"Hello," I say. "Yes?"

"Sir," she says and bobs a curtsy. "My mother sent for me when she heard you had a lady guest, sir. Figured you'd want a girl in, sir."

"Very good of her to take the initiative. Well come, and well stayed." I take a moment to go to my portable desk and scribble upon a fresh piece of paper. When the ink is dry, I fold up the note. "Your name, miss?" I ask.

"Neris, sir."

"Can you read, Neris?"

"Yes, sir. Of course, sir."

"Excellent. Here." I hold out my hand. In it are a letter and a small sack of gold coins. She takes both.

"I would like you to return to your usual household with this and give both to your mistress. The envelope contains an apology letter to your employer, and this should be enough coin to replace the wages she's already paid you this week. I would have you here until you are no longer needed at Turn Hall. And I will pay double whatever your current employer offers. Is that acceptable?"

She smiles, and there must be her father, for Cook's face does not have such fetching dimples. "Oh, yes sir!"

"And I invite you to move your things into the Hall come morning. Unless you have another billit you prefer?" I ask. She shakes her head. "Very well. Ask your mother for Turn-russet livery when you return, and we'll get you set up in the maid's quarters. Though, ah, you may be alone there."

"I'm not afraid of the dark and the quiet, Master Turn," she says, dropping a curtsy and vanishing in that lovely discreet way of lady's maids the world over. It's a vastly underprized skill.

My new guest and I are now alone.

My skin prickles at the thought of being trapped in a room with a person I know so very little about—I am not used to being the one on poor footing—and I go to the window to try to relieve the pressing sense of claustrophobia. It is silly; she is unconscious and, thanks to the poppy milk, will remain so for a good long while. I have nothing to fear from her.

Still. She is an unknown factor, and I do not like those in the least.

There is a *reason* I'm the king's Shadow Hand. Who better for a spymaster than the man who becomes physically agitated when he feels ignorant?

The sky outside has turned an ashy blue. Rain is on the horizon, and the breeze is picking up accordingly. I open the sash just enough to allow in the fresh wet air, but not enough for raindrops when they finally start to fall. The puff of breeze against my chest, fluttering my shirt and Turn-russet robe, gives me a false sense of safety—I have an exit if I need one.

The breeze also flutters the heavy velvet drapes. Dust puffs out of the folds and onto the wooden floor. My mother was of House Sheil, and so much of the décor in her chambers is a deep, dark purple—the throw rugs, the comfortable upholstered chairs by the hearth, the bedding, all of it is patterned with curling designs of lilac and lavender and deepest indigo. It has been years, perhaps a whole decade, since my father had Mother's chambers shut up. I suddenly realize how much I have missed purple.

The cloud cover is blocking so much of the sun that the room has become gloomy, and the details of the woman hard to catch. I make a second circuit for candles, which I light with a twig from the small fire in the hearth. Then I set the kettle Cook left on the mantelpiece onto the hook attached to the flume and wait for it to boil. A hot drink on a gray day is always a comfort, and the air in my mother's chambers is dry from being shut up for so long, so the steam will do us both some good.

Now to take care of this silly fear; I will observe the woman and decipher what I can of her, so that the anxiousness can finally dissipate long enough for me to get some paperwork done. I pull one of the chairs that stand before the fireplace over to the bedside, and settle into the lush padding. Then I *look*.

The first thing that registers is that she is in pain, despite the sleep brought on by the poppy milk. It is obvious by the creases in her forehead and the set of her jaw. Her hair is matted with sweat and other fluids that I do not wish to consider closely. Perhaps I dismissed

Neris too hastily—my guest could certainly do with a wash, if only for her own comfort. But I am not certain that it would not have caused her more agony, so perhaps it is best to wait until the young woman is awake and aware and able to help the maid.

Beyond that, I have no concept of who she is or where she may be from. Any clues that might have come from her clothing were lost when Bootknife cut them off her. Her ears are pierced, but there are no jewels from which to read her origins or history, no rings, no signets, no torques. *How galling!*

Her features resemble those of no family I know, which is impressive, as I have a very good head for faces. Her mouth is a small moue of pain, neither generous of plumpness nor waspish or thin. She has lines around the corners that indicate that she laughs heartily and frequently. Her cheeks are higher than I am used to and smooth, sprinkled with freckles. Her skin is dusky in tone, quite similar to the color possessed by the outdoor laborers from the Flung Isles after a season's work, but not so reddish. Hers is closer to the hue of well-cared for honeywood, made even more yellow in tone by the Sheil-purple of the blankets surrounding her. Her nose is short, adorable in a way that many women curse for being too childish looking. Her lashes are dark, and her eyes sweep upward at the outer edges.

I can tell by the curve of her exposed back, where it swells into her hips and the sides of her breasts, that she's never starved, never seen a rough harvest or overlong winter.

In summary, she must be a well-off merchant's daughter, and quite possibly yet another merchant's wife. I would say a nobleman's, but she cannot be the child of any nobleman I know from court, legitimate or not.

She could be from another, distant kingdom beyond the borders of Hain, but I have met much of the nobility from Urland and Gadot, as well as a few from Brystal, and she does not bear the trademark of any house that I know; her skin is either too light or too dark, her eyes too round or not round enough, her nose too snubbed or too high, her chin too round.

In short, the collection of her features does not come together to spell out her parentage.

Infuriating.

And fantastic. I am intrigued, instantly. How long has it been since I have been gifted with such a *mystery*? And that she was imprisoned by the Viceroy for so long without my knowing he had kidnapped *anyone* . . . was holding anyone *at all*. It was only an accident of circumstance that she was even rescued, that I even know she exists. The Viceroy had been raiding magical archives and libraries the world over, and when I had put together the picture the sorts of tomes he was stealing painted, I ordered my Men to raid and retrieve. That they had also found *her* was sheer coincidence.

At least, I believe it is an accident. I cannot imagine any person would allow such agony to befall them for the sake of gaining my pity and entrance to my Hall. Spies usually do not bleed.

I cannot recall the last time something like this happened accidentally in my work, and my heart flutters against my ribs.

The entire situation is completely astounding. Magnetic. Incredible. And so impotently frustrating that I cannot know more, cannot have my curiosity slaked immediately. I wish she were awake to answer my many questions.

The only thing I can know for sure is that the Viceroy wanted something from her, and she refused to give it to him. I cannot guess what it might have been, for he has the power to take anything he wants—even her, had he so chosen. Mother Mouth did not say anything about signs of a violation, but perhaps she wanted to be delicate while my staff was in the room and means to discuss it with me in the morning. The woman in my mother's bed is pretty enough; the Viceroy likes the pretty ones.

To resist the Viceroy for as long as this woman did, to keep her secrets for so many days that the pattern on her back had the time to grow so complex, must have taken real strength of spirit. As much as she must have been screaming, she'd never told him what it was he sought to learn.

I admire her greatly all of a sudden. There are very few who can keep secrets behind their teeth when Bootknife's art is in their flesh.

That makes her beautiful to me.

It does not matter how her features are arranged; her will is strong. And, as it was Bootknife she was resisting, I can hope that her morals are also true. I allow myself to follow the soft curve of her pain-paled cheek with my eyes, the delicate protrusion of the tendons in her neck, the place where her breast presses into the blankets and is hidden under her body. I am struck with a sudden swelling of attraction, and I stomp it back viciously.

No. A woman as remarkable as this, unexpectedly arriving at Turn Hall? There is only one explanation—she is for Kintyre. Women like this are always for Kintyre.

The kettle over-boils. Water foams into the fire with an indignant hiss, bringing me back to gloomy reality, and I make myself a pot of tea. Then I settle back into my chair, my portable desk on my lap and an afternoon's worth of tedious paperwork stacked on its surface.

The only sounds to break the silence are the sputtering of the candles arrayed around the room, the slow tap of the rain just beginning to fall against the roof of the manor, and the pained, almost inaudible whimpers my guest exhales with each labored breath.

I dip my quill into my ink pot and add the scratch of a nib on parchment to the quiet symphony of pain.

✍

"Oh," the woman whispers, dry lips rasping against the silk pillow casing. "It's you."

I have fallen asleep in my chair, and the quiet murmur of her voice yanks me back to wakefulness so quickly that my portable desk clatters to the floor. Ink sprays across the wood and splashes over the Sheil-purple rug beside the bed. I wince. *Oh, Mother's rug!* It will take my staff a terrible amount of scrubbing to clean it.

There is nothing I can do about it at the moment, so I right the pot, step around the spreading puddle and toppled papers, and go to her side.

"Greetings," I say. "Water?" I'm not certain how I'll get the cup to her lips without spilling all over the pillow or forcing her to sit up, which will be a special new agony in and of itself.

She nods and presses upward on her hands, grimacing but holding herself there until I manage to tip the earthenware cup against her mouth. She sips slowly, grunting as her arms tremble. When the water is gone, she flops back down into the pillow and doesn't hold back the yelp that such an action causes. It makes anger froth beneath the surface of my own skin, to realize that she has learned how to move with such injuries in order to drink. That Bootknife must have *made* her learn.

And that I have been unable to spare her that pain in Turn Hall. I've failed my first task as her guardian already.

She shivers all over, and my first instinct is to cover her snugly with the blanket. But that would irritate her wounds and allow fibers into the open ones, so instead I put the kettle back on the hook, stoke the fire back to life, and close the windows. Air that was fresh and crisp at sunset has become biting.

She watches it all with eyes that are a very normal, boring shade of muddy green, yet sparkle with keen observation. As I first noted, they are ever so slightly cat-like, turned up at the outside in a manner that I have never seen; though, it is even more pronounced with her eyes open. I have never been on the receiving end of such an intent gaze before.

She watches the same way that I watch.

I fidget until the kettle hisses, welcoming the excuse to duck out from under her odd gaze. As I pour the boiling water into the bowl my staff has left beside the ewer, mixing in the room temperature water until the heat is bearable, I cannot help but ponder on the strangeness of the young woman's eyes.

Perhaps it is about her eyes . . . ? I recall that the Viceroy has a sickeningly obsessive fascination with Sir Bevel, who is plain but has eyes such a dark blue that they are an anomaly. The Viceroy often threatens to pluck them out and have them rosined for a cloak brooch. It would be very much like him to pick this woman simply because of the unique almond-shape of her eyes. But, then again, that makes no sense at all, for what would Bootknife have tortured her for if the Viceroy had only wanted to collect—possibly *extract*—a piece of her?

This cyclone of reasoning is near to making me dizzy. Instead of dwelling on answers I cannot deduce alone and cannot ask for now, I sit on the side of the bed with the bowl and a cloth.

"May I?"

"Sure," she rasps. "This is so unreal."

"Your injuries are, in fact, quite real, I'm a-afraid," I say.

She stares at me for a moment, and then turns her head back into the pillow, purposefully obscuring her expression. For a brief moment, it seems as if her eyes are wet.

"I know," she mutters into the muffling fabric. "It's insane, but I know."

I dip the cloth into the bowl and begin to bathe her back, careful not to oversaturate it. It would not do for excess water to slip down her sides and soak into the bedding beneath her. The ointment has dried into a yellowish crust and must be wiped away carefully before reapplying. The warm water soothes her goose-pimpled skin, and she alternates between soft moans of gratitude and small hisses of pain caused by wounds suddenly being exposed to the air or jarred.

"I've never seen you like this before," she grunts as I lean close to concentrate on cleaning around a fanciful curlicue carved into the sweet dimples right above where her back swells into her buttocks. The latter are covered with a blanket to preserve her modesty, and I am careful not to jostle it.

"You've never met me before," I counter without looking up, soaking in every syllable of her speech. Her words are queerly broad. "How can you say that you have never seen me like . . . whatever it is that you mean by 'this.'"

"That's also the longest sentence I've ever heard from you."

What a deliciously strange accent! So flat and lacking the jumps and dips that fill the speech of Hain Kingdom's people. I've never heard anything like it before, which both thrills and shocks me. Knowledge is my currency; so how can she hail from a place that I do not know? How can such a place exist, as every clue she gives up suggests?

I am careful to school my expression, to not appear too thrilled or eager.

"Of course," I agree, "as you've only heard six. Eight, if you count the last one, and this one."

She turns her face into the pillow and groans. "I can't believe this is happening."

"Again, 'this,'" I say, because it's easier to look at her back and work on her wounds than look her in the face. I am ashamed to be causing her pain. It feels like a stab in my own gut.

Useless old Forsyth, as usual. But Mother Mouth asked me to have her fetched in the morning, not in the middle of the night. So I will muddle through, try my best, and hope that she does not chide me too much for the attempt at playing healer myself.

"Master Forsyth Turn, the king's Shadow Hand . . . boiling his own water and closing his own windows. Elgar Reed would be horrified."

I feel nauseous immediately.

Oh no, no, how does she know? No one, save my Men and Mother Mouth, is meant to know. The whole village thinks I am no more than the younger son, left behind to be the Master of Turnshire and surroundings, Lordling of the whole of the small but fertile Lysse Chipping; a man soft and slightly useless. That she *knows*, and speaks of it so *casually* . . .

A Shadow Hand must be secret above all else. The king will have me turned out—might even have me killed—for failing to maintain this secrecy. How can I function as Hain's spymaster if I am known?

"Oh," she says softly when my ministrations stop. "Oh, sorry. Shit. Sorry. I know, I know, it's not supposed to be talked about. I won't say anything else. I just meant, you know, you're the Master of Turn Hall. Shouldn't a maid be the one with the cloth? Shouldn't someone be here to open the windows and boil the kettle for you?"

"I am n-no lay-layabout. I am c-capable of do-do-doing it myself," I say, and I curse all the harder in my head when she cranes her neck around, wincing as the whip-fast movement stretches her wounds. She blinks at me like a stunned owl.

"Did you just *stutter*?"

"Of c-course n-n-n-not," I deny, but my words prove themselves liars. I bite my lower lip and scowl, fingers going so tight around the cloth that it creaks and water splashes down my arms, pooling uncomfortably into the bunches of fabric against the insides of my elbows. I *hate* that feeling.

"Oh my god, you stutter," she says, and her expression is a mixture of horror and amusement. "Reed never said anything about you stuttering."

"I do-do-do *not* stutter," I snap.

"Hey, no, it's cool," she says, rising up as if to turn to face me, but the motion makes everything in her back pull. She yelps again and flops back down to relieve the pain. "*Fuck!*" she screams into her pillow. She slams her fist against the mattress, clearly infuriated beyond coherence.

"S-stop," I say softly, setting aside the bowl and placing gentle hands on her right shoulder, the least cut up one.

She flinches away from my touch so dramatically that it looks more like a full body spasm.

"*Don't touch me!*" she screams.

I flinch myself, springing off the bed to give her the space she so clearly needs.

She goes still, save for her ragged breathing. One of the thin, deep cuts below her left shoulder blade seeps blood. A low coughing sound, muffled by the pillows, fills the air. I realize that she is sobbing.

Oh, Forsyth, you stupid man. You are useless at women.

"P-please s-stop crying." It sounds as stupid out loud as it did in my head, but I have no other way to convey my concern. Clearly my proximity is unwelcome.

I clench my fists and shove them into the pockets of my house robe, impotent in the face of her misery. Why is it that among spies and the dance of court politics I am assured and suave, but the moment I remove the mask of the Shadow Hand and become simple Forsyth Turn, I am such a useless, stuttering sack of skin? I hate it.

Eventually, the tears wind down and she turns her face to me. Her muddy green eyes have become bright, even though the skin around them is red and swollen.

"I'm sorry," she says.

"Why are *you* ap-ap-apologizing?"

"I didn't mean to make you uncomfortable about the stutter. I was just surprised. You never stutter when you've got the mask on."

I only stutter when I am upset or caught off guard. As a child, I stuttered all the time, worse when my older brother teased. But I learned, through sheer force of will, to suppress it. To think about each phrase as I want to say it, to hear it in my head, clear and whole, before letting my tongue taste the words. The Shadow Hand does not stutter because he is a personality I wear, a costume I conceived. I did not conceive him as a stutterer.

I lean down and pick up the bowl. The water has mixed with the ink on the rug, spreading the stain further. My paperwork is also a sodden mess. I will have to begin that report anew. Resentment flares at the thought of having to waste another evening in correspondence, but I cannot blame my guest. It was my own clumsiness that caused them to be on the floor. I should have picked them up right away. Stupid.

"I'm sorry about scaring you, too," she said. "I just . . . don't like to be touched. Anymore. Don't surprise me."

"I understand. No woman enjoys my touch. I will fetch Neris, your maid," I say, and turn toward the door to do just that.

"Whoa, no, wait," she says, and I pause. I take a hesitant step back toward her and her hand shoots out, fingers wrapping around mine. I look down at our twined grip with dumb surprise. I can see her frustration at her inability to move. Warmth blooms against my sternum at the thought that she appears to want to touch me, to physically prevent me from departing. "I didn't say that. Why would you think that? I just meant that it freaks me out when people touch me and I don't know it's going to happen. I never said you have cooties. Stay. Please." I do not know how to answer. She looks up at me and adds: "You're the only one I know. I trust you. Please."

This is enough. I do not know how she seems to know me well enough to trust me, but she does. And I cannot betray that trust. Even though I fear that it might be misplaced. I must do my best not to disappoint her.

"I will stay. I'll put the kettle on again and finish your back," I say. She lets go, fingers brushing against the insides of my knuckles, and I clench my tongue between my teeth. I memorize the ghosting sensation, trying not to let it get too far under my skin.

I can hear her shifting, trying to find a comfortable position. "God, do you have any painkillers?"

"I can mix you a draught with poppy milk, but it will make you sleep again."

"That's fine," she says. "Sounds perfect, actually. Fuck, this hurts."

"That word again." I turn to face her, leaning back against the mantle as we both wait for the water in the kettle to reheat.

It is a good thing it is such a large kettle, or I would have had to send someone to refill it by now, and I believe that the young lady's pain is something she would like as few people to witness as possible. She said she trusts only *me*. Knows only *me*, though how she can know me at all is a mystery. Clearly she knows enough to know my deepest secret, and now my deepest shame, but *how*?

"Fuck?" she says.

"Yes. What does it mean? 'Fuck'?"

She giggles suddenly. "Oh my god, I can't believe I just heard *you* swear."

"It's an expletive?"

She giggles harder, and I take it for an affirmative.

"And what about the rest of it?" I ask. "The things that you say you know and simply should not. Cannot."

She sobers immediately. She turns her head away and goes silent, her shoulders becoming rigid. She looks like she is preparing for a blow.

"Ah," I say. "This is what the Viceroy wanted. And what you would not share." She stiffens further at his name, but otherwise does not move. I walk across the floor to her side, purposefully clicking the wooden heels of my embroidered house slippers against the boards so as to prevent startling her. "I am going to lay a hand on your shoulder."

She nods once, and I do it, carefully, palm cupped on her whole right shoulder blade, fingers curved along her neck. She sighs into the touch, and her tension eases.

"He doesn't know," she mumbles. "I didn't tell him."

"That I am the Shadow Hand?"

She nods.

"Is that the only thing he wanted to know?"

"No." Her voice is scratchy and low, so quiet and ashamed that I can barely make out her words. "But I didn't say anything. Not a thing, after the first day. He never even knew my name."

"That is something of which to be proud," I say softly, and I mean it. "Bootknife is not an easy man to defy. I've never seen such an elaborate carving as yours. You must have made him very angry."

"I did."

"Good girl."

She snorts. "Loosey."

Another strange word. "What's a 'loosey'?"

"I am. It's my name. Ell-you-see-why, Lucy Piper."

"You gift me with your name when all of Bootknife's attention could not wring it from you?" I ask. The weight of what she has just done nearly sends me to the floor with shock. My knees shake, and I have to put my other hand on the bed stand to remain upright.

"You'll protect it."

"I will," I vow. "I will, Lucy Piper." I take a moment to clear my throat and try to keep the tears that have sprung into my eyes from falling. What a great thing she has done. This conversation, her bravery, has left me flayed.

I must turn away, before too much emotion shows on my face. Preparing the promised pain potion is the perfect excuse. Mother Mouth left the concentrated elixir on the bedside table, and it is convenient to turn my back on Lucy Piper as I mix it with a little wine to make it more palatable. Then I help drip some onto her tongue. Lucy Pipers drowses.

When the kettle has boiled again, I resume cleaning her back.

Her eyes slip closed just as I have finished. I rinse out the cloth and spread it across what is left of her skin to keep her warm until I can move on to the ointment, and then stand.

"Try to rest," I say, when the feel of the cloth startles her back to wakefulness.

"Thanks. Hey," she mutters sleepily, worn out by the pain, both the physical and emotional. "You're not stuttering anymore."

"No," I agree. "I am not."

Two

When Lucy Piper wakes the second time, nearly a full day later, Mother Mouth is there to decant broth and watered wine into her. Lucy Piper cranes her head around to watch all that happens over her shoulder, and Mother Mouth obligingly mixes her potions on the bedside table where her patient can see. She follows Mother Mouth's every movement with an expression that reminds me sharply of the looks on the faces of the village children when they see a fairy for the first time: wonder that such a creature is really before their eyes.

It disgruntles Mother Mouth, and, very strangely, keeps her quiet for once. I find I miss her brash laughter and blunt pronouncements. I do not like her silenced, not at all.

When it is all done and her bandages are changed, Lucy Piper reaches out and grabs the healer woman's hand as she packs up her bag. "Thank you, Mother," she says softly.

Mother Mouth's eyes dart to mine, just as surprised as I am that Lucy Piper knows the term of endearment which only the Shadow's Men use.

"You're very welcome, Lucy Piper," Mother Mouth replies and, flustered, wishes us a very hasty goodbye. She doesn't even linger to converse with me in the hall, as she usually does.

"Neris will help bathe you now, if you like, Lucy Piper," I say, once we are alone. "It's too early in your healing for a full tub."

"I'd like that. And just Pip is fine," she says. "It's what my friends call me."

"Pip," I allow. "Am I your friend?"

"Gee, lemmie think. Do I want to be friends with the man who rescued me out from under the blade of Bootknife? Uh, yeah. Yeah I do, Master Turn."

I wonder what my name will sound like in her mouth, and so I offer it: "Forsyth, please."

"Forsyth," she says, obligingly, and I suppress the shiver that crawls up my spine, which has nothing to do with the temperature of the room. *Oh, I like that.* Her accent turns the last syllable of my name into a sweet little lisp.

Neris comes in, clad in Turn-russet livery and carrying a wash basin. I step out of the room to allow the ladies the privacy required. I find I am imagining what Pip's hair will look like when it is clean and dry, spread out upon her pillow, a soft, straight curtain of ebony. I shake my head—and the thought away—and trot to the other wing of the Hall to ensconce myself in my study. I must get caught up on the paperwork with which my position, unfortunately, is filled.

Anyone would think that being the king's chief spymaster would be a duty overflowing with dangerous chases and listening at keyholes, when in fact it is largely comprised of sifting through missives to separate the truths from the elaborations and tracking spending so I may pay off informants. Snowdrifts of paperwork wait for me upon my desk in all seasons, and I shovel down through the layers daily, as best I am able.

If action needs to be taken, I have my Men to do that for me. Very rarely must I don the Shadow Hand's mask and cloak and venture out with a sword strapped to my hip. And even then, I am usually capable of diffusing the situation without ever having to draw my blade—my tongue is a far deadlier weapon, and I have leverage on nearly everyone in Hain.

A few hours pass in this manner, and by the time I am finished, my shoulders have seized up from being hunched over a desk for so long. I stand, stretch, and decide that now is the perfect time to spar to loosen them up, and then to indulge in a hot bath of my own.

Sheriff Pointe's home is the next estate over; when the old man who previously lived there died heirless, the lands and house reverted back to the possession of the Turn estate. As I had more than enough land to supply my own kitchens and tenants, and no need for a second home, I turned it over to the constabulary to be used as both a courthouse and a jail. One of the wings was also transformed into the Sheriff's apartments, where he and a very small staff reside. The outbuildings were made into cottages for the farmers who work the estate's land and pay their rent in food for the Sheriff's table. It is an excellent arrangement, and I have entailed the estate to the constabulary in perpetuity. The estate's previous owner's wastefulness was frustrating—there is no need for a single man living alone in such a large house, hoarding some of the most fertile land in the Chipping when, in the town center, the tenements are rarely large enough to even include a kitchen.

Pointe became both my neighbor and my friend the day I installed him and his family in the newly dubbed "Law Manor." He had been struggling with the rundown apartments he'd kept above the squashed jailhouse in the town square for years. It should have been torn down rather than inhabited, but when Pointe took the commission, he'd not been a wealthy man and could not afford to upgrade the structure.

He thanked me, but I was only doing as the lord of the Chipping ought: provide for those citizens who could not provide for themselves until such a time that they can. I am certain, had he thought of it, that my father would have done the same. Pointe disagrees with me, but I flatter myself that I knew my father better than he. He just simply did not *think* some days, but he was Master of Lysee and Turnshire, and its people were his responsibility.

Thus, when I send over an errand boy with promises of swordplay and supper, the Sheriff is at my doorstep within the hour. He comes bearing a seed cake from his lovely wife. We exchange small talk about his son, just old enough to begin riding lessons come the autumn, until we reach the cavern of my sparring hall. Once, it was the ballroom, but as it has the most pleasant summer sun—and I do not have enough friends for whom to throw a ball—I have converted it into a gymnasium.

"So, village gossip says you've got a pretty young girl shut up in your mother's chambers." Pointe says it without preamble as we both enter the practice room. He strips off a glove at his pronouncement and hits me good-naturedly in the shoulder with it, then the second glove and his jerkin join it on one of the benches that line the walls. The shoulders of his jerkin are damp from the drizzle that persists outside.

I sigh. "What I wouldn't give to have a spy network as efficient and quick as the grandmothers of Turnshire," I say. Sheriff Pointe is one of my very few friends, and the only one outside of my Men and Mother Mouth who know that I am more than the indulgent younger son of a wastrel country lord.

I remove my heavy house robe and velvet waistcoat, leaving just my cream shirt and dark trousers. I tuck the latter into my high sparring boots as I slip them onto my feet. Pointe is already dressed to spar.

"So it's true," Pointe says, swaggering to the center of the room. The weak sunlight streaming through the windows catches on the water droplets collected there, making his silver hair glint like snow. I hear the women of the Chipping find his full head of silver hair very attractive. His lush wife certainly does. A sharp knot of jealousy pushes against my sternum, but I am so used to feeling it when I regard Pointe's easy charm and manners that I am well practiced at ignoring it.

My own ruddy brown hair is already thinning on the top, and I have taken to wearing it slightly longer than a landed lordling ought, in order to disguise my ever-lengthening forehead while I can. Kintyre teases me for it, calls me vain. He wears his own fair hair so long, pulled back into a club, that if he is thinning, I cannot tell. But he is handsome where I am plain, and his hair is the last thing the opposite sex usually notices—they gravitate straight to the width of his chest and thighs, or the sword-calluses on his hands.

I am tall and gangly, and have inherited none of our father's impressive physique. All too soon, I will resemble one of those farmer blokes down in the Chipping, bald pate covered in sunburn and wisps of forgotten youth, a paunch from decades of nightly ale, and a picker's stoop from years of curling my long body over documents and desks.

I envy Pointe his full head of hair and his loose shoulders, even in his late thirties. I stand straighter, determined to at least have excellent posture if I cannot have anything else.

"Yes. It's true," I allow, and salute him with my wooden practice sword. He returns the gesture with his own, and we begin. My admission distracts Pointe, and my buttoned point jabs him lightly in the shoulder. He winces theatrically, and we reset to begin again.

Pointe has always been a good match for me; he fights with the gusto of the street, aiming to end the match effectively and quickly, where I have been taught the stiff, formal rules of dueling combat. One of these days, Pointe will best me, and each time, he comes closer. My twirling, dancing cuts will only protect me for so long.

"Bugger. Hold still, you twittering bird!" he guffaws, as I step out of his reach again. "You'll be the death of me."

"Not with these swords," I say, and I use mine to swat his rump.

Pointe scuttles out of reach and rolls his shoulders, then takes a double grip on the hilt so he can use the wooden length like a cudgel. He telegraphs his intent easily, and I dodge again.

"They also say you abducted her and spirited her into the house in the dead of night," he says, as he turns to the side to avoid my next thrust. He raises an eyebrow, his attempt at sternness ruined by the curl of his mouth. "Am I going to have to arrest my lordling for kidnapping?"

"Hardly," I reply, smacking his forearm with the flat of my blade. "Pay attention. Your footing is still unbalanced. And that's three for me, my friend."

He rubs his abused arm and grins. "I don't know why you insist on playing the useless fop in public," he says. "You could skewer any man in court."

"Oh no, of course not," I argue. "There are men there who have been training with far greater swordmasters than my father ever was, and for far longer as well." I salute again so we can start the next round.

Pointe doesn't salute back, and I am left standing there like an idiot, waiting for his sword to reply. He watches me carefully, lips pursed, eyes roaming my face.

"Why do you talk about yourself like that, Forsyth?" he asks, all levity gone.

I strongly dislike it when he gets serious like this, as if he can actually convince me that I am more than I am. I wave his comment away and jiggle my sword, reminding him that we were in the middle of something.

He rolls his eyes and, instead of lifting his sword to mine, he asks: "Why is she really here, then? They say she's your betrothed."

"Do they?" I am suddenly very irritated. *Gossiping old grandmothers!* I drop my sword back down to rest position with a snap. "Is that what they say? Stupid, bumbling, ugly old Forsyth needs to kidnap a woman to find someone to marry? I bet they're enjoying the laugh."

Pointe's expression softens. "Of course not. The whole of Lysse would rejoice if their lordling finally fell in love. Forsyth, it would please me to no end to see you happy and married. I think you spend too much time shut up in this Hall, alone with memories of your father's favoritism. All you spend time on is your missives, and your staff—"

He reaches out and places a hand on my shoulder. It is meant to be comforting, I'm sure, but it feels condescending, and I jerk away.

"I am *fine*," I spit. "This is the life I ch-cho-chose."

"Oh, you did not, you ruddy great liar," Pointe says. He is trying to keep the conversation light, teasing, but each word stabs at the fragile walls I have built around myself. "That arse of a brother of yours just up and walked off, and left you to do his job. It's him who's supposed to be lord of the manor, not you."

"I li-li-like my life! I li-li-like L-Lysse Chipping!" I stagger over every *l* so it takes thrice as long to say the cursed thing and leaves me sounding unconvinced. Blast.

"Of course you do. But you should be out there, with your Men, staying at court, not trapped between duty to Lysse and duty to your king. If Kintyre had half the brains of a village idiot, he'd be back here fulfilling his pledge as the eldest son. You're too cunning a Shadow Hand to waste your time stuck in the backwaters of Turnshire."

"Wh-what Kin-Kintyre does is m-more important for the king-king-kingdom. Kin-Kin-Kintyre is a *hero*," I argue, because I don't want Pointe to see how badly I resent my brother. How I resent his physique, and the way that adventures always seem to fall into his lap, and how he always seems to come out of them the better for it. I resent the riches and rewards the king has lavished upon him for the monsters he's slain; the women who throw themselves in his direction when he passes through the cities; the lands he's seen; the treasures he's discovered; the loyalty of his little friend, Bevel Dom, who follows him everywhere.

I resent him because he is out there being *marvelous*. And I am here, doing his job, when I have something of my own, something that I should be doing out there, being marvelous myself.

But I am lanky, skinny, and somehow, at the same time, growing to fat. I am book-smart, but life-stupid. Father always said so. *Kintyre* always said so, and he is a hero. He doesn't lie.

Pointe merely sighs and puts his hands on his hips, waiting for me to calm enough for the stutter to vanish. I take several deep breaths and, eventually, my heartbeat slows again. My tongue becomes loose and fat at the bottom of my mouth, once more under my control.

"Forsyth, my friend," he says. "Is this girl your betrothed?"

"No," I am forced to admit. "My Men rescued her. From the Viceroy. She is here to recover, and then, inevitably, she will return home."

Pointe winces. "How's her back?"

"A ruin," I say. "And it is large. Far more elaborate than I have ever seen before. The vines crawl all the way up her left side, from her tailbone to the nape of her neck. She resisted, the whole time."

"That is impressive."

"She is an impressive young woman," I allow.

The smirk returns to Pointe's face. "And attractive?"

"Yes," I blurt, and then immediately wish I had not. "Oh, don't look at me like that!"

"Is she of an age?"

"Yes."

"And you find her attractive and impressive."

"She's only been here two days. Slow down, man. I barely know her."

"And yet you find her attractive and impressive." I swing my sword at him, gamely, and he leaps out of the way with a grin. "So, do something about it."

"She is too good for me."

"That's horse shit."

"It would betray the rules of hospitality. She came to me as a supplicant; she needs succor, not seduction."

Pointe throws up his hands in exasperation. "You are an impossible human being."

"But she does!"

"She is upstairs, in pain but *safe* because of you. You do not think that perhaps she might also be *grateful?*"

I wrinkle my nose at the suggestion. "I cannot take advantage of what Bootknife has done to her, nor my position as her host and rescuer. I am sure she is in a very delicate state at the moment, and I shall not push myself upon her, nor betray her trust."

"I'm not saying overwhelm her. I'm saying *court* her."

"What for?" I ask, hating how miserable I sound. "The moment she meets Kintyre, he will sweep her away, as he always does."

"That was *once*, Forsyth, and Melinda was being seduced by a barrow wraith! It doesn't count!" His voice rings in the echoing silence of the practice hall. Pointe takes a calming breath and says, slowly, "You can't spend the rest of your life showing your belly to your brother."

But I can. That's the problem. I can, and I must, because Kintyre Turn is a legend in his own lifetime, a genuine hero with an enchanted sword with a ridiculous name—*Foesmiter*. Kintyre is a hero who has always appeared as if he stepped straight from a tapestry, and his little brother is nothing more than the village joke.

Having nothing to say to that, I simply salute Pointe once more.

"Yes, fine, I get it, you don't want to talk about it. So, what now?" Pointe asks as we resume trading ripostes and lunges. "You going to try to get her home?"

I am so unhappy with the decision I've had to make regarding what should come after Lucy Piper is well that Pointe actually manages to score a hit off me. He pauses, just as startled as I am that his wooden point has landed in my gut, and then raises his gaze to my face.

"Oh, Forsyth, *no*."

"It was inevitable," I reply.

"It is *not*," he says. "He'd never know if you didn't tell him. There's no reason at all for him to come back here!"

"He's probably heard all about it by now, anyway. It only makes sense to ask him to accompany her on her return journey. She'll need a hero."

"My arse! You stupid *heel*," Pointe bellows. "He hasn't even arrived yet, and you're already acting like you've lost her to him."

"I never had her to begin with," I protest. "It's been *two days*."

"Because you won't *try*." He snarls and throws his sword to the ground, running his hands through his hair. "When it comes to anything with Kintyre, you never bloody *try*, and it drives me *nuts*, Forsyth."

"It is the way of the world," I say, walking back to the sparring rack to drop my sword into its bin. Clearly, our match is over. "Kintyre Turn was built for adventures and winning; Forsyth Turn was built for skulking and spying, and hiding—"

The smack to the back of my head is both unexpected and painful.

"Ow!" I yelp, a hand flying to my scalp to check for blood. I turn to glare at Pointe. He has never struck me unprovoked before, and I am shocked.

He is standing just behind me, the wooden sword he just whapped me with clutched in a white-knuckled fist, his rage making him blow like a bull.

"Shut it!" he snarls.

"I am not cut out for the sort of adventuring this will require, Pointe," I say softly.

"And how can you be so certain of that?"

I gesture for him to follow me, pulling on my embroidered waistcoat and house robe and buttoning both while Pointe dithers. I knot a length of Turn-russet silk in the hollow of my throat, basic and comfortingly restrictive, as I make my way down the hall and toward my study. Muttering under his breath, Point slams his practice sword onto the rack and re-dons his gray jerkin of office before stomping after me.

Spread out on my desk are a sheaf of letters; two hastily drawn maps; a scroll that, until recently, had been buried in an ancient ruin; and no less than five pages torn from five separate, and no doubt eminently price-less, tomes. Behind me are all the books that my Men liberated from the Viceroy when they raided his most recent hideaway and inadvertently rescued Lucy Piper. I will return the books to their rightful owners soon, but I wanted to pull the collection together first, in order to observe what I can of the Viceroy's intent.

My Men have also been collecting what intelligence they can about how, and why, Lucy Piper ended up in the Viceroy's grip. The picture their combined effort paints is one that I am not pleased to have to explain. The carvings in her back were horrific enough. Yet, the sight of the sigil that one of my Men copied from the wall of a summoning chamber in one of the Viceroy's other hidey-holes has made me pity Pip even more than the agony she endured has.

Pointe is not a scholar of magics as I have been, and so it takes longer for the disparate clues to come together for him. I let him scan the papers, his gray eyes flash-ing. I know the moment he understands because he steps back away from the desk and slaps his hands over his eyes, rubbing with disbelief.

"Are you telling me it *worked?*"

"Apparently."

"But that's supposed to be a myth." He drops his hands and stares at me, jaw slack. "That's just a *story*."

"And yet, here is Lucy Piper."

"So, what, you think she was spirited here from a world beyond our own by a few squiggles on the ground, some fairy blood, a troll's toenail, a sparkly stone, and some *chants*? That's . . . that's insane!"

"That's dark magic," I correct. "There are creatures of the night who love a good bribe, Pointe. You know that as well as I. Speaking Words is one thing, but to offer exchanges with a Deal-Maker spirit . . ." I sigh, rubbing my forehead. "This is the worst sort of thing, and I wish I could say that I am more surprised than I am that the Viceroy has turned to this. He grows ever more desperate in his efforts to dethrone our king, and this does seem in keeping with his manic obsession over destroying Kintyre."

Pointe is visibly shaken. "And what the hell must he have offered a Deal-Maker to summon down a . . . what would you even call her?"

"A Reader, I suppose." The term makes me uncomfortable. It is just so otherworldly. And this is coming from one of the few humans who takes tea with a centaur on a regular basis. Humans are inherently non-magical, unlike many of the other sentient species that populate our world. But also unlike them, we can learn the skills, the Words and the gestures, to make reality bend ever so slightly in our favor. But to say that there is a creature that cannot, by all the rules of all the sciences and magics

I am privy to (which is to say, *all of them*) exist, and yet does; that it is out there—well, no, not *out there*, but *in my mother's chamber*—existing . . .

A shiver runs through my blood.

Is this why I find her attractive? Because she has such power over us mere mortals? Or is she simply human, as I am, as she appears to be? She seems so frail, so fragile, so hurt, and so determined to pretend not to be.

If she really did have the power of the Readers of legend, then why would she have allowed herself to be carved upon by Bootknife? How had she even been restrained by the Viceroy?

"She can't be a Reader," Pointe says, and it seems as if his thoughts have been following the same trail as mine. His eyes are trained on the ceiling, as if he fears that Pip will sink through the wood and plaster and float before us like a zephyr. "Nobody could have captured her if she really was one of them."

"And how can we be certain of that?" I ask, my own voice a low and reverential murmur. It seems wrong to discuss this pseudo-blasphemy at full volume. "There are no accounts of Readers, no scientific inquiries. There are only the vague ramblings of mad prophetesses, and the recorded poems that talk about seas of eyes far beyond our skies that watch all we do, that can imagine and conjure us and our world into their own minds, who can change reality by imposing an impression on us and our actions. What if she is as human as you or I?"

"You mean, just some innocent girl from beyond the veil of reality, brought here against her will?" He scoffs, the sarcasm thick in his throat.

"She certainly appears to be," I concede. "Either she plays her part well or she truly is what she seems. And yet . . . she has such knowledge of my life . . ."

Pointe's expression is growing ever more horrified, and the nervous energy of the revelation manifests itself in quick, confused pacing. He flitters about my study like a hawk too flustered to fly to its master's lure.

While he works through whatever agitation it is that has him so unnerved, I drop my gaze back down to the papers. There is a sketch of a necklace, and I know I have seen the piece before. It is quite distinctive, the pendant wrought to resemble a great feather that, were it to be worn by a woman, would dip between her breasts like a quill into an ink pot. It is strewn all over with what the notes assure me are dark sapphires.

Where in the world have I seen such a fantastical thing before? I try to recall, but all I can flash upon is one of those wretched court balls I had to attend as a young lordling while my father still lived. Supremely unhelpful.

"Are you going to let her stay?" Pointe asks, suddenly coming to a stop and whipping about to face me.

"Of course," I say. "If she is a Reader, then my permission would make no difference. If she is not a Reader, then she deserves the care of the best the Chipping can offer, and that is here. Besides, I would prefer she be where I could see her, in case things go amiss."

"Blast, Forsyth," Pointe curses. "Then let me take the lead on security, please?"

"And what is the need for that? You know Pip and I are well protected here."

"Pip?"

I feel the blush painting the tips of my ears and look away. "Lucy Piper. 'Pip' to her friends, whom, apparently, I number among."

Pointe scoffs again and resumes fluttering around the room.

Yes, right, of course. He is correct in his disdain. Of course I'm not really her friend.

He stops a second time. "I want to meet her. Now."

"Give me a moment, then." I cross to the bell-pull and ring for my butler, Velshi. When he appears—tall and silent, with the faint air of put-upon-ness that all butlers share—I order up a tea to be sent to Pip's room and tell him to send Neris to ensure that Pip is in a fit state to entertain visitors.

Pointe and I both take fortifying slugs of brandy from the heirloom decanter and the last two matching glasses on my sideboard. Kintyre and Bevel smashed the other two during a drunken rout the last time they passed through on an adventure, the wretches.

Then, Pointe and I make our way upstairs.

✍

Neris has left Pip propped carefully on a chaise by the hearth. She is wearing my mother's house robe, a

Sheil-purple affair that turns her muddy green eyes browner, deeper, and her olive-toned skin a bit more golden, like she's been in the sun. Pip seems to be lacking the customary white shift that goes beneath it, though. She is wearing the robe backward as well, the lapels left open over the tender flesh of her back, the collar folded under her chin, the shoulders of the robe hooked awkwardly over her actual shoulders. It looks like it is just barely staying on, tied loosely around her waist as it is, and I assume that there is probably only a pair of bloomers covering her modesty below her waist. It seems precarious, but is far more dignified than being squashed face-first against a mattress, and the most logical solution for covering her front without irritating her back.

Just as I imagined it might, her hair shines blue-black in the firelight, a soft sheet of fly-aways falling to just below her ears. It is oddly short, for a woman, and I wonder if this was part of the torture the Viceroy forced her to endure—cruelly chopping off all of her lovely hair. I indulge for just a moment and allow myself to imagine a plait the same color curling over one round, pretty shoulder. I imagine my skinny fingers on the tie holding the plait closed, the sensation of sinking my hands into the living silk of her braid, smoothing it into deep waves that spread upon my pillow as I—*No.*

Damn Pointe and his imaginings. He's almost got me convinced that courting her is an admirable idea. Damn him doubly for talking as if it were a *possibility.*

When I knock on the door frame to catch her attention, Pip looks up and gives a brave, genuine smile, despite how wearied she must be. I step aside to allow her to glimpse our visitor.

The moment she espies Pointe, her expression of haggard suffering clears like a brisk wind blowing away a storm. "Sheriff Pointe!" she says, and she seems genuinely pleased to see him. "It's really true, you are silver all over like a sword."

"Ah, yes, Miss Piper," he says, and folds himself into an awkward bow. His craggy face smoothes into an expression of interest, the crow's feet beside his eyes crinkling into folds of amusement. He is out of practice addressing others with such manners, for I never let him bow to me, and he only receives such courtesies while in town.

She holds out a hand to him, and he takes it, kissing her knuckles. His tongue flickers out, tasting her skin, as if that would help him determine whether she is fully human or not. Maybe it would—I've never licked someone who isn't human before. Pip doesn't seem to notice the abnormality in protocol, and I shove down a vicious spout of jealousy at his daring.

Then, he sits in the chair opposite her and meets her eyes with the sort of practiced earnesty that makes all the victims of the crimes he investigates trust him implicitly. Pip is staring back at him with all the wonder of a child confronted by her first mermaid.

"How are you feeling today, Miss Piper?" he asks, the natural charm of his voice laid on as thickly as lard in pastry.

I sit, unnoticed by either, on the foot of her bed. Forgotten, as I always am, when worthier men are in the room.

"Been better," she says, eyes never leaving his. "Been worse, too. Antsy. Why are you here?"

Pointe's eyes flick up to mine, then back to hers. "Master Turn and I have been sparring."

"Sparring?" She turns her head slowly back over to me, so as to avoid aggravating her injuries, eyes narrowed and thoughtful. "You sword fight?"

"I may not look it," I protest, pulling myself upright, "but I *am* capable. Father taught both his sons the right way to hold a sword."

"Oh, I reckon he taught you much more than that," Pointe says. "Forsyth's brilliant. Kintyre just smashes about with that enchanted sword of his that does all the work for him, Foe-whatsis. But Forsyth's got *grace*. And he's worked hard for it, too, he has." *There*, his expression seems to say over Pip's head, *now she's got to like you*.

And she does look intrigued, studying my face with that same expression of surprised awe that she used on Mother Mouth and Pointe, but has never turned to me before; the look that says I am something special and unexpected. My stomach does a flip.

"I, er, P-Po-Pointe exaggerates, of co-course," I stammer, and then clutch my tongue between my teeth to still it's useless tripping.

"I'd like to see it," Pip says, and she sounds like she means it. "I'd love to see how you fight. I never thought that you would, but, of course, you'd have to, what with your 'hobby' and all."

"You may speak freely of it in front of Sheriff Pointe," I say, turning the topic away from a discussion of her coming down to the gymnasium. I have no desire to make a fool of myself in front of her with a weapon in my hand. "He knows I am the Shadow Hand."

"Oh, he does?" Pip says, and her dangerous, piercing attention is back on him. "I didn't know that."

"We'll probably spar again soon, Miss Piper," Pointe says, cutting me a cheeky look. "You could come watch us then." The little bastard wants to force me to make a spectacle of myself for Pip's amusement. What a wretched friend!

"I'd love it," Pip answers.

"Then it's set-set-settled!" I say, and rise, clapping my hands to ruin the chance of Pointe adding anything more. With extremely fortuitous timing, Neris pokes back into the room with the tea tray. "Oh, your tea is here, Miss Pip; I'm afraid that's the Sheriff's cue to hea-hea-head back to his wife for his own."

"It is?" Pointe asks, forehead wrinkling. "I thought—"

"No, you didn't thi-thi-think," I correct, and shove him with as much politeness toward the door as I can muster.

"Ah, lovely meeting you, Miss Piper!" he calls over my shoulder, letting himself be corralled. "I'm looking forward to calling again!"

"Me too!" Pip calls back, and then I shut the door between them.

"Watch it, good man," Pointe teases as soon as we are in the hallway. "You're acting jealous."

"*Why* would you invite her to wa-wa-watch us?" I moan.

"Because I want the chance to study her more," he counters. "And people are usually at their most natural when they are watching someone else."

I realize what he means immediately. I do my best observations when my subjects are at the theatre. "I didn't realize," I say. "It's a g-g-good ta-ta-tactic. So, what is your initial im-impression?"

"She seems human enough," Pointe whispers, looking up and down the hall as if fearing some spirit is about to jump out of a dusty, stiff old portrait. "But it's sort of a hard thing to judge from just one conversation. A *brief* conversation," he adds, pointedly.

"You see? Nothing to f-f-fear from her."

"Just keep your eyes open, yes? For my sake?"

"Yes, yes," I mutter irritably.

He nods once, as if confirming something to himself, and then shakes his head vehemently. "Just so you know where my footing is, Forsyth, I wanted to say it out loud. I don't believe it. I *don't*, Forsyth, and I don't care what you say. They're just fairy tales made up to scare bad kids into eating their vegetables. There is no such thing as The Last Chapter, there is no such thing as Authorial Intent, and there is no such bloody thing as the Great Writer!"

Three

 see the Sheriff safely out, jump into a cold tub to bathe away the sweat I accumulated during our spar, and change into the blue house robe that Mother Mouth favors because, she says, it makes my eyes brighter. When I return to Pip's room, she is fussing with the tea tray and there is a basket of embroidery supplies tucked behind her knees.

I hesitate on the threshold of her chambers in order to observe, unseen, for a moment. Pip looks exhausted, the lines around her eyes especially deep and tight, and I wonder how fresh the ointment on her back is. Have the numbing effects worn off? Is she ready for another draught of poppy milk? Did we interrupt her chance for pain relief?

I tap one knuckle on the frame to catch her attention, and then I take a step inside the room and close the door behind me. "Are you well enough to stay in the chaise?"

"I'll live," she says.

"And the pain?"

"This ointment is a miracle. I feel tingly and sort of numb, like Novocain all over my skin."

I know not what "Novocain" is, so I assume—probably rightly—that it is the name of the ointment they use in her own Chipping for the same purpose. "The numbness is most remarkable, yes. It will fade within the hour, unfortunately."

"Yeah," she sighs. "I'm also glad to see you. All your servants are so damned *quiet*. It's unsettling. Neris is like . . . a creepy shadow."

I smile at her theatrical shudder. "I am glad to see you, as well," I reply, because it is the truth.

Perhaps it is odd for the Lordling of Lysse Chipping to spend so much time with a healing guest, but I am eager to talk to Lucy Piper; to learn about her, where she has come from, and why the Viceroy wanted her to speak so badly. And why, equally as badly, she wanted to remain silent. I *need* her to tell me, I need to *know*, if only to relieve that small knot of anxiety that still lives beneath my ribs. I hate knowing that I have not yet ferreted out all of Pip's secrets, the story of who she is and why she behaves and speaks as she does.

"Besides that, is there anything more that can be done for you?"

"Not really. I'm pretty damn happy to be upright," Pip says. The freckles on her cheeks are dark against the paleness of her skin, and I think that perhaps she has rather rushed this stage of healing. She should be lying down still, but I cannot deny that if I had spent what were probably months on my stomach while Bootknife carved his signature into my back, I would be eager to sit up under my own power as well.

I cross the room toward her, pausing at the fireplace to stir up the embers. The rain of the last few days has made the air damp and chill, and the crackle of the re-awakened flames is welcome. "I am pleased to hear it," I say, as I place a thick log of hardwood in the middle of the fire. There; it should burn all evening without needing to be fed again.

"I'm also utterly confused." She points to the embroidery basket. "What the heck am I supposed to do with this stuff?"

"Pass the time?" I suggest, sinking into the chair opposite her chaise.

"Right," Pip says, and shoves the basket off the side of her cushion. It bounces against the rug but stays closed, the latch holding. "I don't do that useless lady stuff."

I can't help the smile that curls itself into the corner of my mouth at her indignant expression. "And what would you prefer to do, then?"

She sighs. "Usually, I go jogging."

"Jogging?"

"Uh, I go for a run."

"Where?"

"Sort of . . . around the block? Or around a park?"

"Why*ever* would you do that? Go running in circles?"

"To stay in shape? And for the sheer joy of the exercise. The mild endorphin high. How good it makes you feel. The way it makes the blood flow to my brain."

Lucy Piper is absolutely *baffling*. I cannot imagine the appeal of running with no planned destination, to neither escape something nor to rush toward something else. For "just the sheer joy of the exercise." Then, I consider that it is no different than sparring—moving for the joy of feeling the flex of muscle and the exhilaration of honestly earned sweat.

I am utterly without a bead on understanding who she is and from where she hails, and the more she speaks, the more deliciously confused I become. What an incredible mystery she is. And goodness me, does she run so in the heavy women's chemise and skirts? Or in menswear, where she could walk much faster without the extra weight and swing of the longer robe?

The image of trousers stretched deliciously over the plump bottom I witnessed when Pip first woke sparks into my mind. I shift in my chair, glad for the pooling fabric of my own house robe on my lap. "A jog is, unfortunately, not a possibility at the moment."

"You're telling me. I guess I'd like something to read, then, if that's possible? I know you have an impressive library."

I leave the ever-present question of *how* she knows that I have an impressive library unspoken. She has kept her teeth closed on those secrets for such a long time that I think it pains her to even consider opening them. I am confident that she will tell me what she could not tell the Viceroy, as long as I am patient and allow her to do so in her own time.

Instead, I fold my hands under my chin and perch my elbows on the armrests. It has the double advantage of making me look scholarly, and of hiding the extra flesh under my chin. "You can read?"

"Yes. Obviously. Everyone in Turnshire can read, too, Lord Philanthropist."

"I do fund a free school," I admit. "I feel that it is important for the peasantry to have the agency to be able to manage their own affairs, especially when they venture away from our little Chipping. And it is less expensive to hire one teacher than to send a scribe with each man who looks to make a deal beyond our borders. But we both know that it is rare outside of Lysse for anyone who is not of the gentry to possess the skill."

Pip grins at me, and I am surprised to find myself returning it. "Is this your oh-so-subtle way of encouraging me to talk about my home by comparison, and thus trying to figure out where I'm from?"

I start, surprised to have my secondary intentions so easily caught out. "Yes," I admit. "Pip, you do baffle me."

"Ooookay."

Another odd word. "'Okay'? You say this often, and I take it for an affirmative, or a confirmation of wellness, but what does it mean, exactly?"

Pip shakes her head slowly, amused. "This is weird. If ever I needed a blatant reminder of where I'm not . . ." She raises her hand and circles the thumb and forefinger, then extends the other three fingers. "O-K. It's an idiom taken from military parlance. Zero Kills. All is well."

"Okay," I repeat again, raising my hand to mimic her gesture, and it makes her laugh until the pain causes her to gasp.

"More poppy milk?"

"I don't want to sleep just yet," she says, bent over slightly to relieve the pull of her healing skin.

"I'll fetch a book for you, then."

"No, stay and talk to me," she says. "I've always wanted to just sit down and have a drink with you."

"I am happy to oblige," I say, and pour out the waiting tea. Neris has brought us matching earthenware cups, solid and hard to break, and I find myself pleased with her forethought. I don't trust the strength of Pip's hands to my delicate porcelain just yet. As I pass a cup to her, I add: "But what you hope to gain from conversation with a fat old man like me is beyond my comprehension."

Pip snorts, amused, and takes a sip of the tea. "If you're fat, then I'm a fairy," she chuckles. "You've got about as much extra skin as a hummingbird."

I drink to hide my discomfort. She assesses my expression carefully, and I curse my fair complexion, my inability to keep what I am thinking off my face. This is why I wear the mask as the Shadow Hand: to hide my thoughts as much as my identity.

"No, really, you're not fat," she says, and her voice is surprisingly earnest. Her expression has grown serious, as well, as if she has decided that she is going to try to convince me that this lie is truth. "You're like a whip. You've got barely any wrinkles, except for when you get frowny."

"It is kind of you to flatter me, Miss Pip, but there is no point in lying to me." I try to make it come out straight, but the shame I hear in my own voice cannot be hidden. "I know what I am."

She stares at me for a moment, eyes becoming rounder and rounder until she sputters, "You actually believe that, don't you? I mean, you really believe that you are old and fat."

Her seriousness has me stunned, trapped like a rodent under a basilisk's gaze. One just simply *does not talk about* such things. But what can I do? How can I answer save with polite truth? The faster we get this conversation over with, the faster it will end, so instead of trying to turn the topic to other things, I simply answer: "Yes."

"Jesus," she says. I don't know this word either, but I let her continue instead of asking for clarification, because it sounds like another of those expletives I am learning Pip likes so very much. "You're not old, Forsyth. Not unless twenty-seven is ancient around here."

"I am quite approaching the middle of my life. If I am careful, I shall live to sixty. Perhaps sixty-five, if I am not too frail or too stout."

She stares in silence again. "That sucks." Her tone makes her sentiments clear, even if her actual choice of words do not. She is disappointed. Probably in me. If I were ever to take Pointe's advice seriously, I am certain she would be revolted to have such a useless old man, past his prime of life, the skin around his eyes and mouth crinkled like paper, showing her romantic attention.

"It is a harsh life, farming the Chipping," I agree. "The nobility has it better, of course. Easier lives, better homes, and no shortage of food. They live to seventy, if they are lucky."

"I'm not noble. My parents would be merchants by your reckoning, I guess. I suppose my father is a land-owner, technically, but it's just a house and a vegetable patch, and they both work for someone else for a living. So do I." Pip scrubs the heels of her hands over her eyes. "But *wai po* is eighty-four."

"*Wai* . . . ?"

"My grandmother. Her sister turned ninety last month."

"Incredible." Now it is my turn to stare. "What . . . why do you call her that? '*Wai po*'?"

Pip's high cheeks go faintly pinkish. "It's . . . my mother's language. I don't know how to explain it to you. I'm a, uh, half . . . uhg, this is terrible. I don't even have words to use for you to understand. I'm half of one nation and half of another. How's that?"

"And one speaks one language, that one, and the other speaks . . . ?"

"English. Er. Hain-ish? Like we are right now."

"Fascinating," I admit. "Then, your mother emigrated, and your father wed her."

She blinks at me. Then she chuffs a short laugh. "Right, I forgot how quickly you get things. Yes, nearly exactly that."

"What did I get wrong?" I prod. I can't help shifting a bit closer, nor the way my gaze narrows on her face. Information, at last!

"My parents met in my mother's homeland, and they wed there. He was young, a teacher of, um, the language we're speaking. They fell in love, and *then* they moved to, um, where I live now."

"And what is the name of that kingdom?"

Pip hesitates again. "I . . . I'm sorry, Forsyth, I . . . I don't think I should tell."

I try very hard not to feel resentful. "Wise," I admit, grudgingly. "Very well." A change of topic is required, quickly, to mask my frustration, and I fall back upon our previous one. "You are fortunate that you come from a very long-lived family."

"No," she says, clearly glad for the return to safer conversational territory. "Just a . . . kingdom . . . with better access to the necessities of life. This is what I was trying to say about life-spans and stuff. My family is normal."

"Twenty-seven is not old to you, then?" It feels like stating the obvious, but my curiosity has been piqued like the string of a harp, and I can feel the waves of interest resonating across my frame.

"Well, I'd be a hypocrite if I said it was. I'm twenty-five," she says. "And I've barely begun thinking of settling down and doing the family thing. I just finished my education, and that only barely. I fast-tracked my Master's."

"Twenty-five?" I echo dumbly. She does not look so old. I had guessed that her life had been easy before, when she slept, because of the fullness of her form and the softness of her hands. But to look so unworn at *twenty-five*. "And, I don't understand. *Starting* a family? *Finishing* an education? You have no husband, no children? At *twenty-five*?"

"Shocking, I know," she says, but she says it with a chuckle and a little upward curl of her lip. "I chose not to."

"So, you're a vi-vir—"

"No," she replies, cutting me off. Her smirk has gotten wider. "And I'm especially glad of that, because I know what that means around here."

My panic deflates. There will be no issues with Hands-Right Challenges after all. And no unicorns. Good. Those beasts are always so messy. "But to be, um, as you a-a-are and no children?"

"Prophylactics," she says, as if that word is in any sort of language I ought to comprehend. When I tilt my head quizzically, she adds: "Methods of preventing pregnancy. And not spells, either."

"What a wondrous place you must come from," I murmur, "to have produced a woman like you." I am amazed. Utterly amazed.

"Many women like me," Pip says softly. She flushes, probably insulted by my blatant admiration, and I curse my inability to hold my tongue. Kintyre would never have offended her so thoroughly; he always knows the right thing to say. And I am also terribly, terribly angry at myself. Because it is my duty to *know things*. Information is my reason for being, and I do not know this place Pip comes from. I know nothing about these merchants who live beyond the age spans of even our hardiest kings, where everyone reads and pleasure does not result in a surplus of children. Where women control their own lives. There is an entire kingdom somewhere beyond the borders of my own—*two of them*—and I know nothing of them.

And the Viceroy does.

Pip seems amused that her introduction to the Sword of Turnshire was so brief when we share lunch the next day. "Pointe was charming," she says. "Very charming."

"And very married," I counter. I have tried to keep my tone light, but I suspect the undercurrent of discontent is audible. It is ridiculous, to feel jealous of Pointe, especially when there is no understanding between Pip and I. At all.

And yet, her eyes have brightened and her face has assumed a more healthy glow, her cheeks filling with roses at the thought of her brief visitor. I want it to be me who has made her that content, that effortlessly happy. I am a ridiculous old man.

"Oh, that I know," she says. "No power on earth would make me come between Sheriff and Mrs. Pointe. Not that they would let anyone, anyway."

"Their marriage is quite strong, yes."

Pip smirks at me, the curl of the side of her lip quite familiar and, damn me, something of which I fear I am growing quite fond. "That's a pretty sterile way of saying they're disgustingly in love."

It is a rebuke. I try so hard, but I cannot seem to ever get it right. Every time I think I've mastered the arts of conversation, I realize that there is still so much I do not know, a language beneath the words that I cannot comprehend and do not speak, no matter how much practice I have. Oh, if only people were like spells and arithmetic—easy measures and countermeasures, where knowing the right formulae would fix everything.

I look down at the makings of my small meal (must watch my physique, of course, I run to fat so easily) and sullenly push a piece of cheese around the edge of the dish with my fork. My mother would be horrified, and I stop, hoping Pip hasn't noticed my bad manners.

"I fear that you must find my language lacking," I say softly. "Of course I mean to say that my friend Pointe and his wife are very much in love, but I . . . I am not very talented at . . . poetry."

"Naw, it's fine," Pip dismisses. "Not everyone can speak like a flowery froufrou romantic, like Bevel writes in his scrolls. Not everyone needs to, either."

Oh, to be compared to that hedgehog of a friend of my brother's and to be found *lacking*. I spear the tangy orange cheese on my fork and shove it into my mouth to keep my tongue from stuttering through another ridiculous apology, or an attempt to prove her wrong that will only embarrass us both.

How woefully inadequate I must be to merit comparison with my brother's sniveling little dogsbody.

There is an awkward silence, heavy as lead. Pip shifts in her backward house robe and, in an attempt to return to light conversation, asks: "What's Pointe's son's name?"

"This is one of the things you don't know?"

She nods.

"Lewko," I answer. "After his late grandfather."

Pip freezes on the spot and sighs. It is sad. She puts down the bread she was buttering and nods sagely. "Good name."

"He was a good man," I reply.

"Yes, he was."

Lewko Pointe the elder was the man from whom I inherited my station as Shadow Hand. He trained me while I was a youth, quietly, on the sly, knowing that the best Shadow Hand would be one who was of the gentry, who could gain access to court more easily than a simple Chipping Sheriff, and I'd agreed. I just hadn't expected to have to take over for him so soon. I was only twenty when Pointe's father was murdered.

Unlike Pip, he had not been rescued from Bootknife in time for his cuts to be healed. Pip shifts in her seat, back arching in discomfort, and I know that she knows this, too. How she can is yet another part of the great mystery that both the Viceroy and I are so keen to uncover. Although, not for the same reasons, and certainly not through the same methods, I should hope.

It disgusts me to think that there is a thing the Viceroy and I both desire. That there is anything at all that we have in common. At least I know that, unlike that villain, I can gain it without harming my guest.

Another silence descends upon us, this time sorrowful.

"How are you feeling today?" I ask, resorting to the default question.

"Kinda getting sick of being asked that," she says with a watery smile.

"Apologies."

"Don't apologize. I know you genuinely want to know. It's just . . . I wish people didn't *have* to ask. I can't even *see* the damn thing, so how am I supposed to answer?"

"Honestly?"

"Fine," she huffs. "I feel antsy, and my back feels tight and hot and horrible. I am sick of sitting around, and I am sick of sleeping. There is a whole incredible world outside of these walls, and I haven't seen a single grain of it. I haven't smelled the grass or watched the sun set, or stuck my toes in the river, or *anything*, and it's driving me bonkers."

"I wouldn't advise the latter," I say. "Kelpies nip."

She laughs, and it is a clear, cheerful sound that rings around the vaulted ceiling of our private dining room—no sense in using the big, formal one when it's just the two of us—and I wonder when the last time such pretty laughter was heard by these walls. Surely not since Mother died. Perhaps even before that; my father was not a man known for his mirth, and I wonder how much my mother had to repress her own jovial nature. I recall her soft giggles and gentle smiles, but the memories are always framed by either her chambers or my nursery. I don't ever remember her laughing anywhere else in the house.

I am suddenly determined to make sure that Pip laughs in every single room, at least once. It is a foolish vow, but I make it all the same.

"When does Mother Mouth think that I'll be able to move around under my own power?" Pip asks, breaking into my reverie. "I'm sure Velshi is as sick of carrying me up and down the stairs as I am of being carried."

"The, uh, the wounds are nearly closed over. The ointment is working well. But you ought to rest a week or so more before you begin to stretch and strain the new scar tissue. And you've been bedridden so long, you must give your legs time to adjust."

Every day, her back heals more—the ointment speeds the process, and between Mother Mouth, Neris, and I, it is always fresh and layered over with Words of Healing. The exposed muscle scabs over; the thin slices begin to turn red and close. In a matter of weeks, the whole mess will be puffed with tender white scar tissue, beautiful and horrible.

I wonder if Pip is the kind of woman who will cover the designs completely, ashamed of them, even to the point of sweltering in the summer months. Or will she be the sort of woman who has her clothing cut to display them, proud of this sign of her strength, in the twisted attractiveness of the intricate designs? Perhaps she is neither, and she will dress and behave as if they aren't even there, pretending that it never happened and showing no extra care to either cover or reveal the scars. When her hair returns to its normal length, no one will ever see the pattern under a woman's usual wardrobe, not unless they are a lover. I wonder if, one day, a woman or a man will lay their lips upon the leaf-shaped scar at the very nape of her neck and kiss Pip, tell her that she is beautiful despite the marred flesh. Perhaps even because of it.

She groans. "That seems so long, but, god, really that was actually fast. I can't believe how fast that healed."

Ah, her words tell me so much about her world and where she comes from without telling me a thing. Does she realize how much she gives away in choosing to give away nothing? Perhaps so, and that is why she refused to speak at all for the Viceroy.

"Have you magic for healing where you come from?" I ask.

"None," she says, softly, and spears at her own cheese to, I assume, keep her mouth busy and unable to answer further.

"I cannot guess how long or painful a convalescence it would have been, then," I say, instead of saying what I really want: namely, *But you're a Reader, aren't you? Can you not use your power? Has the Great Writer given you no magics of your own whilst infusing our world with all manner? What are the rules of the world from which you are from?*

"There'd be morphine for the pain," Pip says. "Like poppy milk. But nothing like the ointment or the . . . the Words. How do the Words work?"

"You simply Speak them," I say. "You weave them into the air and lay them over things or people like, well, like spider webbing."

"But you have to know them, first. You have to *learn* them. Who teaches you?"

"Mothers teach their daughters housework Words. Soldiers teach other soldiers the Words to keep their blades clean and sharp, their clothing free of vermin. Fathers hand down books of Words to their sons and apprentices. Farmers teach their hands. Or you overhear and learn."

"But I can't."

This is a startling revelation. "You can't hear them, or you can't weave Words?"

"I tried to repeat what Mother Mouth said. I heard it, but it was like my ears were unfocused. It's all fuzzy sounding, like . . . like an ink drawing that someone spilled water on. I can't make it make sense."

"The Words are perfectly intelligible." I sit forward on my chair, intrigued. "Yet you cannot hear them at all?"

"No." She shifts on her own seat, suddenly acutely uncomfortable, her lower lip jutting out so deliciously that I nearly fool myself into believing it is an invitation to take it between my own. But, no, Pip is *pouting*. Adorable.

"Fascinating."

"I don't think it's fascinating. I think it's frustrating!" she says. She bangs a fist against the table hard enough that our dishware clatters. "I *loved* the idea of Words, and it's not *fair* that I can't even hear them."

I reach out, mindful of her forceful entreaty not to touch her, giving her ample time to move her hand out of the way and demonstrating my intent. She watches warily, but doesn't flinch or move. I take her fist into my own hand, running my fingers along hers until she relaxes her grip and turns her palm up, showing the bright red half-moons cut into the flesh by her own nails. I run the pads of my fingers across them and Speak Words of Healing. Swiftly, the red marks vanish. It was just a shallow hurt, and recently done; the Words have little actual work to do.

I look up and find that Pip's expression has gone glassy and vague. She is staring at nothing, eyes blearily focused on the place where my bowed head had been, which is now occupied by my mouth. I cannot help the involuntary lick of lips. The motion startles her back into awareness, and she withdraws her hand from mine and stares at her blemish-free skin.

"That's amazing," she says, and then swallows heavily. "And really, really terrifying."

Knowing that Pip is too good for me—that, in fact, she is, in all probability, going to fall for my brother the moment she meets him, as women always do—makes Pip's presence both bearable and more frustrating to endure than I anticipated. She is not meant for me, so I may admire, but not want her. And yet I do want her, in a way that I have not wanted another person in years—to simply touch, to savor, to comfort. I have been Master of Turn Hall for nearly a decade, and I have spent too much of that surrounded by servants and employees and spies. No one tender. No one *personal.*

I *ache* for a connection that I cannot rightfully demand of Pip, and yet Pip is the first woman, the first person to be available for it. It is pathetic how attached I have become, and how quickly. How easily a pretty woman has unorganized my mind, muddled my priorities. I am like a lad in a tavern for the first time, head turned by every woman who walks by until dizzy. But there is only one woman, and I needn't make myself dizzy tracking her—instead, I cannot seem to separate myself from her presence, like a magnet and iron.

Oh, but Pip is not perfect, and that is part of what is both enchanting and infuriating about her. She says things, compliments me in ways that are beginning to grow tiresome because I know that they are patently untrue. I cannot decipher why she would want to flatter me with such untruths. What does she believe she will gain from it?

And yet her optimism, the honesty with which she says things she cannot really believe . . .

I do enjoy her company, and so, I endure it. But it has also become increasingly obvious that Pip is unhappy.

"You are missing someone terribly," I say softly.

She laughs, but it is not the mirthful version I have become accustomed to. This laugh is bitter and pained, and for the first time, I wonder if all that kind, happy strength I have seen in her has been a mask of her own. A mask which is now cracking.

"I couldn't even begin to explain it to you," she says.

"I am both a patient and a clever man," I say. "Please try, and I will do my best to follow along." *Yes, yes, tell me. I am desperate. I am parched for this knowledge. Give me a drink.* I have struggled so hard to simply soak in what she says, to absorb her words and press for more, not ask why, or who, or when; not demand that she tell me everything, now, the whole tale, for fear of offending her and scaring her into silence.

The Viceroy had demanded, and Pip had met that with clamped lips. Gentleness and patience seems to have so far been the much more effective tack, and I shall continue sailing that course, no matter how I desire to do otherwise.

She shakes her head, and suddenly her whole body is trembling, her face gone parchment pale again. "No, not yet. Please, I . . . I can't. Not yet."

The disappointment is strong, but her resistance does not surprise me. "Very well," I say. "When you are ready."

"Thank you," she says, in such a small voice that I nearly do not catch it. She picks up her bread and resumes eating. Pip devours the slice of bread still warm from the wood ovens and a piece of melty, soft cheese that had been a gift from one of my tenants. She sets down the bread and takes a moment to swallow before dabbing at her mouth with a napkin. "This is really, really incredible."

With no alternative, I hide my frustration and instead tell her where the cheese comes from. I try to distract her back into genuine mirth by recounting the tale of the first time Sheriff Pointe had this particular farmer's goat eat his prized hat. You would think that Pointe would stop wearing hats when he wandered past this farm, but it seems that he has not learned his lesson, as the goat has taken a liking to this particular delicacy and ambushes him for the new one each time it has the opportunity.

When Pip laughs this time, it looks and sounds real. But I know about putting on faces and assumed personas, so I do not take her renewed happiness at face value. I cannot, not yet.

I conclude the story with my advice to Pointe to simply arrest the goat, and she guffaws. "Your people sure do like you," Pip says. "You're really good to them."

Uhg! More compliments that she does not mean and surely cannot know enough about me to believe honest. I shrug. "It is kind of you to say so, but it's no more than a lord ought to provide for his charges. To make certain their farms are workable, their lives are happy, and their needs provided for. I am the Lordling of Lysse; it is my duty to protect and enrich the lives of those who live within it."

"Not everyone feels the same as you. Not everyone would have given the Sheriff a whole estate to run the law enforcement from. Not everyone builds a school and pays for a teacher for all the children of the Chipping. Not everyone would *want* their tenants educated. They think ignorant people are easier to control." She takes a drink of her watered wine, daring me with her eyes to rebut.

"Possibly they are," I allow. "But they certainly would be more miserable."

"And not everyone would care about their happiness," Pip points out, setting down her cup with an air of finality. It seems to say, *There, see? Don't argue with me.*

I let that linger between us for a moment, take the time to memorize that look on her face, the seeming genuineness of her admiration. Then I fold it up and tuck it away to go over later, when she is gone and I am alone again and in need of consolation.

"Speaking of my people," I say, slowly, "you must know there's been terrible curiosity about you."

"What are they saying?" she asks, amused.

That I ought to gather the stones to propose marriage, I think, but do not say. Even with the speedy meetings and engagements among the minor country nobility, like myself, it is not uncommon for the proposal, and marriage, to come swiftly after a first meeting. Not with titles, lineages, and wealth to negotiate. Marriages are business transactions for heirs. But even so, only three days—and ones where the maiden in question is mostly too ill to rise from bed—is excessively fast. *How desperate must Pointe think I am?*

Instead, I veer the discussion toward safer territory. "If you are feeling up to it, I thought perhaps I might have a dinner for the merchants and their spouses. A little light fare, a little dancing, and everyone can go home with their curiosity slaked and more gossip to turn the mill wheels."

"See?" Pip says. "You're good to them."

"That is not a yes."

She raises a teasing eyebrow. "Oh, were you asking me if I wanted to go?"

Oh, drat, I've insulted her again. Made assumptions, made decisions *for* her, which no one ever appreciates. What a horrific mistake.

"It will only ha-ha-happen if you want it to," I scramble to add. "By all m-me-means, if you don't wa-wa-want to, then I c-c-can certainly—"

"It's fine," she says hastily. "I *really* want to meet Mrs. Pointe. She'll be a hoot."

Pip is unguardedly unraveling more of her secrets than she has in days, and I am devouring it the way she devours the cheese. "You are a mystery, Lucy Piper."

"And I'll take that for a compliment, Master Turn."

She smiles fondly, sets down her wine, and finally leaves the bread and cheese and tucks into the rest of her meal. I am impressed by the delicateness with which she handles her utensils, and self-consciously adjust my own ham-handed grip on my fork in an attempt to mimic the same level of etiquette. It has been a long time since I've dined with anyone but myself, and it seems that my manners have slipped. I wonder if I'll ever remember how to do it all. Then I wonder if she'll even be here long enough for me to need to.

Then I wonder if she actually wants to return home. We haven't discussed it yet. Is there a home for her to go back to? What happened when Bootknife snatched her from that life, that place beyond reality? Who had she been forced to leave behind? What had he destroyed in his wake?

The thought of Pip leaving is sudden and lurching. The boiled radishes make their bid for freedom, and I have to swallow hard to keep them down. A burning lump appears in my throat, and I clutch at the wine cup, swallowing its contents in an attempt to wash it back down.

"We have not spoken of how I will get you home yet, Pip," I say softly.

The change that comes over her is so sudden as to be shocking. Immediately, every part of her begins to shiver and shake like a leaf in a violent wind storm, and her eyes drop wide. Their muddy depths glaze over with horror, and I wonder, fear that she is remembering something terrible. She shivers so hard that her fork drops from her hand and clatters across her plate, jarring. The sound startles her, and she gapes down at her fork in terror.

The shaking of her fingers almost makes a disaster of her house robe, but my astute attention saves the garment; I snatch the wine out of the way.

With no other ideas, I grab her shoulders, intending to shake her back into reason, but at my touch, she screams so loud and with so much animal panic that I jump away and crash into the table, sending both the table and everything on it toppling onto the floor.

Fear for her splashes up my spine, pulls my skin tight, and I am torn between diving for her and scrambling away on hands and knees so as to prevent another terrible spasm in her.

"Pip!" I cry. "What . . . ? Help!"

Neris and Velshi scramble into the dining room. Velshi helps me to my feet, brushing food off my clothing, while Neris goes to Pip. She is about to embrace Pip when I stop her.

"Don't touch her," I order.

"Miss?" Neris says instead, hands hovering over Pip's shoulders. "Miss, can you hear me?"

Pip blinks, and then she is looking, really *looking* at Neris for the first time. Her eyes go wide, and then her whole expression crumbles. She clutches at Neris, buries her head in Neris's neck, and *sobs*. It is the sort of heartbreaking, gut-wrenching sound that makes every human being in the world feel the undeniable desire to comfort the person making it. I press my fingernails tightly into my palms and force myself not to succumb to the urge.

I caused this. I am not wanted.

Neris wraps her arms around Pip, and I am only slightly jealous that Pip has chosen to take her comfort from my maid and not me.

"Miss . . ." Neris says, petting the back of her head, running a soothing hand in circles across the back of Pip's neck, because she cannot do it to her back.

"I'm fine," Pip answers, voice dry and cracked, attempting to preempt any gentlemanly platitudes on my part. "It's nothing. It's silly."

"It's not nothing," I counter. "You were genuinely terrified."

"It wasn't *real*," she insists. "It's over." She looks up over Neris's shoulder to meet my eyes. "It's just culture shock."

I have no idea what that means, but I can guess. "I think it is more than just acute homesickness, Pip."

"I'm just . . . everything is very different, and I . . . I mean, I . . . I'm . . ."

"Alone," I supply softly, throat burning to see the brave face she has been trying to maintain cracking and falling to pieces. "And somewhere strange."

"A—" she tries to repeat, but her voice cracks dangerously, so I snap my mouth shut and just nod.

"But you must tell me of your home eventually, Pip, for I am duty bound to get you back there."

With a frankly admirable amount of self-control, Pip shuts down on the horror. Her whole body goes still, and she closes her eyes, taking deep breaths. For a moment, there is silence—the deliberate, pregnant kind that I dare not interrupt.

My own heart has answered in kind, fluttering and pattering against my bones, and I must deliberately relax out of my suddenly wary posture. There is no threat here greater than Pip's memories; the Shadow Hand does not need to make an appearance, so I tuck him away.

"Do we have to?" Pip whispers, eyes still tightly closed, her voice harsh and small.

For a long moment, I make no answer. And then: "Eventually."

I decide to leave it at that. For now.

Four

ucy Piper's panic attack and lack of desire to be touched is surprisingly gratifying, and relieves all sorts of concerns I had barely even realized I was harboring about her mental state. I have to admit that I had been waiting for just such an emotional breakdown. I have seen men who have been tortured crumble far faster and far more violently than Pip; I am relieved to see that she falls upon the scale of my normal experience. I think it would be unhealthy to express none of the trauma she must have endured.

Neris and I have a long conversation after Pip has been reinstalled in her room and calmed with poppy milk. The serving girl, however, has seen and heard nothing amiss. Pip, it seems, says very little beyond "please", "thank you," or "could you fetch this for me?" to her maid. Neris says that it's likely because Pip has never had a maid before and does not know what she is allowed to request. I ask her how she knows this, and Neris smiles, slyly. "I've been a lady's maid since I was fourteen, Master Turn, sir," she says. "I can always tell when a woman was raised with one. They're the ones who don't bother with their 'pleases.' And you're the only one she smiles around, sir. That genuine smile, if you take my meaning, sir."

"Careful, Neris," I reply, my tone light but my rebuke serious. "That smacks of impertinence."

Neris grins cheekily and apologizes, though she does not mean it at all.

Drat! Has the whole of Lysse Chipping decided to team up and force me to confess that Pip intrigues me? Or worse, that she attracts me in a way very few women have done simply *because* I am intrigued by her mysteries? I cannot allow them to tease me into embarrassing myself. Or worse, Pip.

Of course, Neris must be mistaken. Pip is not attracted to me in return. She must only smile when I enter the room because she is so very bored with sleeping all the time.

I send Neris off for the night, and remind her that we should pay closer attention to Pip's mannerisms. I do not tell her that I suspect Pip to be a Reader. Only that she is perhaps not what she seems, and that we should watch her very carefully without seeming to watch.

As Pip sleeps, arrangements are made for the dinner and dancing I promised her. For all that she is suffering from the memory of her captivity, she did seem genuinely pleased to have been included in these plans. And a bit of merrymaking can only help heal her spirit.

In the morning, the toll the panic attack took on Pip becomes worryingly clear. There are bruises under her eyes. It looks as if she has not slept for a fortnight, despite the rest the poppy milk has forced upon her, and the skin that brackets her eyes and mouth is tight and white. Her lip curls miserably, and one of the larger gashes on her back has split open, the delicate membrane of scabbing dried and half scraped off by what must have been her fall yesterday afternoon.

"Oh, Forsyth!" Mother Mouth scolds as she prepares a long, curved steel needle, sterilizing it in a candle flame as Pip watches warily from her bed. "You know that Miss Piper should not have been rolling around on the floor. Now I shall *have* to stitch it."

"I wasn't rolling, Mother Mouth," Pip protests sullenly.

"It's all the same, for the damage is done," Mother Mouth scolds. "You should not have been out of bed, young lady."

Pip colors, and then Mother Mouth rounds on me. "And you shouldn't be digging into her head when she's barely healed in the flesh. You know as well as me, Forsyth Turn, that you don't poke at a soldier until he's well, and ready to talk about the war himself."

"But Pip wasn't *in* battle—" I begin to protest, but Mother Mouth silences me with one of her furious, blunt glares.

"And you tell me how being tied down to a bed and carved on by Bootknife is *any* kind of different."

"I . . . well . . . fair point," I allow. "Pip, I'm sorry for bringing it up."

Pip tries to shrug, attempting vainly to remain nonchalant while her gaze is riveted to the preparation of catgut and hot water for the process of sewing her up. She winces instead, and seems to shrink further into herself.

"Many and mysterious are the ways of PTSD," she says, and it is so soft that I wonder if it was meant for our ears at all.

"'PTSD'?"

"Post-traumatic stress disorder," Pip says, a little louder. "And damned if I never thought I would ever use that phrase to describe myself. Well, in any way except about my thesis defense."

I've never heard of it before, but I can guess what it is by the name.

I am torn between the juxtaposing desires to go to Pip and offer her comfort, and to leave the room so I cannot possibly say something that will make the forthcoming experience worse. Instead, I move to the other side of the bed, so Mother Mouth and I bracket Pip in, and sit by Pip's head. I am careful not to loom; I do not wish her to feel trapped. I mean to comfort, not confine.

I touch her gently, making sure that she sees my hand moving before I lay it on her arm, not wanting to startle her back into another shivering fit. "I am sorry," I say, my voice as low as hers. "I'm sorry that this had to happen to you."

"Yeah, me too," she breathes. "But, I'll admit, I'm luckier than most."

"How so?"

"Most people die when Bootknife is done with them."

"*All* of 'em, actually," Mother Mouth corrects. "Never met a victim of his that hasn't died of it."

Pip goes paler, shivering once all over and so strongly that I fear our talk has pushed her into another "PTSD" episode. She squeezes her eyes shut and breathes heavily, deliberately through her nose, fingers digging into the sheets around her. I pull back and ball up my fists on my thighs, impotent with the fear of my touch inadvertently starting off a shake. And more frustrated still by my wanting nothing more than to cover her with my own body, cradle her against my lap, curl her into a ball and protect her from the whole world. I wish I had the Words to shrink her down, so I could put her in my pocket, keep her safe.

It is a bizarre, possibly unhealthily possessive compulsion, and I choose, probably wisely, not to voice it.

Instead, I offer up Words of Calming, the sort of nonsense murmurings a parent might use for a small child woken from a nightmare. Mother Mouth shoots me an approving look. Pip's trembling eventually abates. I risk a gentle touch on the crown of her head, and Pip turns into it, seeking further contact. I allow my fingers to slip through the warm silk of her hair and down to the nape of her neck, where the first curling tendril of scarred ivy begins, and then back up. Pip relaxes into the pillows like a contented cat.

"I'm starting now, my girl," Mother Mouth warns.

"Ointment first?" Pip requests. "You *are* going to numb it, aren't you, Mother?"

"It makes the needle too slippery," I answer her. "Believe me, I have experience. Dry hurts more, but with the ointment, it takes twice as long."

"Then the poppy milk?"

Mother Mouth shakes her head. "You need to be awake, just in case I need you to move for me."

Pip grabs my hand so hard the bones grind together, and I wince. "Pip!" I complain. "Please, I need to write with that hand."

"You are not moving, Forsyth Turn," she growls. "You are staying right where you are, and you are going to *distract* me."

"Let me fetch you wine, first," I beg.

She relents and releases me. I am sore tempted to make a dash for the door, but Mother Mouth glares at me with such reprisal that I merely slink over to the credenza by the fireplace and pour out three earthenware cups of wine. I water Mother Mouth's and my own habitually, but hesitate with Pip's. It's a bit barbaric to leave her wine unwatered, but she could use the buzz of the alcohol.

Once I return to my side of the bed, meting out the drinks and helping Pip to raise her head enough to slurp off half of it in one go, Pip resumes her grip on me. This time, she digs her nails into my thigh, and I allow it. The pain she is about to suffer is significantly more than what she is causing.

Mother Mouth suppresses a smile at the intimacy of the gesture, and I barely manage to clamp down on the irritated, *Oh, not you too!* that tries to tumble out of my mouth. Instead, I say, "Well, I am here, Pip. How can I distract you?"

"Tell me," she begins, and then she yelps at the first prick of the needle into her skin. Her nails bite down, scratching at the fabric of my trousers, and I cringe.

"Tell you wh-what?"

"Tell me about you and Kintyre," she grits out between clenched teeth. Sweat appears on her forehead, her face going white and clammy, and I find myself hoping she'll pass out soon to spare herself from the pain.

"Oh, one of my brother's adventures?" I ask. "You know, then, that my elder brother is a great questing hero?"

"No, no, not that," Pip grunts. Mother Mouth ties off the first stitch and re-threads the needle. Pip pants, back heaving, and then Mother's guiding and restraining hand is again on her spine.

Pip's muscles shiver and bunch, like a horse shaking off a fly. I place my free hand on a bare patch of her skin by her shoulder to keep her from bucking when

Mother Mouth pushes the needle back into her flesh for the second stitch.

"Then what?" I ask, hoping to keep Pip engaged in the conversation.

"Tell, tell me—*oh, goddammit!* Tell me a story about the two of you, when you were kids."

"Oh," I say, taking a moment to think. "I didn't think you'd find that interesting."

"If it's about you, I—*Christ!*—I would."

I sort through those few childhood memories that fill me with pleasure, turning a few of them over in my mental hands, watching the light of nostalgia glint off their facets, before Pip's nails dig in harder, forcing me to choose one.

"There were foxes," I blurt, my gasp of pain in harmony with one of Pip's own. "In the covey forest in the bottom of the gardens. The forest is cultivated for hares and pheasants, and the sorts of birds that like to nest in trees and make for good eating. We kept a man back then to hunt game, but father preferred to do the killing for the table himself, where he could. Small animals attract more predators than just drunk old men with crossbows, though, and generations of Turn Hall masters had hunted out foxes and coyotes before. But they always came back."

Mother Mouth tied off the second stitch and took a moment to take a sip of her wine. I used the opportunity to pour the rest of Pip's into her, as well, while I spoke:

"When I was, oh, seven, I think, and Kintyre ten, a mother fox became clever and dug her den under the rosebushes on the west side of the manor. This was directly below my bedroom window, so on the night she whelped, I could hear the kits crying. I didn't tell Father, because I couldn't stand the thought of him bashing in their little skulls."

"See?" Pip slurs, eyes glazed with wine and pain, "You're good to the people in your care." She pats my thigh, right over the nail gashes, and I hold back my wince.

Mother Mouth threads the needle, and I quickly resume.

"In the morning, when I had completed my schoolroom hours, the nanny let me go outside to play. Kintyre was a slower reader than I, so he was still upstairs in the nursery. I went to the kitchen and begged cookies from Cook, and asked for a glass of milk to go with them. She gave me a small cup, and out I went to the rosebush. I left the cookies and the milk by the mouth of the den, for you see, I thought baby foxes would be like baby humans and want sweets."

"Adorable."

"I left milk and some sort of food for ten days. At first, they were barely touched, but then the milk would be vanished and the meat I began to bring entirely devoured. On the eleventh day, while I was laying out some leftover kidney pie and the milk, the fox mother stuck her snout out of the den just far enough for me to see the red of her fur and the glint of her eyes. 'Human kit,' she said, 'why do you bring me such gifts?'"

"She spoke?" Pip asks.

"Oh yes," Mother Mouth said. "Animals can do that, if they want to. Use human speech. If they've lived around humans enough, you know, or we pay one of them enough attention. Master Forsyth's attention gave her the ability. The milk, y'see."

"Amazing," Pip mutters. I can see that the prick of the needle has become lost in the rush of wine and the chemicals the body produces to combat pain. "What did you say?"

"Nothing!" I chuckle. "I'd never heard an animal speak before. I screamed and ran away. It was horribly unmanly of me."

"You were seven."

"My father said it was no excuse. He came out and asked about the noise, and I managed to lie enough to keep him from suspecting there was a den there, but not well enough to keep myself from a thrashing for disturbing him. I went back the next day, and the den was empty. The fox must have moved her litter elsewhere. That's lucky, though, because while I was trying to shove my face down the hole to look at the den, Kintyre came out with a shovel and dug it all up. I guess he had come to see why I screamed. He found the den. He would have killed the kits if they'd still been there, so in a way, my weakness saved them."

Pip's fingers alternate between stroking my leg and digging in. "S'not weakness. You're a . . . a good guy, Forsyth." Her voice is choked and heavy. When I look more closely, I see that she has soaked the pillow under her with tears. Whether they are from the needle or my story, I am unsure. Perhaps just the wine and the pain.

"I suppose," I allow, ignoring whatever kind of look it was that Mother Mouth was pounding upon my bent head just now. I decide not to find out, watching Pip's eyelids grow droopy instead.

Mother Mouth ties off the fourth stitch, and then sits back to clean the needle and her hands.

"You did quite well," Mother Mouth assures Pip. "Didn't cry half so much as most of the Shadow's Men when their turn under my needle comes."

Pip sobs a wet gust of laughter, and I feel everything under my sternum untwist with relief. When Mother Mouth hands me the jar of ointment, I apply it to Pip's back with hands shivering in the aftermath of unused adrenaline. Mother Mouth drops a few pearls of poppy milk onto Pip's tongue, and the young woman falls off into a well-deserved sleep almost immediately.

"Now for your leg, my boy," Mother Mouth says and points to the small red splotches that have risen up through the fabric of my trousers.

"Oh," I admit. "I'd forgotten all about it."

Two days later, Pip is protesting that she won't be well enough to dance, not with the fresh stitches. This has her disconcerted, on top of fearing that she will not know the steps. I assure her that I will make it known she does not wish to be asked to take the floor.

"Did you . . . *want* to learn to dance?" I venture. "You are not disappointed?"

"Another time," she says. "If you're willing to teach me."

I laugh at her joke, but stop when I realize that she isn't laughing, too. "You mean it? You actually want *me* to teach you? I'm rubbish."

She quirks a crooked eyebrow at me. "So am I," she says. "We'll make a good pair."

A good pair. No, she doesn't mean it like that. I duck my head to hide my blush and bite the inside of my cheek to keep from saying something ridiculous.

On the bedside table is the book I'd brought up from my library for her several days ago, and it makes an ample distraction.

"Did you like that book? Shall I fetch you another?" I ask, seizing on the opportunity to escape her smiles. The light scent of menthol and lemon rises from where the ointment is warmed by her skin, and I need a moment to catch a gasp of fresh air to clear my head.

"Well, no. I couldn't *read* it. I sort of . . . expected it to be in English. I mean, we're *speaking* in English, but that's not what's on the page."

"Oh, dear. That is . . . is something I didn't antici-pate. Perhaps something with many pictures? A children's book?"

"Sure, yes, fine," she says, and I duck out of the room without saying anything further. I relish the op-portunity to take a break.

I return with several scrolls of my brother's adventures, as set down by Sir Bevel. They are hand copied en masse nowadays, and the monks who make the scrolls also make hand-carved copies of the original wood-stamp illustrations. Mine are, of course, originals. I also bring another book on the history of Hain, with many reproductions of the royal family. She chooses the latter. It surprises me, but she just grins and tells me that she's read enough about Kintyre to last her a lifetime.

She doesn't realize how profoundly her casual admission affects me. I stagger where I stand, and clutch the spindle at the foot of her bed to stay upright.

Did she just admit it? I wonder, boggled once more by her easy trust in me. *Is she truly a Reader? By the Great Writer, perhaps she has! Or perhaps, no, perhaps I am reading too much into this, finding too much meaning in words carelessly tossed out. Wherever she is from, the Tales of Kintyre Turn may have traveled there, as well. Bevel's stories are always copied down by bards when they hear them in taverns. My brother is famous. It's just that. It's only that.*

"Yes, I suppose you would have," I say, in answer to her probable admission. I don't know what else I could add, and besides, my throat feels too tight to squeeze out any more words.

Instead, I go to the chair I left by her bedside and retrieve my portable desk from the floor next to the bed stand. We have both agreed that she ought to stay in bed today, to try to heal as much as possible before tomorrow's entertainment.

By the time I'm settled in, Pip is watching me sharply. "What did you mean by that?" she asks.

"Nothing," I say, wondering from where this sudden defensiveness has arrived. "Just that . . . well, you must know the stories. Everyone does. Someone must have told you, or sold your father a scroll. Everyone knows of Kintyre Turn and Bevel Dom."

Pip's eyes narrow, and then she huffs a slight puff of laughter. "Right, yes. Of course. That, yes, exactly."

Her words aren't convincing, but it is clearly a topic she fears to discuss, and I'm not about to just blurt out my concerns over her true nature. I may be wrong, and I wouldn't want to look a fool in front of her. And if she is a Reader, I fear how she would react if she felt trapped or confronted, especially while injured. No, this conversation, if it ever has to come, will come later, when she is well enough to defend herself or flee, well enough to feel safe. Or, I think uncharitably, until my hospitality has lured her into trusting me.

Not falsely, I vow. I would never do anything to make Pip think I had tricked her into trusting in me. I want her trust to be genuine, and I want to *earn* it. I hope I have already.

But then, for the rest of the afternoon, while I work at my portable desk in her chambers, she is the one watching me. It is unnerving, the way her muddy green eyes follow me around. Clearly, there is a question in their depths, and I wonder if she knows my superstitious suspicions.

If she really is a Reader, then perhaps she already does, but that is silly, silly twaddle. And she seems more frightened of me and what I can do than I am of her and what she might be able to accomplish.

No one has ever met a Reader; they don't even *exist*. They shouldn't. . . . *But then, why did the Viceroy want her so badly? And what is it that was so important she keep from him that Bootknife carved her so deliberately? If she was a Reader, couldn't she have stopped him? So that would mean that she is not, that she is just human, boring old human, and nothing special. Ah, but if she was nothing special, then the Viceroy would not have.* . . . And around and around my mind has been spinning.

Oh, to simply have an answer!

After Pip retires for the evening with an illustrated book of fairy stories from the next Chipping over, I remember that Pointe and I are to spar tomorrow. I take myself to the gymnasium and practice until my thighs ache and my arm can no longer lift my sword. Pointe will be more handsome on the floor, but I am resolute not to make a fool of myself.

I have not slept well these last few days, my worries too loud between my ears to allow me much rest. I think tomorrow will finally be the day Pointe bests me. I want to put on my greatest performance for Pip, but I can feel the exhaustion of both body and mind pulling at my bones.

I retire to my bed wondering why I care so much for the good opinion of a woman I have known a mere week, and decide that I dare not dwell on the potential answer.

I am pathetic; falling so entirely for a woman with whom I've had only a handful of conversations. She is vulnerable and beautiful, but that is no reason to behave like a love-soaked sot.

☙

Pointe is to meet me in the gymnasium any moment now, and I can put it off no longer. I cannot deny him the opportunity to be devastatingly competent for Pip. I scrape the strands of thinning hair from my forehead, correct my posture, and enter the room. My first reaction is to raise my hand against the light—all of the curtains are tied back, and I've forgotten how much sun the ballroom gets mid-morning. My second is to seek out my guest, but I resist that temptation for fear of seeing disapproval of my attire on her face.

Velshi has informed me that Pip is arrayed on a chaise that has been brought in from the sitting room, and I am flustered at the thought of her seeing me so indecently clad. She'll be able to see the full curve of my posterior, for goodness' sake! No robe trailing to the floor to hide my horrible stork legs. Pointe wears trousers and a jerkin all the time, but that's because he must chase after drunk hooligans and the occasional thief, and robes of station would just trip him up. Every other decent man and woman keeps their bottom hidden.

Hmph. Unless they are Kintyre, who seems to take great joy in flouncing about in leather tight enough to be a second skin and wholly indecent. At least Bevel Dom—who has the sense of a belligerent bulldog, for all that he is a deft hand at weaving a narrative—wears a sleeveless short-robe; it keeps his arms and legs free, but his modesty intact.

I've opted for a formal dueling outfit for today, and Pointe will be wearing the same, seeing as this farce of an exercise began with a mock-formal request. He has, of course, brought his dining robe for after our duel. Silver, as is his wont. The Pointe family is not high-class enough to have claimed a color for themselves, but the Sheriff of Turnshire knows which shades compliment him and uses them to good effect.

Mother Mouth has tried to convince me that I should wear my bold red robe to dinner, but I think it makes me look ruddy. Perhaps I will wear the Turn-russet one that is so dark it appears blackish, no matter that I appear sallow in it. That way, if I spill, the stains will be hidden.

I've always felt faintly ridiculous in official fencing attire. It was designed for heftier statures than mine, and my lapels stick out obscenely over my collarbones. But there is sense to the design; no swaths of fabric to trip up feet or in which to conceal secret weapons. The trousers are so tight that I've had to resort to a pouch instead of my regular drawers, which would bunch awkwardly beneath the thick canvas. I've opted for my Turn-russet ensemble, because then I can wear my normal brown sparring boots, and topped it with a cream silk shirt and the regulation lapelled jerkin with the ridiculous shoulder puffs. Modern dueling fashion has replaced the puffs with loose lacing to allow the shirt to froth out of the arm hole and give the joint itself full range of motion. The jerkin I am wearing today was my father's. It is perhaps too large and too old-fashioned, but I never saw the need to replace a perfectly adequate regulation jerkin simply because fashion dictates it dated.

I am too embarrassed to look at Pip when I enter, and instead, I go straight to the sword rack.

"Whoa," Pip says. "Hi."

"Hello," I say, turning away so she can't see my shameful blush. It feels like her eyes are sliding down my back, and I stomp down on both the flight of fancy and the urge to check.

"Is that what you've been hiding under those robes this whole time?"

I don't rise to the taunt, having learned long ago that it is better to ignore such insults. It's not like I can defend myself, anyway; no matter what I say about it, my body will always be mawkish and flabby. Instead, I turn my attention to the metal swords in the rack. They have been dulled for practice. They will sting when they score contact, but they will not cut, and they will flash more impressively as Pointe and I cut in and out of the sunbeams. Vain, I know, but I can't help wanting to impress Pip.

It may be the last chance I have before Kintyre arrives.

My blush finally under my control, I turn to greet her and am forced to stop, a stupid smile on my face while my tongue pushes at the back of my teeth. I don't dare speak now; I would stutter like an utter fool, and probably embarrassing truths to boot.

One simply does not tell a woman that she is utterly and entirely *divine* looking.

The Words of Healing, combined with the ointment, the stitches, and a day and night of enforced bed
rest has done wonders. Pip is already dressed for dinner
in an ivory chemise with butterfly sleeves and a modest
scooped neckline, overlaid with a stunning blue-velvet
sleeveless robe, belted low on her hips with a Turn-russet
sash. I don't recall my mother ever wearing such an ensemble, so it must have been put together from disparate
items from the wardrobe.

I wish, suddenly, that I had formal dining robes in a
complementary shade.

As Pip shifts, her own blush rising as I mark her
garb, something sparkles over the sash knot. It is a jew-
eled brooch, and this I certainly do recognize as coming
from my mother.

It is the symbol of House Turn, a key lancing an
open lock, suggestively phallic and archaic. That she is
wearing *my* family emblem so close to her most womanly
of parts causes a heat to rise where I want no heat rising
while in such restrictive clothing. I hastily begin men-
tally reciting the names of the rulers before King Carvel's
dynasty in order to bring my blood back down.

Luckily, before either of us can embarrass ourselves
further, the door slams back and Pointe, looking rakishly
dashing, enters. He crosses the gymnasium floor and claps
a hand on my shoulder, a knowing look spreading across
his own features when he catches sight of Pip. I really
wish he'd cease this strange desire to pair me off with
whatever pretty girl comes flouncing through Turnshire.

"Good morrow, Miss Piper!" he enthuses.

"Morning, Pointe," she rejoins, grinning, his good humor infectious.

"Ready?" he asks me.

"Okay," I agree.

There is a very long, very confused pause before Pointe repeats: "'Okay'?"

I cannot help the small smile at my verbal slip. Pip's jargon is delightfully endearing. "Ready, I mean."

We salute one another, and then, in a flash of steel, we begin. The fight itself is little different from our usual sparring sessions, save that I am not stopping whenever he makes a mistake to correct his stance or his footwork. Now, I am taking advantage of these errors. Well, some of them. It would embarrass my friend to have the match over too quickly, so I take perhaps one in every three openings his clumsy style offers.

Our swords clang and clatter as we pace first one side of the floor, and then back again, chasing and running, turning and twirling, lashing out and scuttling back with such intense concentration that I think perhaps I have never had such fun. It reminds me of the great demonstration fights the foreign swordmasters put on for the court, all laughter and witty banter and the mirror shine of the other man's buckles and blades. Serious and not-serious, all at once.

Pointe seems to be as pleased by the fight as I. His face is open, and he laughs with joy when he scores a hit off me, genuinely enjoying the game, and slowly, my fear of Pip's assessing gaze dissipates. She is gasping and clapping, engrossed in the display, and I cannot help holding

my chin higher, puffing out my chest and adding a ridiculous flourish to a ringing backhanded riposte that
would get me disqualified at court.

"Hey, fancy!" Pointe crows as he steps out of the way.
The flourish telegraphs my move terribly, but I don't mind,
because I have an actual follow-up. I bring my point back
around and button him in the shoulder. "Trickster!"

And then Pip screams.

The shrill fear in her voice is enough to root me to
the spot. It is a good thing it does, too, because, with
a whoosh and a dull *thock*, a knife embeds itself into
the floor—*my good hardwood floor!*—right in front of my
foot. Had I turned or stepped toward Pip at all, the knife
would have cut right into my toe! It shivers as it comes
to a sudden halt, and then sways back and forth between
Pointe and I like a waggling tongue.

I am startled by the appearance of the knife, by how
close it came to lodging itself into my boot, and I stumble right into Pointe's sword. He drops it with a clatter
and grabs my arms to keep me from tripping us both.

"Watch it!" Pointe snarls, whirling to address, over
my shoulder, whomever it was that threw the knife. I
know who it was already, of course. I'd recognize that
knife anywhere.

"That little weasel never could fight fair," a new
voice cuts across the expanse of the gymnasium. He guffaws as Pointe holds me upright. "Always had to do that
fancy, tricky stuff. Could never fight face to face, steel to
steel, eh, Bevel?"

"Forsyth?" Pointe whispers in my ear. "You've gone all white."

"Give me a moment," I say, trying to get my shaking knees back under me and breathing in slow, deliberate pulls in order to regain my grip on my temper. *How careless!* I rage to myself. *He could have hurt Pointe! He could have hurt Pip if the knife had ricocheted. What a careless, thoughtless, stupid ape!*

Pointe nods, hands still on my upper arms, and, over my shoulder, hails the newcomers. "Sir Kintyre, Sir Bevel! Well met, again, and welcome back to Turnshire."

"Well met, Sheriff Pointe, Master Forsyth," Bevel chirps obligingly, for we all know that common manners are below my brother, and the duty of fulfilling them always falls to the younger, round-faced man.

Bevel Dom is dishwater bland in every way. Even his short-robe of Dom-amethyst has faded from outdoor wear into a sort of soppy, milky shade. He bears deep lines around his eyes, caused, no doubt, by the stress of handling my brother's ill manners, and a jaw set stubborn from many years of clenching it around rebukes. The only remarkable thing about him is how dark the blue of his eyes are, and that he has remained by my brother's side after being his squire and his apprentice. Now, they are knights together, partners in adventure and in causing my hair to fall out all the faster.

"Forsyth!" Kintyre's booming bellow echoes across the cavernous space. "You look a right prat! What's all this, then? Playing at swordsmanship?"

"Hello, Brother," I say, drooping in every way as I turn to face him. I feel my shoulders hunch back into the curled position I cannot seem to break them of while in his presence, and feel my sword point lowering to the floor. I don't bother extending my hand. He wouldn't take it, anyway. "Just practice."

"And what do you need to practice for?" Kintyre snorts, large hands on his large thighs. The sunlight gilds his blond hair and the gold thread that picks out the swirling Urlandish designs around the collar of his Sheil-purple jerkin. It's silly of him to wear the colors of Mother's house when everyone knows him for a Turn; and yet, he continues to do so. He thinks it's some sort of *disguise*. In the light of my sparring room, Kintyre glows like an ostentatious wood sprite—teeth straight and white, jaw strong, and overall hatefully handsome. "Need sword mastery much, sitting around in your study like a mouse making a fort out of books, eh?"

Not for the first time, I wish I could throw being the Shadow Hand into my brother's stupid, broad, crooked-nosed face. But the king explicitly told me *not* to tell my brother, and goodness only knows what would happen if Kintyre Turn, who is never cautious about what he says, and when, were to tell the wrong person what his little brother does behind a mask.

It would bring the Viceroy down on Turnshire for sure. While my own safety is of negligible concern—the king can always appoint a new Shadow Hand—the safety of the people of my Chipping is not.

For their sakes, I hold my tongue and let Kintyre think what he'd like. Pip cuts a glance between us, a small wrinkle of confusion between her eyebrows betraying her surprise at the manner in which my brother is being welcomed home.

My glance in her direction does not go unnoticed, and both Bevel and Kintyre have the absolutely abhorrent manners to turn their backs on us and gawk at her. Pip straightens self-consciously.

"And who is this vision?" Kintyre asks, holding out his hand to her.

Her eyes go wide with that same childlike awe she seems to turn on everyone but me, and the surge of jealousy is nearly overwhelming this time. Why am I not fascinating to Pip? Why does she not regard me as a wonderful and fantastical thing?

"Uh . . . Pip. Piper! Lucy Piper!" she breathes, stumbling over her own words in her excitement. "And, and wow, you're Kintyre Turn. And Bevel Dom!" I do believe her bosom actually heaves, and her eyelashes flutter.

It has begun.

"And wearing my family crest, no less. A sister I did not know I had? Surely my brother did not wed without inviting me to the ceremony."

"No, no," she giggles. "I'm not Forsyth's wife, no way! Just, uh, a guest."

I wince at the speed of the denial, and Pointe turns to take in my reaction. Well, he won't be getting one. I shut down my face, putting on my Unimpressed Shadow

Hand look. Pointe's own expression sours, and he begins packing up our equipment.

The servants will be in soon to transform my gymnasium back into a ballroom for one night. The formal dining hall is cavernous and usually where the dancing begins, but it always ends in here—the room is more modern, more comfortable, and better lit. And I do not begrudge it for one evening.

"A guest, how lovely," Kintyre oozes. "Passing through, I assume. Come to take in the hospitality of the little lordling."

"Er, sorta," she allows. Bevel, the hedgehog, plops right down onto the chaise beside her and takes her other hand for a kiss.

I think I might be ill.

Disgusted by Pip's sudden degeneration into some maidenly moron by the mere presence of my brother, I turn away and begin to work Kintyre's stupid knife out of the floor. I don't want to gouge the hardwood, if possible, and I rock it back and forth carefully. Pointe picks up both our swords and returns them to the rack.

Kintyre bends over Pip's offered hand and smacks a kiss off her knuckles. Pip giggles. I take a deep breath and do not scream.

I invited them here, I remind myself. She needs a guide home. They came far too early, though, which annoys me. The message I sent out requested his presence in a fortnight, not immediately, but Kintyre is Kintyre, and he takes such instructions only when they please him. They must have been between adventures, for them to return to Turnshire so swiftly. Probably, his travel was speeded with the thought of getting at my private reserve again; at least he won't find it. I've had a second cellar built since his last visit, one to which only I have the key.

Even still, Pip is not yet well enough to leave Turn Hall. I will have to host them for a week, maybe more, until Pip can keep her seat on a horse. And, besides that, we haven't even managed to have a discussion about where her home is without her reacting negatively. It is delicate going, and I was hoping to have answers for Kintyre so he doesn't crush her fragile mental health under his ham-handed attempts.

Blast and drat!

Bevel trots over, and, mistaking my gentleness in working the knife out of the floor for weakness, bats my hand aside and wrenches the wretched thing out sideways, leaving a naked scar of wood splinters behind.

"There you are, Forssy," he says, handing me the knife point-first. I have to twist my wrist at an uncomfortable angle to grasp the hilt, and I resent him the casual cruelty of it. I plaster on my fakest smile and nod, and he trots right back to Kintyre's side, crowding Pip and peppering her with such artificial flattery that I wonder what I ever saw in the woman, if she is lapping it up so.

They have been here five minutes, and already I am so livid I feel that my head might boil. How will I be able to stand them for as long as it will take for Pip to be well enough, and for the three of them to *leave*?

Five

’you have any of that whiskey that makes your stomach tingle?” Kintyre demands as soon as I am able to herd him into the formal sitting room. I would prefer to do my shouting in my study, where the servants are used to me rebuking my Men and so pay the loud noises no mind, but I don’t dare trust my brother around the sensitive documents and priceless tomes my current line of research has forced me to acquire. “The dragon whiskey?”

“No,” I say, and offer him instead a decanter of the standard stuff. It’s actually even a little subpar for Turn Hall, but I wasn’t about to decant the decent liquor, knowing that he would be here within the fortnight. No point wasting it on someone who cannot appreciate it. "You drank the last of it the last time you were here."

It's a lie, but Kintyre doesn't need to know that.

Bevel trots in on his heels. He plunks himself down in the most comfortable chair in the room—that is to say, *mine*—and sweeps his dusty Dom-amethyst travel robe to the side. This liberally smears the upholstery with what is surely months of road-dust. I drop a tumbler of the richly amber whiskey into his hand too, trying not to breathe in too deeply.

"Gentlemen," I say. "May I offer you the use of the servant's bathhouse around the back of the garden before this evening? I doubt the copper indoor tub will be enough for your . . . generous needs."

Bevel snickers at that, sniffing himself and nodding. Kintyre, ox that he is, doesn't understand that I've insulted him. He never does, and it's the only way I can get my revenge for his ill manners—by doing it underneath his understanding. Instead, he simply drains his tumbler and reaches around me for the decanter. *Rude!*

"So, who was that sweet piece?" Kintyre asks, as he helps himself to a generous splash of my alcohol. "Lucy Piper. Cute name. Strange."

I wish I could simply not tell him, could tell him I've changed my mind, and that the person he was to escort on a quest has already departed without him. He would never need to know that it was Pip I was going to send away with him, and he especially would never need to know that I am horrifically jealous of the way she looked at him just now in the gymnasium.

But I owe it to Pip to tell him the truth. I owe it to her to help her try to get home, as her host, as the king's Shadow Hand, and as a man who—*No. Stop it.*

So I sit down across from Bevel, my own tumbler in my hands, and I tell them.

Sending Kintyre and Sir Dom off to their toilette, I go to make my own. They will also be discussing travel plans, and I do wish that I could be present for that. But the price would be having to share the bath with them, and that is more of my brother and his partner than I would ever care to see, or smell.

While we have been talking, Pointe has been availing himself of one of the guest rooms, and he comes into my own apartments now glowing with good health, good exercise, and a good wash. He wears only a thin house robe, and he is scrubbing his short silver hair with a towel so that it stands up in all directions, rather like a hedgehog. I cannot help but grin at him as my valet, Keriens, unlaces my fencing boots.

"Now, there's a change," Pointe remarks, letting the towel fall down to collect around his shoulders like a scarf. Once I am into my own bath, Keriens will help him dress. Until then, he must wait.

"What is?" I ask, stepping behind the modesty screen in the corner so Keriens can work on my buttons. No point in flashing my friend my winter-white bum.

"You, smiling."

I am relieved to be where Pointe cannot see my face flush red.

"I smile," I protest.

"Not enough."

"Keriens, I smile, don't I?"

My valet raises an eyebrow at me from his place beside my stays. "Only lately, sir, and only around Miss Piper."

My staff are all traitors. Pointe makes a small noise of triumph.

Keriens pulls my billowing shirt over my head, and I use that as an excuse to end this topic of conversation. He wraps me in my own thin bathrobe, and I take over from there, tying the belt myself.

Keriens, at my instruction, moves the screen to obscure the copper tub that is already filled with gently steaming water, so that I may continue my conversation with Pointe while getting clean. Pointe wanders over to my valet stand and investigates my outfit while I slide into the water.

"All black, Forsyth?" he asks. "What about that Shiel-purple waistcoat? The one with the, uh, the stripes?"

"With the silver embroidery? No. Kintyre will likely be wearing Shiel-purple."

Pointe snorted. "Kintyre will be wearing Turn-russet. Wouldn't want the Chipping forgetting that he's the late lord's son, would he?"

"Pointe, really," I admonish, scrubbing. "That's unfair."

"I'm not wrong." There's a *clink*, like he's availing himself of the decanter of whiskey I had Velshi bring up from the parlor. Well, that's acceptable. I don't mind Pointe taking some without asking. He needn't. Our friendship is beyond that.

"I never said you were wrong. I just meant that your comment ascribes far more forethought to Kintyre than I think he is actually capable of."

"Oh, vicious," Pointe teases. "Good for you. You're far too nice sometimes."

I sigh and, though he can't see it, wave the comment away with a soapy arm.

"Be off, Sheriff," I say gently. "Go dress, and spend some time with that wife and son of yours before the catastrophe of Kintyre Turn and Bevel Dom at a formal dinner begins."

"C'mon, Keriens," Pointe says, his ever present sword-grin in his voice, and I hear the tumbler of whiskey be set down on the salver. "As our lordling commands."

"Sir?"

"Yes, Keriens, go on," I urge. "I can dress myself tonight. Take care of the Pointes."

"Sir."

"Off we go, Keriens. Might be the last time you have to help my family clean up before dinner."

"Oh, sir?" Keriens asks, polite but also curious as their voices and footsteps move toward the door.

"Yeah. The next formal ball, you'll probably too busy helping the Lordling Turn and *his* wife and son."

"Oh, Sheriff!" Keriens exclaims, giggling.

"Do you suppose the babe will have Master Turn's eyes, or Mistress Piper's pretty green?"

"Pointe!" I shout after him, even as my friend's voice erupts into uproarious laughter. "Do not spread such gossip!"

Groaning as the door closes between us, I lay my head back on the rim of the tub and drape my forearm over my eyes. *Drat and damn that man.*

I resolutely do *not* imagine a plump young babe with Pip's sweet, upturned eyes, and my own gingerish hair.

☞

My own appearance proper and in order, I decide to hazard dropping by Kintyre's rooms so as to ascertain that his own and Sir Dom's will pass muster. I know that Kintyre keeps a few sets of replacement formal robes and road clothes in his apartments, but have no notion of Sir Dom doing the same.

If he requires something, Sir Dom will have to borrow clothing from a nobleman down in the village, for Kintyre is far too large and I far too skinny for him to plead attire from. I meet Velshi halfway down the gallery, and he simply shakes his head at me as he passes, making it clear that my brother and his partner are not, in fact, ready. I repress a long-suffering sigh and, instead, pinch the bridge of my nose to ward off the ache I can already feel growing behind my eyes.

I hesitate at the door, my hand up and my fingers curled to rap on the frame, when I hear Sir Dom exclaim: "Oh, for the sake of the Wri—Kin! Would you *please* put the whittling down and put on your shirt!"

"I don't want it to smell of your pipe," Kintyre says calmly, voice only mildly gilded with petulance. "I'll dress once you've opened a window."

There is the sound of boots stomping across the floor, ogre-like, and the crash of the sash being thrown up.

"Happy?"

"Ecstatic."

There are some softer sounds that I can't parse, and then Sir Dom's voice again, coddling: "How's your elbow? Still stiff? Let me see."

"It was only a twinge," Kintyre replies, and then there is a great sucking hiss, an audible wince.

"My arse," Sir Dom says. "You went flying up that hill in Gwillfifeshire swinging so hard I thought you'd pulled your arm straight from your socket. Foesmiter was a blur."

"She was running toward the children. And you're blowing smoke on me."

A long-suffering sigh, not unlike the one I nearly puffed out in the hallway a few minutes ago, and then the muffled fabric sounds of two men dressing, punctured every so often with Sir Dom's fussing.

I am about to retreat, not wanting to be caught eavesdropping when they emerge, when Kintyre says: "So, what do you think? Is Forssy's quest worth the bother?"

It most certainly is! I bristle and raise my hand again to knock, but wait for Sir Dom's reply instead.

"It's simple enough, a fetch-and-carry. It will be nice, I think."

"And Miss Piper is very . . . nubile."

"That she is."

"Good sport, you think?"

"We'll have enough days on the road to teach her if she's inexperienced. That is the benefit of these rambles. How soon do you think we'll go? Should we—"

"Bev, wait, don't pack up the—leave the dirty stuff out for the staff."

"Oh, clean laundry! That'll be bliss!"

"Pull the bell—we'll have someone do it now."

Now? All of my staff is engaged in preparing for the ball, and they want to pull a laundress away to do their filthy, stinking travel gear *now?* Thoughtless! Rude! Selfish!

Disgusted, and suddenly not caring if my thick brother and his little hedgehog are underdressed and make fools of themselves, I turn on my heel and flee before any of my staff answer the bell and find me loitering and fuming outside of Kintyre's rooms like a thwarted gnome.

Escorting Pip into the dining hall was to have been my honor—ought to be still, as Lordling of Lysse Chipping—but my brother claimed that his elder status and his own accomplishments outstrip my rights. He has taken Pip's arm instead. Bevel, always happy to be one step behind, is right on their tails, nearly treading on their dragging formal robes. I stand in the alcove just outside of the entryway and try to school my expression into impassive nonchalance. Dressed in a rich velvet formal suit of Turn-russet, just as Point predicted, Kintyre's attire compliments Pip's. To my utter chagrin, I must admit that they look *good* together.

The merchantmen and their spouses in attendance are those with whom I must do business daily; I cannot let my ire at my brother make me unruly and moody. I cannot be anything less than calm, collected, and in control. That is what they expect of their lordling, and that is what they must see. I cannot afford to give them reason to move to a new town, taking their business, their money, and the employment they offer to so many away with them.

Kintyre abandons Pip at her seat, not even helping to pull back the heavy chair before cutting over to take his own. It is the height of ill manners, even if Pip was healthy enough to do it for herself. As it is, her back is not whole enough for her to do it, and I step up to remedy Kintyre's faux pas. Bevel seems cheerfully oblivious to the misstep, even if the men and women arrayed around us are not. From Pip's left, Pointe rolls his eyes. His wife, seated to his left with Lewko on her lap, copies the gesture.

I help Pip settle up against the heavy feast table, and then take my own seat to the right of her, at the center—which, thankfully, Kintyre deigned to ignore. He is to my right, Bevel beside him, and one of the merchants' nubile young daughters is beside Bevel. She is fluttering her lashes at him, but his eyes are on Kintyre. I wonder what manner of creature she diced with to have won the seat from the mayor, who was supposed to have been honored with the position.

The other side of the table is empty, so that we have a clear view of the center of the room. On either edge of the space are two great long tables that I've always found ridiculously un-intimate, really just too ostentatious to be worthwhile. My father always entertained in this room, the cavernous formal dining hall, and I dislike it greatly in comparison to the cozy little nook that is the small parlor beside the kitchens, with its modest, battered table and chairs.

The long tables are stuffed on both sides with men and women dressed in every color of a fairy's wings. Their clothing blends into the busy background of the tapestries that line the walls behind them to keep the chill of the manor at bay. They are woven with scenes celebrating local life—farming, harvests, spring crops, industrious tradesmen crouched over carpentry or quills, and women hunched over looms, or children, or dye vats. When my father was in Turn Hall, the tapestries depicted the great battles of dynasties past, but I felt that having to stare at embroidered renditions of the Bloody Battle of Bigonner put me off my pudding. I had them replaced with something more local, tame, and less . . . red.

As far as I can tell, perusing the crowd, my guests' family heirlooms have been left at home. But for all that I specified that this was to be an informal affair, my guests seem to have been unable to resist dressing up just a little. I see many second- and third-best dresses, elaborate hair styles on both sexes, and children with bows in places I am sure will only encourage other children to tug at the tails. Everyone is laughing and happy, the wine already being poured, and it fills me with proprietary pride to know that I have made them so. My people.

Of course, they are all also staring at Pip in that spectacularly subtle way which only people born and bred in a small town are able to achieve—that is, without appearing to at all. (More than once I have brought my Shadow's Men to such evenings and told them to observe the spying techniques of those with more experience than them.)

In short, everyone has turned out to gawk at Forsyth Turn's mystery woman.

Just so.

The floor between the three tables has been specially polished for the dancing that usually breaks out when enough wine has been consumed. The two great fireplaces, which interrupt the line of tapestries on the long walls beside the tables, have been laid, but will remain unlit until the dancing is done. It's not yet late enough in the day to require the extra heating—nor the enormous kettles of water that will be brewed for after-dinner tea. The fourth wall, the stone left bare to bounce the sound down the hall, is lined with a handful of minstrels I have hired to play along with dinner. They have just started to tune their strings.

Once I am seated, Velshi vanishes through the discreet, curtained door behind me to initiate the procession of food from the kitchens to our plates.

The music begins, calm and plinking, and I realize almost immediately the error of taking the honored seat for myself when Pip leans around me speak to Kintyre.

"So, where have you just come from? What adventures were you having, Sir Kintyre?" She giggles a bit, tripping over his name like a stupid milk maid, and I clench my teeth together, forcing myself to make no face over it.

"Miliway, east in the prairie lands," Kintyre says. "My brother's messenger hawk caught up with us just as I was squaring away business with a mountain elf who had a fondness for collecting human eyes." Reaching right across my plate, Kintyre touches Pip's chin and raises her gaze to his own. "He liked green eyes best."

Ugh.

Pip flushes and turns her face away, teeth nibbling coquettishly at the corner of her bottom lip. "My eyes aren't green."

"Not completely," I agree.

Pip grimaces. It looks like she is about to argue, and I keep my mouth shut, her expression broadcasting quite clearly how little she wants to have this conversation. Perhaps it is a sore point with her.

"But I bet they're green in the sun. So lovely," Kintyre says, and withdraws his arm. I take the opportunity to catch up one of the pitchers on the table and pour Pip a cup of wine. Bevel can see to Kintyre, if either of them want it. I'm not serving my damned brother. "We'll have plenty of opportunity to find out."

"Oh, you're staying, then?" Pip asks.

Kintyre sits back and regards me. "You didn't tell her?"

"Tell me what?" Pip cuts a look between us, clearly unimpressed that someone has been making decisions for her and without including her in the discussion.

I clear my throat. "Kintyre and Bevel have come to . . . act as your champions."

Pip laughs. "What for?"

"Wherever it is that you come from, surely you—" I begin, carefully. Pip's eyes go wide, and her jaw tightens. I cut myself off, quickly. "Never mind. Let us concentrate on our company and the evening for now, and discuss the woefully tedious business of adventuring in the morning."

Kintyre flashes me an annoyed glare, but sits back and grunts for Bevel to fill his cup. I relish the small point I have scored off him, that he is reluctant to argue about the tediousness of his chosen profession in front of a woman he is clearly attempting to seduce. I wonder how he'll get his own back.

Velshi, along with a string of other servants borrowed from Law Manor for the evening, appear around the tables in concert, holding baskets of fresh warm rolls and cups of whipped butter. Pip moans as Velshi sets the basket right before her plate.

"Oh my god, fresh bread straight from the oven."

"I know!" Bevel agrees, with a nearly pornographic moan of his own. "We never get this on the road."

There is a moment of blessed silence as Kintyre and Bevel dig in. Pip's joy in the freshly baked bread is less demonstrative but no less enthusiastic.

Lips shining with melted butter, Pip leans around me to waggle her roll at Bevel. "So, I have to ask . . . the Dire Dragon of Drebbin?"

"Yes?"

"It was really a sleeping potion, right? You put it to sleep first? You hid it in the horsemeat, am I right?"

Kintyre smirks cheekily at her, and I resist the urge to copy the Pointes and roll my own eyes.

"Perhaps," he says. "Perhaps the dragon was overwhelmed and swooned."

"Please!" Pip laughs. "Dragons don't swoon!"

"How do you know?" Kintyre asks. And, oh, horrible, he is *flirting* with her.

"I just know." Pip is using that cryptic tone of voice which means that she *does* know and isn't comfortable admitting how.

I would have taken that for the warning it was and backed off, but Kintyre just leans closer, his shoulder jamming uncomfortably against my elbow, and makes some sort of ribald joke about being able to "*get it out of her.*"

Pip immediately stiffens all over, her face going glassy with terror. Her roll drops from her spasming fingers and disappears under the table. She is mere seconds away from another panic attack—Kintyre, the great insensitive lout, has done the one thing I specifically told him *not* to do in my letter. "*Do not make any references to torture, forcing anything on or in her, and do not mention either home or your beloved scourge of the kingdom.*"

"Pip," I say, urgent, turning my face so that my nose is brushing her ear. "Pip, breathe."

There is danger in behaving oddly among near strangers, especially those of a class who are more prone to superstition; if anyone thought Pip was fey-touched, our very pleasant evening could quite quickly turn into an attempt to put off a warlock-hunt. Or a Hands- Right Challenge, come to think of it. She is comely enough that someone might offer to "shelter and offer succor" to her at the price of her hand.

Oh, I am a fool. I am a stupid, old fool. The moment I realized Pip suffered the mental ailment of the returned soldier, I should have called off the event. Instead, I have given her grief the exact audience that we *do not need*. And all under the vain, thin excuse of wanting to satisfy the Chipping gossips and show off to Pip.

Selfish, stupid Forsyth!

"Miss Piper, I'm going to put my hand on your arm now," Pointe says, on the other side of me, realizing at the same time I have that we cannot allow her to have an episode here. For both the sake of her reputation and her shame, of her *safety*, she must stay calm.

I am an idiot child! I wanted to cheer her with a dinner, and instead, I have put her into a precarious position. Why can I not have any forethought? What is *wrong* with me?

Pip nods, a slow up-and-down jerk. Pointe stands, moves around to the back of the table, and carefully lays both square hands on the tops of her shoulders, warm and comforting and stable. The heel of his left hand must brush one of the stitches, for she winces and flinches away, eyes blinking back into awareness.

"Ow," she says under her breath.

"Are you stable now, Pip?" I ask, mouth still hidden in her hair so no one else at the tables—many of whom are now openly staring—will be able to read my lips.

"Yes," she husks. "Yes, I think so."

I press her wine goblet into her hand, and she takes a swallow large enough to set her coughing. Pointe rubs his hands over the back of her neck until she stops. Pip wipes her eyes; I cannot tell if the tears are from the pain, the memories, or the lack of air.

Kintyre has been silent this whole time, and when I finally lean back, I see that he is slouched in his seat, chatting with Bevel, completely unconcerned for Pip's wellbeing.

Arrogant arse, I think. *You caused this, and you didn't even try to help!*

He must notice my movements out of the corner of his eyes, because he turns back around, and, utterly ignoring me, asks Pip if she's back with us. He says it with such disdain that Mrs. Pointe opens her mouth to give Kintyre the tongue-lashing of what surely will be his life. The Sheriff kisses her quickly to forestall it. There is no point in yelling at Kintyre Turn—scolding words do not seem to penetrate his ears. Much better to save one's breath to blow away pixies.

Pip shoots Kintyre a confused glare, offended, but then takes another sip of wine to clear her throat and says, "I'm fine."

"Oh, good. I was afraid you were going to be one of those boring sorts who gets lost in their own thoughts."

He guffaws and slaps my shoulder so hard my teeth rattle. "Forssy's like that, and it's dull as all get-out, isn't it, Bev?"

"Yup," his partner chirrups on cue.

"His face just goes slack, and his eyes stare into nothingness, and he just sits there. For *hours*. I could never get him to do anything fun at all when we were kids."

"And what do you constitute as fun?" Pip asks, but there is a saccharine undertone to her words that I've never heard before. I think . . . I think she's making *fun* of Kintyre. I hold my breath, wondering if Kintyre will notice.

"Oh, stuff. You know. *Boy* stuff," Kintyre admits, and he is oblivious! I whip my gaze back to Pip, enthralled by her daring.

"Of course, *boy* stuff," she echoes. "Running and hitting things with sticks. Crushing the skulls of baby foxes. Not sitting around thinking, surely—I can see that you're the type that doesn't spend too much time on something as boring as *thinking*."

"Too right," Kintyre agrees quickly.

Pip scoffs. "And certainly not reading either. No point in expanding a mind when there are so many things to chop at with a sword."

"Exactly!"

"And why would anyone ever waste time in a library when the world can teach you so much! It's not like anyone actually expects a Chipping lordling to, I don't know, learn from the great leaders of ages past. Surely a lordling born to his role knows it instinctively."

"Of course."

Pip covers her mouth with her hand and makes a noise that sounds very much like stifled incredulity. "Oh my god," she whispers. "Elgar Reed is a moron."

Pointe and I share a startled glance over Pip's head, and this confirms it for me. Pip is teasing Kintyre for being an illiterate goon.

"Who is this Elgar Reed you keep mentioning?" I whisper back, leaning in close to her.

Pip startles as if I had breathed fire in her face. She is up and out of the chair so quickly that it topples backward and smacks into the flagstones. Her muddy eyes are wide, white showing all around like a terrified horse.

The whole room stops to stare. Even the musicians fall silent. Kintyre looks vaguely amused; Pointe already has one hand on the hilt of his sword.

And Pip . . . Pip looks like she is about to weep.

"I . . . I need the . . . toilet," she mutters, and then turns on her heel so fast her skirts whirl out in a near perfect circle. She is out the servants' entrance before I have even pushed back my chair. I flick my wrist at the minstrels, and they launch into a jaunty air to cover the ringing awkwardness that echoes through the silent hall. Slowly, my guests go back to making the droning noises of conversation, though I'm certain I can guess the topic to which they've now turned their noses. I stand and turn to follow Pip, but a meaty paw lands on my arm, halting me.

"Oh, let her go, Forssy," Kintyre drawls. "It's probably just that time in her courses. You know how moody and unpredictable women get on their moon."

I jerk out of his grip, incensed. "No, I do not, in point of fact, *know how women get*. Pip is distressed, and it has nothing to do with moons, so I will go to her."

"She'll just bite your head off," Kintyre says. He makes it sound like it's a warning, like he knows better than me, and I am furious. I hate him, suddenly. Hate him more than I ever have before in my entire life. Yes, he bullied and hurt me as a child, but you do not—you *do not*—harm a guest of Turn Hall. It is just *not done*.

"This is your fault!" I snarl and scurry away before my parting shot can wring any sort of revenge from my brother. It will come later, so I will worry about it later.

The sound of sobs is easy to follow, and I dash along the narrow passageway toward the kitchens, turning when the sound of skin hitting stone indicates that someone has fallen upon the stairs that lead up to my study. I find Pip halfway up the flight, her hands clutched before her and her palms scraped and bloody. She is curled on her side, one leg held out at an uncomfortable angle, and I guess that she slipped on the flags and slid down a few steps on her hands and knees. She probably knocked a kneecap on the way down, and an elbow, but I suspect that her pride is more wounded than her bones.

"Pip, let me help you up—" I begin, closing the gap between us.

"*Don't touch me!*" she shrieks, and it's so loud that I actually back down the steps, ears dazzled by the ringing echo her high-pitched invective makes as it bounces through the small stone hallway.

My hands hover in the air above her heaving back, and I am frozen with indecision. Her sobbing has become so wretched that almost all the noise is being choked out in great, gasping breaths. My own lungs constrict in burning sympathy. It sounds as if her whole soul is being wrung out into each tear, and that such wringing is agonizingly painful.

"Oh, Pip," I say softly, and sink down onto the stone step directly behind her. The chill of it through my trousers sends goose bumps racing across my thigh and up my spine. "Please, please, what can I do?"

She turns, unfolding from her protective curl, and launches herself at me. I raise my arms, ready to impassively accept her angered blows—after all, it must have been something I did to make her rage so—and am startled to realize that instead of punching me, she has wrapped her arms around my waist and is weeping into my chest.

Oh, I think dazedly. *A hug. She wants comfort. From me.*

Terrified of provoking more screaming, I very, very slowly lower my arms and lay them across her shoulders, careful to keep to the right side where the injuries are more sparse. She hitches a breath, turns her face, and buries it against the soft flesh of my belly, and then she screams.

Screams, and screams, and screams, and all I can do is fold my body over hers, muffling her face with my robe and curling over her like a protective blanket, murmuring soothing nothings into the skin of her neck, the back of her ear, the strands of her fragrant hair. "Oh, Pip, oh my poor Pip," I whisper, holding her, protecting her, offering stability, comfort, whatever she needs.

I close my own eyes against the urge to cry alongside her, cry for what was done to her, for the pain it has caused, for the way it has shattered her soul. But men, real men, Father said, do not cry. So I choke back the lump burning behind my larynx and keep my breathing even.

Finally, *finally*, the screams die away to coughs, and then back to soft, hitching sobs. When even these have stilled and the only trembling in Pip's limbs is, I assume, from the exertion and the cold of our perch, I carefully tuck the back of one hand under her chin and coax her up.

Her face is blotched and red, her eyes swollen and shining. She is not beautiful like this, not like they describe crying women in the epics. She looks exactly as she is: wrecked, and heartbroken, and so exhausted with hurting that the pain has become a part of her.

I remove my handkerchief from my waistcoat pocket and mop at her face, slow and tender, cleaning away the tears, the running cosmetics, and the mucus. She turns her face into my touch, eyes fluttering closed, and I obligingly drop the hanky and cup her cheek in my palm. She is burning.

"Who are you, Forsyth Turn, that you can do this to me?" she whispers, smearing the words against the skin of my wrist. "I never told Bootknife. I never told the Viceroy. But when I'm around you, I can't help it."

"Everyone tells me their secrets," I say, tone light and a forced chuckle in my voice, desperate to try to lift this dreadful, oppressive cold of misery that hangs over us both. "It is why I am such an effective Shadow Hand. I have a trusting face, and people don't guard themselves."

Pip looks up then, allows me to help her straighten, flinching and whimpering as her back stretches and pulls against the fabric of her chemise. It must be a riot of burning, and I dearly hope she has not split open any more of the cuts.

"You do, you really do. It's inscribed in who you are. Everyone tells you their secrets because they *have* to, because that's how you were designed." She sighs. And then, as if making the choice to leap off a cliff, she adds, "Elgar Reed wrote you well."

Then she sits back, putting an arm's length between us, and watches my face with such expectant terror that I fear that I am about to spontaneously combust. I do not know how to react. She has told me something, something important in her eyes, but to me, it still makes no sense.

"This is your secret," I say, trying to work it out, searching for the corner piece of the puzzle so that I may build the rest from there. "You are telling me, now, what you wouldn't tell Bootknife."

"Yes," she whispers.

"Elgar Reed is a name?"

"Yes."

Dread slips into my gut, and realization is right on its heels. "It's true," I hiss. "All the stories, they're true."

"I don't know the stories. Tell me."

My own hands shaking, suddenly, I reach out for hers, and Pip twines her fingers through mine. Her grip is strong and real and hot, and now it is I who needs comfort.

"You're real," I say, and it is a stupid, silly thing to say, because of course she is real. I am holding her hands. She is corporeal; she exists. And yet, she should not.

"I am. Tell me the stories?"

"Legend has it—and worldwide legend, mind, not just human legend—that when the world was created, it was done so out of the nib of a pen."

Pip makes a distressed choking sound, but when I look to her, she simply shakes her head. "Go on," she whispers, voice harsh from screaming and some great emotion that has clutched at her throat.

I feel it clutching at mine, as well, and wish I had something with which to wash it away. The oblivion of drink would be very welcome at the moment, because thinking has become terrifying.

For the first time in my life, I am scared of knowledge.

I go on: "They call the one who wielded the pen the Great Writer, and that he created our world, our very selves, with Authorial Intent. That he has a plan for us and our lives, and that our fates are unchangeable. Written down, as you would. And that our world, our lives, will continue along the Writer's plotted arc until the Writer composes our ends in The Last Chapter."

"Dear god," Pip breathes. "It's a genesis myth."

"Yes," I whisper back. Somehow, these confessions seem too important to pronounce at full volume.

She closes her eyes and presses her forehead against my clavicle, warm breath ghosting down the front of my shirt. "And it's . . . it's entirely right."

I should feel more startled than I am. Perhaps I am detached with shock, my emotions so overwhelming that my body has shut them away. Instead of horror, or smug satisfaction that I had deduced her origins correctly, I merely feel the spread of warm acceptance. It makes my stomach untwist, and my limbs and eyelids become pleasantly warm and heavy.

"And you, then, must be a Reader. One of those thousands of pairs of eyes from the realm beyond our skies, who watch us and dream of us, who interprets and imposes."

Pip makes that same wet, desperate, distressed sound again. "Like an angel?"

"I don't know what an angel is," I admit.

"Angels are . . . like Readers. From *our* version of the Writer."

"You are from a created world, like mine?" I ask, and I am only mildly interested in the answer. Pip's fingers have found the cuffs of my shirt under the sleeves of my robe, and are sweeping back and forth along my wrists, soothing and warm. My pulse-points seem to be directly connected to my nethers, for there is a stir of interest, and I am both relieved and sad that Pip is no longer smushed against my lap.

"According to legend," she breathes.

"And this is what the Viceroy coveted," I say. "He pulled you into our world. That much my Men have deciphered. And he did so, so that you could confirm that the stories of the Writer and the Readers are true?"

"Oh, no, no," Pip says and lets go of my hands, suddenly. She struggles to regain her feet, and I rise quickly in order to help. Her knee, the one she barked against the step, trembles and threatens to give out, and I pull Pip into my embrace, emboldened by her confession and this revelation. She allows it, resting her forehead against my chest, speaking to my waistcoat lapels. "The Viceroy pulled me into this world to kill Kintyre Turn."

My interest shrinks in revulsion. I am sure she feels my fingers stiffen on her shoulders, and she clutches even harder at my waist, not allowing me to pull back and examine her expression.

"Ho-ho-how? Wh-why?" I am choking on the words, all my calm acceptance burning up in the freezing concern for my brother's life. He is an ass, but he is my blood.

"I'm a Reader," Pip whispers into the fabric, so softly that I nearly cannot make out the words. "Just like you said. In fact, I'm an avid reader. I've read the books a hundred times. I grew up with them, you see? The first one came out when I was just a kid, and I love the series. I reread them constantly, all the way up to university. Which means . . . I know the most. Maybe more than the Writer himself. I can predict Kintyre's movements, his reactions. I know secrets about his weaknesses and his morals that nobody else has bothered to synthesize."

"But how? Just by reading?"

"By *analyzing*," Pip whispers. "I did my thesis on the books. I know more about the world that Reed wrote than probably Reed, or his editor, or anyone else, because I analyzed all the stuff *under* the words."

"Bo-books? Plural?" I ask, though I can already guess the answer, and it fills me with dread.

"Eight books in all. Together, *The Tales of Kintyre Turn*," she says. "By Elgar Reed."

Six

ow it is my knees that are trembling. Pip pushes me back against the wall, using the stone to keep me upright.

"You're dead pale," she said. "Forsyth, don't faint on me. Not here."

"I . . . I am fi-fi-fine," I lie. "A mo-mo-moment, p-p-please. Just-just a-a-a mo-moment."

"Breathe deep, through your nose," she commands, and, helpless against the rush of fear that has filled my gut, I obey. "Out through your mouth. Yes. Again. Again, keep going. Good boy."

Good boy. Just as Mother Mouth calls me. I make a high, distressed whining sound that I am unable to muffle before it escapes, strange and scary even in my own ears. Pip runs her hands over my shoulders the way I had been doing not moments before to soothe her, saying my name softly, shushing me like a high-spirited dog.

"Shhh, Forsyth, shhh. Just breathe. Breathe. That's it."

"M-my who-who-whole world ex-exists f-f-for my *bro-brother?*" I manage to get out, and it sounds both petulant and wounded, everything I am.

It's not fair.

It's not *fair*!

Kintyre gets everything, *everything*, and now this, too? Pip has read his stories for most of her life, she adores the books, she adores *him*, and it's so staggeringly unfair that I nearly do faint.

The whole world was created for my brother. To serve him. To exalt and glorify *him*.

"Oh, Forsyth, listen, please . . . he's just the protagonist. There's so much, so much that fills this world that is not in the books. Neris and Velshi, you and little Lewko, you're all so much *more*, so much more real and passionate and filled with pain and love and depth. The books may follow Kintyre, but this world is not *for* him. I've been here months, and this is something I've realized, Forsyth Turn: you are all so much more than just background players in your brother's tales. You are *more*, and . . ." She makes a wry sort of snuffling sound. "And you are *better*. You are kinder, you are gentler, you are intelligent and trustworthy and so, so deserving of wonderful things,

Forsyth. And I am horrifically disappointed by my child-hood hero, I can tell you that much. Elgar Reed must be a bigger misogynistic moron than I thought, if a jackass like Kintyre is his idea of the flawless hero."

I cannot help it; the tears come now, and I press my face against Pip's shoulder, my nose at the nape of her neck, and sob.

"I mean it! Kintyre Turn is not a desirable human being, and he's a frankly poorly written character."

Her words stun me, as much as a blow to the head might.

"Ooooh, fuck. I cannot believe I just said that. For-syth, I'm sorry, I'm sorry," she says. She squeezes tighter, pressing every warm, delicious inch of her body against mine, from kneecaps to nose. "He's your brother. I shouldn't badmouth him in front of you."

"Th-th-thank you," I manage to stutter out. "Thank you!"

"Thank you?" she echoes, confused.

"Kintyre *is* a ja-ja-jackass, isn't he!" I crow.

Pip is startled into laughter, and my sobs morph into something closer to the noises she is making than the ones I was before. It's not quite a laugh, but it is nearly there, and it feels good. Oh, it feels so *good*.

Because the woman I admire does not admire my brother. And she thinks I am a better man than he. She thinks I am brilliant! I wrap my arms around her again, then, wanting to express my gratitude. She yelps and squirms in my grip. I have forgotten her injuries.

I release her instantly and jerk back to press my arms against the wall, out of the way.

"Sorry, oh Pip, I am so-sorry!"

"It's fine, it's just . . . really sore, sorry, damn, really sore." She presses her nose against my collarbone, panting heavily, eyes screwed shut against the pain. Tentatively, I lay my hands on the tops of her shoulders, and she sighs into my waistcoat.

"I will get you poppy m-milk."

"No, just the ointment," Pip says. "I don't want to sleep."

"It will only numb the pain for a short while."

"It'll be long enough to go back downstairs and save face," Pip counters.

I realize what she is offering and shake my head. "My reputation will survive. I am more concerned for you. You don't *have* to come back to the dinner."

"I want to," she says fiercely. "I don't want to go back to that room and be alone with my thoughts. I couldn't *bear* it. I want to be wherever you are."

"Okay," I whisper against her neck. "Okay. As you wish."

She laughs against my chest and turns her face up to mine. Her eyes are still red-rimmed, but the mud has given way to such a brilliant green that my breath feels knocked from my chest. "That's funny," she says.

"What did I say? 'Okay'?"

"No, 'as you wish.' It's from . . . this other book."

"Another world like this one?"

"I don't know," she admits, eyes roving my face, searching for something that I would gladly give, if only I knew what it was. "Maybe it's real, too. Maybe it's filled with people who are more than they are on the page."

"Tell me?"

"It was about a girl and a boy, and whenever he said, 'as you wish,' he really meant . . . he meant that he . . ."

Her eyes land on my mouth, and I know what she's trying to say, of a sudden. She licks her lips, and I cannot resist anymore. I dip my head, closing the space between us.

The sudden sound of a shoe scraping on stone above us startles us apart, and Pip jerks back in my embrace so quickly our noses bump. We have touched faces, but not lips. My mouth is dry with the kiss that will never come.

Neris appears at the top of the stair, descending tentatively toward us. "Begging your pardon, sir. But I was setting your brandy in your study, and I heard crying, sir," she says. "Can I help?"

"Yes," I say, taking Pip's hands between mine and squeezing them once, hoping to telegraph my regret at the interruption. Then, I place them in Neris's hands. "Take her back to Mother's chambers, get her cleaned up, more ointment, and then escort her back to the dining hall, please. Pip, are you sure you want to return? There is no shame in retiring."

"No, no," she says. "I'll come back. I won't let your brother get to me."

I nod and, feeling very bold indeed, lean forward to place a chaste kiss on her cheek. Pip turns away, but I can see the back of her neck flush red.

"Neris," I say meaningfully, just as the maid is helping Pip limp down the steps past me. She pauses, and I lean in, making sure my words are only for her. "You *only* heard crying?"

"There was talking too, sir," she says. "But I couldn't make out what you were saying."

"Very good. On your way."

"Yes, sir."

I lean back against the cold stone and put one hand to my forehead. I am so stunned, so amazed, my world so turned upon its ear that it feels as if my brains should be melting, sluicing out through the bone and dribbling down my face. But no, my skin is only wet with cold sweat and tears, clammy and unpleasant. No brains.

That my brother is the main character of the novel that is our lives is no surprise to me. He is exasperatingly outgoing. He can don a charming mask, and is a fairly decent marksman at high speed (though I am more precise and technically proficient at slow). He seems to have magic's own luck.

If anyone was to have to pick which of the two of us to write a series of tales about, it would indubitably be him. This choice is not what bothers me.

What bothers me is that there is, definitively, a Writer.

And that I know his name is Elgar Reed.

✍

"You require cheering up," Bevel ventures. He is talking to Pip, of course, who is settling back into her seat beside me. Her face is clean, and her eye makeup has been reapplied, her hair brushed smooth, and her stained chemise changed. If I wasn't sitting directly beside her and able to witness the redness in the corners of her eyes and around her nostrils, I wouldn't have known that she'd had her crying jag in the stairwell.

I have washed my own face, as well, but I am better at hiding my expressions than she. Pip snorts in reply to Bevel, a definitively unladylike gesture, and something inside me thrills with the way she throws convention back in their faces. Pip is no lady to be coddled or seduced; she is a *woman*, an equal for any man, as Mrs. Pointe is. A personality, forceful and competent and proud. A person to admire and respect.

Oh, how I want to be with her.

Bevel ignores the snort and comes to stand behind her chair. He holds out a hand, which has somehow materialized a pristine white glove. "Dinner will keep warm for us a little longer; will you dance?"

"Dance?" she asks. She exchanges a look with me. "I, uh, I already discussed this with Forsyth. I can't."

"Well, not with Forssy, no," Bevel chuckles. "Nobody can dance with this stork. But I'm an excellent dancer."

Pip's expression clouds with anger, but she whisks it away just as quickly. "Sorry, I wasn't clear. That whole walking around each other in lines thing, where the gentleman touches the lady's hand and they move in the patterns prescribed by the song? I can't do that. I never learned."

Bevel exhales heavily. "I can teach you. It is very easy—"

"Right, I see," Pip interrupts, holding up a palm to halt the flow of his words. Her hand is glistening with numbing ointment and scraped raw. "Being polite about it doesn't work with you. I don't *want* to dance with you. How's that? I don't want to *dance*."

I can see that Bevel is trying very hard to hold on to his scandalized anger, but her sheer nerve seems to be too amusing to allow for the heated emotion to linger. He sighs, a puffing breath that I didn't think stocky men in such tight waistcoats could achieve, and grins, that same open, rehearsed smile I have seen him give a hundred times while apologizing for my brother's mistakes. He presents his hand again.

"Please. As the guest of honor, you must take the first dance with *someone*." He shoots a look at me, which makes it clear in his mind that he is saving Pip from the embarrassment of said dance being with me.

"I was quite clear that Pip doesn't have to take the floor if she doesn't feel well enough," I say, only just loud enough for Bevel to hear.

He makes no indication that he's actually caught my words and flexes his fingers at Pip.

"Oh, for . . ." Pip rolls her eyes and lays her fingers across his, sparing her palm, and allows him to pull her to her feet.

Bevel shoots me the most disgustingly triumphant look, and I wish I had the wherewithal to punch it straight off his little hedgehoggy face. There is no true triumph in badgering a woman into accepting something she did not want in the first place.

Pip limps slightly alongside Bevel as they head out to the middle of the room. The numbing ointment on her back, and I assume her knee, will be enough for her to last out this set, but I worry what will happen if Bevel doesn't return her to her chair quite soon. Pip is too polite to simply abandon him on the dance floor, I think, and I fear he is too oblivious to the tiny signals her body language is sending to read when she will be in too much pain to continue. I will have to watch closely and cut in at the appropriate time.

Pip wasn't lying when she said she had no idea what to do. She is standing in the very center of the hall, and Bevel turns her to face him. Her eyes find mine amid our guests, and there is a sort of embarrassed desperation in them. I nod in what I hope is an encouraging manner. She flashes me a small smile and turns to face Bevel.

The minstrels strike up the first dancing tune. Bevel has requested something light but slow, one of the courting country dances. Pip won't have to do much bouncing about, and that's a relief. Bevel bows, and Pip has enough insight to curtsy. Then Bevel, very deliberately, takes her left hand firmly in his and, turning so they both face away from me, begins to promenade her up the floor toward the musicians. He takes it slow, at a half tempo, and the minstrels follow his lead. His face is toward Pip, and I can see his lips moving, though I cannot hear his words. I can read what he is saying, however, and I am gratified to see that he is talking her through the steps instead of just yanking her along.

When they execute the complicated whirl at the end of the hall and switch directions, promenading back toward me, I can see the bright flush on Pip's cheeks. She is smiling—her genuine smile—and I think this means she is having fun. The blush may be from the pain, however, and her hand in Bevel's is trembling. They execute another complicated over-under whirl at my end of the hall. The dance looks faintly silly with only one couple. However, Pointe plops little Lewko onto my lap and holds his hand out to his wife. They join the dance two beats behind Bevel and Pip, and another couple joins two beats behind them, and then suddenly, the dance has become a beautifully intricate weaving of bodies around and between one another, coursing up and down the floor like waves upon a beach.

It is a lovely dance. One day, I may even have the luck to perform it with someone. For now, I quite enjoy watching it, and I allow myself to relax into the back of my chair and observe, my arms a loose ring around Lewko's waist to keep him from tipping into my plate.

Lewko has got himself occupied with a toy knight and a carved dragon, and both are too large for him to successfully swallow, so I allow my attention to drift across the assembled crowd. My guests are well on their way to being into their cups, and everyone looks pleased and relaxed. Whatever lingering tension there was from Pip's outburst has vanished, and it seems that the danger is past. The music flows on, strangely mesmerizing at this slower tempo, and the dance plays out.

And then, of course, Kintyre stands and makes his way to the minstrels. With Lewko slowing me down, I do not have the ability to stop him before he gets to them, requests a song, and moves to the dance floor. Bevel's choice ends, the dancers applaud the guest of honor and her escort, and as soon as Pip lets Bevel's hand go, Kintyre has got his arm around her waist.

He hoists her into the air as the next song starts. I recognize both it and what my brother is doing. The jump is supposed to be made with the man's hands on the woman's elbows, and it's only a small jump, but Kintyre is showing off. He's got his hands on Pip's plush, lovely arse, and is holding her up, above his head so everyone around can see how strong he is. Her pelvis is being ground into his chest, and my brother is, of course, leering at her breasts, which are now eye level.

"Hey, fucking hands off, buddy!" Pip snaps, wriggling her legs until Kintyre sets her back on her feet. He whirls her quickly to the side to catch up with the rest of the dancers around them. He tucks his hands against the small of her back, right where the worst of the scarring is. Pip actually staggers with the pain of it and *howls*.

The noise is more chilling than the dying scream of any werewolf, and I think she is just as shocked as the rest of the room that such a keening wail of pain was birthed from her own throat. Kintyre fumbles her to the floor and everyone in the entire room screeches into a halted silence.

Kintyre, suddenly the center of very unwelcome attention, does the one thing I have never seen him do: he freezes in panic.

As the wail dies in echoes along the rafters, Pip recovers from her white-faced swoon. Her forehead is clammy with pain, her eyes glassy, as if she is about to faint, but then she snaps, very suddenly, into a sea-foam wall of anger.

"Ow!" Pip snarls, and tries to push my brother away. But his fingers are digging in as he tries to hold her against her struggles. "Let go!"

Her invective startles me back into motion, for I too had been struck as dumb by her cry as the other onlookers. I shove Lewko at Velshi and make my way as quickly as I can to Pip; the crowd of dancers is milling about, unsure how to respond. I gesture the minstrels back into their music and, around us, the dance reluctantly resumes, people scuffling into motion at the request of the lordling. Perhaps it might even be because they respect that the fight I'm about to have is not going to be private, when we all desperately wish it was.

In the center of the floor, Kintyre has not yet relinquished Pip, and she is hauling back her fist and aiming at my brother's oft-broken nose. I manage to catch her elbow just before she lets fly, and crowd up beside Kintyre.

"Kintyre, let go," I snap. "You're hurting her."

"I wouldn't hurt her if she'd stop squirming," he huffs, a gleeful look on his face. I remember that look; it is his "I am hunting, and I have just caught my game" look.

"Pip's been cut!" I hiss. "Haven't you been paying attention? Don't touch her back!"

"Her back?" Bevel repeats, abandoning the partner he'd been dancing with nearby and coming to Kintyre's side. He instinctively maneuvers his body to shield those around us from seeing our conversation, as I have. "So, you mean . . . Bootknife?"

Pip kicks out hard, her heel connecting with Kintyre's knee. He winces and lets go. It would take a stronger person, with a more substantial boot, to inflict any real damage on my brother, but the sentiment behind the gesture is more than clear.

Pip takes a shaking step away from Kintyre and grabs the arm that I offer to help herself remain upright. Together, we turn back to the table, and I help her mince her way past our pretending-to-be-oblivious guests and to her chair. Lewko has got it pulled out for us, gray eyes glittering with pride as he struggles to push it back in for Pip as she sits.

"See, now that's a gentleman," Pip says, ruffling the boy's ashy-blond hair. Lewko climbs back onto my lap, knight and dragon in his small fists, and I settle him against my hip to spare my legs from falling asleep under his weight.

"Your brother is a slimeball," Pip says.

I resist the urge to say, *And this surprises you?* But only just. Instead, I pour us both more wine, cut both with water, and she drinks gratefully. Lewko reaches a hand for my cup, and I let him have a sip. He makes a face and shoves the cup away, and Pip laughs at his antics. The sound is strained, though, tight and high, more obligatory than honest.

The dance ends, and Pointe and his wife return to their seats. I pass off their son gratefully. Kintyre and Bevel both slouch back into their chairs. As they pass, every one of my guests gives them the evil-eye, and I am both honored and shocked that they would be so angry at my brother on Pip's behalf. I think we have accidentally succeeded in ensuring that Pip will be well cared for in every and any house in the village she should deign to visit.

Kintyre sits and descends into what I can only describe as a resolute sulk, arms crossed over his chest. It is embarrassing.

The next course of dinner is served, and the head table eats in intense silence. Only Lewko is oblivious to the cloud that hangs above our heads, ready to rip the air into thunderclaps of argument. I am used to such family dinners, but Pointe and his good wife are highly uncomfortable. Pip is lost in her own head. I chance it and settle my free hand over her own, which has balled up into a fist around the armrest.

She starts, but then flicks a grateful look to me and relaxes into the touch, fingers coming loose so I may lace my own between them. Bevel is watching with narrowed eyes, slurping his wine at an unhealthy rate. He hasn't cut his or Kintyre's with water, as the rest of us have done. Crude. And unintelligent. I can see them both getting drunker by the mouthful.

Velshi, my good, observant Velshi, swaps out their jug of wine for a pre-watered mix. Knowing him, it is probably much, much weaker than standard, as well. *Oh, how I adore my staff.*

When Bevel has imbibed enough liquid courage—I don't know what his gauge is, but he seems to have met it—he stands and sways over to Pip's side.

"Sorry he hurt you," Bevel slurs gently. He's not quite too drunk to be clear, but his lips are tumbling over the consonants.

Dismissively, Pip answers, "Kintyre should be apologizing, not you. You're not his keeper."

Bevel laughs. "Oh, but I am."

"And aren't you sick of it?" Pip challenges.

Bevel shrugs. "That's just Kintyre. You get used to it. It doesn't bother me."

"Well, it bothers me," Pip returns. "Actually, no, you know what bothers me? It's not that he doesn't know the social cues and common practices of politeness. What bothers me is that he observes them around him every day and has decided, however unconsciously, that they aren't anything he needs to bother himself with. That learning to communicate and interact with other human beings is *beneath* him. That everyone will just recognize his superiority and marvel, and obey. *That* is what bothers me."

I am so stunned by the boldness of her words that my tongue seems to be blocking up my throat. My heart is there, beating alongside it, hard and loud and painful. I have never, *ever* heard anyone challenge Kintyre this way.

Bevel isn't certain how to respond. "Listen," he says. "I think we got off on the wrong foot. You're a pretty little girl—" he doesn't seem to catch Pip's incredulous look at the insulting diminutive "—so why don't we just jump ahead to the end of the evening, hm? We promise we'll be very gentle with you, won't hurt your back at all."

"And what happens at the end of the evening?" Pip asks, wary.

I cover my face with my hands. I cannot watch this. Either Bevel will insult and embarrass himself, or Pip will say yes, which will be worse. Either way, I do not want to see her face when it happens. I couldn't bear it.

Bevel leans in close and whispers filth into her ear.

"What? Both of you?" Pip yelps, and her face twists in disgust. Bevel leans close and says something else, and Pip physically shoves him back. "No! No, I'm as happy to have a threesome with two hotties as any red-blooded girl, but you guys are complete sleazes. Get off me."

She shoves him hard enough that Bevel knocks my chair and I *have* to look. He is stunned. I don't know if he's ever been turned down before. And Pip looks like fury incarnate.

On the other side of me, Kintyre raises himself from his indolent slouch and scoffs. "So, I suppose it will be to *Forsyth's* bed you go to tonight, then?"

Pip goggles at him, eyes wide and mouth a scandalized 'o'. "Hey, how about I go to *nobody's* bed, because, one, I am in *pain* because of you, you stupid behemoth, and two, because I'm not a prize that's meted out at the end of dessert. Here's a startling and revolutionary idea: maybe I just don't want a fuck!"

Ah, so that's what that expletive means.

"Maybe you're just a frigid bitch," Kintyre snaps.

Pip rocks back in her seat, stunned. "Oh my god! I cannot even believe I used to look up to you! You're incredible! You're nothing like Forsyth!"

"So, that's what this is about," Kintyre snarls, his bright blue eyes snapping over to me. "Forssy's already got his scrabbly little fingers and flaccid little prick into you."

Pip pushes up to her feet and leans over me, her face puce with fury, in order to threaten Kintyre from as close a proximity as possible. "Don't talk about your brother like that! He's a good man! Better than you'll ever be!"

"Oh, and now you let your woman talk for you, too, brother?" Kintyre sneers, rising to his own feet. "Perhaps she's the man between you? Does she stick it to you? Do you think you're in *love*, just because she hasn't run away from you yet?"

I shrink down in my seat, too mortified to even get my tongue to stop fluttering against the roof of my mouth. I could never make words like this.

"And is there something wrong with taking it up the arse?" Pip challenges. "Does it make you less of a man? Because Bevel seems to like it!"

Bevel and Kintyre both go pale and stagger. Bevel clutches at his chair. "How did you know?" he hisses.

"Silence!" Kintyre booms.

"Oh my god!" Pip says, exasperation written into every feature. "What does it matter what you two do together? Bevel's disgustingly in love with you, you ridiculous moron! He always has been! It's barely even *subtext*! He sets up threesomes for you just so he can touch you! Is that what all this macho manly shit is about? 'Cause there's nothing wrong with loving who you love!"

"Nobody loves Forsyth Turn," Kintyre snarls.

"Qu-qu-quiet!" I snap, standing and pushing Pip and Kintyre away from one another. "E-e-enough!"

"Not here," Pointe snaps, his voice just loud enough for us to hear, but quiet enough that music keeps his words from reaching my guests. He crosses behind my chair to lay hands on Kintyre's shoulders. "You're not doing this here, Sir Kintyre. You're drunk and shaming yourself. Master Bevel, get him into Forsyth's study."

But Kintyre is incensed. He is insulted. He pushes the Sword of Turnshire away and holds a hand out to stay Bevel. "I am shaming myself? Me? You're the one shaming the Turn name, brother! You are pathetic," Kintyre sneers. "Deciding that the first woman to show a grain of interest in you is actually infatuated with you? Look at you. What in the world could she find attractive about *you*? You saved her, that's all. She's being nice to you only because you saved her. And everyone here knows it."

Faces which had been frozen all around us narrow and shut down. Nobody, not one guest, makes a sound in my support. Of course. They are laughing at me, silently, inside. Laughing at foolish Forsyth Turn, who thought he could make this woman fall in love with him.

"Now," Kintyre says. "You are going to apologize and sit down and act like a proper lady, or I will leave you here to *rot* and never take you home!"

"I will not!"

"Kintyre . . ." Bevel starts, plucking at his sleeve, but Kintyre is embarrassed and feeling cruel. He pushes Bevel away hard enough that he slams into the table. Bevel turns hurt, dark eyes up at my brother and goes silent, biting so hard on his lower lip that the flesh turns white.

All the breath rushes from my body. *Oh, incredible, Pip was right.* Bevel Dom *is* in love with my brother, and I never noticed.

Poor Bevel.

I hate the hedgehoggy little lackey, but to be in love with my brother, and Kintyre so in love with women's bodies . . . how cruel this Elgar Reed is. Poor, poor Bevel.

"Sit!" Kintyre repeats, pointing to the chair magnanimously, and Pip throws her own finger into the air, the middle one. It is clearly a rude gesture, but its exact meaning is unclear.

"I am not some docile dog you can order around," Pip screams. "You are an asshole and a bully, Kintyre Turn, and I don't want your help!"

The whole room falls into a screeching hush.

Kintyre goes very, very still. I can't help the involuntary step back as his fingers twitch into a fist. It seems the survival instincts of childhood are still deeply ingrained.

"Good," he grunts, fury in every line of his face, "as you will not be receiving it."

"Kin!" Bevel squalls. "You can't just turn down a maiden in distress."

"I can, and I have."

"I'm not a maiden in distress," Pip snarls, rounding on Bevel, who is utterly unprepared for his own tongue-lashing and stumbles back into my brother's arm. "I'm a *woman*, and I am damn well capable of rescuing my own damn self, *thank you very much*."

"Let us hope so," Kintyre rumbles. "For your sake."

And then he pushes past Pointe and storms out of the hall, Bevel quick on his heels.

Seven

"**H**ave you gone completely *mad?* He was your one chance!" I snarl.

"I told you," Pip lobs back, "I don't need help from some misogynistic asshole!"

I slam my palm against the surface of my desk, and Pip doesn't even flinch. I think she is too angry to react now. Perhaps even too angry to feel pain. I worry for her, for her knee and her back and her hands, but the last thing she will accept from me right now, from *anyone*, is coddling.

"Well, you can't very well do it yourself!" I snap.

"Why not?" she challenges, chin raised and arms crossed over her breasts. "Why can't I? I know this world as well as anyone else! I probably know it better than Kintyre! Why can't I figure this out and go on an adventure by myself?"

I gesture at the papers my spies have collected for me. "There are charts! Spells! Objects that must be collected in the right order at the right time. You don't know the land, no matter how much you may have read about it, and you do not know the temperaments and habits of the creatures you may encounter. Have you even traveled, Pip? Can you start a campfire and direct a horse? Have you bartered for anything in your life? You *cannot* go on a quest alone."

Pip clenches her jaw and says nothing, eyes scanning the papers. I brought her into my study to show this to her, to plot the quest she would have to undertake with as much precision as possible so she would see, so she would *understand* that she cannot do this, she cannot go home without the help of Kintyre Turn.

As much as I hate to have to admit it, she needs my brother.

"I could learn," she says. "You have everything else I need here. God, you're clever, Forsyth, you're really clever. You can lay it all out. You've put half the pieces together for me already."

I have saved my strongest argument for last, and I lay it out before her now with solemnity: "You cannot Speak Words, Pip."

She stares at me, muddy eyes wide, and then, slowly as an old woman, she creaks her way down into the only other chair in my study. She is furiously silent, and I take the respite to fetch us both brandy for our abused throats. She accepts the goblet from me without comment, and without eye contact.

We both sip, and the silence stretches on for longer than is comfortable. Just when I am debating whether to fetch a second glass, Pip sighs and slumps awkwardly into the side of her chair, closing her eyes. The skin around her mouth is white and stretched, and every line of her body screams that she is in pain.

"Let's get you upstairs and put to bed," I whisper, pulling the glass from her slackening fingers.

"Poppy milk?" she whimpers.

"Yes, of course."

She opens her eyes and smiles at me, warm and sad. "You haven't won this argument, you know," she says as I help her to her feet. "This is just an intermission. A pain-delay. Ha ha."

Velshi, who has been lingering by the door to my study as Pip and I argued, ducks under Pip's arm and helps me spread her other across my shoulders. Together, we carry her gently, slowly, up the back stairs to Mother's chamber. Below, I can hear Sheriff Pointe's distinctive voice coming from the direction of the formal hall, calling for the next course, for more wine, for the dancing to continue. He is trying to salvage the night, and I am grateful, once more, that I am able to call him my friend.

Where Kintyre and Bevel stormed off to, I do not know and, frankly, do not care to know. Let them go fling themselves in the river and be eaten by Kelpies, for all I care. All I hope is that they return come morning, when I have talked sense into Pip. I don't want her to go off alone with them, but what other choice is there? Pip needs to go on a quest, and for that, she needs a hero.

That is how these things are done.

Neris takes over for Velshi when we reach Pip's room, tutting at me as we maneuver her over to the bed. She already has poppy milk mixed into tea in her hand, and Pip drinks the whole draught before she sits.

The potion works quickly, and soon, Pip is swaying on the mattress. I toe off my shoes and climb up onto the bed behind her, holding her upright so Neris can begin to undress her. I frame her thighs with my own, my hands on the unmarred forward curve of her shoulders, her head falling back against my collarbones. I cradle her skull under my chin, discreetly memorizing the scent of her hair and skin. Warmth, rose oil, the tang of pain-induced sweat, the lemon-mint of the ointment, poppy milk, and something musky under all of that, almost like vanilla but less cloyingly sweet. Pip.

Within moments, she is breathing deeply, asleep. The strain on her face clears, and I breathe a sigh of relief.

"She shouldn't have gone back down, sir," Neris says, settling onto the floor beside the bed and reaching for Pip's shoes. "It was too much."

"It was Pip's choice," I counter. I make a point of looking away as Neris pulls off Pip's slippers and then, gently, runs her hands up inside Pip's dress to unlace her garters and slide her stockings off.

"She's a stubborn thing," Neris mutters. "She's pushed herself too hard, and you should have sent her to bed, sir."

"I'm not her father, nor her master, to just send her off," I counter, still keeping my gaze resolutely on the wall above the headboard. "But I am yours; mind your tongue, Neris."

Neris sets aside the stockings, folding them neatly, and then looks me full in the face. "Then I beg your pardon for being so bold, sir, but you *should not* have let her push herself like this. And the healer woman would say the same thing if she was here."

I glare down at Neris, angry not at her for her cheek, but at myself because she is right. Mother Mouth would never have let Pip return to the dining hall after her episode in the stairwell, no matter how much Pip herself protested. Pip has a stubborn streak as wide as my Chipping, and if someone doesn't rein her in, she is going to seriously impede her healing. She was not supposed to have danced tonight, we *discussed* it, and all the running up stairs and screaming in my study has done her no good on top of that.

I look to Pip, drowsing against my chest, mouth slack. I give in to the urge to run my fingers through her hair, which is still soft but tangled with her earlier exertions.

"Yes, of course, Neris. You're right. Apologies."

Neris nods firmly, and then undoes Pip's sash and begins plucking at the laces of her formal robe. She peels that off, then goes for the chemise.

"Oh, I should . . . go," I say, but Neris shakes her head.

"I need your help, sir. And while I'm saying things I oughtn't, I don't think Miss Piper will mind, you seeing her in her altogether. Better you than Mister Velshi, hm, sir?"

I cannot disagree with her, except where she seems to be making the assumption that Pip regards me as anything more than her benefactor. The kiss in the stairwell was interrupted and never resumed, and now that Pip and I have quarreled so fiercely, I am probably right in assuming it will *never* be consummated.

Together, we get Pip down to her bloomers and the bandage that winds round and round her torso, binding her breasts nearly flat and protecting the cuts. Where Kintyre grabbed her, all along the small of her back, the bandages are spotted with blood.

"Stubborn, stubborn woman," I mutter, as we lay Pip flat on her stomach and tuck the blankets over her legs. I repeat my actions from her first night here and set up the kettle for tea, while Neris cuts the now-useless bandages off Pip with her sewing scissors.

The wounds low on her back are red and raw, the scabs rubbed away, leaving the muscle exposed and weeping sluggishly. The scars further up her back seem to have held, the skin already knitted together in slim white ridges where the cuts were thin, or forming a pinky layer where they had been wide. The stitches are fine.

The ointment truly is wondrous, for the healing to have progressed so quickly in just one week.

When the kettle boils, I pour water into the wash basin for Neris and place the jar of ointment within her reach on the bedside table. I try to hand her a clean cloth, but Neris shakes her head and says, "I think she'd appreciate you, sir. I'll be just in the hall if you need me."

She curtsies and vanishes before I can say anything to the contrary.

Hm. I am beginning to wonder if the whole Chipping really *is* conspiring to get Pip into my bed, and me into her affections. Well, they are wasting their time.

I clean Pip's back and reapply the ointment, and then, because the brandy and the wine and the emotional turmoil of the evening have caught up with me, I let my head slip onto the pillow beside Pip's. I will not sleep; I just need a moment to rest before I go back downstairs to the party.

It is several hours later when I wake. The process is slow, and more than once, I give it up as a bad job and muzzily contemplate just rolling over and staying abed. An unlooked-for warmth radiates from somewhere close to my pillow, and I sigh, contented for reasons that I cannot yet remember and am happy to indulge in rather than tease out, for now. The inhale of my sigh brings the sharp scent of lemons and menthol to my nose, and I snap completely awake.

I am in bed with Pip.

I fell asleep beside Pip. I *slept* beside Pip! Most of the night, it seems!

My insides curl with the audacity and impropriety of it—and yet I cannot help but flex a few of the fingers of the hand closest to my head, to run their tips gently across the tickling strands of hair at the back of Pip's head. How gloriously intimate.

How bold of me.

I shy back, wriggling slowly to get off the mattress without alerting Pip of my shameful imposition. Pip remains still and silent beside me, the lamps turned down in her chamber and her breathing steady in the thin darkness of early morning. As soon as my socked feet are on the floor, I retrieve my boots from beside the bed—I don't remember removing them, just as I don't remember turning down the lamp. Was it Mother Mouth who did? Or Neris? Or, Writer forbid, Velshi? What *must* my staff think of me now?

Lecherous, opportunistic old man, I scold myself.

Boots collected, I tiptoe to the door. The creak of the hinges sounds loud in the dawn's glow, and Pip stirs.

"Mmm. Fo'sth?" she mutters.

Blast and drat!

"Yes, Pip?"

"Mornin'?"

"Not quite. Go back to sleep," I say soothingly. "I'll, uh, I'll come back with some breakfast and a bath for you later, okay?" Now that most of her wounds have closed, she can be immersed, and I think she will enjoy the treat.

"Mm, yeah, okay," she says, and turns her face the other way on her pillow, burrowing down into the comfort and warmth of the blankets. She inhales and reaches out, hooking the pillow I just abandoned and pulling it against her face.

Just to block out the morning's light, I tell myself. *Not because it smells like me.*

Full of cowardice and shame, I flee to my own chambers. I wait in darkness and silence, alone, for the sun to fully rise. Once it is up, and the hour is a decent one for being awake, I summon Velshi to my chambers, bidding him bring tea and the bathtub. I feel grimy, and a soak sounds divine. I don't think Pip will begrudge me a turn with the bathing tub first.

Cook rounds up an excellent breakfast from last night's leftovers. I nibble and read my Men's reports while I float. Pointe has left a rambling letter about how the rest of the night went, his handwriting difficult to decipher because he was clearly pleasantly drunk by the time he got round to it.

I inquire after my brother while I am drip-drying in my chambers. The servants remove the tub, and Velshi allows all of a single emotion to cross his otherwise butler-blank features: annoyance. He reports that Kintyre and Bevel haven't been seen since they stormed out of the hall, but that their travel gear is still in Kintyre's chambers, so they haven't left yet.

When I'm all caught up on my paperwork, I put on some casual clothing and grab the food tray. Buoyed by the thought of no Kintyre, no Bevel, and no duties save for rest and thus spending the whole of the day with Pip, I take the stairs to her chambers two at a time.

When I get there, I am startled to find the door open. My staff have wrestled the large copper tub into the room, and it is sitting before the hearth, half filled with steaming water. Neris is standing beside the fireplace, outwardly watching the kettle boil but, in actuality, glaring at the bed without seeming to look at it.

Pip is sitting up, a light robe draped over her back as she leans against the tent pole of her crooked knees. She has her arms wrapped around her shins and an expression of thunderous fury on her face.

Before her, Bevel Dom sits cross-legged, his back to me.

I pause on the threshold to eavesdrop. Neris spots me, but I shake my head, warning her against making any move to give away my presence.

"I don't know what to do," Bevel is saying, reaching out to take Pip's hand. She jerks it out of his reach.

"You can get the hell out. That would be a good start," Pip snaps.

"Miss Piper, please, you have to understand . . . this has been a secret for so long. I don't know how to talk to him! He's my best friend, he's my confidant, he's my *partner*, and, because of what you said, because he *knows* now, he won't even *look* at me."

"That's not my problem."

"But it *is* your fault! Please!"

"What do you want me to say?" she asks. "If he's disgusted by your regard, then he's a hypocritical asshole."

"He's not disgusted! He's never been disgusted. When we . . . when we're . . . with women," —he swallows, clicking and sticking, and I find that there is a swell of pity for Bevel building under my ribs— "he touches me. He kisses me. He . . . *lays* with me. But he doesn't love me. He doesn't love *anyone*."

I cannot hold in the ironic snort, and Bevel whips his head around, dark eyes wide with the shock of being caught. Then, they narrow with fury. He shoots off the bed and slams me up against the doorjamb. The tray of breakfast clatters out of my hands, sending breads and cold meats into the air like a spray. He presses his elbow into my throat.

"You think this is *funny*?" he snarls into my face.

"Bevel!" Pip squawks.

He pushes me back hard, snaps my head into the wood; stars bloom in the sides of my vision. I scrabble at his arm, but he is stronger than I, and his strength is doubled by his anger.

"She's ruined *everything*!"

"Bevel, stop it!" Pip cries.

Bevel slams my head into the wall a third time, but then lets go and takes a step back, panting and red-faced. "He makes them fall in love with him, and then he *runs*. He thinks it's *a game*. I did, too. But now he knows, and he's going to run away from *me*."

"I . . . don't," I croak, hands on my throat.

"Don't *what?*" Bevel snaps.

"I don't think it's funny," I admit. There is water on the credenza, and I grope my way along the wall until I can wrap my hands around one of the cups. I gulp, catching my breath, and then turn to face Bevel.

He is standing by the open door, face buried in his hands, shoulders rigid and posture so completely still it is like the adventure where the gorgon turned him into a statue.

"I don't think it's funny, Sir Dom," I say. "And I think it's sad, because I think there is no better partnership than yours. You and my brother were, I think, quite literally written for each other. You balance each other too well. And I pity you, Sir Dom, because you are right. My brother loves no one but himself."

Bevel's renewed anger rises swiftly, and he drops his hands into fists.

"Curse you, Forsyth Turn! *And you*, you mouthy bitch!" he snaps at Pip. "Curse you both!" He runs out of the room, leaping over the fallen tray, and vanishes down the hall.

I am not surprised to hear from Velshi, several minutes later, that Kintyre Turn and Bevel Dom have departed Turn Hall. I *am* surprised to hear that they did so in each other's presence.

✍

"Now what will you do?" I ask Pip.

She is seated in the tub, a layer of bubbles preserving her modesty as I scrub my long fingers and the soap into her hair. I should feel faintly embarrassed that I am acting as her lady's maid, that she is here and nude, but all I feel is the warm glow of companionship and the comfort of a shared secret and respect.

I am also doing my absolute best to block out any sexual thoughts. I am not here to impose my desires upon Pip, I am here to be kind, and to help her with a task she is unable to perform alone. But oh, how I wish this were romantic. How I long to strip myself down, to slide into the warm water behind her, cradle her back against my chest, hug her close between my thighs . . .

I squeeze my eyes shut and force myself to take long, cool breaths. No. *No.*

I am listening too much to Pointe and the part of me that . . . points.

Instead of ridiculous fantasies, I focus on the feel of my fingers against Pip's scalp, and the glow of satisfaction that curls along my spine, knowing that my brother is gone and that he has left in a horrid mood. It is cruel of me, to wish misery on Bevel Dom, but he is not above reproach himself. And there is something satisfying about watching one's tormentors suffer through actions of their own.

I am still worried, of course. He is the only hero I know and have leverage with, and I trusted him—if not with Pip's body and heart, then at least to finish the quest and do his duty as her champion. There are other heroes, but I do not know them personally and cannot vouch that they will be as reliable as Kintyre Turn. And yet, I must contact and engage *someone* to guide Pip on her quest.

When she is ready.

A new flare of warmth floods my insides when I reflect on the fact that Pip will not be ready for any kind of adventuring for several more weeks. Pip has made it clear that she holds no desire for Kintyre, that she will not be my brother's woman, and for the first time, I have hope that I can convince her to turn her eye to me.

Now, if I could only find a way to be less stupid, less gawkish, less of an embarrassment. If only I could prove to her that I can live up to her assessment of me as a great man. I can work very hard and watch what I say very carefully, and be brilliant, just as she says I am.

"Now what?" she murmurs, distracted by the way I am scratching her scalp with my fingernails, light and gentle. "Hmm. Now, I'm thinking that you're going to hand me some more of that lovely soft cheese on that toasty bread."

Neris replaced the fallen breakfast tray, so I rinse and dry my hands and obey. I compose the snack and hold it out for her, but instead of reaching for it, she simply opens her mouth.

Right. Yes. I swallow hard and tell myself, very firmly, that I can do this. That it is not horribly intimate, it is just practical. Pip's hands are wet and soapy.

I press the bread forward, slowly, and Pip closes her lips over half of it. Her bottom lip brushes the very tip of my thumb, and I have to take a deep, slow breath to keep myself from either startling away (which is my first instinct), or dropping the morsel entirely in my shock.

Deliberately, Pip presses white teeth through the snack and nips off half of it.

Pip grins around her mouthful. "This stuff is bliss." I feed her the second half, and she takes it with a flutter of her eyelashes. Her throat as she swallows is wholly unremarkable, and yet I cannot make myself look away.

"I agree," I say, leaning back in my chair and indulging in my own slice of bread and cheese to keep me from pressing the thumb she inadvertently kissed against my mouth. "But what I meant was . . . now that Kintyre and Bevel have declined to be your champions, how will you . . . quest?"

She stiffens slightly in the steaming water. We've been dancing around the topic all day, but it needs to be discussed. I only hope it does not bring on another episode.

There is silence as she contemplates my question. She finishes off her snack and sinks lower in the water. The bubbles on the surface brush her bottom lip when she finally answers: "I want you to write it all down for me. Step by step. How he brought me here, and how I get . . . h-home."

"Pip, we've already talked about this. You cannot go alone."

"I don't intend to." She turns and looks meaningfully at me.

Dread slips under my skin. "Oh, Pip, *no*," I mumble. "No, you are not serious. You cannot be."

"Why not?" she asks, turning over in the water and pillowing her chin on arms she crosses over the edge of the tub. "I've seen how you deal with conflict—you're levelheaded and collected. You're a great swordsman, you're smart as hell, and, best of all, you're the Shadow Hand. You've got enough dirt on everyone in Hain to get us loads of free rooms at inns and help along the journey."

"Pip, I'm not a hero!"

"I don't need a hero. I need a guide. Between the two of us, I think we can get it all figured out. It will be tough, but we can do it."

"But I can't *fight*. I can't best trolls and wrestle serpents and lasso flying horses!"

She frowns. "Am I asking you to? Why would we get into those sorts of ridiculous situations? You're a professional spy. I'm sure we can get everything we need and do it on the sly. The Viceroy won't even know we're doing it, and then I can . . ." She stops and swallows, shaking her head resolutely. "Then I can go home to my family."

I pause at the odd tone in her voice. "I thought you said you had no one at home waiting for you."

She screws her eyes shut and shivers in a way that has nothing to do with the temperature of the bathwater.

"It's all screwed up in my head," she whispers. "I think . . . I don't know what I think. I want to go home, but I'm terrified to think of it. I miss my parents, my friends, so badly, and yet there is something that is keeping me from thinking of them. It scares me, Forsyth. It scares me so *much*. I want to go, and I am scared to go.

It's like someone else is in my head, pushing against the lock, while someone else is . . . barring the door."

I kneel on the floor beside the tub and take her face between my hands, gentle. "Look at me, Pip."

She does, and her pupils are pinpricks of fear.

"You daren't think about your home, and your family, because you were protecting them. I have seen this before in men who have been tortured. Your mind locked them away in a place that Bootknife could not get them from you, and though you are safe, your mind believes that it must keep them under guard. You *are* safe, Pip. You can release them now."

Fat tears roll down her cheeks and over my thumbs, and she sniffles, forcing a smile. "Goddamn PTSD."

"Ah," I whisper. "You have been very brave, Lucy Piper, but your war is over, and you are here with me now. And I will be with you for as long as it takes for you to readjust. Take all the time you need."

She presses her cheek into my palm, and I run my other hand over her soapy shoulder.

"Thank you."

"You are very welcome," I reply. "And then, when you are healed and ready, we will find you a real hero, a smarter and stronger and braver man than I to take you on your quest."

Pip stops nuzzling and looks up at me, eyebrows drawing down into a concerned 'v'. "I already said I want to travel with you."

I smile. "Ah. You weren't serious."

"I was serious, Forsyth. I meant it. Honestly, I meant it." She sits up in the tub, so far that the beautiful valley of her breasts appears out of the snow of bubbles. I wrench my eyes back up to meet her own.

"No, you were not, Pip. You'll reconsider. Stupid, fat old Forsyth Turn is not a good choice. I'm just happy that you'll allow me to be by your side while you heal. Then we'll say our farewells, and you will go off and have your grand adventure."

"Why do you talk about yourself like that?" Pip asks quietly. "Why do you believe Kintyre when he talks about you? You don't believe him when he says those sorts of things about me, or about Pointe, but when he says it about you, you take him at face value. Why?"

"Because it's true."

Pip makes a frustrated sound and grabs both my ears in her hands. It hurts, and she twists them until I relent and meet her gaze. "It. Is. Not. True. Do you understand me, Forsyth Turn? Are you *listening* to me? You are not fat. You are not gawky, or stupid, or useless, or unlovable. You are a good man. You are a *better* man than your brother, and you will stop investing in what he says about you *right this instant*, or else."

It feels like acid poured into the hollows of my ribs. Why won't she stop *lying* to me?

"Or else what?" I challenge, hurting and wanting to lash out, wanting to make her hurt the way she is making my whole world crumble around me.

"Or else I will never kiss you."

I can suddenly taste my heart in the back of my throat, and hear my blood rushing in my ears. I swallow hard and cannot help it when my eyes drop down to her mouth, cannot help envisioning the soft press of her slightly chapped lips against my own, the prickle of my stubble against her chin, the cool touch of her nose nestled into my cheek, the taste of her tongue as it slides over my teeth.

"Ki-k-k-kiss," I struggle to say.

"Not yet," she whispers, and I can feel her warm breath puffing against my face. I let my mouth drop open to catch it. "When we're both ready, I will. I want to. But not yet."

She pulls away, and I have the dignity not to follow her with my face, offering myself up to the promise of her embrace like a minotaur's sacrifice. I slump onto the floor by the tub, resting against the warm metal in order to stay upright. She looks down at me, pets the side of my head with the soft backs of her damp fingers, runs her nails lightly through my hair.

"Maybe it's just the Florence Nightingale effect, but I do like you, Forsyth Turn. Your brother is wrong. Your staff love and shield you from your brother's destructive moods. Pointe defends you, and the people of Lysse Chipping think you're the best lordling they've ever known. They practically worship you. And the Shadow's Men are so incredibly loyal . . . I don't think the king has as much respect as you do. Forsyth, people *love* you. Why can't you see that? Kintyre was wrong. You are *loved*."

"Do-do you l-lo-lov—"

Pip smiles sadly and puts one finger over my lips, halting my clumsy, terrifying question before it can escape out into the open. "I don't know," she admits. "But I think I could. Will you give me the time I need to figure it out?"

I nod. Oh, how badly I want to tell her of the admiration I feel for her, to show her. How I want to struggle against my inherent nature and prove to Pip that her love will not be an unwelcome gift, that I will treasure it, that I will acknowledge how wonderful and rare and incredible it would be to receive it.

But I do not. Because she has asked for time. I am not my brother—I can respect her requests. And because the thought of such a bold action frankly frightens me. Would it really be welcome?

She turns over and leans back in the tub, still mincing like an old woman with sore joints the day before an approaching storm. I return to my chair. We watch one another in mutual, anticipatory silence, and I let my gaze wander over her in a way I feared would be too bold before. I linger on the smooth column of her graceful neck, plan the love bites I will put right there, just under her ear. I admire the curve of her shoulder and breasts, the plumpness of her bottom lip, the round at the base of her chin that shows she has lived a well-fed, good life. I imagine burying my face in her short, silky hair, the feel of her hands on my back, her nails digging into my buttocks, all the things that I would not allow myself to imagine before because before they could never be mine.

Because before, she would never have given them to me.

All the things I have seen as Shadow Hand, through peepholes and around corners, from behind the arras and tapestries, all the things I have never had the privilege of having for myself. No matter how much I may have desired it, fantasized about having someone touch me like that, make me moan and tremble like that, someone that I could slowly pull to pieces the way I have seen other men do, I could not. Because it could never happen. I could not fantasize it; would not torture myself with that fantasy.

And now Pip says that I may. That I will have someone with whom to share all that I've learned about carnality through spy-holes and fantasy and the generous application of my hand to myself in dark, small moments. She will. She has promised. I may have the thing I desire most—the companionship of another person, the love of a good woman—if only I can give her that which she desires most: me. A truer, more honest, more brave me. I can earn her.

And this terrifies me. I have spent so much time building walls and shields around myself. How do I make them crumble? How do I let them go? How do I let myself be convinced of things that I am not certain are true?

What if I can't? What if it's all a lie? What if I'm not good enough for Pip? What if I try and try, and I cannot ever be confident, or smooth, or well-spoken and intelligent and kind and all the things she is pressing upon me? What if I just give up now, stay the Forsyth I know,

remain in the shadows, remain the Shadow Hand, skulking and quiet? It's easier, certainly; it's easier that way. It
is safer. And I will lose Pip, but it won't hurt, will it? It
won't be hard work. I can stay as I am, and I will miss
her terribly, but one cannot really miss what one has not
really ever had, and it would be better, wouldn't it? Pip
could fall in love with a real man, and I will stay out of
her way, and—

"Shut up," Pip says softly.

I look up, my thoughts skidding off the road like a
poorly constructed cart. "I . . . wasn't speaking."

"No, but I can tell what you're thinking," Pip answers. "You don't get to chicken out of this. I'm not
going to let you."

"Pip, you're asking so mu-mu-much of m-m-me."

"Not anything you can't do. I've seen it, Forsyth.
I'm not asking you to change. I'm just asking you to start
seeing yourself for who and what you really are. We're
not reconstructing you. We're just ripping the distortion
off the surface of the mirror, okay?"

"I don't know h-ho-how," I mutter. "How can you
ch-ch-change how I see myself?"

"Easy," Pip says. "We're going to force you out of
your comfort zone. Then, you'll see how amazing you
really are."

"And how will you do that?"

Pip smiles, and it is one of the honest, dazzling ones
that makes me feel like there is no evil in the world at all.

"Because you're going to say yes, Forsyth Turn."

Eight

ip, as it turns out, is an extremely competent researcher.

She says this is because she possesses something called a Doctorate in English. I ask her what reading has to do with alchemy, and she laughs. We spend the most pleasantly fascinating evening while she tells me all about the education system in her world, where there are libraries that reach into the sky and are filled with more books than can possibly be read in a single lifetime; where it is *illegal* for children to not attend a school; that the most skilled and most celebrated of her people are called "Doctors," no matter their healing knowledge, and that they are also, comically, often the most myopic when it comes to their subjects of discourse.

"This is why you are unmarried?" I ask. "Because you are devoted to your studies?"

"I guess," she says, looking up from the enormous roll of blank parchment she fetched down from my cupboard. She blushes and looks away. "But I'm still really young, in my society. Twenty-five . . . that's nothing. Also 'cause, you know, most of the people at my school were jocks. Um, like Kintyre," she adds, when I admit I do not know what a jock is.

"I see."

What I do not see is why she is so keen to scour every book in my library. I think that, if we are to head out on an adventure, we would be better learning how to build a campfire, sew wounds, and practice outwitting elves. The thought of being ill prepared for our journey terrifies me, though I will not allow Pip to see my fear.

"Well, the aim of the quest is obvious," Pip says to me, as I begin pulling the scrolls and books I feel may be helpful off my shelves and into a pile on my desk. Pip has cleared space on the floor and is now crouched over the long piece of parchment. She is methodically scoring it into a grid-work of squares, rather like an over-extended calendar.

"Obvious?" I ask, slipping two blue leather-bound tomes on the native fauna of the northerly Minchin Forest onto the top of the pile.

"We have to summon the same Deal-Maker spirit the Viceroy did to send me home. That part's easy."

"Ah, and we have that spirit's sigil already," I say, retrieving the note with the recreation my Men brought to me when they brought me Pip. I hand it to her, and she lays it to the side of her chart.

"And that's Station One, taken care of. With this sigil comes the rules of summoning, so we also know that this is going to be a collection quest. We have to get stuff and bring it all together," Pip explains, when my eyebrows wrinkle with my confusion.

"I see," I say. "But what . . . stuff?"

"Well, that's what research is for. Which Spirit Poem goes with this particular Deal-Maker? Where is it written down? What is its history? Who has summoned this spirit before?"

"The Viceroy has," I say, grasping her line of reasoning. "Did you see anything?"

Pip stills, hands hovering over a quill and inkpot. "No," she says softly. "No, I didn't see anything in the room."

I wait for another episode of shaking and screaming, but none comes. Pip breathes deep, in and out, for several minutes. When she feels calm enough, she resumes scoring the parchment.

"I'll search the tomes and notes my Men extracted," I say. "And compare them to the Spirit Poems on record. They are . . . ah! Here." I pull them from the shelf.

Pip chuckles. "Only you would have a *record* of known Spirit Poems."

"I am the Shadow Hand," I say glibly.

"Yes, you are."

Over the next few days, I spend many an hour re-reading my Men's letters, and the pages and scrolls they liberated from the Viceroy. When the information within them tangles in my mind, and I need a respite from clue-deciphering, I pick up the chronicles of my brother's adventures, and those of the heroes that came before him. I make notes on the sorts of tools they seemed to find useful, the weapons and provisions they pack when they go on adventures, the clothing they cherish. I'm not certain where to procure all of these items, but thankfully, my Men do, as they often pack as if they're questing when I send them to spy.

No one asks me why I'm having them bring me such items. They simply smile and nudge one another. Gossiping old grandmothers, the lot of them.

Neris floats in and out of whatever room we're occupying, bringing in tea and wine, victuals and fruit and—something that Pip has taught Cook to make and which has quickly become a favorite staple of my afternoons—*sandwiches*.

In a fit of a punchy mood, brought on by perhaps too much tea and not enough sleep, Pip rearranges all the books on the south wall of my study so the colors of the spines create a comical, smiling visage. It is cheerful in the face of her frustration at being impotent when it comes to reading the books she rearranges.

When Pip and I are together, Pip bids me put down the tales of daring-do and instead insists on being talked through everything the Shadow's Men have deciphered about her capture. She cannot read the alphabet of Hain, and so I must read each notation and squiggle to her, which she copies into a small leather-bound book of her own with chicken-scratch markings that I, in turn, cannot read myself.

I am powerfully fascinated by the way she constructs her written language. Knowledge is the highest aphrodisiac for me, and to be offered an entire method of recording thoughts that *sounds* like my language but is not written the same is wondrous. Especially since I will be able to use it as a code for myself; no one else will know this method, so my deepest secrets and most important notes will remain safe.

In the evenings, she teaches me how to read them, the twenty-six letters with so many rules that I am certain I will never get it right.

"English," she tells me, "is a thief language. We steal verbs and nouns from other languages, and so their rules must apply when conjugated. It's terrible. There's this great saying about English lurking in alleyways, knocking out other languages and rifling their pockets for spare vocabulary. I wish I could remember where I first heard that . . . I'm a bad academic. No citation."

Her little notation book begins to live in her pocket. At any time of day or night, I can expect to find her scribbling, her letters messy with ink splotches, her fingers stained from little practice with a quill. Sometimes, she stops mid-sentence and, with a distant look in her eyes, ignores all that is happening around her until her thoughts are on paper.

I find it endearing. Sheriff Pointe, the first time it happened in his presence, found it insulting, for he had been telling a great tale of his father's era as Shadow Hand. I had to explain to him that she wasn't bored, she was working through a problem and something he had said had triggered a thought for her.

Eventually, when I have read every piece of the relevant correspondence to Pip, when she has pulled down every single book I own and demanded I read chapters to her based on the titles in the codex, when several weeks have passed and her little notation book must be nigh stuffed with words that I am only now learning to read easily, she sits back in my study with a glass of unwatered wine rolling between her hands and a smile playing over her lips. She is leaning fully back, reveling in the ability to do so. The ivy is completely healed and only occasionally does Pip wince when one of the still-tight scars pulls uncomfortably.

"You look satisfied," I say, setting aside my bookkeeping for the night. In point of fact, she looks—near as I can tell from my necessarily covert research on the subject—like a woman who has just experienced a thoroughly satisfying orgasm. I shall never say so out loud, however.

"I am," she says, and gestures at her enormous roll of parchment, the one she had been scoring when our research began. It is now tacked to the wall above my study fireplace. In each of the squares, she has scribbled some relevant word or two. "It's done."

"Impressive," I murmur, while scanning the elaborate chart. "I cannot understand it, mind, but I assume it is meaningful?"

"I'm a whiz at Excel," she says, taking a sip of her wine. She is getting drunk, celebrating her achievement, relaxing in a way I haven't seen her do since that afternoon in the tub. "This took a bit longer, since I had to do it by hand, but this is how I charted the storytelling arcs in Reed's books for my Doctorate."

"Baffling," I tell her again, and deny the urge to cross the room and fall to my knees before her, a supplicant to her strange ways and intellect, and kiss that beautiful rounded tummy I have glimpsed so briefly. "Utterly baffling."

"Just a different way of organizing knowledge, my lord Shadow Hand. Here, let me show you."

She stands, taking her wine with her, and with only the smallest of winces, reaches out to explain the process of cross-correlation to me. "And so I understand the exercise," I say, when she is finished explaining how to read the chart. "But what is the purpose?"

Pip turns to face me, and we both startle to notice how closely I am standing behind her. She turns her face up to mine, and I take a small, significant step backward so as not to crowd her. It is difficult, as what I'd really like to do is take a step forward and twine that talented tongue around my own, drink its cleverness into myself. I am about to think something more disparaging about how Pip must not truly want me, as she hasn't given me permission to kiss her yet, but then I recall my promise to try to be more generous to myself, more kind in my own mind, and so I only remind myself that she *wants* to kiss me. That fills my fingers with sparking tingles and brings a soft upward curl to my too-thin lips, and, for now, it is enough.

Pip covers the moment of awkwardness with a sip from her now quite depleted glass. "Most times, in a Quest Narrative, heroes go bashing about until they stumble on a clue or some elderly wise entity points them in the right direction, usually with an ominous half-prophecy," she explains. "Forget that. You've got spies who've done most of the legwork for us. We know which prophecy he perverted, which sigil he used to summon the Deal-Maker spirit, though not which spirit it was. We know what the five objects are that go with the Deal-Maker, and the sigil to make the Seven Stations of the Quest. Reed *always* does Seven Stations," she murmurs to herself more than to me. "Where'd you put the map?"

I steer her toward the pile of papers scattered on my desk, brushing aside scrolls and sketches that I will reorganize later, the detritus of academia. The discarded corpses of more than a few dry ink bottles and nubby quills flutter and shuffle as I move things aside. A map of the known world takes pride of place on my blotter, and Pip sets aside her cup for a fresh quill. She dips it into the virulently red ink she prefers when making notations and begins to scratch at the landmarks.

Kintyre—slew dragon—book 2; *Bevel—sung siren to sleep—book 5*; *Viceroy—lair exploded—book 7*; she writes. Note after note, and with the book numbers circled. I am pleased that I am able to read most of what she writes. My diligence in my study of her alphabet is being rewarded.

"There!" she crows. "Fetch me some other color of ink!"

I retrieve the bottle of Tarvers-green ink I reserve for my business as Shadow Hand from the desk drawer, and Pip starts connecting the red points. Everything that is labeled "book 1," she connects with a solid line; "book 2," with a dotted one; and ah, yes, I see what she is doing. She is laying out the path my brother took on each of his quests. Nearly all begin in Kingskeep, save for the first and fourth, which start here at Turn Hall.

"There, you see? You read the Seven Stations just like a book. From west to east where possible, and always starting north and heading south. Each and every time."

"Astounding. I never noticed. Or, rather, I never thought to bother tracing Kintyre's journey on a map."

"Who would?" Pip asks, setting aside the quill and reaching once more for her wine. Her fingers are spotted with red and green, like she's been dabbling in potions, and I wonder if the ink would taste bitter on her skin. "It's not as if Bevel includes a map with his scrolls."

"So, we shall begin here," I say, pointing to Turn Hall. To date, it is the westernmost point on land that Kintyre's adventures have ever come, so it makes sense. There is very little between my Chipping and the Sunsong

Sea to the west; what little land does exist between the two is technically part of Lord Fimoger's Chipping, but the isthmus of useless chalk cliffs and scrubby trees is no good for anything but drying fish upon, and so neither of us have much bothered with populating it. There are scrublands on the isthmus where round mountains of rock fracture away into sheer cliffs, and great folds of stone that are said to be the bones of a long-ago felled giant. In actuality, they are just bare patches where the swift and salty wind off the Sunsong has worn away the vegetation, where the gnarled trees grip desperately to the rock and blow back away from the sea.

It isn't until the downward slope of the land exhales the sea salt and transforms into my lush little valley that the soil is of any use. "And then?"

Pip turns to study her Excel. "Kingskeep, would be my best guess. The first Station is complete; we have the sigil from when the Viceroy collected his own spell components and did his, uh, *thing* to pull down a Reader." She fights down a shiver, biting her bottom lip for a moment. I have just enough time to wonder if we are going to have to endure another episode, and then the moment passes.

Pip shakes her head, shrugs her shoulders as if to brush away an ill omen, and retrieves her little notebook from her pocket. She flips through the cramped pages until she finds the one she wants. "Right, so," she begins, "this one here talks about calling down a witness from the sky, and that's the one your guys found with me? Hmmm. . . . *The Sigil that Never Fades by the Quill that Never Dulls in salt of the Cup that Never Runs Dry upon the Parchment that Never Fills o'er, all with the Blade that Never Fails upon the Desk that Never Rots*. Yadda yadda, more Tolkien-esque rip-off lyrics with clumsy scansion and then, this: *The Witness shall game with the Spirit Who Never Lies to open the passageway to the sky*. What's a spirit that never lies? If the witness is me, what do I game with . . . like, chess?"

"Word games," I say, grave all of a sudden. "It's a Deal-Maker spirit. They don't lie. But they don't speak in what you and I would consider full truths, either. They are very dangerous to deal with, and they're the only creatures dark enough and powerful enough to call down a Reader. That I know of."

"And you know of everything."

"I do. It's in the job description."

Pip smirks at me. "Well, it's a pretty clear list; even the awkwardness of the way the sentences are put together shows us the order it has to be in—see, we have to get the knife and then the desk. And . . . it ought to be somewhere right around here." She points at a valley in the Southlands.

"By the Great Writer," I say, following her finger. "Then, judging by the prophecy . . ." I retrieve a bottle of blue ink from my desk drawer and uncap it quickly, then catch up the quill. "We will need to stop here . . . then." I point to a small isthmus where a squiggle of river runs right over a painted cliff. "Three ought to be somewhere in this vicinity, by the Salt Crystal Caverns; then back east here, to the Lost Library"—I slash a little '*x*' over the prairie in the middle of Hain—"and then south and west again, along the Long Pond Lake to . . . possibly here?" I tap the map with one finger, where the lake narrows into foggy marshland. "The Valley of the Tombs." I skim south one last time, the thick emerald ink of a forest making the blue line hop and the nib scratch. "And then finally over to one of the Eyrie coves in the Cinch Mountains."

Pip's eyes shine with a kind of abundant glee that makes them sparkle like a child spying the dessert table at Solsticetide. They look greener like this, glittering as they hop over the map, taking it all in. "And we should be able to summon the Deal-Maker from there. *Et voila!* See? All the hard work is *done*. Now, all we have to do is go out and actually get this stuff."

"And before the blue moon." Which, luckily enough, happens to be occurring in two month's time. I squash the very great desire to sweep Pip into my arms and kiss that quick, clever little mouth of hers. "Ah! And the feather!" I say instead.

I retrieve the sketch that one of my Men brought to me the day they rescued Pip. It is the one of the silver filigree feather, all spattered with sapphires.

"See, Pip. The Quill that Never Dulls. I remember where I saw this before—it is a Gyre family heirloom. Lordling Tritan Gyre wears it in his cap, and his mother before him wore it on a torque. They have had it for centuries, though no one can recall its origin. The Viceroy must have been researching it as well."

"Lucky for us that your guys scooped his notes, then. And that this is a world where automatic backups to an external hard drive don't exist."

"Genius, just genius," I whisper. "A hero's quest made the purview of the intellectual instead of the adventurer! How *marvelous*."

"They don't call me Doctor Piper for nothing," she says, and raises her cup of wine in a salute.

I fetch my own cup from where I left it on the mantle and return the toast.

I reach out and brush my fingers across the corner of the Excel on which Pip has scrawled the moon phases. The ink is slightly raised—she mixed it too thick, and it warms me to realize that, as clever as Pip is in the abstract, working with the physical tools of my trade is still a frustration to her. She is clever; she is a Reader. But she is human, and she errs.

"Amazing," I breathe, because she is. Pip is amazing. I have been gifted with a whole new way of learning to think, and beyond that, she has expended all of this talent, all of this imagination, all of this skill on *me*. *For* me. "You've taken what my brother does and . . ."

"And made it something you can do, too," she says, and there is no small amount of drunken smugness in her voice. "There's nothing you can't do, if you can think your way around it."

I am stunned. I am humbled.

"Lucy Piper . . . you enthrall me," I whisper. I take my courage into my hands and lean down to press a sweet kiss on her forehead. I feel the skin there heat under my lips and know she is blushing. I linger perhaps longer than is polite, but for the first time in a very long time, I do honestly believe that I am not imposing, that my continued touch is welcome. It is a thrilling feeling: to be *accepted. Wanted.*

Eventually, I pull away and turn to the credenza behind my desk to fetch up the decanter of wine. I pour for myself, and then bring the jug over to the hearth to refill Pip's cup.

"And now what?" I ask, setting the decanter down on the mantle.

She raises her glass to me in an informal pledge and clinks the side with mine. The low chime that fills my study also slithers into the heat pooling low in my belly.

"Now," she says, taking a sip. "I'm gonna start jogging again. I've been dying to see your gardens."

Later that evening, I go up to her room, hoping to share a nightcap with Pip. I hear the sobs before I ever reach her door and do not bother to knock. I keep walking instead, fingers closed around the neck of the bottle, and return to my own rooms. I do not have the heart to open the wine, and leave it to languish on my bedside table.

Sometimes, I forget that Pip is not here of her own volition—would not choose to be here, could she help it.

Sometimes, I forget that the Viceroy has torn her from everything she holds dear, from everyone she loves, and that Turn Hall and I will always, and only, be that place where she seeks to hide from the misery of missing her old life.

She laughs, and she smiles, and she teases and touches; and she is sad every moment of every day.

🖋

In the morning, Velshi wakes me earlier than I am wont and bids me come to the window. He presses a warm drink into my hand as I obey and stand by the curtain, sipping, waiting for the haze of sleep to clear.

"What am I looking at?" I ask.

"Just watch, my lord," he whispers.

I turn more fully to the window and let my gaze roam the garden, the cup in my palm spreading warmth up my fingers and across my skin. A light mist is burning off as the sun rises, leaving dewdrops in its wake. The manicured lawn and the tight rosebushes under the window appear adorned like a noblewoman, all flashing diamonds and gold in the sunrise. At the bottom of the lawn, where the covey forest begins, I see a smear of red and wonder if it's my fox-mother, or one of her kits. There is the rainbow sparkle of fairy wings above the fishpond in the middle of the lawn, flashing too fast for me to catch a glimpse of the bodies attached. A trout leaps and snaps, and I wonder idly if the fairy escaped or just became breakfast.

All of the plants I can see are green and fresh, and trembling just on the cusp of summer, blossoms held tight and selfish against the last lingering chill of spring. Then, Velshi points. Down, at the very edge of the forest, where the Turn Hall gardens are separated from the first of my tenant's fields by a low stone wall, there is the shape of a person. It is moving toward us, the pace steady as it moves in a long-strided clip along the wall before turning to pace the forest. Not quite a run, but rhythmic all the same.

It looks like a young boy, clad in tight trousers and a cast-off tunic too large for him, and, for a moment, I wonder what village child this might be, traveling to see his lordling or to fetch help, and how Velshi knew he was coming. But as he grows closer, I realize that this is no boy at all. This is Pip.

And she is smiling, too, of all the bizarre expressions to be wearing. She is not running fast. She must be prevented from it by the lingering pain in her back, but she is moving faster than a walk.

"Did you know about this, sir? She's been making circles of the estate for an hour."

"I did," I admit. "I am sorry; I forgot to inform someone. Don't bother Miss Piper. She is merely exercising."

"Exercising," Velshi murmurs, eyes back on Pip's approaching figure.

Pip looks up and catches sight of us, framed against my window. She grins and waves. I wave back, and watch with awe as she makes a tight corner and follows the lawn around to the other side of the house.

"It's normal, where she's from," I say. "Well, apparently." I'm having a hard time thinking of much more to add, because that had just been a brilliant answer to the question of what young women wore while doing this so-called "jogging."

"Very well, sir," Velshi replies. There is a wealth of other things he is not saying underneath those words, and foremost are ones of disapproval. But he is too professional to actually voice them.

"Call for a bath for Miss Piper," I say, turning away from the window. "And bring just an ewer for me. Let her know that I'll meet her in the breakfast room when she's done this morning."

"Very well, sir," Velshi says, and departs.

I linger at the window sill, sipping my tea and smiling to myself.

Pip flops down into the rickety little chair opposite mine wearing a grin as wide as her face. She is still wearing her jogging attire. A thin sheen of sweat wreathes her hairline and soaks the shirt between her breasts, making it cling in a way that forces me to concentrate very hard on the papers spread out on the breakfast table before me.

"That felt great!" she enthuses, as she reaches for the pitcher of water. "And thanks for the bath. I'm going to go up to it in a minute. It was too hot."

"You're very welcome. I still don't see the appeal," I admit, sipping at my third cup of tea, "but if it makes you happy, then I am pleased for you."

"I just missed it, you know? *Moving.* Getting into the headspace. I think I'll have to find better shoes than your old fencing boots, though, and I didn't go for as long as I normally do, but I think I can be forgiven, seeing as I was flat on my face for three months."

I am startled. "My old fencing boots?" I check under the table, and sure enough, she is wearing the ratty brown ankle boots I'd first learned to fence in as a boy.

"Hm, yeah." Pip reaches for a warm roll. "It was the only thing Neris could find in my size. There was no heel, and that's all I wanted."

The thought of Pip wearing my clothing, even my discarded clothing, sends a wonderful, proprietary shiver up my spine. I wonder if I can coax her into one of my house robes, just to know that the scent of me is so close to her skin.

"I was thinking," she says, buttering the roll, "that if we're going adventuring, I don't want to wear dresses. The women in the stories always trip up when the hems get snagged on roots in the forest, or they're mistaken for whores, or princesses, or whatever. I'd much rather have some nice warm trousers and shirts. Can we arrange that?"

"I, er, I can summon a tailor . . . and a cobbler," I add, realizing that Pip would probably appreciate a pair of her own boots, made for her own feet, rather than wearing my old ones. "But, Pip, it's not entirely decent . . . and, according to your notes, we're going to have to visit Kingskeep."

"I can pack a nice dress," Pip assures me. "I just don't want to wear them all day. Surely you can see the logic in that."

And I can. I can envision the logic quite well . . . as well as the way Pip's legs looked in the trousers this morning. I swallow more tea in an attempt to quell my blood and nod.

"Yes, very well."

Pip bounces from her chair and presses a kiss to my cheek. "Thanks!" she says, as she grabs another roll from the basket and vanishes from the breakfast nook.

Oh, dear Writer. If this is Pip healthy and happy, I wonder what I've got myself into. She is still and silent while at work in academia, but filled with the spirit and high blood of exercise, she is as chipper as any squirrel and twice as bouncy. Combined with her by-now-legendary stubbornness . . . I am a doomed, doomed man.

Very happily doomed.

Nine

A fortnight later, when the moon is full and all the right aspects are aligned, Pip and I steal out of Turn Hall on horseback. No one is to know that the lordling and his guest are absent, and so we ride into the forest instead of down the path through the village. We have even arranged with Pointe that he will continue to visit Turn Hall for our sparring matches, so that, for all outward observers, it appears as if we are still in residence.

We have packed bedrolls and first-aid salves, dried rations, water skins, fire-making supplies, and a scroll onto which I have copied all of our necessary information and directions. Pip has the Excel, folded carefully like a map so we can unfold it to specific sections when necessary, and her leather-bound notation book. And, for reasons that I cannot fathom but find eminently practical, Pip has also insisted that we do not forget our pocket handkerchiefs.

We also each have a sword, and now that Pip's back is healed, I have promised her that we will be stretching her skin in sword practice, keeping her scar-knitted muscles limber as I teach her how to defend herself with a blade. If she is going to dress like a young man, I am determined that she will be able to defend herself like one as well.

Our comfortable relationship hovers somewhere between very affectionate siblings—or, rather, what I imagine an affectionate sibling relationship would resemble—and chaste lovers. We have lain together in bed as I read aloud to Pip, her fingers threaded between mine; there have often been affectionate touches, cuddles in the library, muddled limbs and reaching around while packing, knees bumping and pressing together under the breakfast table, but there have been no exchanged kisses, no promises beyond the one to try.

I find this slow courtship remarkably calming. It is rare and odd, and I am enjoying it immensely. There is no pressure to jump into carnality, with which I have no direct experience outside of witnessing the trysts required for Shadow Hand work. Though, thankfully, Pip has—or so she has hinted—enough to make up for my lack of knowledge. And I don't have to deal with any of that "at first sight" fairy tale twaddle. I am able to be just me, and it is . . . a relief.

All the same, I find myself looking forward to sharing a campfire tonight and, I assume, having our bedrolls side by side next to it. Kissing may be in the hazy, unpredictable future, but holding Pip close and knowing that I *may* . . . that is more immediate and will be just, I think, as satisfying.

We make camp a day's ride out from Kingskeep. We stop, right around dawn, in a clearing used often by my Men. The starflowers glowing in the night-darkened meadow are pinpricks of pearlescent luminescence still. No larger than my fingernail, they reflect in the boggy ponds that fill the lowlands, looking like nothing more than a reflection of their heavenly counterparts. The clearing is thick with starflowers, and as dawn approaches, they wink closed, one by one, like shy clams.

As I had hoped, Pip lays her bedroll directly next to mine. I expect the usual "just for body heat" objections that maidens claim in the epic tales, but she makes no such excuses. Pip never makes the usual maidenly excuses for taking what she wants from me, and it is shockingly attractive. I observe from this that Pip wishes merely to be close to me, unashamedly, and take comfort from it.

The rising sun masks our campfire smoke as I spread flat-bread dough from Cook on one of the stones in the embers. This will be our only chance for fresh-baked bread on the road, unless we buy more uncooked dough when we leave Kingskeep. It cannot last more than a day wrapped in damp cheesecloth before it becomes dry and useless. I could have used the room in our packs for something that travels better—dried apple chips, or hard cheese—but I know how much Pip considers fresh bread a delicacy. She says the bread in her world never comes fresh-baked; it is too much hassle. They buy it days old and wrapped to keep from going stale, and never warm.

We enjoy our dinner of bread and fresh stone fruits, mixed with a little of the soft cheese she adores so much, using up all of our perishable provisions in one fell feast, and then take to our beds. I bank the fire before lying down on the ground, a careful distance between us just in case Pip has changed her mind.

She falls asleep before I do and rolls into my side, snuffling against my armpit, so I take this to mean that her intentions remain true. All the same, I wrap my arm around her shoulders cautiously, just in case I alarm her.

I fall asleep to the sound of waking birds, happy not to have to set any magical wards tonight, for I am too exhausted to get back up and do so. The Minchin Forest is populated with only the most non-magical of animals. The older forests are filled with all manner of magical creatures, but this growth is still quite young, planted in penance by a dragon who accidentally destroyed an elder-dryad's copse a hundred years ago. Magical things like old places, and this forest won't be ripe enough for their liking until I am well dead and dust.

That is part of its appeal, of course—nobody likes to wake with gnome-knots tied into their hair or covered in the graffiti of particularly drunken fairies—but the other part is that it means we will have several hours to sleep before we make our way to the capital city. It is vain, but I want to see the look on Pip's face when we steal up to the Queen's Gate at sunset, and the light glances off the great crystal dome of the Palace Keep for which the city was named. It is breathtaking, and I do so want to take her breath away.

☜

Around noon, when I have already woken and am, in turn, waking the embers of our campfire in order to heat a small packet of travel-stew for our breakfast, Pip finally stirs from her sleep.

"Christ, ow," Pip says as she sits up from her bedroll.

"Your back?" I ask, concerned that we have perhaps sped along her healing faster than she could handle.

"My *thighs*," she moans, spreading them wide and kneading the muscles on the insides of her knees with her fists. I drop my eyes back to the business of stirring stew, and do not, do *not* look at the shadow cast by apex of her legs. Pip is wearing her freshly made riding clothes. While I'd agreed with her that dresses were no sort of wardrobe for adventuring, the way the trousers she commissioned from the tailor cling to her legs is moderately indecent. To add to that, she is also not enamored of the knee-length sleeveless robes most people wear—she says they get in the way—and has instead purchased a short leather jerkin like Pointe's.

We have packed both a dark purple short-robe and the fine dark blue dress, just in case we need the clothing to make Pip less conspicuous wherever we end up, but right now, she is wearing only her trousers, my old socks, and one of my old rough-woven Turn-russet shirts. Her boots, and the black leather jerkin, are piled on the ground beside her roll.

I try not to think about how gloriously intimate it is, my clothing touching her body, and instead set aside the pot of stew and stand.

"I could tell by how you took your seat yesterday that you're not an experienced horsewoman," I admit. "I wish I had noticed earlier. I assumed that, as a land-owner, your father would have had horses. I regret now that we did not make time for riding lessons."

"What can I possibly be doing that's so wrong to make my legs scream like this?" Pip asks. She winces and rubs her knuckles along the small of her back, as well, and I know that pain intimately, had experienced it myself before Father taught me the proper way to roll my hips with the gait of the horse. "All you have to do is sit on the thing and let it do all the work, right?"

"Not precisely," I admit, moving to stand directly behind her. "May I?"

She stiffens, the way she always does when she real-izes that someone wants to touch her. And then she nods curtly, just once. I slip down onto the ground behind her and press my thumbs into the spot just above the dimples at the small of her back, right on top of the curlicues where Bootknife's art begins. She groans again, a mix of pleasure and pain.

"Oh my god, you're magic," she says into the tent pole of her knees as she leans forward to give me better access.

"You blaspheme an awful lot," I say, conversationally. "What would your Great Writer say?"

"It's against the rules," she admits. "Thou shalt not take thy Lord God's name in vain, or something like that. But it's not like I've ever heard of anyone being smote with lightning for it. Besides, there's something wonderfully poetic about cussing."

"Your Writer gave you rules?" I ask, slightly disgruntled. "Ours didn't."

"Sometimes, I wonder if my world would be better than it is if ours hadn't give us any, either. Lotsa wars fought over how people interpret what our Writer said to the people he talked to. Not sure how much good it's done, being all about peace and faith and honesty, and then setting people up to fight over the way things are worded." She laughs a little, but it's not mirthful at all. "That's what happens when you write things down. Authorial Intent. People interpret what they want out of things. Readers." She snorts, and it's a wet, sad sound.

"Perhaps Elgar Reed had the right of it," I murmur, not sure if I am now the one blaspheming. "Abandoning us as he did."

Pip cranes her head around to meet my eyes. "You think you've been abandoned by your creator?"

My hands pause on her lower back of their own volition. I spread my fingers wide and press them on either side of her spine. "Haven't I?"

The way she regards me suddenly puts me sharply in mind of the look on little Lewko's face when he'd seen what was left of the barn kitten a horse had accidentally squashed.

She turns slowly, her hips scraping against the inside of my legs as she shifts on the ground. She gets up on her knees, rises until we are eye level, and places her hands on either side of my face. She moves so slowly, like I am a deer she fears to spook, and I do not move because the pace of her movements is mesmerizing. They make my breath stop somewhere low in my stomach, make me forget to take another.

"Just because you're a secondary character doesn't mean you're not a *person*," she says, and her voice is low and intense. "A complete, wonderful, fleshed out person with needs and desires and hates. You are *worthy*, and it doesn't matter what you were made to do, you have found a calling all your own. So *fuck* Elgar Reed, *and* Kintyre Turn. Just be brilliant, all on your own, all for yourself. The books are over. You don't owe anyone anything else. Have a *fantastic* life. Okay?"

I don't know what to say to this. I literally do not. So instead, I copy one of her favorite moves and turn my head so I can nuzzle her palm, run the cool tip of my nose against skin slightly gritty with dirt and fragrant with pine needles, bridle leather, horse, and Pip.

"Infuriating man," she says, and turns back around, plopping back down onto her rump. She crosses her arms over her chest.

"That's what Pointe says," I agree. I am now in an amorous mood, and so I lean down and just breathe in the scent of her hair, where it meets the stale sweat and salt at the nape of her neck.

But no, this is meant to be about horseback riding, and no other kind. I draw my blood down and my professionalism forward.

"He's right," Pip says, leaning back.

I put my hands back onto her lower back and resume my massage, working quickly now so she is loose and warm enough to move on to the actual lesson without causing her pain.

"Uhngk," she grunts, as I attack a particularly stubborn little knot.

I splay my long fingers on her hips, wrapping them around the bones to get a good grip.

"The secret of riding" —I budge up right behind her so I will be able to lead her hips with my own. I cross my knees on top of hers, so the inside of her legs are tight against the outside of mine— "is to not fight the motion. The horse has its own natural rhythm, and you must be fluid. Grip with your knees, keep your back straight and your shoulders pointing in the same direction as your beast, but let your spine be fluid."

"That's a lot to remember," she says, and her voice is suddenly quite breathless and light. Like she's been running and not yet caught her breath.

I push out with my legs. Hers spread a little, until I say, "No, grip the barrel of the horse with your knees." Then, she resists.

"This is . . . Forsyth . . ."

She's a good student. Already her spine has gone a bit liquid, pressing warmly into my thumbs. "You'll learn. You need to roll with the gait," I said, pushing her hips forward in the circle required to stay seated.

"Hmmf," she says, moving with the forward push of my hands. She giggles once, pushing back and rolling forward again, and then resisting the tempo I was trying to set. The roll becomes slower, more deliberate, and her thighs spread further. She raises her legs, runs her feet against the outside of my calves.

"Pip? What are you—you'll be unseated."

She giggles again, and then moves away from me, turning on the dirt to face me. "I suddenly understand the appeal of equestrian pursuits."

"This is serious. We have many days of riding ahead of us, and you may hurt yourself if you don't learn. Don't tease, Pip."

She makes a sound of outraged amusement. "You started it!"

"Started what? You need to learn this. Come back down here."

She giggles again. "Oh my god, your oblivious-shield is on at full strength. You just don't get it, and you are adorable." She pecks a sweet kiss onto the tip of my skinny, large nose.

☙

The sunset was as impressive as I'd hoped it would be.

We watched from a hillock just outside of Kings-keep, and then made our way to the Queen's Gate—the main thoroughfare entrance to the walled city. The portico is tall and thin, to allow carts and carriages to pass through only one at a time or rows of soldiers with upright spears to pass through four across. The entrance flanks a bridge that grows ever more narrow, the alabaster walls coming together in an apex that, unfortunately, rather resembles a woman's—

"Thighs," Pip breathes, eyes roving over the entryway. "Reed's mind was seriously in the gutter. Everything in this world is about sex." She points to the heavy steel gate above us, waiting to be closed at full dark. "And what do you call that? The Chastity Belt?"

I snort. The soldiers look askance at us, and I school my expression into something more resembling the imperious lordling I am meant to be. I convinced Pip to change into my mother's velvet dress during our last rest stop, and am glad of it. While her short hair and the fact that we are on horseback instead of in a carriage does attract unwanted curiosity, the fineness of our clothing and the fact that we both wear brooches from House Turn makes everyone's eyes slide away, uninterested in the nobility from a frankly base and boring country Chipping.

We must wait our turn to enter, a soldier marshaling the end-of-day traffic, and Pip makes a comment about big-city commuting and jam. I am hungry myself, so I don't blame her contemplating the soft fruit compote we had with lunch. When it is our turn, our two horses just barely fit side by side, my knee brushing the stone of the entryway. We make for a small taverna that I know and patronize often when I am in the city, for the windows on each floor are accessible from the roof of the stable. Not ideal, in terms of room security, but perfect for a lordling who needs to steal into the hayloft to change into the Shadow Hand.

As I oversee stabling our horses, Pip pulls out the Excel and reviews the lunar calendar. She sits on a hay bale, unconcerned with her skirts, and chews on her thumbnail as her eyes flick over her coded notes.

"What pretty boys," the stable lad says, as I help him to remove the horses' tack and hang it on pegs inside their stalls. "Who's this, then?"

"Dauntless," I say, rubbing my stallion's nose. He lips at the top of my head, making my hair stand up frightfully. It's a frankly extravagant name for such a well-behaved creature, but I was young and my mind was on silly quests when I named him.

"And this?" the boy asks, jerking his head at Pip's chestnut gelding. The horse is fresh-bought—I acquired him from Pointe specifically for Pip—and as such, he has no name yet.

"Pip?" I ask. "Your horse's name?"

"Oh, I get to name him?" she asks, packing up the Excel and walking over to pet his nose.

"You are his first master; it is your right," I reply, untangling Dauntless's bridle.

Her horse, young and playful, nips at her fingers and she starts back, clearly unused to working with the animals. The stable lad laughs and hands her half an apple.

Her horse takes it from her hand carefully, using his lips rather than his teeth, and Pip giggles at him.

Dauntless takes the other half from me, crunching delicately, as if unimpressed with the younger horse's obvious attempt to curry affection.

"Mr. Ed? Joey? Flicka? Shadowfax?" she muses softly, trying out names. Then, she laughs at herself. "No, no, Karl! His name is Karlurban. How's that, kiddo? You like it? Karl."

"I like it!" the stable lad says.

"Unusual, but, I assume, something of an in-joke?" I ask, shouldering our saddle bags. Pip tries to take hers, but the stable lad won't hear of it and trots along behind us as we cross the stone courtyard to the taverna's entrance.

"I'll explain it on our way up to the Keep," she says.

I feel the frown flit across my face. "Are we not to rest first? I thought we could go in the morning."

Pip shakes her head. "We've only got forty-five days to finish up, er, everything," she says. "I'd rather not waste them when we know how close we are to Station Three."

"Wise," I allow. I'm not happy about it. I was looking forward to a bath and a rest in a real bed, even if it is straw-ticking and rope-framed, but Pip is right. We cannot afford to delay now, when we do not know what impediments might meet us at later Stations. "Then let us hope that young Master Gyre has not retired for the evening."

✍

Smelling rather more of horse and the open road than I usually prefer when donning the costume of the Shadow Hand, Pip and I sneak out of our garret room, cross the thatched roof of the gallery, and wiggle through the thatch to land in the hayloft above the stables.

In a corner of the loft that is so squeezed under the eaves that even the boys who bring their conquests up here for their literal rolls in the hay would not find it unless they were earnestly looking, I have secured a metal chest to the floor with large bolts. It was made for me by the great dwarves of the southern mountains and is clasped shut with three separate enchanted locks that require not only the correct key used in the correct order, but also the breath from my own mouth for the hinges to loosen. The dwarves certainly know their craft.

In this locker, I have secreted all that I need to be the Shadow Hand while in Kingskeep. It would not do to be caught upon the road with this gear in my riding bags or carriage luggage, so I deemed it safer to leave it here. While Pip watches, I don the black boots and gloves, and a many-layered cloak of gray and black. It looks like roiling fog as I walk, a bit too long in the hem for me, as the Shadow Hand before me was a broader man, but impressive still. The sword is of good elvish design. It is straight and thin, and never goes dull, with a hilt that is swept back and curled like the emissions from an old gaffer's pipe. I call it Smoke, but never out loud.

Dauntless's kit is here as well, comprised of a black tabard big enough to drape over his body and disguise his shape, and a cloth mask of his own to blot out the distinctive cream line between his eyes. I have let all his buckles tarnish, so they do not shine and give us away as we travel the shadows.

There is one more thing in the bottom of the box, and Pip reaches in and pulls it from the black velvet pouch. It too is silver, made from the same vein of metal as the sword's hilt and crossguard, but this time by a dwarvish craftsman.

This is my Shadow's Mask, the face that the chief spymaster wears before all but the king. It covers the whole of my features, save for an opening the width of my mouth that begins at the bottom of my nose and runs to the base of my chin, allowing me ease of speaking. The metal is otherwise flat and entirely, eerily, feature-less. There is no decoration, no expression stamped into the metal, and the only concession to the natural shape of a man's face is the ridge for my nose and eyebrows. The eye holes are cut narrow, but through the same sort of planning as one uses on a loophole window, I have use of the full field of my vision.

It is, in short, nothing less than spectacularly in-timidating. When I don this, too, Pip falls back and shivers slightly, pupils blown wide in fear and interest. I straighten my shoulders, adopt the poise and gait of the Shadow Hand.

"Wow," she whispers.

Once Dauntless is similarly attired, Pip tucks up behind me on Dauntless's saddle, tight against my body, head laid between my shoulder blades. My cloak goes over her, and there is so much fabric that she is entirely obscured. I will smuggle her thusly into the palace. She has changed back into her black riding gear so that she may blend into the shadows as well.

We have decided that the fewer people who know of her existence, the better. As much as I have spies in the halls of the Keep, so too does the Viceroy.

The ride to the Shadow's Gate is swift. I push Dauntless through the side streets at a pace that is perhaps a bit reckless, but each turn forces Pip's arms tighter around my waist, her fingers digging into my waistcoat pockets; her breath is warm on my back. I am glad the night is not too close, else she may smother under my cloak.

As it is, I am just beginning to break a sweat behind my mask when I pull up at the small, ramshackle gash of an alleyway that dead-ends several city blocks from the palace. The alley is filled with refuse, both garbage and human. One of the two bums pulls herself up from a hut made of discarded wood and paper and fish-eyes me.

"Eh, there," she says. "Wot you want down 'ere?"

"I am the Shadow Hand, and you will allow me to pass," I say, voice modulated into a carefully untraceable non-accent. I speak Words of Trust under the words of recognition. "The code word you gave me upon my departure last time was '*thatch roof.*'"

No further comment is made.

The other bum shuffles to the end of the alleyway, and, oh so casually, she pushes on a particularly grimy brick. The wall judders and a doorway, just narrow and tall enough for Dauntless and I to pass through, opens. I urge Dauntless forward, and the beggar-woman by the door hands me a lantern. There is a Wisp inside, glowing blue and friendly through the glass, happy to lead us through the darkness of the underground tunnel. In exchange, I drop a brass coin into each of their hands, and they smile and tip their heads, happy to be in my service.

"Drainage ditch," the bum who first spoke says in parting.

"Drainage ditch," I reply, committing the new password to memory. Then, I duck into the darkness.

As soon as the doorway behind us is closed, Pip pushes my cloak aside and I raise my mask to wipe at my brow. In the glass lantern, the Wisp whistles and jitters, coaxing us to keep moving. I take a moment to affix the lantern to Dauntless's pommel.

"*Well*," Pip breaths against my neck. "That was *sexy*, Mr. Commanding Voice."

I chuckle, nervous. *Accept the compliment*, I have to remind myself. *It was given honestly*. What I would really like to say is something to deny it. Instead I say, "Thank you," and spur Dauntless onward.

Knowing the path to the palace, my horse takes his own lead, and I am able to concentrate on Pip.

"How are you doing?"

"Fine," she says. "Happy to be out of the cloak."

"It's a bit stifling this time of year, sorry."

"I don't mind, really. How long until we reach the palace?"

"A few moments," I say. "We'll emerge in one of the hedge maze dead-ends. From there, we will enter the palace through the Shadow's Door, and take an audience with the king."

Pip stiffened against me. "Me too?"

I consider the tightness of her voice. "In fact, I think perhaps it would be best if the king did not know of you. It is possible that word that Lordling Turn has a strange guest has reached him, but I would prefer to keep you a secret from court as long as possible. One never knows where the Viceroy's ears may be."

Pip shivers at the name of her tormentor, and I feel her nod. "Good idea. Although, if we were keeping me on the down-low, maybe that big old blowout we had with Bevel and Kintyre at your house was a bad idea."

"It made perfect sense before you declined to travel with Kintyre; any gossip coming from Turnshire and Lysse Chipping would have said that you departed in the company of a hero, which would have pulled the Viceroy's attention off Turn Hall. Now, with you lacking a champion—"

"Hey!" she said, and pinches the skin of my belly through my shirt and waistcoat. I gasp, shocked by her boldness rather than the pain. "I have a perfectly good champion right here, buster."

"Yes, of course," I acquiesce, not entirely convinced. "The point is that no one knows that you and I have departed Turn Hall, and you therefore cannot be seen in Kingskeep in the company of the Shadow Hand."

"True. Then, why go to the king at all?" Pip asked. "Why not just get in, get the goods, get out?"

"I need to give him my progress reports regarding the Viceroy's latest schemes, as well as the border skirmishes between the lords down in the Southlands, and let him know what we've come for. It wouldn't do for him to allow young Master Gyre to try to challenge me over a small bit of sparkle. The king will keep our theft quiet."

"So, we're just going to, what, steal it from the kid?"

I turn in my saddle to try to find her eyes in the blue-tinged gloom. "You *were* the one who suggested that we avoid the heroic path—sneaking and study, I believed you advocated."

"True," Pip allows. Her bottom lip plumps a bit, and then she sucks it back between her teeth, her pout aborted. "I did. I just . . . I guess I kinda wanted to see what you would do in a sword fight."

"Talk him down, my dear," I admit.

Pip's smile is nearly enough to light the tunnel, and the skin all over the back of my neck and ears goes hot.

"My dear?" she echoes.

"I . . . that is . . . i-i-if you pre-prefer a . . . dif-dif-different pet n-name. O-o-or n-none at all—"

"It's fine," Pip allows, grin softening to something genuinely pleased and content, and then spreading immediately into something wicked and altogether too alluring to be comfortable while I am squashed into a saddle. "Sugarlumps."

"No," I say immediately. "Not on y-your l-li-life, Lucy Pi-Pi-Piper."

"Honeybunches?"

"N-No."

"Pookiebear."

"Pip!"

"Right, well, you'll have to give me time to come up with something else, then," she laughs. Her breath is a warm puff against my heated neck, which seems to just warm it more. At length, she suggests: "*Bao bei.*"

"What does that mean?"

"'My treasured one.'"

"*Bao bei,*" I repeat softly. "Very well . . . my d-de-dear." I clench my tongue between my teeth, annoyed that our moment has been ruined by my blasted stutter. I turn back to face the direction we are heading and click Dauntless into a slightly swifter pace.

Pip squeezes my middle once in answer and lays her cheek against my shoulder blade, her thighs soft and warm where they frame my own. Dauntless plods gamely forward; the Wisp, pleased that we are moving—flighty creatures that they are, they hate being still—trills. For a brief moment, all is perfect with the world.

Ten

I release the Wisp as soon as we reach open air, and the little blob of blue light chitters in happiness, whizzing around Dauntless's feet. My horse is unimpressed, and when the creature zips off to try her metaphorical hand at the hedge maze, he snorts.

"How will we light our way back?" Pip asks, watching the Wisp go.

"Oh, this one likes the lantern," I say, helping Pip descend from Dauntless, and then following her to my own feet. "She won't go far."

Leaving Dauntless in the maze, I lead Pip through the leafy avenues, hand in hand to keep her from getting lost. I cannot quash the joy that shivers across my skin at the feel of her fingers twining with mine, even through my gloves. Even as we are on our way to find the first item that will help take her away from me forever.

I am determined to enjoy my time with Pip, however short-lived it may be, because, and I am certain of its truth the minute I realize this, I love her. And will continue to do so, no matter how briefly I get to hold her in my life.

By the Writer, I'm starting to sound like some ridiculous poet in Bevel's accounts of my brother's adventures. Useless old sop.

Instead of exiting the maze, we turn down another dead-end, and this time, I Speak Words of Revelation into the vines. Pip's eyes glaze slightly as I Speak, her ear cocked toward me, and when I finish, she snaps back, annoyed. "I still can't hear Words."

"It is no great loss." I try to reassure her as we pick our way around the plant life, which has pulled back to reveal a stone viaduct just tall enough for us to pass through on foot, lit by mounds and mounds of overgrown, glowing moss.

"It is," she insists. "I want to hear them."

I have nothing to say to that save platitudes that I am certain would be unwelcome, so I keep silent. We walk in the damp chill of the abandoned viaduct for several long moments until, eventually, we reach a fork in the path. There are three possibilities, and I choose the northernmost, which will take us to the servants' entrance in the palace pastry kitchen. It is empty this time of night, the evening's cakes and pies sent to the king's table already, while tomorrow morning's sweet rolls are left to rise under cheesecloth on the hulking great rolling table.

The room itself is unlovely and perfunctory. The palace is really rather more of a castle, a squat stone thing plopped onto the highest hill of Kingskeep by rulers thousands of years out of memory. The throne room dome is the only concession to beauty, being hewn of jadeite, and is a relatively recent addition, in terms of dynasties. The original builder's concern had been security, not beauty, so the rest of the castle is made of common rock and mortar, and the only adornments to its façade are the green flags and banners that King Carvel Tarvers had mounted around the doors. The rich, jewel-tone green is the Tarvers family color.

It is far more dynamic and attractive than House Turn's boring russet.

The Kingdom of Hain holds a strange fascination with finding the balance between the natural beauty of wild-grown foliage and the human tendency to want to organize chaos. The palace grounds and the outer bailey wall reflect that topiary poetry, the vegetation carefully tended so as to appear to be growing organically, a contradiction of meadow flowers in rigid arrangements and meandering gravel paths that actually spell a sigil of protection with their crisscrossing lines.

The inner bailey is paved with boring limestone, and the castle's original wall remains low and plain. But the outer wall is made of a rare monk-spelled moonstone, so it glows on nights where the moon has waned to its thinnest, lighting the grounds and the town below with enough of a gentle luminescence to allow people to find their way without being obtrusive. This wall is carved with statues of the great kings and queens of Hain, each generation adding a new statue to the wall when the ruler dies. The statues are patterned after a mold taken of the rulers' faces on the day of their coronation—the moment they became king or queen—and the statue faces outward, watching over Kingskeep and Hain for all eternity.

Personally, I find it unsettling. All those *eyes*.

Little of this ostentation appears in the kitchen, though. The only decoration these plain stone walls bear are recipes. They have been scribbled in charcoal or carved around the bread oven, the sinks, and the pantry doors, the favorite dishes of long-dead rulers scratched into the stone for safekeeping by long-dead cooks.

There is also a basket of going-stale breads from this morning's breakfast on the giant worktop. I pilfer one and secret it in a pocket of the cloak for the ride back to the taverna, and then leave Pip seated in the corner of the kitchen furthest from the main entrance. She is in a scullery maid's apron, just in case someone comes in and spies her.

The trip up to the king's study is quick, thanks to the servants' passageways. Like the rest of the palace, the study is perfunctory and purpose built. The bookshelves are carved into the stone walls, and King Carvel—or, I rather suspect, Queen Bretrandy—has attempted to soften the harsh lines with overstuffed furniture, expensive rugs, and elegantly draping swaths of Tarvers-green fabric.

When I am assured he is alone in the room, I step out from behind an arras and clear my throat to catch his attention.

The king, broad of face and shoulder—and now, in his declining years, also of belly—starts. He softens and grumbles at me. "Shadow Hand, you always scare the wits from me."

"Were that true, sire, you would be a village idiot by now." I step into the light of the lamp on his desk and push up my mask. "Well met, sire."

He takes my extended hand in friendship. "Well met, Master Turn. And for the love of the Writer, call me Carvel when it's just us two, aye? What brings you 'round my way? Have you any more news on this dreadful collecting spree the Viceroy is on?"

"Unfortunately, yes, sire—Carvel. It culminated in him finding the means to call down a Deal-Maker spirit."

The king's age-yellowed eyes widen in understanding and horror. "By the Writer. What did he dice for, do you know?"

Uncertain how much to say, I only nod.

"Is it a danger?"

"No," I say. "No, it is not. What they gained, it would . . . not be tamed by him, or Bootknife, and has fled their power. It is no longer a threat, I assure you."

King Carvel nods and sighs, satisfied that if I have told him so, it must be truth. Sometimes, I wonder what kind of power the Shadow Hand holds over Hain. It would

only take one man with one selfish ambition to ruin centuries of devoted service and pervert the king's rule.

"What was the Viceroy after?" Carvel asks, pouring
out a tumbler of whiskey for me from his private reserve. I take it and wait for him to have his own, toast to
his health, and then sip. "And your health, too, Master
Turn. What was it?"

"The destruction of Kintyre, as ever, sire."

"Blast that man," Carvel spits. "For all the good
your brother has done my kingdom, he sure knows how
to make an enemy and foster a grudge."

"I am very well aware, sire," I say, trying to keep the
bitterness of a childhood with Kintyre from my voice.
The king has no need to know that Kintyre has made
himself as much my enemy as the Viceroy's, though far
less viciously.

I take the respite in our conversation to lay new correspondence on the king's desk. Carvel flicks his eyes at
the letters, all sealed shut with Tarvers-green wax and
addressed in Tarvers-green ink, and sighs.

"So much for getting to bed at a reasonable hour,"
he grumbles. "Betts will be annoyed."

"It is nothing that won't keep, sire," I assure him.
"Do not anger my queen over this."

"Happy wife, happy life," he agrees and tosses back
the whiskey. I take this as my signal that the conversation is over, but then Carvel hoists his not inconsiderable
self back to his feet and goes to his liquor credenza once
more. He comes back with the whiskey decanter, and
I sigh inwardly. Tonight is going to be one of those

confession nights, and I am anxious to be away, to collect Pip and get Dauntless comfortably stabled for the night. And we still have to break into Gyre House, too.

Yet, I cannot decline when my king holds out the decanter and offer my still mostly full tumbler for a top-up.

"Speaking of wives," he starts, and I bite my tongue to hold in a groan. "Word from your Chipping has it that you've got a pretty young lady holed up in your mother's chambers."

"She is merely a traveler who grew ill on the road and is recovering in my manor. I don't know *where* this gossip of her being my betrothed comes from. I really don't."

"A woman would be good for you, Master Turn. Get you to, eh heh, *unwind* a bit, see?" He waggles bushy yellow eyebrows at me and smirks over the rim of his tumbler.

Oh, by the Great Writer; romantic advice from my king. I resent the insinuation that Pip exists only for my gratification, and I flip the Shadow's Mask back down onto my face to hide the blush of anger that is climbing up my neck. "I do beg your pardon, sire, but I have one more errand I must perform while on palace grounds, and the night is getting on." I set the tumbler down on the king's desk, right by his elbow so he can partake of it as well, as I know he will.

"Eh, right then, right," he mutters.

"With your permission, sire, I shall take my leave and make my way to House Gyre."

"Oh, there, aye?" he asks, the sparkle of curiosity in his eyes. "What's the boy done?"

"Nothing of note, as is the usual case with the young men of noble birth—" Carvel bursts into amused guffaws, interrupting me, and I wait for him to have his fill of mirth before I continue: "But he has something in his possession which I require for another task. I shall return it through you within the year."

"Very well," the king says, sweeping a fat, square hand through the air magnanimously. "Just don't let me hear that you got caught out by that fop. I'll quell any of his squawking if he realizes the theft."

"My thanks, sire." I sweep a courtly bow, made all the more dramatic by my smoke-like cloak, and vanish back behind the tapestry.

Pip is exactly where I left her, clearly bored out of her mind and surrounded by the crumbs of another sweet roll. I wonder what the cinnamon on her lips would taste like, but instead of asking, I wave her along with me to a different servants' corridor.

The palace is comprised of several buildings on a large, walled compound within the fortified city of Kingskeep. Interspersed with manicured lawns and cultivated ponds are the main castle itself, the stables and livery, the entertainment hall and sporting yard, and the homes of ten of the most titled and wealthy families in the court.

Centuries ago, the queen who'd ruled at the Keep married her three sons and eight daughters off to lords and ladies from as many different Chippings as she could manage, in order to solidify her rule over them. But she'd found it increasingly difficult to be separated from her beloved children, so she had holiday homes built for each of them within the palace grounds. The houses each reflect the architecture and preferred motifs of each Chipping, ranging from very ornate, abstract designs to extremely blocky, geometric lines.

Now, this insular village of the privileged has de-volved into more of a playground for the foppish, and is the chief meeting place of the Noble Marriage Market. I am grateful every day that House Turn was not promi-nent enough to be given a manor on the palace grounds. I have escaped the fate of the silly and sparkling creatures that flit through court, nothing between their ears but schemes for the next title they can add to the litany their family already possesses.

Pip and I cross along an avenue that connects the palace to Gyre House, keeping close to the privet hedges so that our shadows will not stand out in the light of the torch-lamps that run along the walkways. We sneak around to the back of the house, where I know young Tritan Gyre keeps his apartments. The windows are shut-tered tightly, and I cannot tell if there is any light on inside. *Blast it. The whelp may still be awake.*

"Here, next door is dark," Pip says, pointing to what may be a valet's room next to Tritan's apartment. "We can go in there."

"Excellent thinking."

"I'm lightest," she says. "Can you give me a boost, and I can try the latch?"

We both tighten our sword belts, and Pip dons the soft cloth cap she had been carrying in her trouser pocket to disguise her hair. I make a cradle of my hands for her to step onto and boost her high enough that she can grab the sill of the window on the second floor and jam her toes against the lintel of the window below it. She reaches up and pushes on the shutter; sure enough, it gives.

It also lets out such an alarming creak that Pip nearly slips off the stone.

"Shit!" I hear her hiss, and I am about to ask her if she wants to come back down again when the lights inside the room flare to life and Tritan Gyre's squirrelly face appears over Pip's head.

"What have we here?" he asks the night, and then, in a flash, he has his hands wrapped in Pip's jerkin and is yanking her inside and out of my sight.

The last thing I hear Pip yelp as she is hauled bodily into the house is: "Whoa, fuck!"

✍

One of the great advantages of being the Shadow Hand is that when you knock urgently upon a door, the person opening it is usually quite startled to see you on the other side. The butler gasps and falls back a step, giving me room to shove past him and race toward the foyer stairs.

In the upper level of the house, I can hear shouting—a chorus of raucous men's voices, and, above that, Pip's polecat snarl: "Get that sword out of my face!"

"Come on, boy," comes Tritan's reply as I round the landing and shoot up the next set of stairs. "If you're going to lurk about, you have to be ready to answer with steel when you get caught!"

"I wasn't lurking!" Pip shouts.

"And he's not a boy, neither!" comes another young man's shout. Pip squeaks as if pinched and fury darts up my spine, lending my legs extra fuel as I clear the stairs and pound down the hallway. "Not with this arse!"

"Get your hands off me!" Pip snaps. I draw Smoke as I run.

I slam back the door to Tritan's gaudy apartments just in time to slap the back of a young buck's knuckles with the flat of my blade. The youth yelps and withdraws his questing hand, cradling it to his chest.

"*Manners*, Master Vintus!" I snap in my best Shadow's Hand voice, deducing his parentage from the color of his hair—a caramel brown—and the crest sewn onto the breast of his Vintus-orange waistcoat.

"The Shadow Hand!" he replies, inanely, and dives out of the room, past me and down the hall.

The rest of the assembled fops, about ten in total, press themselves against the horrendously busy wallpaper of the salon, eager to be out of sword-reach. All save Tritan Gyre, who plants himself before me, Pip between us, and sneers. He has his own sword drawn, and on his head is a Gyre-blue velvet cap with the silver filigree feather stuck in the hatband as if it were a cheap silk flower. The whole room reeks of candle smoke, too-sweet sherry—a youth's drink—and *boy*.

"Oh, is she one of yours, Shadow Hand?" he growls. "Abysmal spying job."

I ignore Pip in the hopes that Gyre will as well, that we can make this business between just us, and quickly over besides. "I have come to collect an item from you, Master Gyre, and I will not be told no," I say instead.

"Oh? And why should I give anything of mine up to you so easily, spymaster? What good have you ever done *me* in return for something so precious?"

"It is not what I have done," I say, tone carefully neutral behind my mask, "so much as it is what I have *not* said. For example, I have told nothing of Zellista and the lovely, pinching gifts she left all over your nethers to your fiancée, the doting Lady Niffier. If you would care to have me rectify that oversight, I would be delighted to do so."

The boy goes dead pale under his velvet cap, hand shaking on the hilt of his sword.

"You wouldn't!" he snarls.

"I would do many things far worse to ensure the safety of the kingdom I serve," I intone. "Now, put the sword away and come talk to me in your study like a sensible boy."

He thrusts his chin out, insulted, and I realize too late that I have played this situation wrong. I should have appealed to his vanity instead of insulting his virility. *Stupid old Forsyth!*

Instead of acquiescing, as I hoped he would, Gyre tightens his grip on his blade and aims the point at Pip's throat.

"No," he says. "No, I have the leverage. I have something of yours, now, and I won't give it back until you vow that you will never tell Niffier, and that you will go away. Empty handed."

"I'm afraid that won't happen, Lordling," I say.

"Swear and leave, or I will cut her!" he snarls, taking a step toward Pip and scratching her cheek with the flat of his sword.

"Oh, for god's sake!" Pip huffs. "Are you two gonna whip out your dicks next and start comparing sizes? This is ridiculous."

"Quiet!" both Gyre and I say at the same time, though I do it rather more to keep her tongue in her head than as the threat of harm he does.

"No," Pip says, and the meaning of the single word is quite clear: *you're idiots.* "Look, if this has to be a fantasy-hero pissing contest, why don't you just settle this the old-fashioned way, *mano a mano*?"

"What?" Gyre asks.

"A duel."

Gyre's eyes spark with glee, even as I feel dread curling into my gut. Gyre turns away to meet the gaze of a whippet rake in mustard yellow, and they share a knowing look.

I grab Pip's arm and haul her to my side. "Are you mad?" I hiss into her ear. "I'm not good enough to beat Gyre!"

"Yes, you are," Pip hisses back. "I've watched him wave that thing around for five minutes, and he doesn't look like he knows a thing about holding a sword. I've *seen* you fight."

"It won't be Gyre who fights, however," I say mournfully, as Gyre and the rake in yellow turn back to us.

"Accepted!" Gyre shouts, and every man in the room breaks into applause. Gyre waves them to silence, smirking. "My champion against you, my impertinent young miss? Or your champion?"

"My champion," Pip says firmly, pressing her palm to my chest.

"Very well. These are the stakes: if my champion wins, the Shadow Hand will vow never to spy upon House Gyre or its occupants ever again, and swears to burn all correspondence and missives mentioning my family and I. He will also leave here without the thing for which he came."

"And if *my* champion wins," Pip challenges him, "we'll take the item, and *your* vow that you'll come clean to your fiancée. Oh, and that you'll go off the booze for a year, because, dude, I'm sensing some serious alcohol-driven rage issues here."

Gyre's expression grows thunderous, but he holds out his hand. Pip and Gyre shake on it, and then he withdraws his arm and, with a flourishing gesture, announces: "My champion, Under-Duke Quints Zerinus of Gadot, where he is his king's swordmaster."

Pip swallows hard, but gestures to me in turn. "And my champion, *your* king's Shadow Hand."

A murmur runs around the room, and some coins change hands. I can't decide if I should be insulted or not. Especially since none of them seem to be betting on me.

"Let us adjoin to the lawn behind the house," Gyre sneers, and, as one, the assembled party troops down the hall, descends the stairs, and heads out the kitchen exit.

"This is m-ma-mad," I whisper to Pip once more, as we reach the fresh air. The young men begin to hoot and holler, forming a circle around the four of us, prepared, no doubt, to shove us back into the middle if Pip or I try to flee.

"It's not," Pip says back. "Good luck. I believe in you. You'll be fine."

Pip backs away, hand on her own hilt, though what she plans to do with that sword, if she draws it, I have no idea. We haven't even had a lesson on how to hold it properly. Across from me, Gyre backs away, and Zerinus takes his stance.

"I am going to be the man who kills King Carvel's Shadow Hand," Zerinus brags, chest puffed up like a peacock.

"I certainly hope not," I mutter under my breath. But he is younger. Faster. Probably more practiced and more skilled. It is entirely possible.

Before I can even salute with Smoke, Zerinus is jumping forward like a carp after a mayfly. *Cheap! And impatient!*

But, ah, I can see his training there. He must have worked under Sphyres in Gadot, who prefers to teach offense to the point of offense. A fine dueling blade is meant to slash and cut, not stab, which is why Sphyres teaches his students to do just that—it is unexpected.

Except when you are expecting it.

Zerinus's blade aims for my eye slits. I dance to the side, avoiding the clumsily telegraphed lunge, draw my own blade, and bring up Smoke to parry. I add an extra downward slash to rip at the tendon behind his knee, and to my surprise, it connects easily. The rake howls and drops to the ground, clutching at his leg and bleeding profusely into his yellow trousers.

"I yield! I yield!" he screams, and I stare down at him in wonder, shaking with unused adrenaline.

"Oh!" I say, staring down at my writhing opponent. As one, his fellows flee. They have left him to, I presume, make new acquaintance with less unsavory fools. Only Gyre remains, and he stands still as statuary, too stunned to aid his champion.

"That was . . . hmm," I say. I feel the frown form, unbidden. "Why didn't he try?"

Zerinus's wails are suddenly broken up with Pip's obscenely inappropriate giggles.

"Try?" she asks. "Why didn't he *try*? Dear god, your blade was flashing across the sky before his was fully parallel."

"But I beat him," I say, slowly, as one would to an obstinate child.

"Because you're good, *bao bei*," Pip rejoins in the same tone.

"No," I demur, under my breath so none but Pip can hear, "I'm not. I could see that his swordmaster must have been Sphyres, and so I knew to duck. I could not defend, though, not as my brot—"

She smacks the back of my head. "None of that now, Shadow Hand. I thought we agreed, no more comparing yourself to that jackass."

I rub my new hurt and frown deeper. "And so you will reinforce this lesson with pain?"

"If I have to." She is smiling, and it is soft and lovely, the kind that makes the mud in her eyes sink away, leaving clear, admiring green. I want to kiss her so badly it is like a physical ache. Her eyes drop to my mouth.

"Shame. I fear I may be black and blue before this quest is done."

"Of course. Your choice. Though, I can reinforce it with pleasure, too," she whispers, and as if she had been reading my mind, she presses herself up on her toes, tilts her head back, and covers my lips with hers.

Oh.

She rocks back to assess my reaction, as much as she is able through the mask. I lower my head and sip at her mouth.

"Finally!" she groans, and the relief in her tone is just as much a shock as the puff of her air against my chin. I am too shocked by the feel of her arms winding around my neck like tendrils, her fingers spread upon my skull through the hood, to move forward, but Pip doesn't seem to notice. She raises herself up more and pushes another kiss onto my lips, her own cheeks brushing the sides of my mask.

And then Tritan Gyre, the silly whelp, turns on his heel and runs.

"Shit!" Pip says.

I whistle for Dauntless, and within seconds, I can hear the strike of his shoes upon the gravel of the avenue.

"We will catch up to him," I assure her.

"You might not get the chance if he goes inside somewhere and locks the door," Pip answers. She takes off after him.

All that jogging has a use after all, it seems. While Lord Gyre is swifter than Pip to start, her stamina is greater. Before he is even to the end of the garden, I can see him flagging. I would not have been able to catch up to him, when he is such a dot on the horizon, but Pip can.

Pip does.

And then she flings herself at his knees, and they are both on the ground in an ungraceful tangle of limbs and cloaks. Dauntless whickers beside my ear, and I wonder that I was so enthralled by Pip's recklessness that I didn't hear him stop beside me. I mount, then spur my horse toward them, fearing what Gyre's sharp elbows could do to her face or ribs, or the softness of her belly. I needn't have worried; by the time I am at their side, he is face down in the dirt and Pip is sitting on his thighs, his arms wrenched around behind him and wrists captured in her hands.

He is too busy attempting to catch his breath, nose and cheek smashed into the soil, to struggle.

"Ah, my Lord Shadow Hand," she says when I pull Dauntless to a gentle stop. "Nice of you to join us."

"Impressive, my lady," I murmur, and then I crouch down by the young lordling. "You, Master Gyre? Less so."

"What do you want, you blackguard?"

"Nothing too expensive or important, Lordling Dandy. I'll take your cap-feather as my prize," I say, pointing to his hat and making it sound like it was a spur of the moment choice. The young man's eyes widen.

"No," he says.

"Your champion yielded to me," I press, folding my hands over my pommel and leaning down to meet his eyes through the slits in my mask.

I lean down low and pluck the silver quill from his hatband, glad that the mask keeps my expression of wonder hidden as the pendant shivers in my hand like it were really made of feather and cartilage. It is an incredibly wrought masterpiece, moves as if it were real, and I cannot believe it has been gracing the throats and lapels of the spoiled Gyre brats for so many generations, instead of being displayed in a museum.

"You can't take that! It's a family heirloom!"

"Strange place to wear an heirloom," I reply, and tuck the quill into a leather wallet, then bury it deep in the secret pocket built into the inside of my waistcoat, my movements shrouded beneath the many shifting layers of fabric in my cloak. Pip mounts behind me and wraps her arms around my waist, pulling the cloak over her head to disguise herself once more.

"You cheated! You cheated!" he screeches as we leave him in our wake.

"It's not cheating to know your enemy, Master Gyre," I throw back over my shoulder. "Stay sober." Pip presses her face against my shoulder blade to muffle her laughter.

We do not bother with any other stops, just ride back to the maze and, from the secret entrance, back to the tavern.

The darkened stables swallow the Shadow Hand and decant Forsyth Turn.

I pat the leather wallet in my pocket to show Pip it is safe, and then we turn to the warm dining room, drawn to the flickering lamplight and cozy shadows like a pair of sleepy wooden toy ducks trundling along in a toddler's wake. Despite the general aroma of unwashed bodies, burned grease, and cheap tallow, there is something close and homey about the dining room. The tables are rustic, authentic—not ridiculous wealthy recreations of handmade, utilitarian peasant couture. The tabletops are scarred with the scrapes of a thousand metal plates across their surfaces, the dents of a hundred evenings of raucous laughter and pounded ale mugs and joyous drinking songs. The chairs are mismatched, wobbly, and worn smooth from a thousand friends sliding into them across from a thousand other friends, from dozens of lovers shifting them toward one another. The floor is clean swept, the lamps high and smoke-free, and the windows clear. The proprietor clearly takes pride in the establishment, and their love of the place—low, dark ceilings and crowded seating notwithstanding—imbues every bit of furniture and dishware and seems to have been, in turn, absorbed by the patrons.

"Well, that was certainly interesting," Pip says, as we take a seat at a banquette along the front wall of the room. Her eyes gaze out the mullioned window, and her hands stray to the knees of her trousers, brushing away the dirt her tumble with Gyre crushed into the leather.

"Slightly more active than my usual pursuits," I admit. "And perhaps a little less than honest."

Pip wrinkles her nose at me. "You don't actually believe that kid. You didn't *cheat*."

I lean close and lower my voice to a whisper. "Didn't I? I played the game knowing things that Forsyth Turn would not."

"Well, you weren't playing as Forsyth Turn," Pip replies, leaning in and lowering her voice as well. "If he thinks it's unfair that the spymaster of the king won with knowledge he's collected, then the dumbass shouldn't have agreed to play the king's spymaster."

"True enough," I allow, and I am chuckling loud enough that I lean back in my seat and it becomes full guffaws.

Pip laughs too. "And man, the look on his face when you just took it."

"I wish I could have seen the look on his face when you tackled him," I counter, and Pip stretches her eyes and mouth wide, pinching her eyebrows up in a decent approximation of the boy's constipated scowl.

That sets us both roaring again, and half the taverna turns to see what is so funny, only to witness an awkward lordling and a well-heeled boy howling like farmhands.

The serving woman comes around and offers us a choice between ale, scrumpy, or wine. When she catches her breath, Pip elects to try the scrumpy, having no idea whatsoever what it is, and I stick to what I know and ask for the wine. We are given the further choice between beef or duck, and, to make things easy, I put enough money into the good woman's hand to buy a whole duck, the trimmings, and a clean canvas square to carry away the leftovers.

While we wait, Pip unfurls her Excel and the tricolor-marked map, and we plan our route to the next Station, at Salt Crystal Caverns.

We toast to a Station well cleared when the drinks arrive, both in rough earthenware cups. Pip sips hers and her face lights with a grin. "Oh, yum, drunken apple juice!"

Dinner is excellent, for taverna fare, and Pip has a marvelous time eating with her hands. "Unheard of," she says, when she admits her reluctance to just tear at the duck.

"We'll buy a traveling fork and knife," I say. "And the belt-pouch to carry them in. I forgot to pack some for us. I told you I was a rubbish adventurer."

She kicks me under the table and smiles over the rim of her cloudy apple cider. "This stuff is . . . whoa," Pip says. "I think I might be drunk already."

"It's a workman's draught," I say. "And so: potent."

"Yeah, I'm getting that. Umf. I think I need to break the seal."

I furrow my eyebrows at her.

"Use the little Reader's room. The toilet?"

"Ah. They will be around the back, near the stables." I gesture to a door that leads outside, beside the bar. "Are you sure you want to go alone?"

"I'm fine, *bao bei*! It's a whole half a room away. I think I'll survive. I'm a big girl."

"If you insist," I say.

"I do, in fact, insist," she says and sashays in that direction, the alcohol making her face flush and her steps loose.

The men at the bar follow her exit with their eyes, and I find that I am helpless to do otherwise myself. Pip certainly makes for an attractive sight.

It is so wonderful to see her happy.

I just wish the laughter rolling from her tongue would appear in her eyes.

Eleven

The first inkling that our peaceful night of celebration is running amiss is the way Pip's whole face has gone white, her limbs trembling as she shivers her way down into her seat after returning to the table.

"Pip?" I ask. "What has happened?"

Pip's body is oriented toward me, but her face, her gaze, is locked on the door through which she came. Her lips are curled in tight between her teeth; it looks painful.

"Pip?" I try again.

"I saw—by the bathroom, I saw—it was him. I saw—" She stops mid-sentence, tripping over her own words, and makes a small noise like all the air has suddenly been squeezed from her lungs. Her muddy eyes grow so impossibly wide that I fear they will fall right out of her head. She tugs hard on the collar of her jerkin and, with shaking hands, lifts her scrumpy and quaffs half of it in one large gulp.

"Saw who?" I ask, concerned now. "Gyre?"

Pip only coughs in answer, shaking her head. I turn to follow her line of sight, but there is no one there who seems to be glaring back, no one I even recognize. Just groups of men, some still in travel cloaks, mingling and causing a ruckus.

Pip looks a breath away from another spasm episode. What has she seen that has triggered this? The soldiers' ailment didn't jump upon her while she was facing down Tritan Gyre's sword, so why now, in a crowded taverna that is the furthest thing from a battlefield? Unless this is some sort of delayed reaction . . . ?

I reach out carefully and touch her shoulder. "Pip? Are you well? Do we need to retire before you have another fit?"

She rears back as if slapped and turns a betrayed, scared expression to me. Then she withers, curling in on herself, hands on her face to hide what I assume is her shame, breathing deeply. She leans into my touch, seeking a comfort that I am all too happy to give, though it saddens me that it is required.

"Never mind," Pip says. "I thought I saw . . . but it wasn't." Her eyes, when she looks back up, are brilliantly green with unshed tears. "I'm sorry. Ignore me."

"Never," I soothe. "Who did you think you saw?"

"Boot—" she begins, but succumbs to a second round of coughing, like she is gagging on his name.

I am torn between wanting to rub her back, to soothe and comfort her, and leaping to my feet and chasing the villain down. I stand, but Pip shakes her head again, sucking hard on the air, and chokes out: "No, leave it. It wasn't him."

She implores me with a verdant, sparkling gaze, and I conceed. I sit.

She shuffles and squirms, getting her air back. Finally, after a long, tense moment of wondering if Pip will break down completely, if I will have to hustle her from the taverna and up to our rooms, she looks up.

"I'm fine," she lies, and swigs her remaining scrumpy to clear her throat. I run my hand down her arm to take her hand, and she allows me to twine my fingers through her own.

"What brought this on?" I ask softly.

"I'm just tired," Pip says, her free hand touching her neck again, as if someone has just been pressing their hands against it and she can't quite believe that she has been released and can breathe again. "I didn't sleep well on the ground last night, and the running and the sneaking . . . I'm just *tired*, okay?"

"Pip."

"I'm fine!" The more she says it, the less I believe her. "It's just . . . this place. It's . . . exactly the sort of place that Kintyre would love, exactly the sort of place where Bevel would have a massive audience. You know what

I mean, right? Enchanted children with round, adoring eyes sitting all around his feet. Swooning maidens fanning themselves with lace hankies. The whole shebang. I've imagined myself in places like this for years, *wanted* to be here, wanted to hear the stories and laugh and clap along, but I . . . there's no place for me, because I'm not a white face, because I'm a woman, because of the kind of world that Elgar Reed wrote."

The sorrow in her voice is genuine, but it's her certainty that she doesn't belong here that grips my heart so hard between cruel fingers that I actually feel it as a physical pain.

"Oh, no, Pip, no. Of course there is a place for you here." *With me*, I want to add, but can't. Instead, I hold her hand more tightly, pray that she understands what I cannot say with words. "You are so clever, so kind."

"You don't really know me," Pip says, but squeezes back. "This me, here, this isn't really me. I'm saying things that I wouldn't normally—" She gasps again, free hand going to her chest, and takes a deep breath, forcing air back into her lungs. She drinks, and I watch the level of her cup carefully. I'm not certain she should have more. Then, after a long moment, she mutters: "I don't want to talk about who I am anymore."

"Very well," I say. "Very well. It is fine. Let's talk about something else."

"Let's talk about *him*," Pip says, jerking her chin at man at the bar who must be of dryad blood. His hair is tangled through with hawthorn and holly, his skin cracked and brown like bark. "Why are the only people who are non-white also non-human?"

"There are humans with darker skin, down south," I say.

"Ah, yes; pirates and savages, harems and harlots," Pip mutters bitterly. "Spice merchants with pet sand-worms. All exotic *others*, and never the hero, eh?"

She is not incorrect, so I do not know how to respond. Instead, I sip my wine.

Pip runs her palms over her face again, scrubbing at her mouth with the back of her knuckles.

"Never mind me," she says at length. "I'm just tired and cranky."

"Shall we retire, then?"

"Yeah. Christ, I'm done," Pip says. "Let's just go. I'm drunk-ish. I just wanna . . . go to bed." She does not say *with you*, or make any further amorous advances, so I take her words at face value. And she *does* look exhausted. Between the riding and the fighting, and the less than successful sneaking, I feel quite worn out myself.

Besides, I still need to investigate the quill we acquired, and I am hesitant to do so while we are on the open road. I release her hands, reluctantly. I summon the proprietress with a look, and she packs up our meal for us. I pass her a coin under the table for her discretion.

Together, we make our weary way toward the stairs.

It doesn't occur to either of us, so full of wine and scrumpy, victory and the glow of mutual understanding, that, in order to achieve our rented room, we will have to pass the group of rough men who are blocking the stairs.

I push past first, daring any of them to comment, and none do. It seems as if their rowdy geniality has found other outlets. Until Pip has her foot on the first stair.

She yelps suddenly, and whips around on her heel, smacking at the hand of the man closest to her.

I pause and turn, dinner under one arm and a hand on the hilt of my sword. "My lady?" I ask her, deliberately formal, but my eyes are on the hooting, howling pack of unwashed miscreants.

"Some scumbag just pinched my ass," she snarls.

"How unfortunate," I growl, my fingers wiggling on the hilt of my sword to attract the blackguard's attention to my threat. It is not Smoke, but it is still sharp. "Care to point out which one?"

There is a moment where the hooting ebbs, the men now watching warily to see if Pip will single one of them out. I can tell they are wondering if there will be a brawl. And, by the looks on some of their faces, if there will be an opportunity for more intimate groping in the crush.

Pip scowls, and the howling laughter resumes. The man who pinched her, emboldened by our lack of response, reaches up—this time toward her breast. Pip cracks her hand across his wrist and he just laughs harder.

"Don't touch me," she snarls.

"C'mon, princess," the man slurs. "Lookatchu, all airs and graces. You liked it."

"No, I did not *like it*, in point of fact," Pip says. "Now go away. You're drunk."

"I'd still be a better roll than that twiggy little lordling shite," he says, and, even from the step above

Pip, I am doused with the fumes from the beer he's consumed. "They all have tiny little quill dicks."

I bristle at this affront to my virility, as any man might. Before I can draw my sword, though, before I can decide if Pip might *want* me to stand up for her, Pip waves me down. I desperately want to defend her virtue, but she is already speaking.

"Don't do this," Pip says. "We're leaving. Just forget us."

She turns around again, scowling and muttering something about "*Schrödinger's Rapists*." And then she yelps again, eyes wide. The drunk is pulling back his hand, and I can tell that he has pinched her somewhere far more intimate than her bottom. It fills me with absolute rage that he would take such liberties, not just with Pip but with *any* other person.

My ability to be calmly detached evaporates in the heat of my anger.

"Enough," I snarl, putting on my best Shadow Hand voice and almost wishing I had the mask to go with it, just to scare this useless sack of flesh sober.

Pip turns back around to face the drunk, hand on the hilt of her own sword and her jaw so tight that her words are a hiss between her teeth. "Touch me with that hand again, and you will be drawing back a bloody stump. *Do I make myself clear?*" she snarls.

I viciously stomp down the urge to applaud.

"It's not my fault you're pretty," the man mutters, as if he is blaming her for exactly that.

"Oh, you're hella charming," Pip says, voice rife with sarcasm. In case the man in discussion misses it, she adds a very blatant eye roll. "Your mother must be so proud."

"Silence, hussy."

"Oh, from princess to hussy? Just because I said no? Even more charming. You sweet-talker, you."

"Shut your cunt!"

"Holy fuck!" Pip laughs, the expletive startled out of her by the drunk's words like a bird from a bush by a hound. "Oh my god. When was the last time that worked for you? Seriously? Has that *ever* got you laid? And let me be clear, by 'laid,' I mean consensually."

Now I tense. Pip is starting to take the condescension too far. Slowly, I draw my sword. The Schrödingers put down their various cups and mugs and all turn to face us. The taverna goes suddenly, unnaturally silent.

The spokesman straightens. "I dunno what 'consensually' means—"

"Clearly!" Pip snorts.

"—but someone needs a lesson in manners and to learn their *place*," he snarls, spittle catching on his tobacco-stained beard, his cheeks turning puce.

"Yes," Pip agrees. "But as I don't like teaching drunken idiots, I'm going to spare myself the headache, and you the jargon." Without looking around, she says to me: "We're leaving, my lord."

She takes a step back, crowding against my front and forcing me up the stairs behind her, one riser at a time. We both keep our eyes on the crowd below us, our hands on our swords, and the drunk man seems to decide we're not worth the trouble. He spits demonstratively on the bottom step, wipes his nose, hitches up his trousers in a move that is clearly meant to be obscene but only looks ridiculous against his generous gut, and turns away.

I sheathe my sword as soon as we are around the corner, out of sight of the crowd. Only then do Pip and I turn our backs to the staircase. I am not too proud to admit that we hike down the hall at a fair clip.

When we reach our cramped garret room, Pip is so nervous and tense that her hands shake as she shuts and locks the door behind us. "That's too easy to break down," Pip murmurs, and so, together, we shove the sturdy clothing cupboard in front of the entrance, to act as a further barrier should the Schrödinger and his friends change their minds.

When it is in place, and the windows locked and shuttered tightly, Pip drops down onto one of the two narrow rope beds. She chooses the furthest from both entrances and puts her face in her hands. In the light of the fire the landlord left banked in the hearth at Pip's back, the room looks almost decent. The cracks in the thickly applied plaster melt into shadow, and the floor appears even. At least the room is clean. It smells pleasantly of lavender and fresh straw—that must be the mattresses.

The meager light is enough for me to see Pip by, as well. Her shoulders are shaking and, for a moment, I fear she is crying, disturbed and frightened by the fight we almost had. It makes my heart seize to think that she has just strategically placed herself in the most tactically advantageous position in the room. That she has sat herself in the place where she will be able to *see* her assailants coming if they do choose to break down our door and rape her. How terrified she must be.

But when I take a step toward her, it is not crying I hear, but giggles.

She is laughing!

"Oh my god!" she says, throwing back her head and meeting my gaze. "That was *insane!*"

I cannot help the smile that crawls across my mouth, and so do not fight it. Her mirth is infectious, and soon, I find myself giggling alongside her.

"I thought we were going to get *pummeled*," she says, and it is with glee, entirely absent of the kind of fear that most people have in the face of a physical beating. It occurs to me that Pip might be the kind of woman who seeks out thrill and adventure, who is addicted to that surge of *alive*ness that being in danger offers, and it makes a curl of lust snake through my gut.

Her face is flush with excitement and laughter, her eyes bright and her grin wide, and I cannot help it, I cannot help myself anymore. I swoop down and mash my lips against hers, inelegant and desperate, almost more of a bite than a kiss.

Pip's hands are in my lapels immediately, pushing me away, a muffled sort of yelp escaping from between our mouths.

"Sorry, sorry," I say, following the commands of her hands, shame pulling at my insides. *Oh, what have I done?* To attack her with my affections is utterly base, and no better than the drunks on the stairs!

I try to take a step back, but Pip's hands tighten on the plackets of my traveling robe and she grabs my knees with her legs, pulling me off balance and back against her. Her lips are swollen and pink, wet and stretched into a grin of poetic proportion.

"I'm not opposed," she says.

"I should have asked."

"Then ask," she says, cheeks pink with mirth.

"*May* I kiss you?"

"Yes," Pip says, and this time, she meets me halfway. Her mouth tastes like apples and laughter, and she slows the kiss, touches the tip of her tongue against my bottom lip, sweet and gentle, showing me what she likes. I mimic the movement, lick the seam of her mouth, and she lets me in. She is all heat and slickness, and I tighten my arms around her neck, draw her closer because this is everything I have yearned for, everything I *want*, and I have waited so long, been so *patient*, and it is *wonderful*—

"Whoa, whoa, I'm right here," Pip says softly, pushing me away gently and wiping her chin with the back of her hand. "Slow down. There's no need to go caveman on me."

I blink at Pip owlishly.

"*Possessive*," she explains. "I'm not going anywhere. Shhhh."

Admonished, I stretch my neck and peck a chaste kiss to Pip's lips. She pulls us both backward, and I settle down on the bed beside her. She leans into me, curling against my side like she was written to fit there.

I wrap my arms around her tentatively and ask, "How are you?"

"Fine."

"Because those men—"

"Forsyth, I'm okay. Really. Don't think I'm going to let them make me feel ashamed," Pip scoffs. "They're just troglodyte assholes with hands that shouldn't be going places they are."

"True," I allow slowly. "And it is quite common in a taverna setting, and the men probably—"

"Whoa," Pip says, hand outstretched and palm in my direction. "Stop right there before I lose all respect for you. Just because it's 'quite common' doesn't make it *right*."

Her admonishment strikes me between the eyes, stilling my rushing thoughts for a moment. *Well, then. Of course.*

I nod, slowly. "Just as slaying dragons to steal their hordes under the guise of rescuing maidens was common, but wrong, and was eventually outlawed."

"Exactly," she says, and awards me with a stunningly lovely smile that makes my toes curl in my boots and my lips tingle with the memory of her kiss. "God, your world is slowly driving me bonkers, Forsyth. I love it, but the ingrained sexism is *astounding*. When I first got here, I—" She interrupts herself with a hiss of pain. She had lifted her arm to push her hair back off her face.

"What bruise is this?" I ask, catching her hand before she lowers it. "This is new."

And it is—there is a rough, red welt around her wrist, fresh enough that it can't have happened more than a few hours ago. I slide my palm carefully down around the marks, and, yes, it is the exact shape of a man's hand. Pip flinches and tugs her arm out of my grip, cradling the hurt against her breast.

"Ouch," she says in reproach.

"Did Gyre do this?" I ask.

Pip shakes her head, slowly, looking up at me again with eyes darkened brown in the low light of our room, imploring me to understand . . . *something*. But what that something is, I do not know.

"It's . . . from downstairs."

"The drunk? The . . . what did you call him, the Schrödinger?"

Pip snorts a laugh. "You heard that?"

"Heard it, yes, but did not understand it." I kiss the welt and lay her hand down carefully on her stomach.

"Oh, you know, 'a no is just a yes you haven't made her say yet.' Guys who act entitled, like of course every woman they see exists solely to give them something sweet for the eyes or somewhere to wet their dick. No, there's no human being under there; women aren't *people*, so you don't owe them respect or consideration, and you certainly don't have to take no for an answer. I especially can't stand the ones who get *angry* at me when I tell them to fuck off. Like I'm breaking some law by policing my own body."

She tries to raise her injured wrist again, but I catch it, keep it down by twining my fingers through hers. Her grip on my hand tightens to near pain, but I don't let go. I won't abandon her while she is this lost and angry.

"I . . . I never thought of it like that," I admit.

Pip rolls her eyes. "Well, of course *you* wouldn't, you're a man."

That stings quite a bit more than I thought it would. I turn my face away, unsure of how to reply. Pip makes an exasperated sound. I let her turn my face back, let her touch the side of cheek with her palm, and try not to wonder if she knows what even such a gentle touch does to my insides.

"No, no, I didn't mean it like that," she says softly. "It's just, you've been *taught* that the world and everyone in it belongs to you, only exists for you, because you're a man with power. Finding out that the rest of us disagree with you is tough."

"But how can the attention be so unwelcome? You are beautiful. Don't you deserve the adoration? Don't you enjoy it? It is not your right, as a woman?"

"I do enjoy it," Pip admits. "From people who are genuine. But forcing me to engage when I just want to walk by isn't awesome. It's all . . . invasive and . . . yuck. It feels like grime on my skin, you know? Instead of a real compliment, which feels like . . . silk."

I am reminded, suddenly, of being a very gawky fifteen-year-old, desperate for the approval of a brother who had just returned from his first quest with a new friend, a new sword, and a title bestowed upon him by the king himself. I was growing into my body then, uncertain, self-conscious, ashamed of my height and my new skinniness, and covered with spots and bruises from falling all over my newly enlarged feet. And my brother, sure and broad and comfortable in his own skin, his own muscles, his own confidence and virility, chided and heckled me from the side of the paddock as I tried to saddle Dauntless. His commentary was invasive, hateful, humiliating. The words were those of encouragement, but the tone . . . it made me feel like a monster, inhuman, the barest scrap of *nothing*.

It made me feel like a piece of furniture, or sculpture, or *meat*. Nothing *human*. Nothing with *feelings* and thoughts and frustrations of my own occupying me. No, I was only a flesh-puppet put in that paddock for his entertainment.

"Let's say we're in a coffee house, and you want to buy me a coffee as a way to get permission from me to sit down and flirt with me. If I say no, I don't want a cup of coffee, and you insist on getting me one anyway, and make me uncomfortable enough that I feel guilty and have to drink it, then . . . what else are you not going to accept no as an answer to? You've proven to me once that you don't listen to me, so if you want a kiss and I say no, then what? If you want sex and I say no, what happens then?"

I reach up and take both her hands between mine. "That is a dilemma I never considered. How difficult it must be, to try to discern between genuine interest and pushiness. It makes it difficult for me, as well, I suppose . . . for how am I to approach a woman without terrifying her, if she has already had such a negative experience?"

"It's extremely hard, on both sides." She raises my hands and kisses one of my knuckles. "But I really appreciate you listening."

I cannot help the twinkling, cheeky grin I offer up. "Well, someone told me once that I was written to be an attentive and thoughtful listener."

Pip kisses each of my other knuckles in quick succession.

And then my hands go cold between hers. It never occurred to me to try to decipher whether Pip was as interested in me as I was in her. Everyone had pushed me toward her because that's what happens to heroes— meet a maiden, fall in lust (or sometimes love), and do it quickly. The maiden reciprocates, because why wouldn't she? You're the *hero*. Only Pip has a mind of her own, and desires, and such fierce intelligence. Pip is her own person and will not be dictated to or told where to feel and how.

I wonder, suddenly—do I really love her?

Or is this something brought on by either the Authorial Intent of the Writer, or my own desperate loneliness mixed with the "helpful" suggestions of my friends.

No, I do love her. I really do. Wherever it is that the emotion began, I love her now, and there is nothing to be done for it. Except to decipher whether Pip feels the same for me.

Because, if she does not, I will not be one of those men who take it as a challenge. I will not be a Schrödinger.

Oh, how I hope this will not be the end of it!

"I've scared you," Pip says. "I didn't mean to."

"N-No," I reply, as quickly as I'm able. "I just re-realized that per-perhaps I ne-ne-need to re-reevaluate how I've appro-proached . . . u-us."

"You think about an 'us'?"

"I ... I d-do."

Pip smiles softly, sadly. "Have I given you any indication of being unwelcome?" She underscores this query with another kiss to my knuckles.

"Well, n-no."

"Then don't worry. Trust me, I'll let you know when you're not welcome. You'll know where the line is before you can accidentally cross it." The grin she gives me then is revealing, and salacious, and everything that is wonderfully promising.

But then the smile falters, and she yawns, and I do not think that should be as cute as I find it, her pink tongue curling like a kitten's. I am filled with a sudden surge of warmth and light, because, after all she has said, after all the grief and agony and anger she has exorcised tonight, after all the explanations, she has still chosen to allow me to pursue my feelings for her. She has chosen me, and it feels so freeing, so wonderful, because I do not have to guess. I know now. I know.

She wants me to want her. It is freeing.

"May I kiss you again?"

"One more," she says, and so I comply, but I am careful to stop when she pushes away to yawn again. "Sorry. I promise you're not boring."

"I understand. Dinner?" I ask.

"I'm not hungry anymore," Pip says. "Still tired and drunkish though. Sleep with me," she pleads softly.

"*Sleep*," I echo, feeling a stirring in my trousers and the back of my mind that probably shows on my face.

"Just sleep," Pip clarifies. "I need . . . someone beside me."

Reassurance, she means. Despite her bravado, she is still shaking. The face she puts on is determined and brave, desperate to not allow her fear of what happened downstairs to taint what we have now.

"Very well," I say. "But you'll have to let me go long enough for me to undress."

Pip laughs and releases her hold. I rise and shed both my boots and my robe, but leave my trousers and shirt, being a gentleman. Pip gets herself into a similar state of undress, and we burrow under the covers. She maneuvers us so that my body is between her and the room's only two exits, and I allow it because she needs it, and I say nothing about it because she also needs the illusion that she is fooling me. She wraps one curving, beautiful arm over my chest, palm splayed against my pattering heart, and together, we drop into sleep.

I want to make love to Pip, to hold her close and lavish her with my affection. But tonight, she needs a body between her and her fears, not between her legs. I am proud to be that body.

✍

I wake when slim fingers thread through the thinning hair above my ear. The light is soft and blue-orange, and when I open my eyes, it gilds the rise of Pip's cheekbone, the shell of her ear.

"Hello," she murmurs, her face bare inches from mine. A smile curves into a dimple on the visible side of her face; the other side is resting on the canvas pillow.

"Hello," I croak back. *Water. I would love a cup of water. I might even gleefully commit murder for a cup of water.*

"Drink too much, did you?" she whispers.

"I'm not hungover," I protest, struggling to sit up, to untangle myself from the bed and her limbs. She reaches up, straining against the awkwardness of the position, and puts a finger over my lips.

"Lay back down," she says.

Stunned and ashamed of the possibility of my tripping tongue, I obey. She throws her nearest arm over my shoulders and wriggles until her side is pressed all the way up my chest, our ankles crossing. Her hand splays between my shoulder blades and she sighs, a contented sound.

"You smell nice," she says.

"You too," I reply, though I am more commenting on the memory of her scent than the present version. There was a lot of running and riding yesterday, and I can smell stale horse and old sweat.

She wrinkles her nose. "Well, maybe not this morning."

Emboldened by her embrace, I bury my nose in her hair and inhale noisily. Pip giggles.

"Even this morning," I murmur against her ear. I feel her squirm, and I cannot tell if it is born of ticklish glee or arousal.

She moves onto her side, so that we face one another. "Kiss me, then," she says and wriggles forward.
Our heads are both still on the pillow, and it seems silly,
but I stretch my neck and do as I'm bid.

It is a light peck, and she makes a hearty sound
of disappointment. I jerk back. "So-sorry." I crawl out
of the bed, standing by the side, looking down at her,
ashamed that this is another thing I just can't get *right*.
Pip sits up, frowning.

She reaches up and twines her fingers along the back
of my neck. "Oh, you will be sorry if you don't kiss me
properly, Forsyth Turn," she says, and yanks my face back
down against hers. This angle is better; we snap together,
and it drives all the breath from my lungs, all the fight
from my limbs. But it could be better, it could, and so
I pull back, turn my head the other way, and try again,
playing with angle and pressure. I have always prided
myself in being a quick learner.

"Much better," Pip breathes between kisses, and it
doesn't matter that her mouth is dry and morning-stale,
because, with each kiss, she tastes more and more like me.

"I . . . I th-thought . . ." I manage to stutter, breathing my confusion into her mouth each time we part to
realign ourselves, to experiment, to be scholarly about
the push and pull, the drag of noses across cheeks, skin
against skin, working to find the most comfortable tilt,
the place where we simply slot together. "I thought you
wouldn't want . . . after last night . . ."

"I'm allowed to want it, you know, *bao bei*," Pip
teases, eyes emerald in the pre-dawn light stealing across

our bed. "I'm allowed to be a sexual person. I *want* you. I want to *own you.*"

A surge of lust and affection crawls up my chest, so powerful that I fear opening my mouth lest it come out in a ridiculous torrent of words that are too strong, too meaningful. One simply does not say such things the first time. Instead, it bypasses my mouth and crawls in behind my eyes, making them warm and wet.

Fearing that I will be undone by the pleasure of her hands pulling at my waist, trying to press our skins together tighter, I bury my face against her neck and lavish attention there instead. I am suddenly, powerfully desirous of leaving a very visible love bite under her ear, a warning to others that Pip belongs to another. She gasps and wriggles, getting her legs around mine as I do my best, sucking on the skin and nibbling with my teeth, patient and too slow for Pip's liking, if the way she is pulling at me is any indication. But I will not be rushed, and I crowd her back against the mattress, my palms on either side of her shoulders to keep from crushing her.

I push aside the hair at her nape and do the thing I had envisioned so many weeks before: I lower my lips to the skin there and kiss one scarred puff of flesh, carved carefully to resemble the small, tender leaf of an ivy plant.

Pip arches up off the mattress and shimmies against my legs, pressing that shadowed place at the apex of her thighs against my knees, insistent. I never thought my knobby knees could be erotic, but the way they get warm and watery and threaten to go out from under me makes me revise my judgment.

Knees: definitely erotic.

"Come on, come *on*," Pip growls into my ear. "Get back down here."

She pulls with her legs, and, this time, I am not strong enough to resist. The cradle of her thighs is glorious and hot, the ridge of her hip smooth, and her fingers are pulling at the laces at my throat, impatient.

"Lemmie," she pants.

I return the favor as best as I'm able, propped on one elbow to give us both the space to work, our arms banging into each other's elbows, fingers tangling, laces smacking against cheeks and necks as they are whipped from their grommets.

Pip is suddenly laughing again, and the feel of her soft belly bouncing against my own is a wonder in and of itself.

"This is ridiculous!" Pip crows. She tightens her grip on my hips, sliding one leg up so the inside of her knee leaves a trail of fire along my thigh, the heel of her foot digging into the flesh of my rear. "We're not going to grope around in our clothes like a pair of teenagers!"

And yet, she doesn't release me so that we may undress, just pushes at the shoulders of my shirt until the fabric falls away, down to my elbows, where it becomes pinioned by our combined efforts to get each other naked. I falter, balance lost, and fall against her.

Pip lets out a wuffing breath, her breasts crushed between our chests and two layers of rough-spun shirts. I scramble to my hands and knees, and she lets me go, laughing. I stand and make quick work of my socks, and then hers, relishing the opportunity to slide my fingers up the back of her calves. She shivers all over, the mirth falling away even as her mouth parts and that delicious pink tongue licks at her bottom lip.

She sits up, and we part only long enough to allow our shirts room to be removed over our heads, her mouth back against mine the minute the fabric has passed them. She takes my hands and presses them against her breasts, and I am stunned by how soft and warm they are. Something scratches the centers of both my palms, and I realize that it is her nipples, growing hard. I cannot resist the urge to flick them with my thumbs; Pip arches and makes a guttural noise of approval that I find so breathtakingly endearing that I do it again before withdrawing to attack my own trousers. My knees are on the outside of hers, but the moment she has wriggled out of her trousers she reverses the position, her legs outside of mine, her sex bared and wet and on offer.

My fingers go numb on my flies, and I am left trying to fumble the laces open, finding that I am too moved by the beauty of the sight before me to finish the job.

Pip grins up at me, a cheeky smile caught in the corners of her mouth, a retort on her tongue, but it fades as soon as she catches sight of my expression. I can only assume it looks a bit shocked and frightened and awed, for that is how I feel. Pip is giving me the most intimate part of her, is allowing me the privilege of being *inside* her, where I could hurt her. She wants to take me into her body. She *wants* me.

No one has ever wanted me before. No one has ever wanted *me*.

My hands begin to move again, but only to shake. I want to command them to stop, to play themselves along Pip's hips, to worship the muscle that is the result of hours of dedication to her own fitness, to explore the one part of a woman that I've never touched before. That moist heat . . .

Instead, my hands ignore me and simply shake.

Pip sits up and takes the laces from my fingers, finishes the job of undoing the ties and spreading the sides of my trousers away from one another. Quietly, slowly, as if I am a horse she seeks to placate, she leans forward and presses one soft kiss against the small trail of brown-red hair that spreads downward from my bellybutton.

"Shhh," she says, kissing up and down the trail, kissing my hip bones, the join between my stomach and thigh, the little crease at the top of my pubis. "It's okay. It's okay."

"Pip," I say, and I try to pack as much meaning into her name as I am able. Try to tell her that I am honored, that I am grateful, that I am excited and scared all at once. That I don't want to hurt her. That I am overwhelmed by her trust. That I am terrified that, like other skills possessed of heroes, I will be unable to master this one. That I will be terrible. "Oh, Pip."

She pushes the fabric of my trousers down, her grip gentle, the delicate skin on the underside of her wrists brushing with such lightness against my bottom that I shiver all over. She urges me to my feet with small touches, and I rise, my hands on her shoulders for balance, my feet sinking into the cheap, straw-stuffed mattress. With her head bowed to concentrate on sliding my trousers off my legs, the whole of her back is exposed to me.

It is beautiful, Writer, so tragically beautiful, that I cannot help myself. I curl forward and kiss her shoulders, first one and then the other, and then I kiss that little ivy leaf scored into her skin at the base of her neck again. So strong, my Pip. So stubborn. She is worthy of her own epics, deserves the attention of Bevel's quill far more than my brother ever has.

I lift each foot in turn with Pip's urging, lavishing affection on her scars with my mouth as she finally strips away my trousers.

"Look at you," Pip says, sitting back and raising her face to mine. There is something shining in her eyes that I cannot quite place, but I think it might be pride. "Nothing useless about you. I told you, Forsyth. You're beautiful."

"I'm weedy and gawkish," I reply.

"You're handsome and kind, and this," she says, placing a kiss on the side of my arousal, "this is just perfect."

The sensation of her pink lips, swollen and wet, against the side of my cock nearly threatens to topple me. "Pip," I groan, both a warning and a plea.

She kisses the tip, and then peppers a trail of them along the underside, and I begin to shake so hard that I must grip her shoulders to stay upright.

"Come here," she says, face offered up, mouth parted, and I slowly sink back down to my knees, obliging, obeying.

"What d-do I do n-now?"

Pip wraps her arms around my neck and her legs around my waist, and then hoists herself up my thighs until her breasts are pressed against my chest, her sex leaving a trail of slick moisture across my stomach. I groan at the sensation, my cock twitching against her bum.

"Haven't you ever . . . ?" she asks, words smeared into the skin of my jaw as she kisses down to my shoulder and leaves her own love bites in retaliation.

"Never . . . never a-all of it," I admit. "Ne-never a-all the way. Nev-nev-never with someone th-that wan-wanted m-me t-to—" I stop there, too overwhelmed by the heat of her in my arms to continue. "I've seen it-t, th-though. A-all my kno-knowledge of car-carnality comes from be-being Sha-Shadow Hand."

"Shhh," Pip says again, her kisses soft rather than insistent. She lets go of my neck with one arm and reaches behind her. "Lots of illicit trysts in corners, eh, *bao bei*? Lots of tossing off alone after? Trust me, this is better."

I jerk in surprise and rock forward when I feel her hand close around me.

I moan, louder than I mean to, unable to resist the instinct to snap my hips forward, which creates lovely friction between the skin of my stomach and the folds of her entrance.

"Slow, slow," Pip pants. "Jesus, hold on, fuck, hold on."

I obey, wrapping my arms around her waist as she raises herself slightly. Something warm and wet and *amazing* presses against the tip of my arousal, and then

Pip lets herself slide down, swallowing me, consuming me, body and heart and soul. It is wonderful and hot, and the most incredible pleasure I've ever experienced. I would kill a hundred Schrödingers, slay ogres and pay fortunes to stay here, right here, like this, forever.

"Pip, Pip, Pip," I am panting against her neck, and I kiss the love bite I have left there over, and over, and over.

She squirms in my arms and pleasure shoots through me, striking my insides like summer lightning. And then, slowly, she begins to rock.

My head falls back and my throat opens, and a moan unlike any I've ever heard from myself escapes. And then Pip's lips are there, under my jaw, licking at the little dip between my collar bones, her hands splayed on my chest for leverage as she rocks back and forth, lifting just that little bit more with every return thrust of her hips, sinking back down.

"Forsyth," she pants in reply. "Holy—ffuh!—yes, Forsyth. God, c'mon, move. Take me, take it, take it, take it! C'mon!" she moans, and then sighs in pleasure as I pitch us both forward. She lands on her back on the bed, raising her legs to hook her ankles against my spine. "Come on, *fuck me*."

I do not need be told a second time. I withdraw just enough to tease the folds of her with my head, and then I drive back in, decisive, an opening parry that has her arching up off the bed to return the volley.

"Yes, right there, *right there*," she pants, urging me to move, and I begin thrusting in earnest.

Her moans get higher, breathier with each slam of my hips against hers, and I take the opportunity to explore her breasts with my mouth, careful not to bash my nose against her ribs. This leaves her writhing and red-faced.

Pip's hands curl against my neck and the small of my back, nails digging in, leaving marks that will hurt in the morning, rubbing against my collar and the back of my saddle, and it is *delicious*. It's a struggle to lift my head far enough to look at Pip, to just drink her in. She is flush and gleaming with sweat, rosy and soft and shaking and wonderful, tensing and relaxing by turns, growing tighter with each thrust, straining, reaching for her own climax.

Pip looks helpless with her own need, fighting it as much as she is striving toward it, tears in her eyes as she tries to make it last, writhing against the cheap mattress like a sacrifice on a marble altar. Her throat is bared like a flag, flying an invitation to debauched battle.

Sweat drips from my eyelashes to roll down between Pip's breasts. At least, I think it's sweat. I don't think I can spare the breath to cry, though I can feel sobs pooling at the back of my throat, pleasure and joy and gratitude and something else, something *so much more* trying to get out, to be said, to be shared and understood. It's beyond bearing, the feeling of our bodies juddering together, hardly able to breathe. I reach out to sweep away the tendrils of hair that stick to Pip's cheek, brushing them away from the bruise I left on her throat, wanting to watch as it gets darker, redder as she gets closer. The hair clings to my hand, tiny begging tongues of silk, and with a shuddering cry, I am dragged under by the first convulsions of orgasm.

Pip follows me quite soon after, and I collapse to the side, skin alight with sensation and sweat; I haven't even withdrawn from her body. The way she turns into me, eyes closed and lips curled in satisfaction, makes me think that she does not plan on letting me go anytime soon. I am quite all right with that. I would like to stay here, buried inside her, protected and wanted, trapped in the cage of her limbs, a willing prisoner to her pleasure, until I grow hard and insistent again.

Pip smells like apples and leather and effort. She tastes like salt and sex and cider. She's warm and heavy, smooth and sweaty and earthy, *real* in a way that I'm not sure I've ever entirely believed in before. She is a Reader. She is a creature from beyond the veil of the skies, and yet she is here, curled against me, holding me. I can feel the ebb and flow of her breathing as it slows, the patter of her heart returning to a more normal rate in counterpoint against my own, and the idea of ever letting go of her is such a physical pain that I shove all thoughts aside and pull her closer, ignoring the stickiness of our combined efforts.

Instead, I lift my head to nuzzle, seeking Pip's lips mainly by feel, wanting to kiss her until we forget how to breathe by ourselves, forget that we were ever once two separate people.

"Well, and a good morning to you, too, Master Turn," Pip sighs contentedly against my mouth.

Twelve

our days later finds us standing at the edge of a sheer waterfall, Pip pouting over the rim at the impossible drop. "Some goddamned Yellow Brick Road this has turned out to be! There's *gotta* be a way down," Pip says.

"Yes, there is," I repeat, exasperated and still pointing eastward, the map half unfolded and dangling from my hand like a banner. "Two days' ride that way."

"I mean *here*."

"And even if we could climb, what of the horses?" I ask. "Dauntless might find his way down to us, but I doubt Karl is well-behaved enough to follow him."

"Well, we'll have to come back up for them, then."

Her hands are on her hips, her chin thrust out, jaw clenched, and, in that moment, I wish she were a man, wish she were Pointe, so I could just punch her and be done with the argument. Though, I've never actually punched Pointe, either. *Infuriating, infuriating woman!* Instead, I say, "Pip, you're being ridiculous."

"Am I?" she seethes. "Fine, fine!" She casts around for a moment, clearly looking for another argument or some way of convincing me. In the end, she just drops Karl's reins, making it clear that she has no plans to remount. He takes this as his permission to wander over to a bit of scrub and start nosing at the summer grass, and Dauntless strains against my hold to join him, jealous. I let go, as well, and simply glare at Pip.

"Why are you making an issue of this? It's only two days. That will still leave us forty days to finish the quest."

"Because we are here, *now*," Pip insists. "Who knows what we'll run into between the cave and whatever lies on that path. The cave's right below us, and it seems stupid to go all the way around!"

There is something in her voice, in the insistence of her words, in the way she refuses to budge from the lip of the river, that makes me pause. Her feet are planted, heels dug in, as if she is resisting some unseen force trying to press her backward. Her fists are clenched, firmly held away from the sword at her belt. Something is very wrong.

"Pip," I say slowly. "What is it really that has you so upset?"

Her eyes flash to the east, where the path I prefer continues along the slate-rock edge of the cliff, squeezed between the brambles of the dim forest and the open air. Perhaps I am mistaken, but an expression of utter terror seems to flit across her face—just a glimpse—before she screws her eyes shut and shakes her head hard, as if trying to dislodge something tangled in her hair.

"Nothing," she says, but the word comes out strangled. She raises her hands to her throat, tugging at the collar of her shirt, as if it is choking her, and coughs once. When she speaks again, her voice is normal, if filled with annoyance. "I just don't want to waste any time."

"Pip, what's wrong?" I take a step forward, hands raised with the intent of checking her throat, making sure some magical creature hasn't lodged itself against her skin, but she steps away. Alarmingly, it is backward, closer to the lip of the cliff, as if threatening to jump if I lay hands on her. I freeze immediately.

"Nothing's *wrong*," she lies. She stares at me with such desperation in her eyes that I fear I have missed something vital. With a flash of annoyance, I realize that my brother had been correct; Pip's eyes do shine emerald in the sunlight. "Just. Just, *please*, can we try to find a way down here?"

"Yes," I say, immediately, hands out and palms up, begging her not to take another step toward the roaring water. "Yes, of course. As you wish."

"'As you wish,'" she sighs back to me, and takes two giant steps forward, eating up the gravelly ground between us, flinging herself into my arms. "Thank you."

"You're very welcome, Pip," I say. "Although, I must say, I'm confused as to why this is an issue at all. What is happening with—"

I am interrupted with a kiss that is passionate and just as desperate as the look on her face was earlier. She begs, with every thrust of her tongue, with every inch of her pressed against me, for me not to complete my question. Not to ask it at all, in the first place.

"Okay," I whisper into her mouth as we part for breath. "Okay. Okay, I understand."

"Thank you," she whispers back. She unwinds her arms from around my shoulders, steps past me, and goes to fuss with Karl's bridle, clearly attempting to end our conversation.

I am unsure how to feel about it. Pip has been, by turns, sullen and thoughtful, and then gleefully affectionate. She does not regret our encounter it seems, and has, in fact, demanded an encore every night since. And yet, there is something . . . regretful about her, something contemplative and perhaps guilty which hangs in the air around her when we ride. When we talk, she is filled with happiness and the desire to connect. But when she thinks I am not looking, she is sad.

I am reminded, sharply, of the times I caught her crying in Turn Hall. I thought it was loneliness then, or a yearning for home and hearth, but now, I'm uncertain. This new sadness might be the same as the old one. At first, I thought it might have been a result of our intimacy—regret, mixed with uncertainty and the joy of our coupling. The demand for more kept me on the back foot, as it were, and so I wait each night for Pip to initiate. She has, inevitably, and it has been marvelous, but still the sadness lingers.

Is it something I have done? Something I have not done, or am not doing correctly? I am very new to lovemaking; perhaps I am missing something. But Pip is coming to her climax each time—and truthfully, as far as I can tell—leaving her grinning and lax with satisfaction.

So what is the problem?

I suggested we begin her sword lessons last night, during the portion of the evening Pip lovingly called the "afterglow pillow talks" (even though I reminded her that neither of us were resting our heads on pillows, per se), and even that had not cheered her. And yet, this morning, when I spent the hour it took for breakfast to cook over the fire showing her how she ought to grip her sword, and the beginning of her stance training, she was giddy with happiness.

"This is going to be so useful!" she had crowed. "I can't wait to hack at something."

"We shall have to get you armor if you plan to go about hacking things," I'd said.

"No steel bikinis," Pip had rejoined immediately, chuckling. "Those are useless—they actually deflect the blade *toward* the heart, if there's only a metal cup molded around each boob."

"Steel bikini? What's a 'bikini'?" I had asked, and couldn't help but become amorous when she described the standard armor for women in her land. "Worse than useless, and uncomfortable to boot, I'd imagine," I had agreed with her. "But an attractive fantasy."

She had begun to reply, a joke on her lips, I could tell. But then she had clutched her throat again and turned away, sheathing her sword. "Enough practice," she'd said. "Let's eat."

"But you haven't learned to—"

"*Enough.*"

"Very well," I had sighed. And now, comparing that behavior to this new insistence that we *not* go east, and an even greater insistence that we do not speak of it . . . even to the point of, well, not *threatening* to throw herself off the side of the waterfall, but implying . . .

Every time we broach a topic that she is uncomfortable with, she clutches at her throat. Yet I see nothing there that could possibly choke her.

Pip's behavior is becoming increasingly frustrating and erratic, and I fear that Kintyre may be right— women become irrational the moment you bed them. Then, of course, I must admit that it is *Kintyre* who gave that advice, and I cannot expect that much of what he says is viable.

But how else am I to account for Pip's behavior?

And what else can I do, for now, but watch? I dare not bring it up again, not after she stepped toward that water, not after the way my heart had leapt up into my throat. Keeping my lips shut around my concerns, I join Pip at the horses. She is running her fingers over Karl's bit guard, over and over again, thoughtful.

"Does it hurt him?" she asks, when I get close. "I mean, in his mouth? To be controlled like that?"

"No," I say. "Not if it fits properly, which, if you see here . . . see this gap and how this sits just flush, here? It's fine. He has probably forgotten it's even there."

"Forgotten," Pip muses. "That might be nice. To forget."

She rubs the back of her neck this time, fingers brushing over the small ivy leaf scar, palm against the love bite I put there four nights ago and have renewed every night since. Does she not like it? Is it that which she is hoping to forget?

Blast! All this second guessing has me turned around like a will-o-the-wisp.

She shivers once, eyes fluttering, and then galvanizes herself. "Right. Rope, water, some nibbles . . . gloves? Yes, gloves. What else do you think we'll need?"

"Swords," I say. "The legend of the cave is murky and old, at best, and I don't know which version to believe. Enchanting sylph, angry sea-witch, a sea serpent's long-held princess, the ghost of a captain's wife waiting for her husband to return from sea? Take your pick, the Salt Crystal Caverns have been haunted by every kind of water-ly thing, if you go back far enough in the stories."

Pip retrieves the Excel from her saddlebag and lays it down on the grass, where Karl and Dauntless can neither nose at it nor step on it. "But all of them female," she says. "Which means, for Reed, that this is probably going to be some sort of word puzzle. A riddle, or a question we have to answer, or maybe we'll have to track down information in exchange for the Cup that Never Runs Dry. Or sex."

She wrinkles her nose. I try very hard not to find her distaste adorable.

"If I ever meet Elgar Reed," she mutters darkly as she unhooks her water skin from the side of her saddle-bag, "I am totally going to make *him* wear a steel bikini; I swear it. The one from the Boris Vallejo rip-off cover fan-art."

She turns to fill the skin at the river, and my heart hammers against my larynx. I lunge for the skin and whip it from her hand. "I'll do that!" I squeak, and then I grimace at how desperate it sounds. "I mean, I'll fill the skins. Can you pack up some of the travel biscuit?"

Before she can answer, I am halfway to the river-bank, both of our skins clutched in my hands. *By the Writer, what is wrong with me? Why am I so panicked?*

I take my time filling the skins, looking over my shoulder at Pip as she fixes a small bag of travel rations—biscuits, apples, jerky—and then begins to coil a rope for transport. That done, she rises and looks around for more to do, deciding, apparently, to try to find some-where to tie up the horses. She takes Karl by the bridle and gently guides him further away from the river, to the line of trees where the giant gray stone slates of the bank begin to give way to scrub grass and then, finally, to thin, malnourished trees.

I don't like Pip out of my line of sight. I try to pre-tend that it is because I am madly in love with her and I want her beside me always. But in reality . . . no, I dare not even think what I fear in reality. When she is gone for longer than I expect, the uneasiness blooms into small terror. She's in the forest. She's in the forest alone, and I cannot see her. I don't know these forests. They're not like the ones at home, where the most harmful thing is a querulous gnome or fox, or a particularly stubborn unicorn.

What if there are ogres in this forest? What if there are *wood elves*? Dear Writer, everyone knows what wood elves like to do with pretty humans. . .

And then, suddenly, I realize why my skin is crawling and I cannot seem to calm my nerves; it feels like we're being *watched*.

"Pip!" I catch myself blurting and snap my teeth closed around the rest of what I was going to say before it can rush out and embarrass us both.

I cap the skins and rush into the forest through the same gap she took. I crash my way through a thicket of undergrowth, tripping on the snarled roots, shoving aside thorny branches, and stumble out into a clearing. There are red scratches on my hands, snares in the sleeves of my traveling robe, but Karl's flanks and Pip's hands are fine. They must have found a way around the brier. They are standing on the far edge, near a trickle of a stream, both looking up at something in the canopy.

"Pip!" I call again, and she turns to face me, confusion on her face. Karl nickers.

"What's wrong?" she asks.

I lean against one of the trees in the clearing, panting with relief. "Nothing," I say. "I just . . . didn't know where you'd gone."

Her eyebrows crumple, and she makes another aborted gesture toward her throat; how can I not have noticed before how often she does so? What has happened to my vaunted powers of observation, the skillful glances of the spymaster, since Pip has come into my life? Or is she merely my one blind spot, where everything she does and says is cataloged but found to be so full of conflicting messages that I cannot parse her?

The feeling of being watched surges, and Pip turns her face back to the branches. "Sorry," she says to the air, "you were saying?"

"Humph!" a voice croaks from above, sounding so much like the disgruntled caw of a farm bird that it takes me a moment to realize that there are actually words amid the squawks. "Rude. I says, yeah, there's a way down, but you gotta know where to start, dear, you do, you do."

Oh, no. A riddling raven. Really? This sort of irritation is the last thing we need right now. The blasted things talk at you for hours, promising answers and never giving them. Sometimes, they even work in tandem with hungry bears, making sure their sentient prey is kept immobile long enough to be made into a meal, the scraps left over for the raven itself.

"And do you know where this starting point is?" Pip asks.

"I do, I says, I do! There's a stair, there is. I says there is!"

"Oh, don't encourage the blasted thing," I say, crossing the glade to stand beside her. I look up, and a massive, inky raven looks back, cocking one glass eye at me.

"Rude!" it caws again. "Rude man, rude!"

"What's rude is to answer questions with questions, and to take up our time. You probably don't even know where the best place to start the descent is."

"I do, rude man, I do! I says!" the raven protests.

"Don't get it worked up," Pip hisses at me. "If it gets in a flap, we won't get anything useful out of it."

"You won't get anything useful out of it, anyway." I grab her hand; she splays her fingers and entwines them possessively with mine. Something tight and miserable within me loosens to be so welcomed, even after our quarrel.

"I bet I can, *bao bei*," she counters.

"Bet you can't!" the raven challenges. It ruffles itself up like a porcupine, indignant and fluffy with rage.

"Raven," Pip says, posture and voice suddenly formal. "Please show us the way to the head of the staircase that will take us down the waterfall."

"Why should I, I says, I says?" the raven cackles. "Why shou—"

Pip doesn't let it finish, rolling over its protest: "Please show us the way to the head of the staircase that will take us down the waterfall. Please show us the way to the head of the staircase that will take us down the waterfall."

The raven pauses, stunned, and deflates miserably.

"Follow me, please do, please do," it caws unhappily.

Pip leans over to kiss me on the cheek, and I can't help but feel that it is slightly smug. She mounts Karl and holds out a hand for me. I take the hint and swing myself into the saddle, tucking up tight behind her, rearranging the lay of our swords so they don't jab at us. I am reminded of that first morning, when I was showing her how to roll her hips to compensate for a horse's gait, and realize of a sudden what had made her so amorous before. I blush hotly, and bury my face at the back of her neck, kissing the leaf scar to hide my embarrassment from the raven.

"Ugh, love," it caws, and then takes to the air.

Pip jerks at Karl's reins, throwing us into a gallop after the bird. It seems to be punishing us for forcing it to tell, taking the most convoluted route through the forest, squeezing us between trees and through briers, but Karl seems just as determined as we are to not let the bird out of his sight, and, eventually, we emerge into the daylight.

The cliff here is even more sheer, and I force my paranoia quiet when Pip detangles herself from the saddle and peers over the edge, directly beneath where the raven is circling.

"Here it is, it is, it is!" the raven caws. "I told you so, I did. I says I did!"

"It looks like a straight drop," Pip accuses. She gets down on her belly and hangs her head and shoulders over the side to be sure, and I crouch beside her, one hand on her belt, just in case.

"Sideways, sideways, I says!" the raven caws.

Pip wriggles herself out over the cliff more, and I tighten my grip but don't comment, fear pulling at my throat. She turns her head to the side and exhales a chuckle. "Well, I'll be damned. Wide enough for the horses, too. Hell of a *trompe l'oeil*."

"A what?"

"Eye trick. Look." She wriggles back, and I lay down in her place. When I'm in position, I can see it, a staircase cut into the side of the cliff. "Wide enough, but we'll have to go slow. There's no rail," I comment.

"Wouldn't care if you fell, I wouldn't, I wouldn't!" the raven cackles. It drops a shit over the side in demonstration.

"Well, thank you for showing us, all the same," Pip says, more polite than I think the damned bird deserves. "We appreciate your help."

"Rude humans!" the bird screeches, but turns its beak into the wind and flaps away. "Rude, cheating humans! Rude, rude, rude!"

I stand and brush the gray chalk off the front of my robe. "We'll have to go back and fetch Dauntless and our supplies, but I think we can be down the staircase in a day."

"We can camp there, then," Pip says, and points vaguely to the tree line. "It'll be dark by the time you go back for him and get here."

"I'll get lost alone in the forest, without the raven."

"Walk along the tree line—the waterfall is that way." She points west, eyes still on the shrinking black speck in the sky.

"You won't go down without me?" I ask.

She turns now, to assess my expression.

"Do you think I would?"

"No."

Her muddy eyes widen. "You do. You're scared."

"I'm not," I say. "I trust you."

"Do you?" she asks. She rises on her tiptoes and presses another one of those just-this-side-of-chaste kisses to my lips. Hungry, but not heated enough to start anything more insistent than a low spark of lust in my gut.

I cup her hips in my hands and bend my neck for a second kiss, amused by the way my lank, travel-dirty hair flops across her forehead. She reaches up and brushes it back with her fingers.

"How did you do that, with the raven?" I ask as we part a second time. I am tempted to steal a third kiss, but the day is getting on, and I need to fetch my horse and our supplies if we're going to attempt the stairs in the morning. "I've never seen a riddling raven bested so swiftly, or so easily."

"It works in threes," Pip said. "You did notice that, didn't you? With anything in these stories, all you have to do is ask them three times. And then they tell you what you want to know. But it only works so many times during a journey, and never on the villain, more's the pity."

I am too perturbed at my apparent blindness to the rules of my own world to answer. And yes, perhaps I am sulking, just a little bit, too.

"No, I didn't notice," I finally manage to mutter. "I bet Kintyre knows, though."

"He doesn't."

"He's a *hero*; he should. I'm just—"

"No, we're not having the old and fat conversation again, Forsyth," Pip snaps. "You're not being fair. I've *studied* your world, okay? I've made my whole academic career about knowing these things. You can't be expected to know as much as I do."

It's true.

But it doesn't mean I have to like it.

✍

"Ugh," Pip says as she returns from the trees, cinching her belt. In the darkness around the campfire, it looks as if she has just materialized from the blackness, like a living shadow.

It reminds me uncomfortably of Melinda, the woman whom I'd loved, who had been seduced by a barrow wraith and subsequently by Kintyre after he rescued her from suffocating to death in a wraith circle. I open my arms to Pip, and my thighs, and she returns to help me drown those memories in the scent of her hair. She leans back against me, as if we are back in a saddle, and I rest against the tree at my back and rewrap the blanket around us, snug.

"Ugh?" I ask.

"Just . . . that's the one thing they never talk about in the books, is it? The unexpected aches, and the dirty realities of . . . questing. I mean, nobody talks about needing to take a crap in the woods, and the smell of dirty hair, and days' old breath." Pip holds up a sprig of mint she apparently found while she was communing with nature, as it were. I take the hint—and the offer—and chew on it. Pip is doing the same. "I would give anything for some hand sanitizer and a massive Jacuzzi tub with bubbles."

More words I don't understand, but the gist is clear enough. I'm pretty ready for a hot bath and a real bed myself. Bevel's preoccupation with fresh-baked bread and feather mattresses suddenly becomes far more sympathetic.

Thinking of Bevel reminds me of the last time I saw the poor man. He was miserable and terrified of what Pip had forced Kintyre to confront, angry and hateful and so in love with my brother that it hurt to watch.

"Where do you suppose Bevel and Kintyre are now?" I ask. "Have you read this?"

"I think we're past what I've read," Pip admits. "I don't know what adventure they might be on. There were so many that Reed just never wrote down. He alluded to them, but he only focused on the big quests. Like the dragon."

"Poor creature," I murmur against her head.

"Yes! I thought so, too!" Pip says. "I didn't think anyone else from this world would agree."

"She was just protecting her clutch," I say. "I wish Bevel had tried to get Kintyre to talk to her more."

"She might have moved on peacefully," Pip agrees. "At least the dragonets are well cared for, in that reserve."

"They would be better cared for if they had their mother."

"True."

We fall into a thoughtful, comfortable silence, and I take the opportunity to run my lips across the bruise on her neck. It is dark enough that I didn't feel the need to refresh it, and a possessive swell of pride fills me as I feel the roughness of the suckled skin around it. I like this, having this here, proof that Pip is mine, that she has chosen me, that she has let me in, let me have her, when she hadn't allowed anyone else.

I am just considering whether it would be excessive to put a matching bruise on the other side of her throat when Pip speaks.

"Do you think they're okay, Bevel and Kintyre?"

"Why do you care?" I ask, determined not to let her ruin my swiftly growing amorous mood.

"Because I outed Bevel in front of your entire Chipping. It was sort of an asshole move on my part. I feel guilty."

"You shouldn't. He deserved it."

"Nobody *deserves* getting their heart broken," Pip protests. "Especially not publicly."

I let that sink in for a moment, running my hands up and down her arms. She shivers, and I am uncertain if it's from the cold, from arousal, or in self chastisement, but regardless, I encourage her to burrow even more deeply into my embrace, her lovely bottom against my groin, and she complies. She takes one of my hands between both of hers and runs the tips of her fingers along each of the lines in my palm, nails scratching so lightly it is practically a tickle.

"How did you even know about them?" I ask. "Save for Kintyre, I should like to think I know Sir Dom best, and I didn't know."

"You're not his friend."

"No, but I have many reports from the Shadow's Men."

"Why?"

"Because he is my brother's companion. Whether my brother and I are on good terms with one another or not, he is still my brother. I protect what is mine."

"Am I yours?"

"If you want to be," I say, and kiss the leaf on her neck.

She says nothing in response to that, and I try very hard not to be disappointed. This is probably where a bolder man would propose marriage, but I can't stand the thought of being rejected, not so soon after I've managed to strengthen our ties as far as I have. If she turned me away, I might die. I couldn't stand it. So I will be patient. Instead, I say: "You haven't answered. How did you know about Sir Dom's love?"

Pip sighs. "Honestly, it was sort of a guess. It's just that, in the traditional hero Quest Narratives, there's always some sidekick or cousin or something that comes along and records the quest. There's usually a huge amount of hero worship involved, genuine admiration from a younger person to an older."

Yes, I remember that feeling. The little brother of a hero, so proud of his accomplishments, his strength, wanting so badly to have his approval that I practically quivered with it when he looked at me. Kintyre has quite effectively killed that admiration, however.

"There's always sort of been this . . . homosexual undertone to a relationship like that. I mean, in the ancient Greek stories, it's real. They really were lovers—Achilles and Patroclus, Heracles and Iolaus. Some of the samurai stories. In my culture, lots of gods slept with humans, or gods, or even animals of the same gender. Ha! They even say the great Imperial dragons had a bit of a kink for mature human men."

She cuts a sly glance at me.

"I'm not certain I'd be any dragon's type," I say, and it comes out slightly strangled. I am torn between fascination and curiosity, warring with being flattered at the thought that a ruler of any sort would find interest in me, and horror that it might be a creature so large and . . . *armored* as a dragon. "But if these stories exist, why would Reed . . . ?"

"Mostly, the tales come out of cultures where homosexuality is accepted and the norm. But those stories influenced the way we tell stories in our culture, and homosexuality is . . . still not accepted as much as it should be. Especially in older generations, like Elgar Reed's. So that hero worship I mentioned gets jammed down into a platonic kind of intimacy, but the affection in it still bleeds through. You get these great bromances that are totally straight, like Sherlock Holmes and John

Watson—er, a famous crime-fighting duo like Kintyre and Bevel—but there's such strength of affection there that it reads with homosexual subtext, and people latch on to that."

"Why?"

"Because sex sells. Or maybe because, sometimes, people think that the only expression of such a passionate and deep friendship *has* to be sex. Maybe because the actors have great chemistry. Maybe because it's fun to imagine two hot guys doing it."

I shudder.

"Well, I guess you wouldn't," Pip laughs. "Especially if it's your brother. But you fantasize about two women, don't you?"

"Yes," I admit.

"Hmm," Pip says and turns in my embrace, still ensconced under the blanket. Her eyes spark green in the firelight. She rises to her knees and runs her hands down my chest. "I'll tell you my threesome fantasy if you tell me yours, *bao bei*," she whispers against my mouth, and then takes my bottom lip between her teeth.

I smile, stretching the skin in her grip, relishing the little ache of it.

Thirteen

"One of the greatest pleasures of spending the night, you know, is getting to cook in the morning," Pip says from the other side of the campfire, where she is rolling up our sleeping accoutrements and packing our things in our saddlebags while I get clean. "I miss it."

"The campfire is right there," I say, as I pour a bit of our precious drinking water over my head. I am crouched on the other side of our little clearing, bent over to spare my clothing, though I suspect I will be damp enough from the plumes of mist when we reach the bottom of the waterfall. But Pip is right, the smell of dirty hair is off-putting. As soon as we have this cup, I'm putting us on the road to the nearest town large enough to have an inn, and I don't care how many days out of our way it makes us. "You could warm up some of that travel stew."

"I miss actual *cooking*," Pip corrects. "With an oven, and a microwave, and a dishwasher. Bacon and eggs and fried tomatoes. Or, yeah, *wai po's* Nigbo Tang Yuan. Yummers."

"You do realize that when you speak like that, I don't actually understand the things to which you are referring, don't you?"

Pip laughs. "And what do you miss?"

"Home," I say simply, and the word is nearly too small to encompass all that I feel. "I do not regret the privacy of traveling just with you, the intimacy of your being the only other human with which to interact and converse—"

"Oh, you old romantic, you."

"—for whom to *care*," I amend. "But I miss Sheriff Pointe and his terrible footwork, and worse jokes. I miss his wife's seed-cakes and his son's unreluctant giggles. I miss the usefulness of Velshi and Cook's terrible attempts to get me to eat more vegetables, and how Keriens has no ability at all to retain a professional distance and teases me. I miss walking into town and being known to everyone, knowing everyone. I even miss the Shadow's Men, always hanging about underfoot after providing their reports, telling lovely lies about being travelers passing through or farmers coming by to pay their tithes, flattering Cook into giving up some of her famous rabbit pies. But not half so much as I would miss you, if you were to—" I stop myself before I can continue because it hits me, right then, like an ogre's club to the side of the head, that I *am* going to miss Pip.

Because she is going to leave.

The whole *point* of this little adventure of ours is that she is going to leave. That is the endgame.

"Oh," I say, feeling too dazed by the realization to say much more, and sit on the ground.

Pip appears beside me, kneeling on the deadfall to meet my eyes. "Forsyth," she says, a low tone of urgency on her lips. "Forsyth, you did *know*."

"I did," I admit. "I just . . . forgot. I suppose." I grope for her hand, and she lets me take it. I squeeze as hard as I dare, as if I could fuse our flesh together, prevent her from vanishing. "I wish I could keep you."

"I'm not a thing to be kept," she scolds, but it is soft, and sad, and kind.

"I know," I say. "You know what I mean. I don't have the right words."

Pip sighs and wraps herself around my shoulders, head against my ear, chest flush to mine. "I know what you mean. English seems woefully inadequate. Maybe the Germans would have a word. They always have good long words for complex feelings."

"Still, I wish," I say. "I wish I could take you back to Turn Hall with me. Make you its mistress."

Pip laughs against my ear. "Are you proposing to me, Forsyth Turn?"

A blush crawls up my face, and I feel the bottom of my stomach drop out, because I hadn't meant it like that. Except that I did. I actually do want Pip to marry me, stay with me, be my wife, my companion, perhaps even the mother of our children. A grandmother. I could pass the Shadow Hand on to our eldest child, if he or she proved to be adept at spying, and we could spend the rest of our days managing Lysse Chipping together—going to harvest festivals together, presiding over court cases together, sleeping late on winter days together.

"M-m-maybe I-I-I a-am," I admit.

Pip pulls back, and the pity in her eyes is suddenly infuriating.

"Do-don't lo-lo-look at me l-li-like that," I snap. "I-I-I kn-know the dif-difference between fa-fan-fantasy and-d-d re-re-reality. I-I just w-wi-wish, th-tha-that's a-a-all."

"You don't like it, but you do what should be done," Pip says and sits back, sighing. "No wonder you're the Shadow Hand. You're so damned *good*."

"I ha-ha-have to be. Some-somebody in this bla-blasted kingdom ha-has to b-b-be!"

Pip takes my hand again, tangling our fingers together, and her touch is hot, so hot, igniting so much under my skin and under my ribs that the enormity of it steals my very breath away. I am drowning. I am suffocating in my love for Pip, and it will kill me; surely, it will kill me, because I do not know if I can live without her. Without everything she has given me: belief in myself, the truth of my brother, a purpose, a meaning, and the knowledge that I am desirable, that I am *wanted*, body and heart, by another person. That I am not just a dirty great brain that the king exploits and the people of my Chipping rely upon. That I am a whole person, and that whole person is *wanted*.

Pip makes me more myself than I have ever been, and I am scared, in the same way that little children are scared of the monster in the clothing cupboard, and just as full of conviction in the truth of it, that I will never feel alive again after Pip leaves.

Pip tilts her head in for a kiss, stroking her tongue along mine until I am calm enough to speak without stuttering again. "I just wish, is all," I say once we've parted. "That's all it is."

"Be careful what you wish for," she whispers against my mouth. "You might not like how you get it."

"It would not matter. I would have you. The rest is just d-details."

She stills against me, and I want to pull back to assess her expression, but I do not think I could bear even that much space between us at the moment. "And what would you do if I did agree to stay?" she asks, voice studiously bland.

"Then, I will fulfill my vow," I say, pressing my lips to hers once more.

"What vow?" she asks when we part.

"Oh, it's silly," I say, wishing immediately that I had not brought it up.

"Forsyth," she says warningly, and I relent. I promised to stop thinking so little of myself, to not allow the fears and put-downs to bottle up and fester.

"It's just that . . . the afternoon before my brother arrived at Turn Hall, you laughed."

Pip frowns and rubs her hands in circles across the small of my back. It makes every pore of skin there prickle deliciously, and I dive back toward her mouth for another kiss. A kiss that she willingly gives up.

"I laugh all the time," she says. "So what?"

"But the small dining room . . . this may sound a bit foolish, but, no woman has laughed in that room since my mother. I was so happy to hear you laugh in there that I vowed to fill every single room of that rotting great mansion with your laughter. That is what I want. I want to laugh every . . . *fucking* shadow out of that depressing place."

Pip stares up at me for a moment, eyes emerald with lust, and I can actually see her pupils dilating. She tangles her fingers into my collar and jerks me back down to her mouth so roughly that our teeth clash and our noses bump, and it is *wonderful*. She is kissing me like she wants to crawl into my mouth and bury herself in my skin, and I do not mind it one bit.

"I can't," she says as we divest one another of clothing, festooning the leaf mold with fabric. "I can't, I can't, I can't."

"I know," I say, and the words are smeared into the skin on the back of her neck, an invisible scar left behind, overlapping the puffy white ivy leaf.

The hewn staircase is wide enough for the horses, as Pip guessed, and the descent winding but not so steep as to be uncomfortable for Dauntless and Karl. There is no ledge between us and the open air of the gorge, however, and that makes me more nervous than I can say. At first, I thought Pip and I ought to tie our saddles together, or tie ourselves on, but she pointed out that that meant that if either of us or our horses went over the side, we'd all go. So we pick our way down carefully and slowly instead.

We reach the bottom in mid-afternoon, the damp of the mist that fills the river basin clinging to our coats and hair like jewels. Karl is restless and unhappy that we remain by the river, and Dauntless seems to be bracing himself for some sort of blow.

"Whatever is behind that waterfall, the horses sure don't like it," Pip says, unnecessarily. We tie them to a large piece of sun-bleached deadfall and, after a hasty lunch of provisions for us and nosebags for our trusty mounts, we approach the base of the falls.

"Now what?" I ask.

"Now, we find your mystery woman. Ten bucks says she's behind that." She points at the raging curtain of water. "They always are."

"How do we get through without getting crushed?" I ask, voice raised so as to be heard over the crash of water splashing into the basin.

"Open sesame?" she shouts.

"What?"

"Nothing, worth a try." She frowns at the water. "Come this way." She heads around to the side of the falls, staring up the sheer cliff face beside them. She raises her hands, running them over the jagged stone, digging her nails in between crevasses, and I realize she is looking for a door.

"Speak friend, and enter! *Mellon!*" she shouts, pushing at the wall of stone, but nothing moves. "Dammit. Right, think like Elgar Reed," she mutters to herself, turning around and scanning the riverbank. It is just as bleak as it was at the top of the cliff, comprised of massive slabs of slate and mossy scrub. The forest line is nearly a mile distant now, as if the roar of the falls has scared the trees away.

"Tell me the story of this place again," she asks, coming up beside me and cupping her hand around one of her ears to better hear me.

"The stories are old!" I call back. "There is a woman who lives in the Salt Crystal Caverns beyond the Falls of Never-ending."

"And these are those falls? You're sure?" Pip asks, looking over her shoulder at it.

"Yes!"

"Grand name," she scoffs. "They clearly end."

"They're not named for the falls themselves," I say. "They're named for the woman . . . or the cup, it's unclear. Maybe both. The Cup that Never Runs Dry, that's what the prophecy says, right? So you can see why it's an attractive thing for a hero to have on an adventure."

"An endless supply of water."

"Yes. And the woman, she's an immortal of some sort. Undying. Or undead. Or already dead."

"And she guards the cup, I assume."

"Yes."

"Against heroes?"

"And villains."

"Right. And she's some sort of magical thing?"

"A ghost, or a sylph, or a wraith, or a fey. Something."

"Right, damn, right," Pip mutters and walks over to the bank. She peers hard at the water, eyes darting back and forth, watching the way the whitecaps churn on the jumble of stones erosion has pulled from the lip of the falls. "Elgar Reed, Elgar Reed, who uses every hoary old fantasy cliché that ever was."

She whips around and stares at the deadfall we tied the horses to.

"Oh!" she exclaims, her mouth a perfect circle of revelation. "Of course! Clever!" We sprint over, and Pip drops to her knees beside Karl's foreleg. "Ah ha!" she proclaims, reaching her hand under the great bleached stump.

I push the horse aside and peer down at her. "What's that?"

"The old entrance-through-a-hollow-tree shtick," Pip crows. "Only this tree got old and fell over. The hollow is still here, though, and it smells damp under there. So . . .tunnel."

"Incredible," I say, unable to keep the word back even if I had wanted to. Which I didn't.

"Get out your Wisp lantern," Pip says. "Let's go."

The tunnel is indeed damp, and low-ceilinged. I am forced to stoop, though Pip, holding the Wisp aloft, is able to walk unencumbered. I can't image the tight squeeze it would be on Kintyre's shoulders and head if he and Bevel were to try to navigate this passageway.

We walk in silence. There are no twistings, no turn-ings, just a straight line that goes down, and down, and down. We must be under the basin by now, deep under it, and I try very hard to remind myself that there is enough air in the tunnel, that I do not need to gasp in great noisy breaths, that the way back to daylight is open if we need to retreat. I don my Shadow Hand persona, forcing myself into calmness.

And then, as quickly as she found the entrance to the tunnel, Pip stops. She waves the lantern about a bit, making the Wisp roll over against the glass. It lets forth a chirruping sound of reproach.

"Sorry," Pip apologizes to the creature absently.

"Why have we stopped?" I whisper. I don't know why I'm whispering, surely the creature knows we are in her tunnels by now. But there is something about the quiet darkness of the place, the sense of reverence with which we have been approaching this magical woman, that seems to demand it.

"Look at this," Pip says, and points. Above us is a rounded lintel, made of a pale stone that sparks and shines in the Wisp-light. It is carved with a dizzying knotwork pattern that resolves itself into waves and clouds. "It's beautiful. Do you recognize it?"

"No," I admit, and it fills me with an eerie uneasiness. "It could be an old Verdashlish design, but that culture was lost so long ago . . ."

"So, maybe that does make our mystery woman a ghost. This could have been a safe house, or a hiding place."

"Or a tomb," I add, and immediately wish the words back. They fill the air with an uncomfortable and sudden weight.

"Er, yeah, that too," Pip whispers.

"We won't know for certain until we get there," I say, and take a step forward. Pip doesn't move, as I expected she would, and I end up stepping right into her. She leans back against me, knees to shoulders pressed against my front, and takes a deep breath.

"Pip," I say. "Let's go."

"Yes," she says. "Right. Yes." But she does not move.

"Why are you hesitating?" I ask. Something occurs to me, and I wonder why it didn't occur to me sooner. The answer is that I would never have expected what I'm about to say to be true. But it is. "You're scared."

"No," Pip denies, and it's a lie.

"You are. Why? None of the rest of this quest has scared you so far. Why this?"

"Because . . ." she gestures helplessly, flop-limbed, at the darkness beyond the lintel. "Because there's a *thing* in there."

"Pip," I admonish. "That's unkind."

"No, not like that. Well, sort of like that, but I mean . . . it's a creature. It's a *magical* creature, the likes of which I've never . . . I've read about them, and it's all well and good to have read about them, but we haven't actually *met* any magical creatures, yet. Not-human people, I mean."

"Nonsense," I say. "Three of the dandies in Gyre's apartments weren't human. One was a selkie, and two were halfling fey."

"I didn't know that. They *looked* human."

"Humanish," I allow. "Then what about the riddling raven?"

"It's still just a raven," Pip said.

"You are holding a Wisp."

"It's just a blob of light."

"The dryad in the tavern?"

"Set decoration. I never actually spoke to him."

I narrow my eyes at her, imparting my incredulity with a glance.

"But the creature before us . . ." I prompt.

"Exactly. I have no idea what to expect, and I have no experience, and . . . and that scares me. Because it . . . it proves it."

"Proves what?"

When I crane my neck to catch sight of her expression, Pip's eyes are wide and wet, and her bottom lip is trembling. "That . . . that I'm really here. That I'm really and truly . . . here."

That hurts more than I expected it to. "You have always been here, Pip." I lay a gentle hand on the back of her neck, telegraphing my every gesture as much as I am able in the half darkness, so as not to startle her. "You are real. I am real."

"And whatever is beyond this doorway is real, too," Pip breathes. "I just don't know if I'm ready for my first fantasy monster."

"She may not be a monster. She's just a woman," I say. "And from all accounts, a sensible one that we can have a conversation with. There's nothing to fear from the arrangement of her biology."

Pip snorts. "Easy for you to say. You grew up around talking foxes and unicorns, and summer trips to the seaside with mermaids and seal-men. You're used to this."

"And you will get used to it as well," I say, whispering straight into her ear, trying to fill her with confidence decanted from my own meager stores. "Now, let us go in and see who waits for us. I have no desire to return to the surface after sunset."

Pip nods once, fingers flexing on the handle of the Wisp lantern, and takes a step forward. Her boot makes a hollow scraping sound against the ground, and she lowers the lamp—there is a floor here, smooth and made of crystal, just like the lintel. It throws the brightness back at us in a scattershot of white and violet light.

"It looks like it goes down forever," Pip breathes. "That's gorgeous."

The tunnel widens around us as we walk, the walls bowing out and the ceiling rising to become a great dome. We must be inside the cliff by now, possibly under the exact place where we made camp last night. Amazing.

The tunnel, however, does not branch and does not become a large room. It just goes and goes and goes, onward forever.

"I'm starting to think your idea of a tomb was right," Pip says. "Nobody would just build one long hallway if they planned to live down here. There's nowhere for beds, or to store food."

"Perhaps it was meant to be a treasury instead?" I suggest.

"Correct," a third voice cuts into our musing, and Pip freezes on the spot so suddenly that I bash into her.

I take a stumbling step backward, and then another, ensuring I have enough space to draw my sword without slashing Pip, if it proves to be necessary. A stark white light flares at what I assume can only be the end of the tunnel.

Pip makes a high-pitched sound of distress and scrambles backward so fast she knocks me straight over. She trips over my flailing legs, and, with a combined yelp, we tumble back onto the smooth crystal floor. The Wisp lantern smashes against the stone, and the little creature zooms off, whistling with terrified indignity.

The light settles into something more tolerable to human eyes, and once the spots have cleared from my vision, I get Pip and I sorted and standing again.

"What was that?" I ask.

"That light, it looks just like the light that . . ." She tugs at her collar and clears her throat. "Nothing. Never mind."

Any other time, I would press the issue, because it is now completely clear that there is something Pip is deliberately hiding from me, something important. Now, however, my attention must be on besting this hurdle and getting what we came for.

"Who spoke?" I ask, raising my voice to pitch an echo around the tunnel.

"I did," the other voice says again, and it is female, the tones dulcet and just a little bit sultry. "Though, I must say, I'm not very impressed. I've never seen a hero fall over before."

"I'm a scholar!" I protest.

"And what is a scholar doing down here?" the voice asks.

"We seek the Cup that Never Runs Dry," Pip says.

"You're here for the Endless Chalice?" There is a breathy sigh, and suddenly, the light contracts. It becomes dense and cylindrical, and then, with an irritated pop, turns into a woman.

Her skin is vaguely bluish, clad only in the swirls of her dark green hair, and she looks very, very annoyed. Her hair moves in a strange, suspended sort of breeze, and it takes me a moment to realize that it is moving about her body, protecting her modesty, as if she were being gently rocked by underwater currents.

And hers is quite the body to be protecting.

Pip clears her throat, and, with a jolt, I realize that I have been staring.

"Apologies," I murmur, dropping my eyes to the floor, chastised.

"Ha!" the woman chortles, and her voice sounds far less ethereal now that it is coming from a physical throat. "I've never had an apology before, either."

"We are sorry to intrude," Pip says. "But we do need the cup. Please."

The sylph—for that is what she has to be; there is no other explanation for her appearance—turns her pale fish-eyes to Pip. She blinks, and two sets of eyelids draw down over her gaze before darting back up.

"And a woman," the sylph says. "Dressed like a man and wearing a sword. How unconventional."

"You'll find I'm not one for the screaming and dashing about role," Pip says, keeping her voice even.

"Refreshing," the sylph allows.

"Look, this small talk is great, but we're sort of on a timeline," Pip says. "I really hate to rush you, but we need the cup, so go ahead and do what it is you usually do to heroes who come to try and take it, so we can beat you and get out of here."

"Beat me?" the sylph growls.

"Well, not physically!" Pip amends. "I mean, I'm not gonna punch you or anything."

The sylph's heavy gaze cuts between Pip and me. Confusion crawls onto her face. "She speaks for you, hero?"

"I'm not a hero," I remind her.

"But you are questing."

"Yes," Pip cuts in. "And I can speak for myself."

The sylph wrinkles her nose. "That, I see."

"Look," Pip says. "Can you please just give us the cup?"

The sylph frowns. "And why should I do that? It is *mine*."

"I need it to get home."

"That is not my concern."

"It's just for one summoning," I add. "I can bring it back to you straight after."

The sylph looks surprised. "You would return it to me? Personally? When your task is completed?"

"Yes, of course," I say. "Why wouldn't I? It's yours, isn't it?"

"None of the other heroes have returned it," the sylph says warily, as if looking for a trick.

"I'm a scholar," I press. "Please."

"And manners, too," the sylph murmurs. She floats closer to us. "You intrigue me, scholar," she says. "If I give your woman the cup, what will you leave behind to ensure that you keep your end of the bargain?"

She lifts her hand, and her flesh is cool and damp as she palms my cheek. I cannot help leaning into it.

"Hey now!" Pip snarls, grabbing the sylph's wrist and shoving her away. "Mind your grabby hands."

"Oh, does he belong to you?" The sylph laughs, and there is music in her voice, a tinkling that I want to hear again. I try to move toward her, but Pip is in the way, trying to brace me bodily. "Is he a slave? A servant? Or . . . oh, I see, your lover?"

"Shut up," Pip snarls.

"Pip," I say, and my voice sounds funny, all far away and light. My head is yearning to follow it, to bob across the ceiling like a buoy and circle around and around the sylph. She's so beautiful. "Be nice."

"Oh, yes, *Pip*," the sylph admonishes. "Do be nice."

"Forsyth?" Pip says. "What the hell is wrong with you? What did you do to him?" she asks sharply.

"Nothing," the sylph says, and the way her shoulders ripple in a shrug is like light dancing across the finest alabaster statue. I am filled with the urge to run my tongue across them. "Nothing that I do not do to any other man."

"Please, don't do this," Pip pleads, and her words are low and harsh, and I cannot think for a second why I ever thought her laughter was lovely, why I ever thought I'd like to fill Turn Hall with such a crass, braying voice. "We don't have to do it like this!"

"Like what?" the Sylph snaps, and oh, how my heart flutters. I reach for her, but Pip's rough arm is in the way, shoving me back down with all the manners of a garden troll. "You've come to take something of mine from me. Why shouldn't I take something of yours in payment?"

"We only need to *borrow it*," Pip says. "Please!"

"Then I shall borrow him, until you return it."

"I can't finish this quest without him," Pip snarls. "I need him. Let him go!"

The sylph opens her arms to me, and I push, oh how I push past Pip, shove her aside, shove her down, step over her, clearing the last hurdle before the bliss of falling into my sylph's lovely, rounded arms.

"Let him go, let him go, let him go!" Pip commands from the floor.

My sylph's beatific expression shifts to sharp-toothed fury so suddenly that even I am startled. A haze drops away from my mind abruptly, and I sway on the spot, darkness encroaching on the corners of my vision. Pip jumps up, and I grab on to her to stay upright.

With my other hand, I scrub at my eyes.

"How did you do that?" the sylph snarls, and her voice is now like rocks churning at the base of a waterfall, caught in the hollow of her throat.

Pip draws herself up to her full height and lays a hand on her sword.

"Three times," I manage to grind out. *Oh, how my head aches!*

"Three times," Pip confirms. "And now that we've bested you, give us the cup."

The sylph snarls, baring a mouth full of fish-hook fangs at us. "Make me!" she sneers.

"Lend us the cup, and I swear I will return it to you, unharmed," I say, and I infuse my speech with a secret layer of meaning, filling the silences between sounds with Words of Trust, Words of Honesty, Words of Compulsion. The latter is a bit underhanded. I don't like using Words of Compulsion; it verges on dark magic. Luckily, there are so few who know how to Speak such powerful Words. "Give me the cup, give me the cup, give me the cup."

Pip raises her hands and claps them against her ears, shaking her head and staring at me groggily.

The sylph shrieks in fury. But she does as I compel. Another bright flash of light that has Pip flinching backward, and there is a small, unassuming chalice in the sylph's hand. It is short, the stem fat and barely there, and the bowl is rough-hewn on the outside and a boring, dusty gray. I'll admit to some disappointment in seeing it—I had expected it to be grander.

The sylph hurls it at my head, and I just manage to catch the cup before it makes contact with my skull. The contents splash my face, and my eyes begin to sting, immediately.

"Salt water?" I ask, incredulous, licking my lips to confirm.

"Useless for your stupid quest!" the sylph snarls hatefully. "I hope you die of thirst!"

"If you can't drink it, then what good is it?" Pip asks, lowering her hands.

The sylph sets her chin at a defiant angle.

"Please tell me," Pip says. "We really don't want to hurt you, I promise. Just make this easy for us and we'll go away."

"Easy?" the sylph howls. "You ask me to give up the prophetic powers of my soul, and you want me to make it *easy* for you?"

"Soul?" Pip asks, as I yelp: "Scrying!"

The sylph turns away, putting her back to us and shuddering with rage.

"Scrying?" Pip echoes.

"I can use the water to make a scrying mirror. How clever!" I say. "That is why people seek the Chalice."

"Are you going to have to scry when we summon the Deal-Maker?"

"Possibly," I admit. "I thought the pieces might fit together, and that the solution would become self-explanatory when we got to the final Station."

"I hope so, too." Pip looks at the cup in my hand, dubious. There are just a few drops of water in the bottom, but it appears that more water is sweating out of the stone interior, collecting in the curve of the bowl. I expect the cup will be completely filled again within hours.

I wonder how we're meant to travel with a constantly full cup of water. We can't put it in the saddlebags. I'll have to tie it upside down from my stirrup, to make sure the droplets fall out onto the ground instead of all over our camping supplies and rations.

"You have what you came for," the sylph growls. "Now leave."

"Thank you," Pip says, and she sounds suddenly sad. "And . . . I'm sorry."

"Leave!"

"I will return the cup," I assure her. "As soon as I'm able."

"Even if you don't keep your promise, it will come back to me," the sylph says sadly. The tunnel around us is growing dark, the sylph fading back into the shadows. "It always comes back to me, one way or another."

Karl and Dauntless are pleased to be quit of the river, and I cannot say I blame them for the haste with which they make down the bank. Pip seems a bit stunned by their insistence that we move at nothing less than a canter, clinging to the rim of her saddle, her face white.

When we're far enough away that I cannot hear the waterfall anymore, I reach out and give Karl's reins enough of a tug to slow him down into an easy amble. Dauntless follows the unspoken command and keeps pace with him, allowing me to get close enough to bump knees with Pip.

"Are you well?" I ask.

Pip shakes her head, sucking on her lower lip.

"Pip."

"I'm fine!" she lies. "I'm just . . . just leave it, okay?"

I reach out again, intent on pulling Karl to a stop, but she jerks to the side, making him dance out of range.

"Stop it with the pity face. I said I'm fine!"

"You are clearly *not* fine," I shout back. "What is *wrong*, Pip? We won!"

"At her expense. Taking the cup *hurts* her."

"It will return to her, she said so."

"And until then? God, I can't imagine the agony of being separated from a part of your soul. She needs it."

"*We* need it."

"That doesn't make our need more important than hers!" Pip spits. "I feel like an asshole. It's like we raped her, or something, and there was nothing we could do because we asked, we *told* her three times. Christ, you even used Words against her."

There is nothing I can say to that, for now that Pip has said it out loud, I realize that perhaps I feel the same way. We ride in miserable silence for another mile. For most of that time, she looks thoughtful, as if she is trying to formulate the perfect phrasing for whatever it is she clearly wishes to admit. Finally, she says:

"I wasn't any help."

It takes me a moment to realize what she is referring to, and another moment after that to comprehend what she is actually saying, because I simply cannot understand why she is even saying it. Surely she doesn't expect me to agree.

"Had you not been there, I might have been lured in by her charms," I say. "You saved my life."

"You're smart enough. You would have gotten away."

"You prepared me for the verbal test—your Excel warned us in advance of the sort of trial this Station might provide, and I have learned my lesson of the riddling raven as well. Both are things I would not have known without you."

Pip balls up her fists on her thighs, and I can see that her frustration is so overwhelming that it's making her hands shake. "But I didn't *do* anything."

"You taught me how to survive it."

"But *you* did it! I thought . . . fuck, never mind what I thought."

"What did you think, Pip?"

"I thought *I* was supposed to be the hero!" she blurts.

"You?"

"It's my quest, isn't it?" she complains. "It's my destiny! But that's three Stations now where you've done all the work. Your Men found the sigil, you fenced for the quill, and you demanded the cup! And all I did was stand there like some . . . some dumbass princess in peril, and I *hate it*."

"You tackled Gyre," I correct. "You taught me the way of winning against the sylph. You are no damsel in distress."

"So I'm the sidekick then," she mutters. "Not much better. It's not fair! I've wanted this my *whole life*, and I don't even . . . I don't even . . ."

She trails off and turns her head away, but I can tell by the way that her jaw is shuddering that she is sucking back tears. Pip hates for anyone to see her cry, so I simply wait her out, using the time to remove my gloves and try to rearrange my hair into a less lanky wet tangle. When she has calmed herself again, she turns her face back to mine.

"I can't Speak Words," she confesses. "That's the problem. I can't be the hero because I can't Speak Words. I will *never* be the main character, and that's what's *killing* me, Forsyth. Because I want it so badly."

"It's a skill," I say. "I can teach you."

"It's not like picking up a sword and learning how to stick the other guy," she says sadly. "I can't *hear them*."

"But—"

"I can't. And that will never change. And the more we quest, the more I realize that I can't be here. That I don't belong. That I ha-have to go . . ." Her eyes flash emerald for a moment, as she turns them forward, her gaze on Karl's footing as the horses pick their way across the slate stone banks. "I have to go home."

My heart breaks a little more. "I still don't want you to," I say softly. "But I understand. I just wish . . ." I reach out and grab her hand. She uncurls her fist enough to tangle our fingers together. It is awkward, but I try to make Dauntless keep pace. Eventually, the footing forces our horses onto different levels, and I have to let go.

"I love this world," she explains. "I've played here, in my imagination. In the games of childhood, when other kids were being Hobbits or Harry Potter or Iron Man, I was here, wielding an enchanted bow and arrow beside Kintyre Turn and Bevel Dom! I was besting the Viceroy and throwing Bootknife off cliffs and having fencing practice with the queen! And it hurts, Forsyth, it *cuts* that I love this world so much, and it won't open to me. It refuses to give up its deepest secrets. Your world doesn't *want me here*."

Fourteen

We spend a pleasant two days at a high-quality inn, playing at being newlyweds on their marriage tour and indulging in a large tub of bubbles and a good night's rest on real mattresses.

In the afterglow of some particularly enthusiastic playing, I ask if Pip plans to get up in the morning for one of her horrendous "jogs." We haven't been in the same place two nights running since we left Lysse, and she hasn't had the opportunity before. She shakes her head, buries her face against my neck, licks at the sweat under my jaw and says, "Riding horseback is enough of a core workout. I don't think I've ever had such cut abs. And such sore thighs."

I take the opening for what it is, and when the massage turns into something more, we both sigh and groan, and dig in nails. She tugs my hair as I kiss the place on her that I am very rapidly coming to count among my favorites.

Later that night, Pip and I sit on the inn's flagstone terrace, sharing a bottle of excellent southern wine. Pip's head is tilted back, the base of her skull cradled on the back of her chair, and her eyes are wide. "There's so many stars," she whispers. "It's overwhelming."

I think "overwhelming" is a bit of an understatement. The magnitude of the stars, and the unfamiliarity of their arrangements in the sky, makes her go quiet every time she makes the mistake of looking up at night. Her mouth always drops open, and her eyes go distant and watery, as if, for just one moment, she has forgotten that she is not where she was born, and the sky pierces her.

"Pip," I say gently, bringing her attention back to the table between us.

Pip lowers her gaze and resumes frowning at her Excel. A half-eaten apple is partway to her mouth, the flesh slowly growing brown as it sits in her hand, suspended between the conception of action and completion.

She parts her lips and nibbles at the ragged edge left by her white teeth. She folds and unfolds herself on the chair, knees up, then down again, shifting, searching for physical comfort when it is something more cerebral I suspect she seeks, something that I'm not certain she even knows she can find. Her back might be sore, as well; I haven't asked. The twinge of new scar tissue twisting in muscle is, I've heard, irritating. I will offer a back massage smoothed by Mother Mouth's ointment later tonight.

"I think I'm missing something," she says finally. "I don't know what, but this has all seemed too—" She interrupts herself by slapping her hand over her mouth. "I can't believe I was just going to say that out loud."

"What? That this has all been too ea—?"

She lunges across the table and slaps her hand over *my* mouth.

"Don't you say it either," she says. When I nod, she withdraws and sits back down, but not before rapping her knuckles against the wooden planks of the table with a grin. "To avoid bad luck." I copy her and pour us both a fresh cup of wine.

When she thinks I am otherwise engrossed with the task, she rubs her palm across her throat, an action she has been doing more and more often. I have tried to be discreet about my curiosity over the gesture, but I have not been able to decipher any reason why she does it. Her shirt is not too tight, and there is no jewelry around her neck; she does not even wear a scarf. She has not developed an ague, as far as I can tell, and her voice isn't rough from irritation.

So what is it?

It takes four days to ride to the next Station. We travel across a plain that was once home to a prosperous, ancient city-state, ruled by a warrior-king in the lost age before Hain became one land with one ruler. The outer bailey is fallen, the walls long ago broken apart by enemy siege machines and the resultant rubble hauled off by enterprising peasants to make barns and wells. The marks in the ground where they once were are still visible, however, as a low grassy knoll with the occasional naked stone bared to the world like bone through a wound.

Whatever buildings lay between the wall and the castle have long since been burned to ash or have decomposed into the ground, the wood returning to nature. The castle itself I know very little about, save that there are rumors that the tyrant still walks its crumbling, torn halls, having taken a vow never to die until he is revenged on those who broke his rule. Whether it is true or not, Pip and I decide not to test the tale, and camp under the stars far from the shadow of the crumbling ruin. Pip tells me a story of wraiths and rings that night, a fantasy in her world and a cautionary tale in mine.

Once we arrive at the next Station, it takes another two days to figure out how to even approach the Lost Library. The vegetation is so thick around the sprawling complex that I doubt even a rabbit could get in.

"Let us go to the Shadow's Gate," I say, as Pip stomps around the campfire on the evening of the second day. "The growth of the plant life is especially tangled around the main entrances. Perhaps the spellcaster didn't know of the Shadow Hand's entrance, and we will be in luck."

"Have you got your own secret door to every palace?" Pip asks, still pacing around the fire, footfalls growing less hard, sounding less like a tantrum on the approach.

"Essentially, yes."

"How do you know about them?"

"The Shadow's Mask," I say. "The accumulated knowledge of Shadow Hands past sort of . . . sits in the mask. Not details, not facts, but . . . where the doors are. Where the knowledge depositories reside and how to get in them. Who is trustworthy and why. You don't know the details, but you can look at a man and know yes or no. Not the meat of the job, but the mechanics, at least."

"That's . . . kinda creepy," Pip says. "So, you just put on the mask and you *know*?"

"Yes."

She stops beside me. In the firelight, her eyes are glinting emerald, and I run my tongue along my lower lip. I know what that means. "What if I put on the mask?"

"If I pass it to you, then yes, it would work." I stand and move around behind Pip, stroking my thumbs along her shoulders.

"But if not?"

"You mean if you stole it or if you snuck around behind my back?" I tease.

She turns her face up, and, for an inscrutable second, it seems horrifically blank, devoid of all emotion. It is a trick of the firelight, because, in the next second, a winsome smile is curling into the side of her mouth. I chase it with my own.

"I wouldn't steal it," Pip says. "You don't even have it with you."

"I prefer not to travel with it," I say. "Just in case my bags or home are searched. Unlike my predecessors, I am perfectly content with communicating with my Men without the mask. I've set up Forsyth Turn as the Shadow Hand's intermediary. The Shadow's Men don't even know that they are speaking directly to the Hand when they speak to me. It seemed . . . more convenient."

"But don't you worry that someone will find that chest in the hayloft and steal the mask, if it's so valuable?"

"Nobody knows it is there but you, my dear," I breathe into her ear, then nibble on the lobe.

"But if someone did?" she insists, pushing back on my chest enough to allow her lust-greened eyes to slide over my face, looking for something, something I cannot guess at. I let all the affection I feel for her flood my expression and hope that it satisfies.

"It still would not work," I say, serious now. "There is a pass phrase that I must tell my successor."

"What if you die before you can tell them?"

"Then the mask and sword melt into mist and return to the elves and dwarves that cast them. They can reforge both, knowledge intact, and re-gift them to the king, who then chooses a new Shadow Hand." Now it is my turn to study her expression. "Pip, where is this coming from?"

Lust diminished, her eyes are nearly brown for the first time; less like deep pools, as I've heard other brown eyes described, and more like flitting, living shadows.

"Nowhere," she says, a bit too quickly. "I'm just curious."

"This goes beyond curiosity," I say sternly.

"I'm worried, then, okay? I don't like the idea of Boot-knife getting at your Shadow Hand stuff and using it."

"He would never be able to open the chest—the locks are magic and require my physical presence to open."

"But he could steal the whole thing."

"I suppose. But I am confident that they don't know where it is, at all."

Pip wraps her arms around herself. "It just scares me. The thought of the Viceroy with all that knowledge."

"The mask would not accept him," I say confidently. I wrap my own arms around her, and am only partially surprised to feel that she is shaking. "Are you cold?"

"Yes," she says, and her voice is a croak. I watch carefully as we arrange ourselves under a blanket beside the fire, but she does not put her hand to her throat this time. I lean back against a stone, and Pip takes up my favorite of her positions when we cuddle—her back to my front, snugged between my thighs, surrounded by me. It gives me unencumbered access to her neck, which I am finding increasingly pleases me. I had not expected to be as possessive as I am, but Pip doesn't seem to mind when I leave love bites on her skin, or when I breathe in the scent of her where it is at its most concentrated, just below her ear, and cage her with my limbs.

She is happily kept.

For now, at least.

✍

The Shadow's Gate is blocked by thorns, but they are not as thick a tangle as they are around the other entrances. When Pip asks why, I admit that I cannot know. The Library was cut off from the rest of the world centuries prior—perhaps it just means that the spellcaster who enchanted the Library did not know of the Shadow's Gate, as I'd hypothesized.

"Why did he do it? Cut it off?" Pip asks as we stare at the bramble and try to plan our strategy.

"The spellcaster?" I say, rubbing at the sweat that has collected under my hairline. That inn and its glorious tub suddenly seems much further away than eight days. What I wouldn't give to cuddle with Pip in my favorite position in a soapy soaker right now, instead of being out here in the summer sun, dust and pollen sticking to our skin. "He was a mage, spiteful and prideful and jealous of the information in the Library. He wanted it for himself, wanted to keep his rivals ignorant, so he shut it up with this spell."

"How did he get in?"

I shrug. "Another spell, I assume."

"Where is he now?"

"Centuries dead," I admit. "And the spell never wore off. The Library forever waits for him, and remains lost to the rest of us. I admit I am extremely excited at the prospect of perusing its shelves. What spells have we lost to memory? What tales? What songs?"

Pip smiles and rolls her eyes. "Spoken like a true academic. You know we only have time to fetch the vellum."

"Yes," I agree. "But once we decipher a way in, I can come back again. I'll have lots of time to read once you're . . ." The words dry up in my mouth, and I can't finish the phrase. I don't want to.

Pip seems to understand anyway, for she comes over and places a soft, sweet kiss on my lips.

We lean into one another and consider the wall of greenery. "There's a fairytale, where I'm from, called Sleeping Beauty," Pip says. "About a princess who was cursed to sleep until her true love came and kissed her awake. Or, you know, had at her while she slept and the agony of childbirth woke her. Depends on the version of the fairytale."

"Charming," I say dryly.

Pip laughs, a sudden jolt of mirth startled out of her. "Yes! That was the prince's name. Anyway, in some versions of the story, the whole castle fell asleep with her, and was then overrun with thorns and brambles, like this. Magic ones. In some versions, Prince Charming has to hack his way through them, and they fight back. In others, they recognize him for who he is and part for him."

I raise an eyebrow at Pip. "Is this you being scholarly about the hero's quest again?"

"Well, think about it," she insists. "Kintyre would just have at the brambles with his sword. A villager might go at it with an axe. And knowing Elgar Reed, they would probably fight back. In all likelihood, the mage has spelled the plant life to fight against intruders."

"But if we are not intruders . . ."

"Exactly. I think if we wiggle through without inflicting damage, it might let us."

I lean down and press another sweet, affectionate kiss to her mouth. "You are a wonder."

Her expression turns wry. "I wish you'd stop saying that."

"Why?" I ask, turning to Dauntless and stripping off my sword belt. I hang it from the pommel of his saddle, and he noses me affectionately.

"You don't really know what I'm like, away from here," she says, and copies me, removing anything from her person that the plant life might consider a threat and leaving them tied to Karl. The cup hangs from her saddlebag, leaving a wet patch on the grass by Karl's flank, but removed enough that the horse isn't getting splashed. The cup fills so very slowly, so by the time one drop of seawater falls, the previous one has already been sucked into the ground.

"You jog more, I assume, and quest less," I tease. "And spend time with your family. Beyond that, what is different?"

"Loads," Pip says, but does not elaborate.

✍

It is a tight squeeze, and slow going, but Pip's guess is right. As long as we don't harm the vegetation, it remains quiescent and does not return the hurts. For the first time in my life, I am genuinely grateful that I am not robust like my brother. He would never have been able to scramble through some of the narrower gaps.

There is a tense moment when I accidentally break a young branch off the vine, which tightens hard enough around my waist that I feel the thorns prick through my clothing and press into my flesh. "Pip!" I gasp.

"Hold still," she says. "Don't move; I'll come to you."

I do my very best to obey, terrified of the thought of the thorns sliding into my skin, gouging and flaying. When she reaches my side, Pip begins to brush her hands over the vine that has me trapped. It is about the width of my wrist and brown with age. Slowly, gently, she is able to pull the gap open wide enough for me to free my clothing from the thorns' grip and wiggle free.

Sooner than I expected, we come to an end of the foliage. I realize that, while the wall of greenery is dense, it is not wide. "Oh," I say, standing and brushing the leaves and twigs from my clothing and hair.

"Yeah," Pip agrees. "That was . . ."

"Huh."

"Yeah."

Together, we make our way to the building before us. It is squat and yellow, made up of uneven blocks of the local sandstone, with very little ornamentation. It is three stories high, but absolutely sprawling. Wings and additions reach in every direction, unplanned and seemingly organic. Whenever the Library required more space, it seems the builders just chose an open area and dug in. I shudder to think of the shelving system. If there is one, at all.

"You'd think a library would be a bit, you know . . . more grand," Pip says, staring up at the thin windows in the main building.

"Why?" I ask. "It's what's on the inside that matters."

"I'm just thinking of your origin story," she admits, as we walk the overgrown path to the front entrance. "If you all think you came from the pen of a writer, shouldn't libraries be, I dunno, temples, or something? Revered?"

"Libraries are just a place to store books," I say.

Pip puffs out a laugh. "Right. Okay. Practical. No organized religion, huh? No centers of worship? Of course not. Poor worldbuilding, Mr. Reed."

I do not bring up our conversation about how I feel our world was abandoned by our creator. We have had it once, and I could not bear repeating it.

We pause together before the doors of the Lost Library, brown wood and black fittings and looking entirely too normal for my own ease. I wish I had a weapon with me. Pip turns the handle slowly, carefully, pushing the door open. We are both on edge, breathing quietly and listening intently. The hinges groan in protest, probably rusted, but otherwise, there are no sounds.

"Could it be booby trapped? Like, with magic and stuff?"

"Possibly," I allow. "Let me go first."

"Why?" Pip asks, bristling with self-righteousness. "So you get flambéed instead of me? I don't need a protector, Forsyth."

"Because I will be better able to detect charms and wards," I explain patiently. Her anger is cute, especially when she's defensive about being mollycoddled. "Unless you have made a thorough study of the signs?"

She huffs. "Right, fine, go ahead."

I enter the Library first. The narrow windows let in enough dusty light for us to see where we are going, but not so much that the books would be damaged or fade. The beams of light don't even touch the shelves and only illuminate the passageways. Clever architects.

Slowly, with every step we take, it becomes clear that there is nothing in this Library but ourselves—no spells, no traps, no wards. If they were once here, they have long ago crumbled with age.

"So, the Parchment that Never Fills . . ." Pip asks, as we traverse the length of the Lost Library. The dust is so thick on the ground that we are actually leaving behind footprints. "Do you know its story?"

"No," I admit. "This is something I know nothing of."

Pip pulls me to a stop with a tug on my sleeve, and I turn to face her. "So, it might not even be here?" she hisses, aggrieved. "Why did you pick the Lost Library, then?"

"It seemed the most logical place for a magical piece of paper to be stored."

"Okay. Right. That makes sense," she says, but her brow is furrowed. I lean down and brush a dry kiss across her forehead, and the wrinkles smooth away. "So, where would it be?"

"Either hidden or on display," I say. "That is what I would do if it were my artifact and my library. It would be in a very safe place deep underground, in a dry area where the damp and the rot could not reach it, or it would be in a glass case in a place of pride."

"Let's start with the place of pride, then," Pip suggests. She turns in a circle, taking in the design of this central building, and then points up. "There," she says, her voice echoing slightly through the muffled hush of the abandoned building.

The Library itself is open, the second and third stories really just overlarge balconies that allow us a view of the roof from the ground floor. On the second level, there seems to be a sort of platform built against the wall. There are no bookshelves on the platform, and only a bit of red swagged curtain, rotting on its pole, tied to the ornate railing of the balcony. If I were to show off a treasure, that is where I would place it; right within eye line of anyone entering the Library.

Together, we make our way through the shelves to a spiral staircase carved out of stone. I very heroically resist the urge to run my fingers along the spines of the books we pass. It would leave more of a trail for anyone who might be following us—not that I suspect that anyone is—but worse, it might damage the books themselves. They are old, old beyond memory, and might easily crumble to dust the moment they are touched.

If—*when*—I return here, it will be with archivists who can Speak Words of Preservation, and gardeners who can Speak Words of Calming. We might not be able to clear away the protective vegetation entirely, but perhaps we can convince the foliage to leave a gap in the barrier for the public to use. It would be fantastic to be able to reopen the Lost Library.

A little of the worry and caution that has been flooding my body as we walk ebbs away. I am growing slowly more confident that we really are alone in this massive complex. The floors don't even squeak, made of highly polished black marble as they are. I feel like a ghost, able to move unseen and without affecting any of my environment, invulnerable. Which is why I am so badly startled to see a monster when we reach the second level.

It is large, and hairy, and is sitting on the floor watching us with luminous dark eyes.

"Shit!" Pip yelps when she sees it. I can't help the involuntary step back. My heel hits air, and I wheel my arms, grabbing Pip to keep from tumbling back down the spiraling stairs. We both regain our balance, and then, with the instinct of a small rodent faced with a predator, we freeze. I slide my hand to my hip, the movement hidden from the creature by Pip's body, and resist the sudden, furious urge to curse—*I left my sword behind! Foolish!*

Terror swims up my spine. *We are defenseless!*

The monster shifts on its haunches and sneezes at us. Dust billows up around it, poofing off its lanky, long fur, but otherwise, it seems unimpressed with our appearance. It is blond-brown, a sort of sandy color that matches the stone of the Library, and I wonder if some magic birthed it from the Library's walls. Beyond that, I have no idea what sort of creature it is. It rather resembles a bear, but also a great dog, and also again a lion. There are no distinctive characteristics, like with a chimera; just a big body with limbs and ears and a snout that recalls one animal or another, but is not firmly of each.

"It's . . . not attacking us," Pip says.

"I ca-can s-s-see th-that," I say.

"No, *why* isn't it attacking us?" Pip asks, exasperated by my fear-induced obtuseness.

"Because we ha-haven't advanced toward the p-podium yet?" I move my head slightly to the right to look at the curtains and the raised platform, trying to do it as slowly and unobtrusively as possible so as not to set off the creature. As I suspected, there is a single plinth in pride of place, right beneath a skylight. There is also another swag of rotting red velvet draped over the top of the plinth, to protect the contents from direct sunlight.

Pip takes a step forward. I tighten my grip on her arm, ready to haul her back down the stairs if I must, and wait. The creature cocks its head to the side, watching us, but does nothing else.

This tension is *horrific*. I feel like an overwound child's toy, ready to spring into a chattering dance and being held back forcefully by cruel fat fingers locked on the winding key. I wish something would let go, wish something would just *happen* so I can react.

Pip takes another step, deliberately aiming her body toward the podium, and I am forced to take a shuffling step as well to keep her within arm's length. The creature tenses now, preparing to stand. Pip takes one more deliberate step, and that's it, she seems to have crossed some line. The creature lets forth a sound that blasts against our ears, a rusty pulley sort of roar, short and sharp.

"Stop!" I say, and pull Pip back against me. "Don't move."

The creature heaves itself to its feet, weight equal on all four legs, so it is not bipedal, as I feared it might be. It cannot wield weapons of its own. Of course, having four legs means that it could definitely outrun us. And there are its teeth to consider. Things like this always have *teeth*.

It chuffs another bark, and I feel the purring growl beneath it slide across my skin, a clear warning.

"What's that?" Pip asks, pointing at the floor beneath the creature.

I look, but there's nothing there. No vellum, no trap door, no indication that the creature was guarding something else. Just a clear patch of wear-polished marble where the dust has not settled upon the ground.

Hmmm. Now that I am looking, there is no indication that the creature has been here for long, save for all the dust collected on its fur. There are no bones of previous meals, no water dish, no piles of feces, and yet clearly it has been here, sitting in one spot, for days, weeks, possibly *years* going by the thickness of the dust on the floor around us.

What an utterly incredible creature the mage has conjured.

And utterly terrifying, for it is completely unlike any other beast of the world, entirely untouched by the needs of biology and time. If we were to strike it, would it even bleed to death? Or would it just keep coming?

Pip seems to be just as in awe of the creature as I am, but unlike me, Pip's stubborn curiosity is drawing her closer. I wonder if this is another moment like that in the Crystal Caves, if the creature is somehow bringing Pip in toward it. Because I can honestly say that no power in the world would make me get closer to the massive thing of my own volition.

"Pip!" I hiss. "Don't get any closer!"

"No, look," she says, not looking back over her shoulder. "It only gets agitated when we step toward the platform." She takes a step to the right, breaking my sweaty grip on her arm, and the creature snarls. She takes a step back to the left, and it quiets. Then she takes a step toward it, and it perks up one floppy ear, like a curious puppy.

"Can you talk?" she asks it.

The creature makes no sound, just cocks its head in the other direction and flips up its other ear.

"Non-magical animals only learn to talk when they spend a lot of time with humans," I remind her. "I don't think this, ah, fellow, has been around people in a very, very long time."

"What's he here for, then?" Pip asks. "Just to guard that?"

She gestures toward the plinth, and the creature barks. She quickly draws her hand back to her side. Thoughtful, Pip reaches out toward the creature. I clamp down on the urge to rush forward and yank her back.

The creature opens its jaws and a rolling pink tongue lolls out. Something sweeps the floor behind it, and I realize with a jolt of amusement that it is wagging its tail.

"Are you lonely?" Pip asks it. "You poor thing."

"*Poor thing?*" I hiss.

Before I realize what she is planning, Pip walks right up to the creature—*the fool!* She only comes up to the bottom of its snout, and with a twist of its head, it could easily bite off hers.

We all freeze again, the three of us eyeing one another and trying to figure out which of us will break first. The creature is assessing her, nose wriggling as it breathes in the smell of her hair, her jerkin. I look around wildly, desperate to find *something* to use as a weapon, but there are only books within reach, and they are all precious.

More precious than Pip's life?

I dither, and then am appalled by my indecision. Of *course* Pip's life is more important than some old book!

But by the time I have made the split-second decision to fetch a book to hurl at the creature, Pip has got her hands in its ruff, giving it a good scratch.

"Who's a good boy, then?" she asks it, and the creature's eyes roll up into its head in bliss. The creature slumps down before Pip, holding her between its massive front paws and rumbling the whole balcony with the force of its purring. Pip laughs and digs into the fur beside one of its ears with both hands, making it twitch.

She is still focused on the ground, though, her eyes on something that I still cannot see from my vantage point.

"Forsyth?" she says, her voice still lilting and pitched as if she's praising the creature. "Now's a good time." She jerks her head toward the podium.

"Oh!" I breathe. "Right! Clever."

With the creature distracted, I sneak as quietly as I can over to the plinth. I barely touch the velvet swag, but it still crumbles dramatically, falling to threads and patches in the afternoon sunbeam. Thankfully, it also crumbles *silently*. This reveals a glass case, just as I suspected it might, and there does not seem to be any latch or keyhole on the plinth. I risk a look at Pip—the creature is lying on its back, wriggling happily. I cannot help rolling my eyes.

Of course the big scary monster is just an affection-starved puppy.

But then, would any other hero have discovered this? Would Kintyre and Bevel have taken the time to really look at the creature, see how it had been left alone, and guess that it might just need a good pet to bypass? Or would they have just slain it? An indignant rage curls in my gut. The creature is obviously sweet—it would not have deserved to die.

I try lifting the glass, and it comes away easily. Underneath another swag of red velvet, this one intact, I find a scroll of age-yellowed vellum. It is thick, and smooth, and it does not feel like it's ever been shaved down to be written upon. It is not like a palimpsest, which has been used over and over again. "Is this the Parchment that Never Fills?" I ask. "It looks normal to me. If only there was some way to be certain!"

And of course, the moment I begin to despair, the scroll clutched in my hand, is the moment the creature looks up at me. It is on its feet in a flash, snarling and snapping, racing toward me, and I jump back behind the plinth, hoping it will offer at least a small modicum of protection.

There is a metallic rattle, and then a high-pitched yelp, and the creature jerks backward. Pip is screaming! No, no, it's not Pip, it's the creature! It lunges at me again, and then yelps a second time, yanked back once more.

There is something holding the creature back. A spell? I straighten behind the plinth, uncertain how to proceed.

Snapping and snarling in fury, the creature rounds on Pip. Silly Pip, who did not run when she had the chance.

"Forsyth!" Pip screams. The creature swipes at her with one massive paw and pins her to the ground. A meaty *thock* fills the air as Pip's head smacks off the marble.

"No!" I cry. "No, I'll leave the vellum, stop!"

The creature turns to me, narrowing its eyes, and I am struck with the realization that though it did not speak to us when Pip asked, I do believe it *can* understand what we're saying. The creature sits back down on its haunches, Pip pinned, waiting.

I lay the scroll back onto the plinth. *Blast!* We are at an impasse.

And then Pip, with only the slightest of hesitations, reaches up and brushes aside the dusty fur along the wrist of the paw holding her down. I catch the shine of metal. This is what Pip had seen before. It is a cuff. A manacle.

The creature shifts slightly, and the metallic clank rings out again. Chains. Lost somewhere beneath the dust and the creature's excessive fur, there are chains.

"Oh, you poor thing," Pip says softly.

The creature makes a sound of indignant dismissal and lets her up. Pip gains her feet slowly, but instead of backing away, she reaches out and rubs its snout.

"Pip!" I say, and am dismayed by the actual crackle in my voice, brought on by both my shock and fear. "Please, please do take a careful step away!"

She turns to me, eyes wide with confusion. "Forsyth . . . you're not actually scared of it, are you? It can't hurt anyone. It's *chained*."

"It can still hurt you!" I say. "Come here, we'll find another way down."

"No," Pip says, stubborn. "No, we're going to free it."

"Free it?" I echo. "Have you gone *mad*?"

"Have you ever been tied down against your will, Forsyth Turn?" she snarls, her voice almost as loud and filled with fury as the creature's earlier roars, and I am so startled by her sudden temper that I cannot even get my tongue to form the word "no." Instead, I just shake my head, shocked. "Then you can shut the fuck up. I'm letting it go."

"And what if it eats us?"

"Look around," she snaps. "It doesn't eat. Obviously."

"It's a figure of speech!"

The creature seems amused by our back and forth. Pip firmly turns her back to me, making it clear that our argument is at an end, and reaches for the cuff. The creature lifts its paw obligingly, but its eyes are narrowed and still on me. I resist the urge to fidget like a child under a headmaster's gaze. With the blasted thing watching me, there's no way that I'll be able to secret the scroll inside my travel robe and sweep the velvet back onto the plinth to disguise its disappearance.

"Listen," Pip says conversationally. The creature's ears twitch toward her, but it keeps its eyes on me. "There's a screw on the manacle here, and my hands are small enough. I can get it undone, and then you can get out of here. I'm sure you'd like that. Go lay in the sun, take a bath in the fountain out in the courtyard, wash the dust off your fur, take a walk around the hedges."

The creature's whole hide shivers in desire.

"And I'm gonna free you whether you agree to this or not, because it's not right to keep you a slave here, alone and unable to communicate to others that you're not here by choice. I know how that fe—ahem. Shit." She shakes her head once, and then continues. "So, I'm not going to make your freedom conditional on your cooperation, but . . . we really need the vellum. It's for a quest. And Forsyth has already agreed to return the things we've collected elsewhere, so I'm sure he'd be just fine with returning the Parchment that Never Fills to the Lost Library as soon as we're done. So, what do you say? Will you let us take it?"

The creature cuts a look between me and its paw. Finally, slowly, it nods.

Pip grins up at it and sets to work, digging her fingers around a screw on the manacle that would be too small for the creature to manipulate, but is big enough for her to wrap her fist around. It takes an inordinate amount of grunting and cussing, but eventually, Pip loosens the thing and it rotates free. The manacle creaks open and drops away.

She drops it to the ground and backs up a step, waiting to see what the creature will do. It lifts its paw to its face, licking the fur that has grown thin and matted under the weight of the metal cuff, whining slightly. Then it stands, and, seeming to ignore us, makes its large way down the spiral staircase.

Slowly, in case it changes its mind, I wrap my hand around the scroll. The creature doesn't roar or rush back up, so I take that for a sign that our bargain is struck, and that we are free to take the Parchment. I tuck it carefully into the pocket on the inside of my travel robe.

"You're a mad bastard," I tell Pip, and she turns her face up for a kiss that I am all too happy to give when I reach her side.

"But it worked."

"It did," I say, and follow her back out of the Library.

The creature is indeed in the courtyard fountain, as Pip suggested it might like, rolling and frolicking in the water.

"Aw," Pip says, the corners of her eyes crinkling in delight.

"No," I say immediately. "It's not coming with us."

"Spoilsport," Pip pouts. Her tone and expression are victorious and joyful, but there is something tense about her posture, about the way she has her hands jammed firmly into her pockets and refuses to budge them.

As soon as the creature realizes we are outside, it bounds over, water flying everywhere, and butts its head against my shoulder, clearly seeking pets. I rub my hand between its massive ears, trying not to think about how its eye is the same size as my whole head. One good shove, and I would be on my arse. Dear Writer, what if this beast decides that it loves us and *wants* to follow us about? Never mind the quest, the thought of the kind of damage it could do to Turn Hall, to Lysse Chipping, is enough to give me spasms.

Content that it has been thoroughly scratched, the creature bounds toward the tall hedgerow that keeps the world out of the Lost Library. It rubs up against the vines, rushing back and forth, wriggling and panting. Great drifting clouds of shed fur tangle in the thorns, making it appear as if the vines have sprouted hairy sand-colored blossoms. I am half tempted to snatch some down and use it to stuff a mattress. I am sure it would be heavenly soft.

When the creature has finished grooming itself on the plant life, its fur now bright and smooth and glossy, it paces over to the place where the entryway should be and swipes at the foliage.

The vines part under its claws, and I am struck again with how close Pip and I came to being gutted on those razor-like blades. The plants try to fight back, to curl into the space that the creature's paw cleared, but it yowls at them and they shiver and clump into an archway.

It turns to us, triumphant, and beyond the hedgerow, I can see Karl and Dauntless tied to their tree and dilating their nostrils at us expectantly.

"Good boy!" Pip coos at the creature and rubs its snout. "Thank you!"

The creature rumbles out another purr, and then head butts her out the door. I follow close after, wary still that it might try to renege on our deal. But the creature only licks the back of my head in passing.

It is hot and slimy and disgusting!

Pip turns to wave goodbye and bursts into full-bellied laughter, pointing at the no-doubt hilarious new configuration of my hair. *Ugh!*

Fifteen

e decide to make camp in the courtyard of the Lost Library. There is talk of doing so inside, but we both fear the effect of too much human interaction on the ancient books, and we don't want to leave the horses alone outside with the creature, just in case. On top of that, we are both terrified of what might happen if we had to light a fire around all that paper. Accidents do happen.

The courtyard is sheltered from the wind, and we don't mind sleeping outside again. Also, we seem to have acquired a guardian of our own. The creature is currently pacing the grounds, clearly searching for threats and reacclimatizing itself to its territory. That Pip and I, and the horses, are now apparently a part of said territory is only slightly discomforting. I do not fear its teeth any longer, but I do fear what might happen if it decides to sleep next to us and rolls over in the middle of the night.

The late afternoon sky above us is an endless ceiling of vaulted blue, and I cannot help but raise my face to the sunlight and smile at the scent of honest vegetation and book-dust. I stretch my shoulders back, and they make a pleasant pop as I work out the kinks of weeks in the saddle and an afternoon of sneaking about, slope-shouldered and cautious.

The water in the fountain is clean, still bubbling up from some underground well after all these centuries. We refill our drinking skins and the travel pot we use for campfire-tea, and then I decide to be the first to brave the brisk temperature to wash away the travel grime. The fountain is a far cry from the warm bath for which I have been yearning, though. I seem to be spending every blasted day of this quest lusting for a good shave and a hot bath. It's starting to get farcical.

Pip is sitting on the edge of the fountain as I bathe, turning the vellum over and over in her hands.

Something has been niggling at me since our encounter in the Library, and instead of tumbling it about in my head, I finally ask: "What did you mean, that you know what it feels like to be tied down? To be a slave?"

Pip jerks back from me so quickly, eyes so wide, that I wonder if something has bitten her. *Surely my words couldn't have been that shocking?*

"Nothing," she lies, but it is a knee-jerk reflex. She catches herself in it and sighs, her whole posture deflating. "I mean, you *know* that I . . ."

I hadn't wanted to bring it up, especially since it's been so long since Pip has had a fit, but I desire clarification, and so I say, slowly, "The Viceroy?"

Pip goes stiff all over, eyes tight and the skin around them translucent with fatigue. "Yes," she grinds out between clenched teeth.

Then she cries out. She drops the parchment and jams the heels of her hands against her temples, fingers balled into fists.

"No, no," she moans, staggering back a step.

I am up and partway out of the fountain before she holds out her hands to halt me.

"I'm fine," she wheezes. "I'm fine. Just . . . stay there. Over there. For a minute. Please."

I stand in the fountain, my nudity forgotten, waiting, goose bumps crawling up my legs, clenching my thighs. Eventually, Pip seems to regain control of herself, shaking out her limbs and rolling her head back. There is a pop loud enough that even I can hear it, and then she sighs, long and drawn out and weary. I feel the tension flow out of her frame from within my own.

Like a slowly unfolding marionette, she reaches down and retrieves the scroll, then checks it over for damage. It's fine. She turns it over a few more times, as if hoping that its fall has jostled some more information from it.

With a grunt of frustration, she goes to her saddlebags and withdraws a pot of ink and a travel quill. Decisively, she draws a stroke across the top of the scroll. She watches it for a long moment, and then draws back, eyes wide.

"Pip?" I call, galvanized into stepping out of the water. I pick up the towel I left on the ledge and scrub at my skin. "What's wrong?"

"I figured out why it's called the Parchment that Never Fills." She holds it up to me. It is blank. She draws another line down the center of the scroll, deliberately showy. Slowly, the ink is absorbed into the vellum, like water being drawn up into a sponge.

"Friggin' useless!" Pip says. "This quest makes no sense, Forsyth. All this stuff, and I don't know what we're supposed to use it for. Maybe I didn't do the chart right."

She sits on her bedroll and digs out her Excel, spreading it out to its full length on the ground. I pull on my trousers and move to stand next to her, careful not to drip on the chart.

"I was so sure I had it all figured out," she says, face in her hands.

I crouch down and lay a soft kiss on her cheek. "You are clever, Pip. We read Bevel's scrolls together; we marked the map together. I don't think we're wrong."

"Then why all this?" Pip says, throwing out her hands in frustration. "I can't for the life of me figure out what we're supposed to do with a bit of jewelry, a cup that's always filled with useless water, and a piece of vellum that won't hold on to any words!" She deliberately drops a spot of ink right into the center of the vellum, savage, and it too is sucked down into the page.

"That's why they are riddles," I say. "Besides, we don't have all the objects yet. There's one left to collect, the knife, and then we have to go to the Eyrie. Maybe it will become clear when we get there."

"I hope so," Pip mutters.

"It's just not clear yet, that's all. It is no reason to fret." I sit beside her and pull her into my arms, trying to soothe, but she shoves me away, prickly and irritable.

"I *always* have it figured out by now!" she snaps. "I *always* guess the ending right after Station Four!"

"But it is different when you're reading it, isn't it? Different from being right in the middle?" I ask. "Does Reed give you hints? Does he foreshadow or give you the villain's point of view?"

Pip deflates and curls into my chest, ear pressed against my heartbeat. The summer sun is comfortable, now that I am without a shirt and refreshed, and Pip is small and wonderful in my embrace. I press my knuckles into the small of her back, massaging the place where the worst of her tension sits, digging in around the curlicues of scar tissue.

"I hate this," she gasps, only partially in relieved pain. "I hate not knowing what's going to happen next. I hate not being able to figure it out. I hate feeling like I'm an idiot. It's all hateful."

"You're not an idiot," I soothe, curling and flexing my fingers against the soft welts of her ribs.

"I am. I'm so book smart, but I can't figure out real life. Even this," she says, one of her fists knotting around my belt, possessive, as if she fears I will dissolve into mist if she lets go. "I can't figure out how *this* happened."

"You kissed me," I remind her, and, yes, my voice is a bit smug, but I feel that I deserve it. "Believe me, if you are unsure of how or why we have become . . . this, as you put it, then do understand that I am twice as confused but half as likely to question my good fortune."

"Good fortune?" she asks, one fingertip starting to circle my nipple.

"Unf," I say, trying to keep my mind on the thread of our conversation. "Ah. No one has ever chosen Forsyth Turn before."

Pip looks up at me, startled. "No one has ever chosen Lucy Piper before, either. Not to date. Not to keep."

"I'll keep you," I say. Her skin is so soft, so smooth against the palms of my hands, her cheeks warm to my touch and flushed, eyes wide and embarrassed and in awe. "I'll keep you for as long as you'll let me."

I fear it's too much to say, to admit. But then she licks her way into my mouth, chasing the confession to the soft velvet wall of my cheek, trying to pin it down to taste, to feel. My skin tightens all over and I stop massaging, pressing my palm against her back instead and running it up the ridges, shivering at the sensation. Pip moans loud against my mouth, bites at my lips, but doesn't speed us along.

I choke back an oath at the way she swings one thigh over my lap and rolls her hips, delicious and hot.

"One of these days, I'm gonna get you to swear in bed," she breathes into me.

"Find us a bed, and I will comply."

I pass my hand across her scars again, sweeping back and forth, reveling in the way that Pip squirms and ducks away from my touch, and then presses herself back into it like a particularly finicky cat: not sure if she should enjoy the sensation or not, but clearly desperate for the experience of it all the same.

The kiss is soft, and slow. I tuck her upper lip between mine, and then her bottom lip, gentle, gentle. Her tongue is soft, tentative in a way I find endearingly girlish. Pip's eyes slide closed, her head falls back to give me all the access I could want, a low, soft moan fluttering up out of her throat.

I peel her out of her clothing slowly, and Pip laughs in delight when I raise a naughty eyebrow and pitch each and every garment over my shoulder and into the fountain. When we make love, it is languid, careful, but not at all lazy. Pip's eyes, flushed emerald with lust, never leave mine. *Please, please*, she mouths into my skin. The lines on her forehead scream, the nails she digs into my shoulder blades beg, and her breath on my skin demands: *Please love me.*

I love you, I say back with the flick of my thumb, with the press of my palms, with the snap of my hips. Pip lays back and tangles her fingers in my wet hair, brings my mouth to her sex, teaches me the art of kissing a woman's entrance as I would kiss her lips, bringing her pleasure with my tongue and tasting the results of my successes.

And when I drive her to climax, she wriggles and writhes and pants, hips jumping up impatiently to meet mine before she settles back against the bedroll with a long, low moan of sinful satisfaction. The look of genuine gratitude and admiration in her eyes sends me over, and I lock my arms around her, hold her still, hold her to me, and she pets my shoulders, my neck, kisses my ear, tangles her fingers in the sweaty curls at the nape of my neck, all the while murmuring: "Yes, yes, oh, good boy, Forsyth, yes. I've got you, *bao bei*. I'm here. Let go. Go on."

When I am able to move again, when my vision has recovered from being washed white and my lungs have remembered to breathe, I lay my head down on the pillow of her breasts, ear pressed against her racing heartbeat. I breathe in the reek of sweat, and sex, and *us*.

"You've gotten good at this," she says.

"Good teacher," I admit.

"God, you're wonderful," Pip moans, stiffening and shivering a little as I slide out of her, growing soft and too sensitive to stay joined. And wasn't that a surprise when I first experienced it. "How did I get so lucky?"

"How did *I*?" I say, kissing the nipple beside my mouth because I can't not, because Pip is magnetic and I want to be touching her all the time, for the rest of my life.

I should get up and fetch my towel to clean us up. The bedroll will be stained, but I don't care. By the Writer, I profoundly do not care. I just want to roll her up in my embrace and stay where we are forever, content as a pair of cats in a puddle of butter yellow sunlight.

"And I just got clean, too."

"The fountain isn't going anywhere. Nap now." Pip yawns, and throws one of her arms around my shoulders in return.

My body seems to agree, for I yawn, and my eyelids droop before I can make any conscious decision to follow Pip into sleep. I cannot help the goofy grin that seems to have taken up permanent residence in the area of my mouth. It *had* been wonderful.

And it had felt a little bit like saying goodbye.

✍

The nap extends into the evening, and we wake in full dark only long enough to light a fire, drink some water, and feed the horses before we collapse back into one another like magnets. Then we tumble back into sleep.

A sense of unreality pervades the following morning. For a long moment, I am not certain that I have actually woken up. Mist lays heavily on the ground, and the creature has indeed snuggled close to us in the night. Its fur is clean and warm, and its lion-like tail is curled around us protectively. Carefully, I extricate myself from Pip's possessive limbs, and then tuck my blanket in beside her. She squeezes it to her side immediately, accepting the substitute, and I push away the ridiculous sensation of being jealous of cloth.

Walking softly, I make my way over to where we tied up the horses, on the far side of the fountain from our campfire and the creature. Karl and Dauntless are both awake, ears pricked at the opening in the hedge, pawing the ground and snorting softly.

"What is it, gents?" I ask them, running a hand down Dauntless's nose. My shoulders are warm, and there is discomfort, a burning across the skin of my back when I extend my arms. *A sunburn? Ha.* If so, it is well earned.

Dauntless knickers, and I turn to look over my shoulder. All I see is mist beyond the hedgerow. Whatever has them uneasy is not something I can spot.

Reluctantly, I go and wake Pip. Whatever it is must be met seriously, and that means being prepared. She crawls back to wakefulness grudgingly, snuffling adorably into my blanket. But the moment she realizes that I am awake and tense, she is on her feet, climbing into her jerkin and belting on her sword. The afternoon sun did its work on her clothing, and it is all dry again, thankfully. The creature stirs with us, black eyes wide and alert.

Within seconds, it is on its feet as well, growling softly at the mist beyond the Library boundary, the tip of its tail flicking back and forth, the now short fur along its spine bristling.

"I don't see anything," Pip admits after a long, tensely silent moment.

"Nor I," I admit. "But there's something . . ."

As soon as I utter the words, the horses seem to forget their anxiety, and the creature flops down onto its stomach and begins grooming one huge paw.

"Ooo-kay," Pip says, her grip loosening on her sword. "That's not even remotely disconcerting." The sarcasm is so thick it could rival the mist. "Well, now that we're up . . ."

She digs around the campfire, coaxing the coals that are blanketed by protective white ash back to life, rousing them from their beds. There is more than enough deadfall by the hedgerow to feed another fire, and it feels strange to feel no anxiety when Pip stops within grabbing range of the vines to collect some up. The greenery trembles, but then the creature growls and both go still.

For the next hour, there is tea, and fire-warmed bread, and the last of the hard cheese. The creature licks the rinds from Pip's palm, and she obligingly keeps her fingers flat to avoid its teeth.

I am surprised by the affection she shows the great beast, and say so.

"He reminds me of my parents' dog," she says. "I miss the fluffy little bastard."

How is it that I can know so much about Lucy Piper, and yet know nothing?

The second day on the road, the creature stops tailing us and turns back to the Lost Library. It moans in that sort of rusty machinery way that it has, and then the heavy underbrush behind us rattles with its passing. It is retreating into the forest, heading back the way we came. Pip stiffens in her saddle, and I reach out to grab her hand to keep her from turning around and beckoning the thing to follow after us.

"It's a lovely pet," I say, circling my thumb over her knuckles. "But I suspect that it is magically bound to the Library. To take it with us may be to kill it."

"I know that; the color of its coat matched the stonework. I'm not a complete tourist," Pip snaps, yanking her hand back, but the ire in her words had not been directed at me, so I let them pass unremarked upon.

I also do not remark on the fact that Pip's cheeks are wet, her eyes red.

She is very quiet for the rest of the afternoon, and instead of curling into me when we tumble into our bedrolls that night, instead of skimming her hands up under my shirt and taking me apart with her tongue, she simply presses her back against my front and tangles our ankles together, cuddling my arm miserably. I spend the evening with my mouth against the ivy leaf, my nose under her ear, breathing in her skin, and scent, and sorrow. Eventually, her breathing slows, and I assume she has dropped off to sleep.

"Why us?" I whisper against the leaf. "Why do you love my world so much that they would pick you for this?"

"Because that's the magic of being a fan," Pip whispers back. I had not realized she was still awake, or I would have kept my musings behind my teeth. She shifts against me and repositions us, tugging gently on my shoulders until I am resting atop her, pressed from knee to nose. I hold myself upright on my elbows, wary of crushing her, but Pip gathers me against her chest, pressing my cheek into the pillowy valley of her breasts. Her heartbeat is slow and sure in my ears, soothing and comforting, the sound of *home*. I curl and wrap my arms around her ribs, enchanted by the way they retract and expand, an even metronome of life.

"Being a fan?" I ask, watching as my breath brushes across the nipple right in front of my face, peaking it under her shirt.

"Unconditional love," Pip says. "No matter what happens, no matter what the characters do or how the author twists, no matter the surprises and the heartbreak and the joys, you love something—with all its flaws and all its diamonds. Being a fan means being devoted. It means daydreaming, and flailing with joy, and proudly showing your colors in public with pins and scarves, t-shirts and bags and costumes. It means being part of a tribe, having a place and a people to belong to. Being a fan means being obsessed, but in a good way. It means learning to love— wholeheartedly, honestly, proudly, crazily love."

"You love us?" I ask, turning my face so I can gaze up at her from under my eyelashes.

Her breath catches in her throat, her cheeks pinking and her pupils dilating. "I am a fan of *The Tales of Kintyre Turn*."

I smile, warmth spreading under my skin and lacing through my torso. "I love you, as well."

Pip threads one hand into the hair at the base of my neck and gently, gently uncurls me, bringing my mouth up to hers. "That's not what I meant," Pip breathes against my lips, but she doesn't explain, and I am too content with our lazy kissing to want to ask.

The next week is spent on the road. We manage an inn three of the seven nights, and a farmhouse with a very loud, very generous, very prolific family on the fifth.

On the eighth morning, and well before the next blue moon, we pull our horses to a halt at the crest of a hill. A chill wind unfurls from the valley below, brushing back our hair and summoning goose bumps along my neck. I snuggle down into my robe. Pip flips up the collar of her jerkin and cinches it tight at her throat.

"This is cheery," she says.

"It's a graveyard. I'm certain that it's not meant to be cheery."

"Was it chosen to be a graveyard because it's spooky?" Pip asks. "Or did it become spooky because it's a graveyard?"

"Scholar," I accuse her warmly, and she smiles back. "The chill comes from the way the mist bottles in the valley. I suppose they chose this valley because the bodies wouldn't rot as quickly, giving them time to construct the tombs."

"You suppose?"

"A man can't know everything."

"Doesn't stop you from trying," she points out amiably.

True.

The horses prance, and Karl tosses his head, displeased with our proximity to the mouth of the valley.

It is all white below, like staring into a bed of clouds, impenetrable to the eye and chilling to the soul.

"We've gotta go in there, don't we?" Pip sighs.

"Eventually, yes," I allow. "The tomb we're searching for ought to be in direct line with the rest of King Chailin's dynasty, but I don't know how far along the river that begins. We could travel alongside the valley, but then we might have to backtrack when we decide to descend into it." I point out the faint white mark of the path cut into the chalk cliffs by the millions of travelers who had decided to bypass the Valley of the Tombs rather than take the swift road through it.

"Which means starting at the beginning," Pip accepts. "Damn."

Without waiting, she nudges Karl into motion. Dauntless, unhappy at having to follow, clips up after Karl without my say-so.

The odd tip of a stone spear or helm, the top of a carved head, or the spire of some great tomb intermittently punctures the mist that rolls along the ground. They poke above the clouds like stones in a harbor, the wash of ash-gray breaking and swirling around them in a tide ever receding, yet never leaving. The air is perfumed with petrichor and dew, crushed grass and damp wool. It tastes wet and mossy.

"So, what can we expect?" Pip asks, once Dauntless has brought us up to flank her. "Info-dump me, Mr. Exposition."

Her forced cheeriness and understanding of the situation makes all the tension and worry I was harboring about the commencement of this Station lessen. It doesn't vanish entirely, though, because Pip's Excel says that this is going to be the Station where the Unexpected Twist occurs, and my mind is racing across the possibilities of lichs and poltergeists.

"This valley is no-man's-land," I explain obligingly. "It is midway between the Three Kingdoms—Hain, Gadot, and Urland. It is where each royal household buries their dead. They say it is so the great rulers can learn to make peace with one another in the afterlife, in the hopes that their descendants will somehow benefit from this knowledge."

"That makes no sense," Pip points out. "Not unless their kids, you know, *commune* with them afterward."

"Which I've never heard of any royal attempting," I agree. "Hmm. Possibly because they fear it will actually be successful, and then they'll be scolded."

"Nobody wants their dearly departed Daddy telling them what to do?"

I shudder once. "I certainly don't."

Pip goes quiet for a moment. "I'm sorry," she says, eventually.

"Don't be," I say. "I'm not. Had I the bravery, I might have pushed him down the stairs myself, instead of waiting for the drink to do it for him. He was a hateful man, with a horrible addiction, who spawned an equally hateful son. At least Kintyre is addicted to adventure and sex, and not the bottle."

"And what are you addicted to?" Pip asks. "Addictive personalities are sometimes hereditary."

"You," I say, trying to lighten the topic. My lungs have become a hot knot behind my sternum, and I can't seem to get enough of the cool, damp air to make them expand again. I shake my head, and water droplets from the condensed fog fly off into the gloom. I wish, suddenly, for the over-warm summer sun of the Library courtyard. I even miss the sunburn that plagued me with heat rash and blistered skin for the last few days. The lack of heat radiating from my shoulders is felt twice as keenly in the damp cold that is reaching slimy fingers under my collar.

"Books, secrets," she offers instead. My honesty seems to have made her uncomfortable, so I take the work-around.

"Secrets, yes, I suppose," I allow. "I am addicted to knowledge. An addiction that I hope, unlike with my brother and my father, will not prove fatal."

Pip bursts into peals of bright, sharp laughter that echo around the valley, slapping back at us from the slabs of marble tombs, from the water of the river that is so slow and deep that the surface is veritably still. She swallows the sound swiftly, stunned, and on guard.

I tense, but nothing seems to have heard Pip; or, if it has, it hasn't decided that her laughter was the perfect signal to attack. After the last echo fades away, I whisper, my voice perhaps too low: "What was so funny?"

It's a bit ludicrous to be whispering—if anything was going to hear us, it already has—but Pip also drops her voice and says: "Knowledge. Fatal. We're on a hero's journey *because* of our curiosity. So yeah, I'd say that this is a pretty dangerous addiction."

I have to concede the point. Then I ask her if she has any addictions of her own.

"Jogging," she says. "Endorphins and adrenaline and all those hormones that make you feel incredible after sex. Books. Stories. Academic debates. Being proven right." She smiles wryly, her lips twisting into her cheek. "You."

I manage to get Dauntless to walk beside Karl long enough for Pip and I to engage in a swift kiss.

"So, who are we looking for?" Pip asks, turning away to squint into the fog as the first monument rises to our left. It is a vain atrocity of raw marble, large enough for all four of us to camp in for the night and have room left over for the Library Lion. The further along we go, the more ornate the tombs will grow, though they won't get much bigger. There is a limit to the size of slab a group of workers can transport, after all.

"King Chailin was the first of his dynasty," I explain. "He was king of Hain two dynasties before the present one. Before that, he was the Minister of the Right, and he was appointed ruler in the field, after King Spiche fell in battle against the Centaur Horde. Spiche had no heirs. Chailin called a cease to hostilities and brokered a peace with the Horde, and, in return for the lives saved and his wisdom in calling for peace, the dryads of the forest—in which the battles were mostly taking place—presented him with a gift."

"The Blade that Never Fails?"

"Yes. I don't know what it looks like, though, but one can assume that a gift such as that would be buried with Chailin. I know it was not passed down to his heirs, or His Majesty, King Carvel, would have it."

"He could have it, and you just don't know about it."

I level a look at Pip that communicates my thoughts on that possibility.

She giggles again, but it is more mindful and subdued. "Right, yes, of course, Master Shadow Hand. Obviously not. So, we're just going to go and take it?"

"Borrow it," I correct. "I see no reason not to return the enchanted knife to the dead king when we are done with it. I'm returning everything else."

"Which is a damn sight more polite than most heroes do," Pip points out.

"It is polite," I say. "It's the right thing to do."

"Still, most people would want to hold on to a knife that can't fail, whatever that actually means."

"It does not belong to me," I counter.

"Chailin is dead. It's not like he's going to mind."

I can't help the shivers that crawl up my spine. "You can't know that for certain," I say. "It is safer to ask permission, and to return the knife. Who knows if any curses have been laid upon it?"

In our last village, I made certain to obtain a charm to repel the dead for each of us—Pip and I are wearing ours around our necks, and Karl and Dauntless have each had the charm braided into their manes. I hope that is enough forethought for the Station that always surprises the hero, because I cast no spells save for Words, have no tricks beyond the strength of my blade, and no wards save those I was able to buy.

I am frankly ill-prepared for battling the darker sorts of magical creatures: ghosts, vampires, lichs, and zombies. In this, Bevel Dom's preparation and knowledge far outpaces my own.

Not that there are probably zombies amidst the tombs of the kings—they are always lain to rest with the rituals and wards to protect their mortal remains from that very thing. I can't imagine a vampire would choose to make his home amid the tombs, either; mortal travelers are too few and far between to sustain a vampire's diet, and the creatures are such utter hedonists that I can't imagine one *wanting* to live somewhere without velvet and silk, humidors and rich wine. If there are lichs, or ghosts, in this graveyard, they are not those of the great rulers of the past. They would be the leftovers of travelers long lost, or thieves who deserve their fates for trying to rob royal tombs.

I shift uncomfortably in my saddle. Pip and I have come to be thieves, too. What spells will lash out against us, I wonder. What foes will we have to face?

For the first few hours, it seems that the answer to that question is merely boredom and cold. No other opponents materialize to challenge us, and the most put-upon thing I must do is try to nudge Dauntless far enough up the slope of the valley to read the names of the kings and queens carved onto the lintels aloud to Pip. He always dances back to the path with a sense of urgency and relief, and it is becoming harder and harder to convince Dauntless to obey the press of my thighs and knees with each successive tomb. Very soon, I might have to start dismounting to check, and the thought fills me with trepidation. I'd rather remain seated, if I can— Dauntless can run very fast, and his hooves are shod in good dwarven steel, excellent for bringing down upon the head of a creature seeking to attack us.

The sun barely penetrates the gloom at the bottom of the valley, giving the light a watery blue quality and making it virtually impossible for me to guess the time of day. We ride until my stomach begins to rumble for its lunch. But neither Pip nor I are willing to dismount to eat, so we munch on dried fruit and meat as we persuade the horses to move further and further along the river.

There are only the sounds of hooves on gravel and grass, our own breaths, my heart in my ears, the shift of leather and clothing and tacking. No birdsong. No rustle of the wind. Not even the sound of anyone following us, which might or might not have actually been welcome, at this point.

Time passes—slowly, quickly, I cannot tell—and everywhere, skin-itchingly thorough silence. Pip is waiting for it, too, whatever it is going to be, the great plot twist, eyes rolling left and right so often now it almost appears as if she is watching a metronome.

If only the infuriating *waiting* for it would be over, I might just welcome this horrible twist.

"Intolerable!" I finally hiss. The sound of my voice cuts across the laden air, and Pip jumps in her saddle. "Apologies," I say. "I didn't mean to surprise you."

"There's the next tomb," she says. She tries to coax Karl off the path, but he refuses to go.

"I will look," I say, and Dauntless takes a bit more heel than is usual for him to obey.

I have to read the name three more times before I am certain that it is King Chailin's tomb. But it is. We have found it. For some reason, this all feels too simple. Too easy. Perhaps too much of a trick. But the name doesn't change on each successive read, and the styling of the tomb is correct for Chailin's dynasty—all organic shapes and curved lines, the product of an era obsessed with nature and the attempt to recreate her in precious stones and delicate filigree. The plinths look like oak trees, and the panels of the door have been carved with leaping stags bearing tree-branch antlers, blossoming fruit trees, waving garlands, and nymphs and satyrs at play.

Such optimism Chailin's rule had ushered in. The Spring King, they had called him. The man who began what his great-great-grandson, my King Carvel, has continued: the prosperous peace between the races. It is this that my brother enforces with his quests, routing the bad apples from humanity and the magical races alike to ensure that the peace prevails. While I may not prefer my brother's methods or attitudes, I cannot deny the worth of his deeds and the benefit it has had on Hain. On all of the Four Kingdoms.

When I return to the path, I don't get lost, or enchanted, or even tripped up. Pip is even right where I left her. Together, we dismount and draw our swords, just to be prepared. Pip is getting better with her own weapon, but always seems to halt our practice just as she is beginning to pick up a new technique. It is almost as if she fears becoming too proficient, which is a strange thing indeed to worry over.

We approach the tomb, but the wind does not pick up; there is no fateful moaning, and nothing screeches in to block our path.

Some of the stone of the portico's knotwork has eroded so much that there are holes in the sculpture, and we loop the horses' reins through one such gap, not at all confident that they won't follow their clear desire to be elsewhere and abandon us if given the option.

I retrieve the Wisp lantern—repaired at the last village and supplied with a new Wisp—and gently stroke the creature awake. Once she is conscious and glowing, I close the glass door to protect her from the damp, and she jostles against the side of the glass, lifting the lantern in the direction she wants us to go.

"Bossy," Pip says, but she says it with a smile, and I get the feeling that the Wisp approves.

At least the little thing isn't scared of the gloom which stains the valley.

Pip tries the door of the tomb, and it, surprisingly, is not only unlocked, but easy to shift. It swings outward soundlessly, the silence of the hinges more eerie than a rusted squeal might have been, as it was the latter for which we were both braced. Swallowing down my fear and raising my sword, I hold the lantern aloft.

The shallow chamber beyond the threshold is just deep enough to hold a large stone box, roughly the length of a man, with enough clearance around it for mourners to attend the sarcophagus without banging their elbows into the walls. A row of shelving, at eye level, runs the entire perimeter of the tomb. Upon it, someone has placed those things which must have been sentimental for the deceased: a favored bow and arrow; small paintings of a woman and three young children; a second painting of the young children looking significantly more grown-up; a small chest opened to reveal a games set; a second chest framing a signet ring, a crown, and a chain of office not unlike the one I wear during official business as Lordling of the Chipping, but significantly more finely wrought and laden with a merchant's wealth of precious stones; a child's cuddly toy, the nap of the fur loved into patches, the glass eyes dull and cracked from thousands of childhood adventures; and a hundred other things that my eyes skim over.

Pip stops beside the toy and tentatively, carefully, rubs one of the round ears between her fingers. "Still soft," she murmurs. "He must have loved this teddy bear a lot when he was a kid. It's sort of sad that it's not in the coffin with him."

I make a noncommittal sound, and make my way over to the sarcophagus. As I expected, there is a bas-relief carving of King Chailin on the cover. His eyes are closed, as if in slumber, and for all that he was a crowned king when he died, he is dressed in the comfortable, simple clothing of a scholar. His house robe is patterned with the royal crest, however, and on his brow is a circlet made of actual gold and woven with green and yellow gems. Pip takes the lantern when I hold it out to her and stands by the head of the sarcophagus, inspecting the mosaic mural that fills the entire wall.

My eyes are for the dead king's carved belt—and yes, there, on his hip, sits the dagger given to Chailin at the end of the Bloody Battle of Bigonner, which signaled the end of the human-centaur wars forever. His palm rests over the pommel, obscuring its shape, fingers loose against the guard, symbolizing both the peace this blade represents and his preparedness to use it to strike at those who would threaten it. That it was carved into the tomb lid gives me great confidence that it was buried with him. Now, to simply open it up without breathing in too much grave rot, or triggering any curses.

I check the seams of the sarcophagus, but there doesn't seem to be any spells or wards carved, or melted into wax and placed along the seal. I give the lid a bit of a shove, pushing with both my arms and my hips, and am startled when the lid gives easily. There is no sucking pop of a broken seal, but I hold still all the same, listening, waiting, fingers curled on the lid and palms tacky with sweat and tomb-dust.

Silence.

A breath.

Nothing.

Relief floods through my limbs, but is very quickly chased away by dread.

Why was the seal so easy to break? And *why* were there no wards to rupture? I do not like the answer that occurs to me, and make haste shoving the lid all the way to the side. Pip hands me the lantern back, and I peer into the box. *Oh.*

No.

By the Writer, no. The coffin has already been shattered. The lid has been punctured by what appears to be a sharp blow, the dark wood scattered out of the way, the light wood exposed like vulnerable flesh.

King Chailin's hand is visible, and if it was ever preserved before, the careless, crude, *rude* way in which his final sanctuary has been violated has let in the damp air. The hand is bloated and gray and half-turned to slime.

The smell hits me hard, and I reel back, gagging, trying very hard not to make the inconceivable sin of vomiting on a king. Pip makes a choking sound and turns her face away, both hands covering her nose. I bury my own in the lapel of my robe, which I bring up to shield my mouth and nose, and screw up my courage to look into the coffin again.

The knife was carved over the king's right hip, which is where I assume he probably wore it in life. It is the right hand that is dissolving. Using the tip of my own sword, I nudge it aside at the wrist, and it leaves a smear of watery flesh and fat on the clothing in its wake. I half-brace myself for the hand to suddenly become animated, to clutch with unholy strength at my blade, or to try to reach up and throttle me. It only falls to the side, the bones breaking free of the meat like they do from an overcooked chicken.

I see the belt now, and with a second nudge, the scabbard of the dagger becomes visible.

Only the scabbard.

"It's gone," I manage to squeak. "Dear Writer. Pip! The knife. The scabbard is still here, but it's empty. Someone's already taken it."

"What?" she says. "Let me see!"

She leans over the lip of the sarcophagus, her shirt pulled up to protect her nose, and moans. She directs my sword into more prodding. "Someone got here before us!"

"Yes, but a long time ago. Years, it seems. Maybe even decades."

"Son of a bitch!" Pip snarls. "How's that for a plot twist! *Goddamnit!*" She slams her palms against the side of the sarcophagus, making the whole room boom with her frustration.

"Careful, Pip," I caution. "Respectfully, if you please."

"Right. Sorry," she apologizes to the king's corpse. "That was out of line. I don't suppose you want to tell us who took the Blade that Never Fails? We'll fetch it back for you."

She peers down into the abyss of the coffin for a long moment. The king makes no reply.

"Well, it was worth a try." She sighs and rocks back on her heels.

"Now what?"

"I don't know," I admit. "Can we skip this and move on to the next Station? Maybe keep our ears out while on the road, see if we get another clue?"

"No," Pip says. "It has to go in order. We have to find the knife first. Dammit, I *thought* things were going too well."

And that's when a flash of gold leaf on the wall catches both the light and my eye. I take a step closer, and the colors reveal themselves to be a mosaic of Chailin and a dryad. Between their fingers is balanced what can only be the Blade that Never Fails.

Incredulity swoops into my gut so quickly that the world actually spins under my feet. I have to lay my free hand on the corner of Chailin's tomb to remain upright.

The knife in the mosaic is blocky and crude, the hilt gilt and patterned with precious stones that are arranged to mimic blooms.

But, above all, the blasted thing is *familiar*. The last time I saw it, it was slightly tarnished, half of the precious stones missing, and embedded in my ballroom floor, scant breaths away from my fencing boot, waggling at me like a taunt.

Sixteen

 cannot manage to make the campfire grow beyond a sizzling, popping misery of smoke and embers, which is probably a good thing. We are chilled, but the light of the fire would probably attract some of the less savory denizens of a graveyard, if there are any.

There is not enough time before nightfall to backtrack out of the Valley of the Tombs, and I don't know how much farther it is to the exit on the other side, either. Neither of us wanted to be caught here after dark, but we have no other options. We are too heartsick, and the horses too tired, to go on.

Desperate for shelter but still wanting to be respectful, we build our campfire and lay our sleeping rolls on the marble balcony of King Chailin's portico. It is just wide enough for Pip and I to wind together under the blankets without fear of tumbling down the three steps to the ground. The fire is at our feet, and the horses are crowded up as close as they are able to come. Karl and Dauntless refuse the gray-green grass and must be nose-bagged. They champ warily on oats and watch the mist, flanks shuddering.

What little light the fire offers is reflected in the sparks of precious metal that have been hammered into the veins of the marble around us. It throws up a sort of eerie luminescence that makes it hard for me to fall asleep. Pip drops off as soon as she's snugged in beside me, head on my shoulder and knee hitched up along my hip, breathing even and slow, if shallow. She is tense in my embrace, ready to wake at any moment.

I don't recall drifting off, which is why, when I awaken, it takes a moment for me to figure out what's changed. I can hear Pip—her soft, low moan, the unbearably sexy intake of her breath—but the blankets beside me are cold, thrown back to allow the chill in. I shiver all over and stand, pulling on my boots and wrapping my belt around me, adjusting the fall of my sword against my leg as I trot down the stairs. Pip makes that incredible hitching sound that always lodges in her chest when she is close to her peak, and I am both aroused and confused as to why she is making such sounds elsewhere.

Surely she hadn't decided to wander off, alone, into a potentially haunted graveyard to pleasure herself, when all she had to do was wake me if she was feeling like she needed attention. Surely?

"Pip?" I call softly, hoping she'll be able to hear me over the sounds she's making. I can only just follow them, the noises strangely muffled by the mist.

Another moan, this time louder, almost as if in answer. I pluck at my flies to relieve the pressure and round King Chailin's daughter's tomb. "Pip, what are you doing out here? Come back to bed."

This time, the moan sounds like a word: "No."

"No?" I echo, and peer around the corner, smiling, ready to tease. "Why do you say—"

I stop. Shock slams into me, so profound that it feels as if my feet have been grabbed by corpses and I am being pulled under the topsoil.

Pip is standing, half curled over a man's arm in the moonlit mist. She has got her hands in his pale wrist, digging in with her fingernails and drawing blood. Her face is hidden by the ebony fall of her hair, but what little of her neck and jaw I can see is red with rage, or arousal. She is sobbing; I am close enough to hear it now, pained and frustrated. And, clearly, it has been going on for a while. It reminds me sharply, shamefully, of the terrible crying jags to which I had accidentally borne witness in Turn Hall. It occurs to me that I am a stupid twat for believing they had simply stopped as soon as we'd begun our adventure together.

Pip's knees are so bent that it's a wonder she hasn't fallen to the damp grass, and it can't just be her grip on the man's forearm that keeps her upright. No, now that I am looking, I can see it—a thin black chest. She is kneeling on it.

I recognize it as easily as I recognized Kintyre's knife in the tomb mosaic. It is my chest. The one from the hayloft; the one with my Shadow Hand accoutrements secreted inside. The one that no one but me can open.

It remains closed, the locks and hinges scuffed and gouged from someone's unsuccessful attempts to force them. The bolts which once secured the box to the loft are still hanging from the sides, splinters of wood clinging to the fist-sized screws.

I return my eyes to Pip, whose whole frame is shuddering and jerking, her head shaking so hard back and forth that I fear she may harm herself.

"Pip!" I call.

"Ah, and here he is. Good lovie," the man says. He reaches out to pet Pip's hair, cradling the back of her neck like a lover, and fury flashes through me so hot and so fast that I am three steps toward him, my sword jumping into my hand before I realize that I recognize him.

"Well, this is certainly not the man I expected to be the Shadow Hand, is it?" Bootknife says. His grin is wide and gleeful and hatefully white in the moonlight. "But here you are, Lordling Turn. 'Course it would be the pain-in-the-arse's useless little brother. It's all so po-po-poetical," he mocks.

"Pip!" I yelp. "Come away from him!"

Bootknife pets the back of her neck again. "Oh no, no, she ain't going nowhere, my little lovie, now is she?"

Pip shivers and gasps, and if I didn't know any better, I'd say she was on the verge of an orgasm.

"What are you doing to her? Let her go."

Bootknife laughs, his ferret-features wide and happy, his dark eyes squinched shut. The tail of his queue brushes along his shoulders, hair dark and greasy. His elvish ancestry lends his eyes and cheekbones a swept-back tilt that, in the shadows, translates as ominous.

"Now, why would I do that, tell me? Got her right where I want her, I do. Though, she's being bad, she is. Not *cooperating*." He jerks her hair hard.

"Fuck you!" Pip sobs.

"So I'm punishing her, I am. Aren't I?" With one pale, slender finger he draws aside the veil of her hair—a white, puffed tendril of scar tissue moves, *crawls* along her cheek, brushing the bottom of Pip's ear and wrapping itself around her throat. She makes that familiar cough, that choking sound I've heard so often of late, and tries to hold perfectly still.

It falls together in my mind quite quickly after that. "The ivy," I say. He doesn't need to confirm it; I already understand. But I can't think of anything else to voice, save for demands to let her go, and Bootknife doesn't like to be told what to do. Instead, I say, "She can't open the chest for you. And even if she could, the Mask would never accept you."

Bootknife reaches down and retrieves his namesake from the sheath he wears in his left boot. It is flat and very thin, and, I know, very, very sharp. It shines in the watery light of the moon, almost like a Wisp itself, alive and thirsty.

"But you can do both. My little lovie told me all about the mask and how it works, didn't she? Didn't you, lovie?"

"Y-yes," Pip moans. "I'm sorry, Forsyth. I'm so sorr—uck!"

"None of that," Bootknife admonishes, and Pip reels backward but cannot break from his light embrace. "Up, up."

Pip stands, limbs stiff and unnatural, joints nearly at the wrong angles, like a poorly strung puppet.

"Go kiss your man hello, lovie," Bootknife sneers. His free hand makes a flinging motion toward me, as if he is spraying water, and Pip jerks forward, closing the gap between us. Her cheeks are flushed with misery and fury, and damp with tears. She fists the lapels of my robe in clumsy, resisting hands, and presses up on her toes.

She mashes her mouth against mine, barely a kiss, and then drops back down.

"Now kneel," Bootknife commands, grinning.

And Pip, looking as surprised as I still feel, kneels.

"No!" I yelp, and hold on to her shoulders, keep her arms from being able to rise to my belt.

"Why not?" Bootknife asks. "You've never minded before, have you now?"

"Before?" I look down at Pip, but her face is turned away. She is *ashamed*.

Bootknife taps the flat of his blade across his palm, one foot on top of my Shadow's Hand chest like it is a prize of war. Perhaps it is. "Have to say," he drawls, "she's got some neat tricks tucked away in that pretty little 'ead, my lovie. Even I learnt a thing or two from her, didn't I?" He taps the pommel of his knife between his own eyes.

"You've been in her *mind?*"

"Among other places." He makes another gesture, and Pip jerks as if something has shoved its way inside her, and I suppose it has.

"Let her go!" I growl.

"Oh no, Forssy, no, no, no. That's not how it's going to go." He takes a step toward us, putting himself between me and the chest. He points the knife at the back of Pip's neck. The threat is very clear. One flick of his wrist, and she's dead.

"How then?"

"You're going to come over here, open the chest, and give me the mask. *Give it* to me, you hear? Proper like."

"This is what you wanted all along?" I say, and it's not a question, not really, because I know I'm right. It takes every fiber of my not inconsiderable self-control to not simply lunge at him, sword up. But then, the Writer only knows what he'd do to Pip. "To know who the Shadow Hand is, and to steal his secrets?"

"As you say," he admits easily, shrugging.

"So, why the quest?" I ask. "Why let it get this far? Why not just . . . right after?"

"Because this way is more fun," Bootknife taunts. "Because the more you thought she loved you, the more you told her. And the more you love her, the weaker your defense. But we're at an end, now, aren't we?"

I adjust my grip around my sword. "Because the knife is missing."

"Of course the knife is missing!" he thunders, the rage and the volume both appearing so suddenly that I nearly take a step back. I catch myself in time. Bootknife jerks Pip again, in a fury. "It was mine! *Mine*! I was the one who read the legends and came! I was the one to battle the ward spells, who broke the castings! I was the one that nearly died for that knife, that perfect knife, *my* perfect knife. It was made for me, my tool, the extension of *my hand*. And *your brother*," he snarls, foam flecking his lips in his puce-faced rage, "he *took it*! *He took my heart*!"

I swallow heavily and make no movement, no noise, fearing to set him off again. Bootknife takes a great, shuddering breath and seems to unruffle himself without even moving. He sighs, and it is filled with an unsettling, romantic longing. "And, of course, it's Kinny-Kinny-Kintyre who's got it, isn't it? Just my luck, little lovie, just my luck. But once I've got the Shadow's Mask, we can go finish up the quest together, can't we, lovie? Are we gonna summon us up a Deal-Maker, eh?"

Pip fists her hands in the knees of my trousers and whimpers. "No," she coughs. But the vines make her nod. She is fighting them, I can see, fighting them so hard they are starting to glow green with Bootknife's power and effort.

Their grip on her loosens enough for her to gag, seethe, and, finally, from between clenched teeth whisper: "Yes, we will, sir."

I am staggered. That Bootknife has used Pip as a conduit for his spying is clear enough; but that he has invaded her mind, her personality, so much that he can even make her speak as he wishes . . . it is horrific.

There is a riot in my stomach all of a sudden, a scream fighting with bile to be the first thing out of my mouth. I swallow hard and try to firm my stance, but I cannot seem to get my body to want to stay upright, to stay planted.

How much of what Pip has said to me was even her? How much of it was Bootknife, speaking with her mouth, touching me with her hands, making love to me with . . . I take a slow step backward, and Bootknife throws back his head, cackling in delight. Pip makes another desperate sound, and I immediately wish that I had not moved at all.

Bootknife's laughter ratchets higher. "Oh, you're disgusted! Cute, isn't it?" I find myself suddenly wishing this graveyard *was* full of zombies and lichs and vampires, and that every single one of them would be attracted to the sound of his hateful, *hateful* glee.

"Go on, then," he says, gesturing to the chest. "Open it up, my boy."

"No," I say. "Not until you let Pip go."

Bootknife makes another gesture that has Pip on the ground in a second, back arched so high that only her heels and head are touching the grass, a scream so loud, so agonizing, so profound escaping from her throat. I stumble, my back and calves slamming into the freezing marble of the tomb behind me.

"*Now!*" Bootknife commands.

I stagger toward the chest, because I can't bear to go in any other direction. Bootknife graciously steps aside, gesturing like a bullfighter, and I only spare a second's thought for what might happen the moment the Shadow's Mask is in his hand and my back is still turned.

But Pip is screaming, *screaming*, and I can't . . . I can't not . . . so I blow on the lock, and the hinges whisper and pop. I drop my sword to palm open the lid, and Bootknife kicks it away, back the way I came, and that's fine, because there's another sword in the bottom of the chest, under the cloak. I can almost feel Smoke yearning for the curling intimacy of my palm, ready to jump to our defense.

Bootknife just wants the mask, has his eyes on the prize, and I will let it distract him. I pull it from its velvet pouch, hold it aloft. He pinches it between two fingers, but he doesn't pull.

"And the password?" he asks, too shrewd for my panicked mindset.

I mumble a few Words of Trust, and he grins. I let go.

The Mask hovers between us, glinting in the shadows, and then he lifts it, crowing in triumph. Pip goes completely slack, so deathly quiet that my heart skips ten beats in my chest.

Not dead, I plead. *Please, not dead yet.* But I wouldn't put it past Bootknife.

I turn to face him, fall back against the chest, one arm buried up to the elbow in the fabric of the cloak inside it, trying hard to look as if I've swooned in horror. The horror is genuine, at least. It is a wasted effort, though—Bootknife isn't even looking at me. He's got the mask up to his face already, the greedy bastard.

The second he's got the mask against his skin, he begins to scream.

I wrap my hands around Smoke's hilt and lash upward. The tip of the blade catches Bootknife under the chin, knocking the mask into the air, but unfortunately leaving no more than a shallow scratch on the bastard's face.

Perhaps I should have thrust Smoke through his chin and into his brains.

The mask flips end over end, flashing like a firefly in the ice-water moonlight, pinging off the wall of a tomb next to us and landing in a scruff of weakly glowing starflowers.

"You lied!" Bootknife howls, hands to his cheeks. I can see between his fingers that the flesh has reddened, burned. Perhaps I should have left the mask on him longer, instead, so it could have eaten through his face.

I am too kind.

"I have not," I say, climbing to my feet and keeping Smoke up and pointed at him. I retrieve the mask, drop it back into the chest, and then kick the whole thing closed. The lock engages with a soft click. "I told Pip that the mask requires a pass phrase, but that it will also only accept as master a *good man*. Which, I am very pleased to say, Bootknife, you *are not*."

He giggles. It grates upon my nerves like the screech of a bleeding hawk, raking up the flesh of my spine, making the hairs on my nape stand out, and my shoulders hunch in an effort to cover my ears without dropping my sword. I bare my teeth at him.

"Nope, not a good man. I am not," he agrees. "I mean, lookit what I did to your girlie girl."

I don't take the bait and turn. He drops one hand and gestures. Pip makes a gasping sound (*alive, thank the Writer*), and I can hear the shift of fabric, the soft thunk of her boots on grass.

"Leave her be," I say, thrilled that she is alive, but carefully containing my relief so he won't see.

"Oh no, can't do that, now, can I?" Bootknife laughs. He drops his other hand, the one still holding his knife, and shakes it at me, admonishing. "She's too good a tool."

"She's no tool."

"It's not an accident that she survived, you know?" Bootknife says, posture and tone a study in forced non-chalance. He is picking his teeth with his dagger. "It took restraint on my part, it did. Didn't like it, but did it. Good work, huh? And all that lovely medicine-magic floating 'round in her blood—great world she comes from. Builds 'em resistant, don't it? Aren't you gonna ask *why* I didn't kill 'er outright?"

"Why not?" I grit out, obliging.

"Cause my master said not to. Good idea, huh?" Bootknife giggles again. "That's why he's the boss man, he is. If she won't tell us herself, he says, we use her to get other people to tell instead. Everyone likes a damsel in distress, he says. Nobody watches their mouths around pretty, silly little maidens. They're a good prop to any scheme, he says. So we let her go, he says. But make sure we can control her, can see through her eyes and hear through her ears. Make sure she gets rescued, right? S'a good spell, isn't it? Took me weeks to carve it against her spine, into her marrow and muscle. And she screamed, oh, how she screamed. But I had to take my time, I did." He turns his attention to where she has walked up between us and makes a gesture with his hand that pulls the glowing vines tighter across her neck. Pip makes an ugly, guttural choking sound, eyes going impossibly wider, skin turning puce. "She's a screamer, this one. Or maybe you already know that?" He leers at me.

I feel sick, all the way down to my toes, a rolling ball of hate and nausea.

"How much of what she did was you?" I ask. I don't want the answer, not really, because I am terrified that it will be: *all of it.* "How much of what she said and how she acted was you pulling her strings?"

"At first, nearly none, wasn't me. She knew you all by herself, betrayed her to us all by herself, she did, yeah? Wrote up that map, that chart thing, did all that research and told you so much, all on her own. But then she felt me pullin', pullin', so she shuts up, stops askin' questions, and so I have to make her, I do."

Smoke quivers in my hand, and I have never wished more than I am wishing right now that my sword was like Foesmiter, enchanted into never missing its mark, so that I could just throw it and have it pierce his heart.

But my aim is not that good, especially not with Pip's life poised between us like a sacrifice waiting to happen.

Bootknife says: "She's a fighter, too, doesn't do as she's told, she doesn't. Bad girl, very bad little pet. But then I started"—he twitches his hand in another complicated pattern, and Pip is dragged forward by her own body, the scars writhing and glowing such a vivid green across her shoulders that I can see them through her shirt. They wriggle down her arms, making her hold them out to me in a parody of an invitation— "to find other ways to make her obey. Squeezin' the air out of her, that's fun. Then she talks, my lovie. Then she says what she's supposed to, doesn't she? Give us a demonstration, yes?" he says to her. "Tell him you love him."

The vines around Pip's neck slide away, slithering back down under her collar. She gasps hard, as if her lungs are being compressed, but bites down on her own lips. Blood blossoms under her teeth, a rivulet sliding down her trembling chin, her eyes screwed tight and leaking.

She swallows hard, trying to drown the words, trembling, *fighting*, but Bootknife barks: "Do it!"

She goes slack, defeated.

"I-I love you, Forsyth." She chews on the words, as if she can grab them with her incisors and keep them from escaping her mouth.

The twisting agony in my entrails tightens, leaving me equally breathless. *No, Pip, no. Tell me that wasn't him that made you say it.*

"Tell him that you think he is a brave, strong man, yeah?" Bootknife is laughing. He waves his dagger in his air as if it's a lady's fan, mocking. "Tell him he's worth something. Lie to him and tell him he's a *hero*."

"You're a good man, Forsyth Turn," Pip breathes, voice cracked and strained. Her head rolls back, eyes fluttering, and it takes effort for her to raise it, to meet my gaze. *Believe me*, her eyes plead. *Believe me!* "You're a hero, *bao bei*. You are strong and intelligent. And you can outsmart this son of a bi—*aarrgk!*"

Bootknife clenches his fist harder, and Pip's whole body spasms in agony.

"Now, now," he scolds gently. "Don't go putting words into your own mouth, lovie."

"Fuck you," she sobs.

Quiet, Pip! I beg, hoping she can see my desperation in my expression. *Don't antagonize the man who literally holds your life in the palm of his hands.*

"Cry, lovie," Bootknife sneers. "Go on, make it a good performance. Make him think you're really that weak, that you need protecting. Appeal to his manly pride, you."

She weeps on command, tears springing up in her eyes and rolling down her cheeks, fat and pathetic. She is as miserable and horrified as she sounded in the stairwell of Turn Hall.

"You're an absolute bastard," I snarl.

Bootknife laughs again. "Yes, I am. Tryin' to insult me with the truth? I already know my parentage, I do. Got on an uncooperative elfmaid, I was."

"Let her go!"

"Might," he admits. "She's been a good little spy; told us all sorts about the Shadow Hand, the secret passages in and out of Kingskeep, even the domestic problems between Kintyre and his little loyal boy-hole. Even about that healer, Mother Mouth; good hands on her. The master might offer her a job."

"Mother Mouth would never work for you," Pip sobs.

"Then she'll die for declining, won't she, lovie? Shut up." Pip's tears abruptly dry, her wails ceasing, though the full body shudders remain, wracking her frame. The skin around her eyes is red and raw, her shoulders slumped, knees slack, wrists holding her upright as if she's been lashed to a whipping post. "Good at twisting my commands, this one is. Clever little lovie. Always says just a bit too much. Tell our hero what you really think of him, lovie."

"As you wish," she snarls through gritted teeth. My heart swoops into my stomach and lodges in my guts. I don't know what she means by that. Is it a message? What does it *mean*? I can't remember.

"Stop it," I command, but Bootknife just sneers.

"You think you can tell me what to do, do you? But you ain't so smart as you think, Shadow Hand. You took her for face value like the trusting, shallow idiot you are, yeah. And gave us everything we wanted in return. So much to work with. She's been so good to us, this one. Might not even kill her; might reward her instead. You've had her, you have, so we have the knowledge to reward her proper, too. Now we know what she likes."

"You will not! Release Pip from your compulsion at once!" I raise Smoke, not entirely certain that my skill would be enough to skewer Bootknife before he can do Pip irreparable harm. Worse, I don't even know if his death will loose his hold on Pip—perhaps it will just transfer to the Viceroy. Perhaps it will kill her.

But what else can I do? I cannot reason with him. There is no blackmail on which to draw, nothing I can say, no words I can turn to weapons. Not against this man.

Forsyth, Pip mouths, her voice stolen from her and exhausted fury in her frank, muddy gaze. *Do it.*

"You gonna stick me, Shadow Hand? You don't have the guts. Played you like a fiddle, didn't I?" Bootknife sneers, and—*ah ha!*—he is watching Smoke instead of my shoulder, like a proper swordsman ought. The sword doesn't telegraph the move; the torso does. I flick my blade back and forth, watching his gaze stick to it, trying to figure out how to use his lack of training and knowledge to my advantage.

"I will only ask one more time, Bootknife. Release Lucy Piper from your compulsion, please, and Unspeak your Words of Control." I drop the point of my sword to the ground, as if in surrender, while raising my arm, steeling my elbow and shoulder, drawing back on the string of muscle so that my sword can jump forward like an arrow loosed from the bow at the right moment.

He just snickers, a high-pitched giggle worthy of the biggest hacks and hams to ever grace King Carvel's playhouses. "Played you for the lonely, desperate, shriveled little rat you are. Played you a patsy, I did. Just like everyone else in your life."

"Silence!" I snarl, rocking onto the balls of my feet, following the script he knows, he craves, giving him the dialogue that makes him think he is the director of our drama. *Soon. Just give me an opening, you self-confident ass!*

He feints, and I follow, slashing out. We both step left, I trying to jump around Pip to get at him, and he dancing around behind her, keeping her between us. A searing flares against the side of my face and I stagger back, startled, and gasp. The hand Bootknife was holding his dagger in is now empty. I resist the urge to raise my hand to my face to check the extent of the damage; I dare not take my attention away from him, even for a second. Liquid heat slithers down my cheek, and I realize belatedly that I am *bleeding.*

I am struck next with the nose-wrinkling thought that he had just been picking his teeth with that dagger. *Disgusting.*

"What, truth hurts? Ha!" He points at me, and, shadowed dramatically against the white mist, even I have to admit that his gleeful menace would have filled me with dread were I not already too full of fury and scheming. "You think Pointe is your friend? He's just waiting for his turn at the Shadow's Mask. And your brother thinks you're so far beneath his contempt that he don't even talk about you, does he? Bevel hardly writes about you in his braggart scrolls, and you can't even tell when your servants are lyin' to you, can you? No, you can't!"

He cackles, head thrown back, confident that he will be able to counter any move I make, with my sword at so awkward an angle, hilt raised so high and wrist inverted. Instead of waiting for him to look at me again, as would be polite, as Kintyre would have done, I lunge.

Now!

Bootknife's laughter escalates into a full-fledged scream as I twist the sword forward through the air, arcing it high in a circle and using the momentum of gravity to slam the sharp of my blade down hard against his spellcasting wrist. It crashes into bone, juddering my arm and nearly wrenching my sword from my grip. Bootknife screeches even as I jerk back out of his reach, taking my sword and half of his hand with me.

His wrist is half-cleaved, his thumb and first two fingers shorn off, and he is screaming, *screaming*. He stumbles to the ground, falls onto his back, face pale and other hand grasping at the ruin of his hand, tearing the already ragged edges wider in his disbelief and shock. Gore slicks my blade, my boots, soaks into the greedy dry earth of the tombs below us. I spare a moment of thought to hope there is no blood-magic spell waiting to awaken at a fresh lick in the graves underneath us. Then I put my foot on Bootknife's chest and get his attention by tapping the point of my sword against the tip of his nose. It leaves a red smear.

"Bootknife," I say. "Release Lucy Piper."

"She is released. She is released from me!" he screeches.

I spare a glance to where she is now crumpled on the ground, her breath coming in pants so shallow and quick I fear she will asphyxiate herself. She is having another panic attack, most probably, but I cannot go to her side and soothe away the fear, not yet.

"I am going to let you live, Bootknife," I intone. "Not because of any ill-conceived notion of mercy, nor because I fear taking another human life. You are less than human to me, you swine. But I am a hero on a quest, and it is *the right thing to do*. Because I am *better than you*. Do you understand me?"

He mewls and nods. I crouch, digging my knee into his solar plexus, the flat of Smoke still against his nose, point aimed at his eye. I grasp his ruined wrist with my free hand. He screams again, and it nearly drowns out my Words of Healing. The blood flow slows, and then stops, the open wound scabbing.

Then I wipe his blood off my glove and onto his coat, and stand. "Now go away, Bootknife, and know that if you ever harm me or mine again—and that includes my worthless brother and his equally worthless friend—I will come back for the rest of you."

He scrambles to his feet, scratching in the dirt for his severed fingers.

"Leave those!" I hiss. "They're mine, now!"

He lets them go and turns on his heel, running like a dragon is on his tail. I watch for a long time as his silhouette grows smaller, fainter, and then vanishes entirely into the mist of the graveyard.

Then, and only then, do I wipe down my sword and sheathe Smoke in the holster already attached to my hip. And *then*, I go to Pip.

She is lying on the ground, curled in on herself, and the moment I lay my hands on her shoulders, she flinches away. I let her go. Her skin must be one single long stretch of agony.

"Don't touch me," she snaps. She looks up at me, and I am startled to see that her eyes are brown. Plain, dark, boring brown, not a hint of green within the flecks of her iris.

"Your eyes," I begin, but then don't know how to continue, so don't.

"I know," she growls. "I goddamn know. They're green."

"No, not anymore."

She blinks. "No? They're . . . give me a mirror!"

I have no mirror handy, but I have the mask. I retrieve it from the nest of glow-starved starflowers. She snatches at it before I am properly within reach, fumbling desperately to turn it toward herself and keep it from tumbling to the ground at the same time. When she finally has it stilled, she stares at her reflection with the sort of abject horror that one usually reserves for when one is confronted with a corpse. The horror breaks, suddenly, like the sun between rain clouds, and she releases a shuddering sigh, her expression transforming to one of careful, cautious joy.

"Oh god," she says, voice all shivery. "It's gone. The green is gone. I'm *free*."

She hands the mask back, and I tuck it into its velvet bag, taking advantage of the time to reorder my thoughts. "So, every time you said that your eyes were not green . . ."

"I was trying to give you a hint."

I let that sink into my skin, frowning, torn between the impulse toward self flagellation for missing such a clue and the odd thought that Pip wouldn't want me to be so hard on myself. Only, was it Pip who scolded me for not gaining control of my self-confidence? Or was that Bootknife?

Am I now going to spend the rest of my journey with Pip second-guessing everything she has ever said to me? I turn to ask her, but realize she is in no mental condition to answer. She is curled up on herself, arms around her shins and chin buried behind her knees, still and small like a terrified rabbit.

I retrieve the Shadow's Cloak from the chest and swing it over her shoulders, tucking it in carefully around her legs, being certain not to touch her. I do not think it would be welcome, for all that the cloak may ease at least some of her shivering. She nuzzles the fabric, and hope sparks in my heart that she is seeking out the comfort of my scent.

"Why do you have to be such a good guy, Forsyth?" she says softly. "Why did you have to *fall* for it?"

I don't know if I have the words to explain it to her, but I try anyway. "It was inevitable, you see? You were . . . more. Different. Something . . . unknown. A damsel. In distress, even. It was . . . inevitable. You see that, right? It was . . . written. Everything you are calls to everything I am."

"But I wasn't *me*," she insists, trying to shove some metaphorical space into a wedge between us, even as she pulls my cloak closer around her, digging her fingers into the diaphanous layers.

"Everything?" I ask. "Every gesture of affection? Every kiss? Every touch? It was all them?"

"This is dub-con in the worst way," she whispers, fingers balling in the fabric of the cloak's layers. "It's *dubious*. I don't even know how much of that was me. I can't . . . I can't touch you without thinking of *them*, of what they were saying in my head, of what they made me say, and do, and *want*." She shakes her head hard. "I don't even know how much of the *want* was mine. Was any of it? I don't know."

"We can find out." I lay a soft kiss against her cheek, and she flinches, actually flinches away as if I struck her.

"No." It is small, but it is firm. I sit back.

"Pip," I whisper. "Pl-Please, look at me."

"I'm not . . . don't . . . you can't kiss me like it means something. Please. Don't look at me like you love me."

"But-t I d-d-do."

"You *don't*. It was *him* you loved, him saying those things and making my h-hands move. None of it was me, and I didn't get any say in it at all!" Her voice is wretched, absolutely ragged, torn from her throat like a scorched battle flag.

"Pip, I understand, I really do—" I begin, but then she is there, in my face, teeth bared like a harpy, all rage and pain so large, so beyond the scope of anything I have ever seen in another human being. My fat tongue stumbles into terrified silence. I take a deep breath. "*Bao bei*," I whisper.

"Fuck you!" she snarls, poking one finger into the dip between my collarbones so hard that I nearly choke. "Don't you try to comfort me, Forsyth Turn. I have been proved wrong! Do you know what that means? I have been proved an *idiot* by the world I love most."

She arrows to her feet, stomping in a circle, somehow avoiding my outstretched arms, my attempts to reel her close and soothe her, without actually looking up at me.

"Please, Pi-Pip."

"I have written essays, blog posts, sat on panels at conventions; I have devoted literally *thousands* of hours, *millions* of words to this kind of thing, and what happens? I spend my whole goddamn academic career championing female character agency, fighting against lazy writing that falls back on epic fantasy gender stereotypes and utilizes rape as a back story excuse, against the half-assed conflation of strong female character with violent female character, screaming myself hoarse about visible minorities in fiction and the normalization of queerness, and what does the world I love best go and fucking do the *goddamn millisecond* I get here? Slaps me in the face and ties me down! Calls me a useless, silly, vain little girl who has wasted everything! Money, time, thousands of sheets of paper, hundreds of ink cartridges, dozens of online flame wars, *everything*: tells me I have *wasted my life trying to make everything better!*"

She cuts the sky with a shaking fist, misery embodied. The air is thick with suffering and betrayal, salt water and drying blood, fog and fury.

"Pip, no—"

"I have been *betrayed* in the harshest, *cruelest* way possible. Bootknife, and the Viceroy, and Kintyre, and Bevel, and *even you* have literally stomped on my childhood dreams! On the very basis of what I've imagined for myself. So fuck you, Forsyth Turn! Fuck you, and fuck the Viceroy, and fuck Kintyre, and fuck Elgar fucking Reed! Don't you tell me for a *second* that you *understand*! You—you white male privileged asshole!"

She jerks to her feet and swirls away into the darkness, the cloak shadowing her and the mist swallowing her up.

"Pip, please, stay close!" I plead.

"Like I have anywhere else to fucking *go*!" she screams back through the fog.

I stumble in her wake, unable to resist the lure of her, the magnet of her, and nearly bump into her back when the cloak suddenly resolves itself to my eyes. Her back is to me, spine a comma of defeat, and I reach out, desperate to comfort, to soothe, to *connect*, but she jumps like I have flayed her a second time, like the merest touch of my hand has laid open her wounds all over again.

"Don't touch me! Just leave me alone!" Pip snaps.

I am torn between reaching for her and backing away, but her eyes suddenly spring wide and she *screams* again, shoving at me. We tumble to the wet grass, and I roll to get her under me, to pin her arms to keep her nails from my face. *What is happening now? Were we wrong? Does Bootknife still control her?*

"Behind you!" Pip shouts, and I roll us to the side again, all instinct, and it is a good thing I do. The blade of my sword—my Turnish sword, not Smoke—slams into the grass where we'd been, skewering the edge of the Shadow's Cloak, pinning Pip down.

I roll off Pip and kick—my heel lands solidly in Bootknife's ribs and he stumbles back, his blood-slicked grip on his stolen sword fumbling.

In the time it takes me to gain my feet, he manages to wrench it free of the turf. Pip scrambles away from us. Bootknife raises the sword again, and, just as I'm about to lunge forward, something big and metal bashes into the back of Bootknife's head.

I assume it is Pip, and say, "Bravo! Thank you!" But the voice that answers back is deep, amused, and very much the last one I want to hear right now.

"You're welcome, little brother," Kintyre rumbles.

Bootknife flails around, trying to get his vision to focus and shaking his head.

"Two Turns!" he slurs. "No, four!"

Kintyre doesn't wait for him to come to his senses enough to fight back; he swings Foesmiter at Bootknife again. In foolish instinct, Bootknife raises his good arm to protect himself, and Kintyre's enchanted sword takes it off at the elbow. Following through, allowing his weight and momentum to pull him onto his front foot—a rather elegant move for my bash-about brother—he turns and swings at the other arm, and Foesmiter severs what's left of Bootknife's spell-hand. There is a spurt of arterial blood that is almost beautiful in the moonlight, steaming ruby glitter on frost-laced grass.

Bootknife scrambles backward, falling to the ground upon his back, wailing and flailing his matching stumps.

"Oh, look, an artist with no hands," Bevel says, with a snort. I risk a quick look over my shoulder and see him crouched on the ground next to Pip, his arms over her shoulders, his hand firmly on her head, keeping her face turned into his chest so she can't see what's about to happen next. "Useless sort of torturer now. And what is it that your master does to the useless, eh, Bootknife?"

"He won't get the chance to find out," I decide. It's the work of half a step and a swift plunge of Smoke through flesh to end Bootknife and his reign of torture entirely.

My aim is true, though Smoke does brush against Bootknife's ribcage, sending a jolt up my arms and through my own core. I hope Bootknife still has a heart to destroy, and it seems that my hopes are not futile. The monster's eyes widen impossibly, and then simply go empty. There's no spluttering or cursing or even bloody foamy gasps. He is simply present in his body one moment, and absent, eternally absent, the next.

I pull back my sword and wipe the gore off the blade with Bootknife's clothing.

"Watch it, Forssy," Kintyre says, cleaning blood off his own blade before sheathing it, not at all affected by the fact that I just killed a man. "That's a bit bolder from you than I expected."

"The Shadow Hand has the right to execute as he sees fit," Pip says, and seems to relish the way that two sets of blue eyes pop at me.

"Shadow . . . wait, *you*?" Kintyre chokes.

"Do close your mouth, brother dear," I say. "Now is hardly the time."

Seventeen

I t isn't until several long hours later, when the sun is struggling to brighten the edges of this cotton-wrapped world, that I realize my cheek is bleeding. Or was bleeding, at any rate. And even then, it must be pointed out.

"Your face," Bevel says from somewhere beside me, and I don't know how long he's been sitting there, for me to have forgotten him entirely. His voice sounds close to my ear.

The warm touch of Bevel's fingers on my cheek startles me back to myself. Now that he has called my attention to it, it hurts like an absolute son of a bitch. My skin is freezing, and I seem to have been sitting beside the fire without properly wrapping up. I have lost the thread of myself in my desperate attempt to just *not think, not think, not think.*

Not think about Pip. Not think about what this means for my feelings for her. Not think about how horrible and scared and furious she feels. Not think about the fact that I have just killed a human being. Not think about the possibility that it might not be the last time I do so on this adventure. Not think about the fact that we have now completed five Stations, with Kintyre and his knife here, and that that means we are one step closer to sending Pip home. Not thinking about a life without Pip.

"It's sort of rakish, Forssy," Bevel says, and then there is something thick and wet and tingling against my skin. He caps the jar of healing ointment and returns it to his pack. "Or it will be rakish, when it heals up. Especially with this." He taps the hilt of my sword, making it rattle against the scabbard.

For a moment, I am caught in that liminal place between being Forsyth Turn and being the Shadow Hand. My face smells of thyme, lemon, menthol. A mixture that only Mother Mouth uses. Where he managed to get a jar of Mother Mouth's ointment, I don't know. Maybe Kintyre is on better terms with her than I thought. I let my gaze fall to my frigid fingers. Smoke is at my hip still.

I am both Turn and Hand, Forsyth and Shadow, and for the first time in my life, the dichotomy doesn't feel as though it is about to tear me in two.

"Thank you . . . Bevel," I say, making free of his first name without having been invited to do so. Bevel Dom has been calling me by my brother's nickname since he was a squeakling squire hard on Kintyre's heels, and I feel that perhaps I have finally earned the right to address him so. That he doesn't correct me confirms it.

I look around. We are back on the portico of King Chailin's tomb, the door still wide open and the fire, somehow, burning much higher than I managed to make it climb before. At some point, someone wandered back to fetch my Shadow chest. It seems foolish to haul the chest around now, when two of the four things it was meant to keep hidden are currently in use. I stand slowly, my knees popping in protest at the cold and the workout I just recently put my body through. I go to the chest and put the mask into the inner pocket of my travel robe, snugged up close against my heartbeat. There. Dauntless's cloak and tack can remain behind.

Bevel watches closely, his dark blue eyes narrowed, flicking over the Shadow's Mask, where it lies hidden against my ribs.

"Well, if that don't just beat all," he says. "Forsyth Turn, the Shadow Hand."

"Surprise," I say glumly. Bevel knows, and Kintyre knows, which means I've violated one of the few direct edicts the king has given me. Well, Pip has, at any rate. Which amounts to the same thing.

"It sure was," Bevel says. "Seems to be the moon for them."

"Agreed. And, speaking of surprises . . . you and Kintyre are still traveling together?"

Bevel looks down, focuses on putting away his healing kit. "It wasn't easy," Bevel says softly. "But . . . there was too much to throw away, you know? Too much . . . history." I realize, tellingly, that Bevel's usual Dom-amethyst short-robe has been traded in for a Turn-russet jerkin.

"I see." And I do. They have been good, close companions for so long. Surely, this one change in their relationship couldn't be the death of all that. "And where is my brother? More to the point, where is his knife?"

Bevel snorts and hunkers down by the fire, clearly happy that my question has closed the previous topic of conversation. I feel strangely compelled to threaten to break his legs if he hurts my brother, but it is a moot point after seventeen years. And, of course, if Bevel hurts my brother, Kintyre can very well break his legs without my help. Bevel pokes at something with a stick, and I realize that there are four leaf-wrapped parcels charring on the embers along the outer edge of the fire. Bevel and my brother providing dinner? Enough for all of us? That *is* surprising.

"Burying Bootknife," Bevel says. "Doing it all proper-like, too. Kin, that is, not the knife. Though that'd be a sight."

"Kintyre is burying Bootknife?" I don't know why the thought of my brother offering his slain enemies repose surprises me, but it does.

"What else are we meant to do?" Bevel asks, head cocked quizzically in that way that makes him look like the gimlet-eyed rodent I always compare him to in my head. "Leave him to rot? No, that's what makes zombies and tempts necromancers. Besides, the people who fight Kin and lose . . . they've got balls, yeah? So, they deserve a bit of a good rest. They've earned it, taking on Kintyre Turn."

"And Bevel Dom," I add, voice hushed.

He blushes slightly, almost fetchingly, and I am stunned again that Bevel is the sort of man who flushes when complimented. Or perhaps it is just that my brother doesn't do it often enough for me to have ever seen it happen. Though, I am as much to blame as Kintyre for that. I don't think I've ever complimented Bevel to his face before now.

"And where's Pip?" I add, because Bevel doesn't seem to want to talk about his joyful new ties to Kintyre, and because, coming to understand the depth of my own misery when I compare his luck to my own, I don't want to hear it.

"Miss Piper," he starts, and then stops. Instead, he jerks his head back toward the tomb. "The king is keeping her company. And he's the more jovial of the two."

"Have some consideration," I hiss at him. "She's been through a greater trauma than anything any of us has ever had to suffer. Be *kind* to her Bevel Dom, or I swear to the Great Writer that you will—"

He holds up a hand. "No need for threats, Shadow Hand. I can see how wrecked she is just as well as you. We'll tread carefully. I've no desire to be torn to ribbons by her tongue again."

Satisfied, I turn my back on the campfire and make my way to the end of the mausoleum. Pip is still balled up in the farthest corner of King Chailin's tomb. She has jammed herself there, covering every bit of herself with my cloak, a pile of black and gray cloth radiating misery.

"Pip?" I say softly. "May I sit?"

She makes no response. I dither for a moment, wondering if I should repeat the request and risk her denying it, or ignore her non-answer and sit away. Which would make her feel more comfortable? Which would make her feel less like I was writing my own desires over hers? *Augh! I am overthinking this. I think. Maybe?*

I sit slowly, giving her the chance to tell me to go, but she remains silent. I lean back against the sarcophagus, noting absently that someone has shoved the cover-stone back into place, giving Chailin his seclusion and us a respite from the reek of his rotting flesh.

It is cold in here, and I still haven't wrapped up. I'm not about to get up and abandon Pip to fetch a cloak, though, nor am I going to ask Bevel to bring me one and let him invade our privacy. So I sit and shiver in as much silence as I can force from my clenched jaw.

The silence stretches on, heavy and damp. Eventually, I gather the courage to say, "Pip. Pip, it's cold. Please. Look at me."

She shifts in her cloak, but only to pull it farther over her head.

"Tell me what to do," I say. "Tell me how I can help."

"There's nothing," she says, and her voice is raw and small and dry sounding. "This isn't something you can just *fix*."

"But it can be fixed?"

"I'm not broken," she protests. "I'm still whole."

"But you are hurting."

"Don't I have a right to?"

"I don't want you to."

"You don't get to dictate that!" she flares. She throws back the hood to glower at me.

"But I want to know. The things he said. That he taunted you with—"

"Were meant for me! You don't have to know *everything* about me, Forsyth. I'm allowed to have secrets! I don't exist *just for you*!"

"Not about this," I plead, hoping to import the gravitas of what I am feeling, the desperation. "Please. Not about this."

Pip's entire face narrows and shutters. Closes off. Closes up. "Fuck you," she says, and buries herself in the cloak again.

Her invective echoes around the marble, and I let it die off, stinging from the rebuke. I am an ass for pushing. Now is not the time. It will perhaps never be the time, and Pip is correct. I have no right to demand she relieve my curiosity. But it is also dangerous to be uninformed.

She sighs wetly and shifts again under the cloth.

"I'm sorry," I say gently. "I just despise seeing you suffer. At least come back to the campfire with me. Get warm. Eat something. We can . . . we can figure this out. Please."

"*Figure it out?*" she snarls, sitting up, righteous indignation painted across every line of her body, her expression. "What else is there to say? What's *left*? I have given so, so *fucking much* of my goddamned *life* to this . . . this stupid, undeserving, shallow world of yours, and I *can't*, Forsyth! *I can't* give it any more. It's taken everything. You all have. And I just . . . I just *can't*."

"No one is asking you to be cheerful or untouched tonight," I say softly. "No one is denying your right to be in pain. Just . . . do-don't ha-harm your-yourself fu-fu-further. P-p-please."

Carefully, in case she pulls away again, I raise my hand and wrap it around her wrist.

"I'm sorry," I say.

"It's not your fault," she replies, and slouches down. Defeated.

My body vibrates in what I realize is a slow, long shiver, the kind that comes from being dangerously close to hypothermia. Pip slides close to me and swings part of the cloak over my shoulders, tugging it into my lap. She presses close against me, her arm and leg a brand against my own. I curve into her body heat, but stop just shy of resting my head on her shoulder. It is too intimate.

"I am still sorry," I say. "And I don't say it to beg forgiveness for my part in it. What a horrendous thing to suffer."

"It was," she agrees softly. "And I defy anyone who uses something like this as back story to survive it better."

Pip shutters her expression, eyes cast down at my clumsy hand, which has somehow wrapped itself around hers. She untangles her fingers and looks away.

"You know the worst part of it?"

I make a noncommittal noise, certain that if I interrupt or answer either way, I may inadvertently derail her confession.

She buries her hands in her hair. "I hate that you fell for it. I hate that they dangled me, sex with me, like bait on a lure. I hate more that the way Elgar Reed wrote this world means that it was always going to work on you, too. But what I hate most is that I needed *you* to get me off the hook. It's that I didn't even get to save myself. After all of that, I still needed a man to save me. Men, plural. God."

Now I do rest my head on her shoulder, pushing my face against her neck. Not for sex, not for intimacy, but because it is the only close comfort I can offer her. Because she is warm, and I am sorry, and I don't know how to say it in any way besides the safe curve of my body around hers, guarding her from the world, shielding her from the hurt. She turns her own face to my neck, in turn, the fabric of the cloak settled around us like a cloud, and though she does not do it demonstratively, she cries. Hot saltwater prickles against my neck and the ointment on my cheek rubs against her ear, and it is horrible, the way her nails dig into my back and hold on.

Because I must be the last body in the world she wants to hold, to smell, to taste. My body is the one that was used to rape her. But mine is also the only one she knows she can trust.

I find myself in the midst of a very real conflict. My newfound enlightenment dictates that I must obey Pip's wishes in her recovery in every way. And yet I feel insecure, desperate to ensure that I do not lose her. I struggle with the noble desire to let her be whoever she wants to be, to do as she needs to do to heal herself, versus the fear of being left. And it is absurd, because what is the endpoint of this quest, but her departure?

"I'm sorry," I say again, apologizing for what, I'm not sure. For what happened to her? For what she suffered? For the way my creator wrote me? Wrote us? Wrote this whole, unfair world?

"I know," she sobs back. "I know."

When she stops crying, when her limbs are loose with misery and exhaustion and the wet patch on the skin of my neck has dried, she lets me help her to her feet. I detangle myself from the Shadow's Cloak and tug her gently toward the fire outside. It is less sheltered from the cool breeze, but the fire has grown high and inviting in our absence.

Bevel throws my heaviest cloak at me as soon as we're in the open air, and I swing it around my shoulders, grateful. There is also a scarf somewhere in my pack, and I before I can break off to go rummaging for it, I see that he's laid it by the fire to warm up. I sit down beside it and happily wind it around my neck. I can see why Kintyre appreciates traveling with Bevel so much. I can only wonder how considerate my brother is to Bevel in return.

Kintyre is sitting on the opposite side of Bevel, eyes intent on whatever it was in the leafy package, chewing. His other hand is dangerously high on Bevel's thigh, possessive and sweet in a way that I never expected from him. He too is wearing a modest jerkin in Turn-russet, rather than his usual ostentatious Sheil-purple one. He greets our entrance with a flick of the eyes and little else. *Boor.*

Pip sits on the other side of me, as far away from Bevel as the fire allows. The cloak settles around her like a storm cloud, and she pulls up the hood again to cover her face.

"Kintyre," I say, and his hand jumps away from Bevel's leg. The flash of hurt in the smaller man's eyes is brief, but sharp. "I need your knife, please," I say, holding out my hand.

"What for?" he challenges, puffing up, ready for another go-round with me. *Writer, why is everything a bloody competition with him? Why can't he ever just do as he is told?*

"We need it for our quest," Pip says softly. "It's one of the objects we need to collect."

I point to the mosaic just visible inside the tomb, the gold leaf on the wall reflecting our firelight. "The Blade that Never Fails," I say.

Kintyre hesitates.

"I'll give it back," I promise. "Though, I think I really ought to return it to King Chailin when this quest is through. Just to be on the safe side."

Kintyre balks. "It was stolen from a dead man?"

I find myself frowning. "You didn't take it from the sarcophagus?"

"I took it off Bootknife," Kintyre says. "After he carved up . . . um." He trails off, staring at me, remembering suddenly that I still have Smoke on my hip, jutting out behind me on the marble.

"The previous Shadow Hand," I supply. Every tendon and muscle in my body seems to be frozen with this horrible revelation. I shrug, trying to loosen up again, and make light of it: "I see. Well, Bootknife would be the sort of fellow who would want the best tool for his job. I suppose the world ought to thank you for relieving him of it."

"Dammit, Forssy, this isn't a joke!" Kintyre erupts. "I can't believe you let the king bully you into it! It's a blasted dangerous job!"

"Nobody bullied me!" I lob back. "The last Shadow Hand offered it to me—to *me*, you understand—and I accepted! He had faith in me! And I'm quite capable of taking care of myself. Have done so for the last seventeen years, while you've been off swanning around the world!"

"I wasn't swanning!" Kintyre snarled back, his pride challenged and his chest puffing up like a partridge. "I was doing a valuable service to the king!"

"Which anyone else could have done!" My fists curl on my thighs, and I want to hit him, Writer, how I want to hit the smug, self-important asshole! "Any farm boy or squire could have taken on those tasks, could have found your sword, could have become a hero! You had no right leaving Lysse! You had a *responsibility* to your Chipping!"

"Father had it in hand!"

"Father was a drunken idiot who spent more time slapping me around than with his books!" I bellow. Kintyre reels back as if I actually did strike him, eyes wide and all the color draining from his face. I should stop now, but I am feeling cruel and badly used, and I want him to *understand*, finally. "And you *left Mother and me* to that. Although, I suppose I should thank you—I wouldn't have been half the Shadow Hand I am today if I hadn't learned how to watch his body language, learned how to walk without making a sound, to defend myself without looking like I was."

"I . . . I didn't know . . ." Kintyre says.

"Would it have changed anything?" I sneer, resentful and hurt. He isn't supposed to *feel sorry* for me. I don't need his *pity*. I don't want it!

Just as Kintyre takes another breath to wind back up, Bevel reaches out and takes Kintyre's hand, and Kintyre deflates mulishly. I wish I could ground myself in the touch of Pip's hand. Instead, I flex my fingers across my knees, breathing deeply, trying to build a wall of calm in the face of my brother's ignorance.

Quietly, almost apologetically, Kintyre says: "I'm proud of you."

I scoff. Dishonesty sits uncomfortably in his voice.

"Forssy, I'm serious. No, you've been Shadow Hand for years, and I never knew. So, I'm proud of you, and the good you and your Men have done. And I . . . I wish I had known about Father." It's not an apology. But with Kintyre, it might be the closest thing I ever get.

"And you've done a really good job with the Chipping, too," Bevel adds. He scratches the back of his neck. "The school—that's fantastic. The people, they really like you, you know? Pointe, too. He's got so much respect for you. Doesn't let Kin get away with anything in Turnshire, you know?"

"I'm proud of you, too," Pip says softly, voice a mere whisper in the shadow of cloth around her face. She reaches out and squeezes my fingers once before retreating again.

I long to follow them with my own, to kiss the tips, and I can't, I *can't*, and I almost wish she hadn't touched me at all. The yearning is worse now, for having been granted a taste of her affection and having had it removed again so swiftly.

The back of my eyes burn, and so do my ears, my cheeks. I don't know what to say in the face of this influx of compliments. I didn't even know that Bevel and Kintyre paid attention to what I did as lordling. I didn't even know they *knew*. I duck my head and resume my calm breathing, because I am tempted, so tempted, to deny, to turn back their words, to dissemble. But I promised Pip—a lifetime ago, it seems now—to accept compliments, and to believe them.

To believe that my brother is proud of me.

Bevel, trying to break through the heavy atmosphere, hands one of the leaf-wrapped packages to me, and the other to Kintyre. Wordlessly, Kintyre holds it out to Pip, and Pip, equally wordlessly, takes it. I take my own from Bevel, accepting the temporary truce, and it is still hot; it singes my fingertips a little. It steams as I unwrap it, and

I am pleased to see that it is a sort of roll made up of meat wrapped around dried fruit. It is juicy and delicious, and I realize how hungry I am on the first bite.

"We've been doing this part of adventuring wrong," Pip moans around her own mouthful.

Bevel pinks again. "I've had a long time to practice. Luckily, Kin was willing to put up with my experimentation."

"And I'm lucky Bevel actually enjoys cooking and was willing to experiment," Kin says around a mouthful. "We got sick of standard travel fare pretty quick." He pats Bevel's thigh in a companionable manner, but then he leaves his hand there, sausage fingers curling into that tender, intimate place behind Bevel's knee. Bevel's expression blooms into something that resembles quiet happiness.

I look away, throat suddenly tight. I am pleased for them, for both of them, because happiness is a rare thing to find, and rarer still is a love who compliments you without overwhelming you, or being overwhelmed. But I am also bitterly jealous of their happiness, solely because it is in such juxtaposition to my own.

And I hate them suddenly. Before, they annoyed me, vexed me, embarrassed and infuriated me, but suddenly I *hate* Kintyre Turn and Bevel Dom. Because here they are, *again*, with everything I want for myself, everything I can't have, and they don't even know it. They don't even understand how much it makes me seethe to see them together, happy, in love; and I, I who have been the dutiful son, the excellent lordling, the proficient spymaster, I who finally managed to have an adventure of his own, and who, for such a short, beautiful time, was in love with a woman who loved me back, I have *nothing*.

And I am so horrifically jealous that they can have that and I cannot, that I stand. I am unable to look on them anymore, lest I say something that I'm going to regret, something that will destroy the tenuous truce between Kintyre and me; something which will hurt Bevel in ways that I don't want to and that he doesn't deserve.

"I need to clean up," I say, instead. "I just . . . I feel grimy."

"I felt that way after my first kill, too," Kintyre says.

I stare at him, uncertain how to respond. How did he know it was my first? And did Kintyre just admit to feeling filthy guilt? *Oh, Writer. Is he trying to* bond *with me?* Desperate to just *be away* before something horrible spills out of my mouth, I grab my pack and rush down to the river.

Pip doesn't follow me—of course she doesn't—so I strip perfunctorily and splash around in the shallow water. It is chilled, but not freezing, and I scrub under my arms, across my face, and I soap and rinse my hands over, and over, and over. The blood is gone—it's been gone for hours, since I wiped my sword and hands on Bootknife's shirt—but it still feels like it's there, digging in like shards of red glass between the whorls of my fingerprints.

When I am as clean as I am going to get without a proper bath, I pull out my shaving mirror. It is small, round, just enough for me to use to scrape at my sparse beard every few days. The water is colder than I'd like for a shave, and my cheeks still smooth enough that I am not annoyed by the prickle. I can wait. Besides, it's not as if Pip is going to complain of stubble-burn anymore.

I am on the verge of replacing the mirror in my pack when I realize that I also, accidentally, brought along the Endless Chalice. It was tied upside down to one of my pack straps, so that the saltwater could bead out onto the grass.

I untie it and turn it rightside up before I consciously decide to follow through on the half-formed notion that has popped into my head.

Dare I?

There is so much that Pip hasn't told me, so much she refuses to talk about, so much that she doesn't say. I am consumed by an overwhelming urge to *know*.

I dart a look around, but nobody has come to the riverbank, no one's eyes watch from the mist. Can I do it? Kintyre would, without a second thought, but in this instance, perhaps Kintyre is not the best role model for choice-making.

But then again, maybe he is. He wouldn't allow anything to remain between him and information vital for his quest, and I don't think I can allow it either. Even if Pip might hate me if she found out. And she was right; knowledge is my addiction, and I am desperate for a fix.

She hates me already, anyway. At least this way, it will be for something I've done, instead of something someone else has done to her through me.

And she is correct to call me a privileged asshole, because I have no right to do this after I have asked her and she has said no, but I *need, I need* to understand what she suffered at the hands of Bootknife and the Viceroy if I am to . . .

To win her back.

I can't do it—I can't send her back to her world hating mine, hating *me*. And I cannot stand to watch Bevel and Kintyre, knowing that Pip and I could have had that, *might* have had that for real, for ourselves, if the Viceroy hadn't interfered.

I *need* this.

So, feeling vindicated, and trepidation, and like the worst kind of slime, I pour the accumulated water from the Cup that Never Runs Dry onto the surface of the mirror and say Words of Scrying.

"Show me," I tell the mirror. "Show me the first moment Pip arrived in our world."

In the mirror, there is a bright flash of light and the impression of shattering glass. Sounds are distorted in scrying glasses, muffled. Like the reflection of a sound, instead of the sound itself. Rather like, now that I think on it, what Words must sound like to Pip—the aural equivalent of an ink drawing left out in the rain to puddle and run.

When the bright light clears, there is a young woman on the floor, hunched ungainly forward on the flats of her forearms, wrists up at an awkward angle, as if to spare herself a possible break as she skidded out. Her waist is twisted, her right leg uncomfortably under the left, practically perpendicular to her spine. She pulls herself upright gingerly, getting her knees under her.

It is Pip.

Her hair is shorn already, short like a page's, just kissing the nape of her neck and the bottom of her ears. She is clad like a boy, as well; knee high boots, tight canvas trousers not unlike my formal fencing-gear bottoms, a sort of v-necked chemise with buttons, and a jerkin with attached sleeves and a wide slit down the front like a house robe. In short, thrillingly indecent and entirely exotic.

My curious perusal of her clothing ends the minute she flicks her hair back from her face and I see the tear tracks on her cheeks. Mirror-Pip is shocked. She is terror-pale, and her lips are trembling. She is staring around at the dank, underground chamber with fear and confusion mixing like a storm across her features. The torchlight in the chamber is feeble, and I see her squint into the shadows.

One of the shadows obligingly detaches itself from the wall.

"*Hello?*" Mirror-Pip says. "*Who's there? I . . . I think there's been . . . I don't know what happened.*"

"*You fell,*" the shadow says, and goose bumps march up my spine. I've only heard the Viceroy's voice once before, while he was fleeing my Men, but it is a distinctive baritone: smooth as custard, sticky as honey, and as poisonous as venom.

He steps forward, all lean lines and slim-fitting jacket, a wave of dark hair and a face that would otherwise be attractive if it wasn't so void of humanity. His eyes flash gold in the lamplight, calculating, cataloging, ever moving, never stilling, eerie.

"*I don't remember,*" Pip says.

"*No, I expect not.*" He crouches and puts himself within her eye line as she struggles to sit upright. His thighs are on either side of her shoulders, obscenely close, but she doesn't seem to notice.

Her gaze catches on the gold of his jacket, on the spiking lapels that he favors, and sticks like a fly in amber on the glittering gold brooch at his throat. I can't see it from this angle, his shoulders are blocking my view, but I can see Pip's expression morph as she recognizes it.

Wonder. That same childlike awe. A small smile. A sudden relaxation of the shoulders, because she thinks she knows what is happening. What it all means.

My poor Pip!

She grins up at his face, logic clicking into place, only it's wrong, it's all wrong, and perhaps she knows it, but her mind is scrambling for the most realistic answer, because the easiest one can't possibly be correct. Reality doesn't work that way. "*Sorry, sorry. Did I interrupt a cover shoot?*"

The Viceroy shakes his head. "*Why would you think that?*"

"*Well, you're Drew Mayfair, aren't you? And you're all done up in your costume, so . . . oh, but I don't remember walking into. . . . Dammit, what happened? How did I get here?*"

"*I brought you here. You fell.*"

A slow blink, and confusion writing worry onto Pip's brow. "*No, I don't think so.*"

"*Who am I?*" the Viceroy asks. "*Name me.*"

"*Drew Mayfair.*"

He pulls her upright, off balance on her knees, and shakes her once. "*No.*"

"*You're Drew Mayfair, the cover model from all the books. I know you.*"

He shakes her again. "*No. Name me.*"

The awe falls away, and Pip starts to look scared. Her gaze flickers from his brooch to his face, and suddenly, she curls her arms back, as if she could bat his grasp away and hold her wrists above her face to protect it. A dark stain cuts through the cuffs of her strange, too-open jerkin, and I realize with a start that her wrists are bleeding. She must have rubbed the skin off as she fell into the harsh dirt.

"*No,*" she says. "*No, I won't. This isn't possible.*"

He shakes her harder, and even in the scrying mirror, I hear the clack of her teeth slamming together. "*I have called you down; you will do my bidding! Name me!*"

She closes her eyes and shakes her head. "*This is a photo shoot, you're just in character, you're trying to prank me. This isn't real. Stop it, you're scaring me!*"

"*Name me.*"

"*Let me go!*"

"*Name me!*"

"*Stop it, you're hurting me!*"

"*Name me!*"

"*The Viceroy!*" Pip screams.

He lets her go, and she sags backward, eyes round with horror, mouth a slack hole. She cradles her wrists over her heart and swallows hard, several times.

"*Yes*," the Viceroy hisses. He snaps his fingers, and another shadow peels out of the darkness. I know this silhouette as well, and it appears that even back then, Pip did too, for she shrinks into herself the way a mouse does to avoid the gaze of a night time predator.

"*And him?*" The Viceroy asks.

"*Bootknife?*" Pip whispers.

"*Very good. Bootknife, our new friend is hurt. Bind her wounds, please.*"

The Viceroy turns his back and smiles. His face is even more hateful to me, then, because he looks content. He looks smug. His horrible knife-slice features, that mop of dirty black hair, all of it is more terrible because he looks *pleased*.

Behind him, Pip screams again as Bootknife shoves her onto her back, and, with the slim silver knife for which he was named, cuts away both her jacket and her shirt. Beneath is a strange contraption that hugs her breasts, like a small corset set too high up, and this Bootknife leaves. He rolls Pip from left to right, carefully shredding her clothing without cutting her skin, avoiding the blows she tries to rain onto his face and settling his full weight over her pelvis so she cannot throw him off.

Bootknife tips Pip onto her stomach, pressing her face into the dirt. She kicks—oh, how she kicks—but Bootknife is not a small man, and when he is settled on the small of her back, she lets out a grunt and goes still.

Bootknife rips strips from Pip's destroyed chemise and wraps them around her wrists, first binding the wounds, and then binding her arms together before her like a captured lamb.

He rises, and Pip struggles back to her knees, panting heavily and crying as quietly as possible, teeth cutting white crescents into her lip. How my heart aches. How I long to reach through the mirror and wrap her in my arms, to shield her from this. My poor, abused, strong Pip.

The Viceroy turns to face her again, hands clasped casually behind his belt, and leans down to meet her eyes, bends double at the waist like an acrobat. Or a snake.

"*You know about me. About all of us. I brought you here because I want to know what you know. Tell me.*"

Pip sucks her lips in between her teeth and sets her chin at that defiant angle that I know so well and find so endearing. To see her make such a gesture here, before the Viceroy, is like a punch to the stomach. I find myself gasping in admiration.

"*You're a Reader,*" he says. "*Tell me about what you read.*"

Pip bites her lips harder and shakes her head side to side. "*No. If you're really him, I won't. I won't help you. I can't. Never.*"

"*Tell me the name of our book,*" the Viceroy snarls.

Pip clenches her jaw and closes her eyes. The backhand across the face is not unexpected, at least from my end, but Pip looks startled. I wonder if she'd ever been hit before. She probes her cheek with her tongue and spits blood onto the dirt floor.

The Viceroy sneers and points to Bootknife. "*If you know who he is, then you know what he likes to do to people who do not answer.*"

Pip pales so suddenly it is as if she had been bitten by a fairy. Her whole face goes parchment white. She nods, once. Bootknife paces around the two of them like a hungry wolf pup, grinning and picking his teeth with his horrible blade.

"*Tell me the name of our book*," the Viceroy demands.

Pip says nothing. In front of her, she wrings her hands, trying to free her wrists, but the binding doesn't budge.

"*Tell me!*" the Viceroy shrieks.

Pip flinches back, and then ducks her head, contrite. She makes a gesture as if she wants him to lean close, to whisper, and I see what she is about to do a half second before it happens. She has loosened a strip of the fabric between her hands, and as soon as the Viceroy's head is beside her own, she has it up around his neck in a flash and is pulling.

She spins around behind him, his shoulders between her legs, and she *pulls*. The Viceroy flops to the ground like a landed fish, face already going purple as he struggles for air, filthy fingers scrabbling at the fabric.

He is laughing. The lunatic is actually suffocating and *laughing*.

"*And now . . . now what?*" he hisses.

"*I will throttle you*," Pip snarls. "*I'll save Kintyre the trouble!*"

Then, of course, Bootknife's blade is at her throat, the glinting tip pressed just enough into the soft spot below her chin to drag a pearl of blood to the surface.

"*I'll carve you a new smile if you don't let go,*" Boot-knife whispers into her ear, his free hand coming up to steal around the bottom of her throat. It slides up to wrap into the short hair at the nape of her neck. He curls his fingers in, and Pip winces.

"*You'll carve me anyway, even if I do,*" she hisses back. "*Might as well do your world a public service and take this son of a bitch with me.*"

Bootknife laughs into her ear, and Pip screws her eyes shut and wrenches back harder on her improvised garrote. The Viceroy wheezes, and Pip's arms begin to shake. I find myself rooting for her, but even as I am, I can see her resolve crumbling. Her expression of determination is slowly eroding away into moral agony, and I can see the question she is thinking as clear on her face as if it had been painted there.

"Can I do it?" she is asking herself.

The answer, it turns out, as I knew it must, is "no."

She sags backward, into Bootknife's waiting arms, and releases her hold on the Viceroy. He struggles to his feet, hissing and spitting, face dark with rage and lack of air.

"*I hope you're done trying to prove your little point!*" He coughs, and he sounds as if a bullfrog has taken up residence in his throat. "*Tell me the name of the book!*"

Pip only relaxes more in Bootknife's grip, as if leaning against a lover in a moment of stolen quietude. She glares up at the Viceroy, impassive and defiant in her determination to do and say nothing.

"*Oh, so that is how it is going to be?*" the Viceroy asks. "*Very well. Your choice. Bootknife, darling . . . up-stairs. The Rose Room, I think. Don't you?*" He turns in a dramatic swirl of glittering gold and black, and stalks out of the ring of light cast by the torches. The darkness swallows him back up.

"*Oh, this is going to be fun!*" Bootknife howls, redoubling his grip on Pip's hair and dragging her by it, out of the view of the scrying mirror.

The vision fades, and I sit back away from the glass, the chill echo of fear and grief playing across my skin. Something hot and wet lands on my arm, and I let my burning eyes slide downward to catalog it.

It is a tear. I am crying.

Oh, my poor, strong, incredible, heroic *Pip*.

Eighteen

he first thing I hear as I near the campfire is Kintyre's voice: "Eighteen days left?"

"Blimey," Bevel adds. "And you just have to get to . . . ?"

The sound of paper rustling drifts in the mist, and I can well imagine Pip spreading out her Excel to show them. "The Desk that Never Rots. Oh. A bit clunky, that epithet."

"I can't read this," Bevel says.

"It's written in my alphabet."

Kintyre makes a sort of confused sound that I haven't heard from him since we were boys. "But you're nearly done, and you're only on day forty-two?"

"Incredible what can happen when you research and *plan* a quest, instead of just heading out and bashing things, eh?" Pip is smug when she answers, and it is good to hear something beyond detached suffering in her voice, even if she is deliberately winding my brother up.

I stop a few paces away, still hidden by the mist, to see how Kintyre will reply.

"Yeah, well. Leave it to my brother, then, to take all the fun out of it." He sounds sullen.

Pip actually makes an aborted sound that might have been the beginnings of a laugh. "Roaming the wilds, fighting trolls and battling monsters and duplicitous princesses is 'fun'?"

"Part of it," Bevel says. "The rest of it is the adventure, you know? Never sure where you're going to go next, where the next step will take you. What lands you'll see. What people you'll meet! What things you'll learn!"

Pip hums. "Yes, I can see the appeal. But we are on a bit of a . . . deadline." There's a sound, like uncomfortable shifting from all three of them: shifting fabric, a cleared throat, an aborted attempt to speak before Bevel finally groans.

"You can't stay?" Bevel finally asks, breaking the silence.

I can't help my swiftly indrawn breath, and close my lips around the hiss, hoping none of them heard it.

Because, yes, Bevel, yes, ask her—ask the thing that I cannot, dare not. Ask, and make her answer.

Nobody calls out, so perhaps I am safe. I shouldn't eavesdrop. I should go up there, be brave, face this conversation myself, but I am still too shaken by what I saw in the mirror, and too curious as to how Pip will answer. I know how I *want* her to answer, but what will she say? Will she lie?

"I can't," she says. "I don't . . . I would have said before that it's because I can't, I can't taint this world. But now, it's because I don't *want* to."

I'm sure one of them must hear the crunch of the frosted grass as I stagger back a step. The pain that blossoms under my sternum is sudden but not entirely unexpected. Still, nobody calls my name. Nobody comes.

"Huh," Kintyre says. "That'll shatter Forssy."

"As if you're concerned about him!" Pip snaps.

Kintyre makes another confused sound. "Why wouldn't I be concerned?"

Pip scoffs. There is another pregnant pause, and I twist my hands around the straps of my sack, dithering. I want to see his face, I need to know what his expression is betraying, but I am afraid. I am afraid of what I'll see, and I am afraid that, if I interrupt now, Kintyre will shut down and not explain. And I *need* him to explain. I need to *hear* it.

Something that I can't see happens, an exchange of expressions and eyebrow waggles and stretching or pouting lips. A whole conversation happens in the silence that strains across the star-dappled, mist-muffled sky.

"You actually do like him," Pip says, at length. Her voice is low and breathless with awe.

"Of course I do," Kintyre allows, and his tone says, without saying: *You're stupid.* "He's my baby brother."

They are discussing me, I think all of a sudden, which is absurd. Of course they are. I can hear them, but I cannot fathom it. Why? What is appealing about me? Why am I the center of their discussion? Is it only because they all know me, that I am the only thing, really, that they have in common?

Imagine, anyone at all deciding that Forsyth Turn is a worthy topic of discussion!

"Well, you sure don't act like you like him when you're around him," Pip snaps.

I edge closer, crouching around the side of the portico to peer over the steps at their faces in the orange glow of the flames. Kintyre shifts on his bedding, looking distinctly uncomfortable. He shoots a desperate look at Bevel, who shakes his head stoically and purses his chapped lips. He's not rescuing Kintyre this time.

My brother sighs, sounding put upon. His hands, however, have wound themselves around and around the tail of his shirt, bunching and twisting the fabric between white fingers and knuckles. I realize, with a start, that he is *embarrassed.*

"Our father wasn't very . . . fond," he says, pursing his lips around the word as if it were sour.

Pip snorts. "The alcoholic, abusive father background shtick. I wonder if men get as annoyed with the lack of depth in fictional father characters as women do with the virgin-or-harlot trope. I mean, not every father in the world is an unmitigated asshole or Clark Kent. There's gotta be something in the middle."

"Who?" Bevel asks.

"Never mind. How is this the elder Master Turn's fault?"

Kintyre clears his throat. "He showed his sons affection in only the roughest sense. Claps on the back, carousing, shouted insults. Father was a soldier first and a lordling, second. He took mastery of the Chipping only when *his* father forced it on him. Perhaps if Mother had survived the fever, there would have been some more . . . kindness." He tugs on his ponytail, fussing over the broken ends of his hair as an excuse to avoid Pip's gaze. "It's just . . . Forssy uses these big, stilted words that I don't understand and makes pronouncements on what you're going to do simply because it's what's good for you. He never asks, he just *tells*. I hate it." His face screws up. "I know he means well. It just . . . drives me mad when I go home. I don't want to fight with him all the time. So I don't. Go home, that is."

"You're not perfect yourself," Bevel says, and lays his hand on my brother's thigh. "You scrunch your feelings so far down inside of you that you try to pretend they don't even exist. And then, when you get mad, or hurt, you blow up, and it surprises you that you feel so much, all at once."

Kintyre turns an affectionate glance to Bevel. "And you wear every emotion and thought on your face. I always know what you're feeling."

"Not always," Bevel retorts indulgently. "Took Pip telling you straight out for you to know my most hidden feelings."

Kintyre curls himself down and ghosts a kiss against Bevel's mouth. Bevel makes a noise of satisfaction, a purr in the back of his throat, as if he were part leo-kin. Jealousy, sharp and cruel, stabs at my gut. I bite my lip to keep all sound in. Pip just looks away, misery painting her skin pale in the firelight.

"That doesn't answer my question," Pip says, after giving them enough time to remember they have company.

Kintyre shrugs. "He's my brother. He's smart. He's . . . my *brother*. We're all we've got. What else can I say?"

"Why haven't you said any of this to Forsyth?"

"It's hard," Kintyre wheedles, and I feel myself bristle.

Hard! Hard to tell your brother you like him! Hard to behave as if you do like him while in his presence, instead of just treating his home like any other rough waystation or taverna on the road! Hard to respect him! Ha!

"It's not that hard," Pip counters, speaking my own thoughts. "You could, I don't know, be kind to him when you see him. Ask him about his work. Respect his household and his guests." A pointed glare, and Kintyre resumes twisting his shirt. Bevel's ears go pink again.

Kintyre is right. His companion is terribly easy to read—Bevel is currently remembering the disaster of a dinner party, and his role in causing said disaster.

"We are sorry," he mumbles. "We behaved . . . inappropriately."

"If you're aware that you did, why did you do it in the first place?" Pip asks, the line of her shoulders and the tone of her voice screaming exasperation.

"Because Forssy's skin is so thin," Kintyre says. "Because it's fun to wind him up."

"He doesn't think so," Pip snaps. "I don't think so, either."

"I was trying to toughen him up," Kintyre says, defensive. "He was always into such . . . smart things. Books and maps and studying things. It made Father think he was a sissy. Made him . . . a target, I guess."

"There's nothing wrong with Forsyth," Pip says. "And there's nothing wrong with being cerebral instead of physical, or being an introvert instead of an extrovert. It's just how he's built. You have to accept that."

"He has to—"

"He doesn't *have* to do anything," Pip interrupts. "Except to accept your faults and work harder to make you understand that he loves you, too."

"Does he?" Kintyre challenges. "He's certainly never told me he's proud of anything I've accomplished! None of my tapestries are on display in the family hall! He doesn't ask Bevel to tell any stories."

"Probably because he's sick of hearing them. He has them, though. Every one, every single scroll—the expensive illustrated ones, too. They're in his library."

"He does?" Bevel squeaks. "Really? That's . . . that's surprising. And, um, flattering."

"He *is* proud that his brother is a hero," Pip presses. "He just wishes you'd let him get a word in edgewise."

"I would if he would ever get a damn word out!" Kintyre challenges. "He just stoops and stutters like a stupid old man, and it drives me mad! And how do you know how so much about my brother, huh? Just because you've slept together?"

"Kintyre, hush!" Bevel scolds.

I feel my own stomach twist at the mention of our forced intimacies. This is *not acceptable*. But before I can stand and begin to scold, Pip jumps up and points a sharp, shaking finger at his face. The gesture is doubly dramatic in the firelight, with the Shadow's Cloak billowing around her like smoke.

"We've known each other for months," Pip says. "We've spent most of that together. And unlike *you* with *your conquests*, I actually *talked* to him after! You can't say the same. I've seen the look in his eyes when he talks about you. He *is* proud, and when you come in and shout him down and get all me-me-me, he gets angry, and he can't say anything."

"Well, he doesn't *listen*."

"He listens fine. Do you listen back?"

"Of course I do!"

Pip laughs. "You don't even know what you've done to him, do you?"

"What have I done?" Kintyre sneers. "Please, go on. Tell me how I've ruined my brother, if you know him so well."

"You've made him feel *worthless*, that's what you've done," Pip says. "And I hope you're happy about it. Because all that stuff you don't like about him? The lack of self-confidence and the stuttering and the stooping? That's your fucking *fault*. You and your useless father."

That's it. I've heard enough. I cannot let Kintyre embarrass himself further. And I cannot let Pip defend my honor when I should be doing it for myself.

I step from between the pillars of the portico, back into the firelight, and wait for them to notice me. Kintyre and Bevel's gazes hop over to me immediately, their warrior's skills serving them well, and Pip's follow a fraction of a second later when she realizes they're looking at something behind her.

"Forsyth!" Kintyre exclaims, dropping his shirt tails and trying to smooth them out against his wide thighs. "Er . . ."

"How much did you hear?" Pip asks, lethally calm. Her eyes slide back to Kintyre, and I am warmed to see that the judging expression in them is leveled at him, and not me.

"A-a-all of it-t, I th-think," I say. "E-e-enough, a-at any ra-rate."

Bevel turns to stare at Kintyre, and my brother is gawping at me like I am one of his slain monsters returned to life. Then, surprisingly, Bevel kicks Kintyre sharply in the calf. Kintyre shoots to his feet at the reproach and skirts around the fire to stand directly before me. I have to crane my head back to meet his eyes. It occurs to me, for the first time, that we have the exact same expressions when we're nervous and choosing our words carefully. I have seen that same slight dip of the eyebrows, the stubborn thrust of his chin in my mirror at home many times before.

And then, without any warning, he launches himself at me. I put up my hands to defend against the attack, but he wraps his arms around my back at the elbows and *squeezes*, and I am unable to get my hands up to protect my face. I think he is going to bite my ear or my neck, because he sticks his face right into the hollow behind my jaw and presses his cheek against my hair. And then he doesn't move at all, save to incrementally increase the pressure of his hold.

Fuck, I think, feeling that Pip's favorite expletive is entirely appropriate. *He's hugging me!*

Carefully, slowly, in case I am wrong, I raise my own arms at the elbows and wrap my skinny hands around the small of his back. He gives an all-over shudder when my palms settle against him, and with horror, I wonder if he's begun to cry. The back of my neck is damp with his moist breath, so I can't tell if there are tears there, too.

"I'm sorry, Forsyth," he mutters against my skin. "I'm so sorry. I'm sorry."

"Y-y-es, well," I bluster, because I have no words, *literally* no words to express how I am feeling right now.

I want to scream. I want to punch him. I want to demand he tell me why it took this long, why it took the scathing accusations of a woman who isn't even a part of our family—not the way Bevel is— to force him to admit the way he feels about me. To force him to begin to evaluate his behavior over the last two decades.

I want to yell, to tell him everything I've kept bottled up since childhood. I want to tell him that he is my older brother and he is supposed to *love* me. He was supposed to *protect* me, that's the way of the world, that's how it's supposed to *go*. He is my brother, so he is supposed to defend me against those who attack me, either with blades or words; that is his duty.

And that he *didn't*.

That it hurt all the more when he *joined* my tormentors instead of chasing them off. That he abandoned me with our callous father's heavy hand when he went off to have his adventures, and that it made me feel *worthless*.

That it made me feel even more worthless when he came back from those adventures with Bevel Dom in the place that ought to have been mine—squire, apprentice, eventually partner in arms and friend; stupid, stolid Bevel and his dishwater hair and hedgehoggy eyes and unwavering loyalty. I want to tell him that I could have been that loyal, that good, if I had only been given the *chance*.

I want to tell him that he is my brother, and I love him anyway, and he is forgiven.

I want to tell him to get out of my sight and never, *ever* try to see me or talk to me again.

I want to tell him to shove his apologies up his ass, and that he can suffer as I have suffered. I want to tell him to go throw himself on his sword.

Instead, I say the only thing I can: "Right. Yes. Of course. You can let go of me, now, Kintyre. I'd quite like to have my feet back on the ground, please."

I shutter my expression in time for him to meet my impassive Shadow Hand mask when he sets me down and pulls back. He flinches, as if the set of my mouth was a slap across his face, and I feel vindictively pleased by his miserable slump.

Pip is watching my face closely, her expression as closed and unreadable as my own; but her hands betray her. They are folded together between her knees, her knuckles white. She is anxious, and hopeful. She wants me to relent, to accept Kintyre's apology and work with him to repair our broken filial bond.

I am feeling so much, am so overwhelmed, that I cannot feel a thing. It is like a whirling storm behind my larynx, and I fear that, if I open my mouth, it will all come out in a swirling, screaming mass.

I will try to say all of it, and, in doing so, say nothing. And ruin *everything*.

Until I've had the time to sort out exactly what I would like to say or do next, it is best that I say nothing. I nod slowly, once, to Kintyre, and then I step out of the circle of his arms and make my way over to my bedroll. My body is cold where the heat of his touch vanishes, and my knees shake with unspoken emotion, but I manage to make my steady way there and fold myself into the blanket.

Then I pull it over my head and bite down hard on my bottom lip and hope against hope that the crackle of the fire is enough to muffle the sounds of the rolling sobs that wrack me.

In the morning, Bevel announces their intentions to join us for the rest of the quest, and I admit that I am not surprised by the assumption that they would be welcome. Of course they *are*, the more party members, the safer we are, but it is the lack of asking that rankles.

The skin around my eyes is raw and tender to the touch, and probably red enough that they can all see what I did when I went to bed.

My cheek is equally tender, warm from the ointment and the healing, and itchy as all hell. Is this how it had been for Pip, but all over her back? I can't imagine how she didn't go mad, trying not to scratch.

Pip had slept on the far side of the fire from me, Kintyre and Bevel between us. I had woken groping across the marble for her, missing her warmth and the comforting wonder of waking beside—and entangled with—another human being.

I am torn between telling Bevel and Kintyre to shove off, that this is my quest and I don't want them with us, and thanking them for staying, because they know better than I do what needs to be done. If news of Bootknife's death hasn't reached the Viceroy already, then it will soon, and I would much rather have my brother and his Foesmiter between me and that maniac. But Kintyre and Bevel are also between me and Pip, and if they weren't here, I might manage to have a private conversation with her, see if I can smooth things over. But then again, perhaps *not* being alone with me is the best thing for her, for the healing process, because of what happened and what the sight of me must represent for her.

Ugh! Too many thoughts!

In the end, it's all moot anyway, because there is literally nothing I can do, perhaps beyond the devious use of some Words, to keep Kintyre and Bevel from following us to the next Station.

And so, we begin the day with another of Bevel's stunning culinary masterpieces. For all that I am annoyed by their closeness, I am inordinately pleased that Bevel has chosen to take over the preparation of our meals. While Pip and I had done our best, Bevel's cuisine is extremely delicious, and makes use of the abundance of wild vegetation en route. I haven't had as much time as Bevel to study which plants are edible, and which are poisonous; which have tuber roots that can be cooked; which have berries, and how to prepare them; and which nuts are easy to harvest and consume on horseback.

Morning ablutions are done swiftly in the stream. Pip takes the first turn, alone, and I desperately do not want to her to go, but Kintyre holds me back with one meaty paw on my shoulder and a sad, slow headshake. "Give her some breathing room," he suggests.

Loathe as I am to follow any advice given to me by my brother, Bevel backs him up, and so I stay. I sit stiffly on the steps of the portico, one hand on Smoke's hilt, one ear turned toward the water, honed to the distant splashes and the soft, sharp gasps and cusses the chill of the stream wrings from Pip. Bevel laughs at me, dark eyes dancing, but the laughter is, for once, not cruel.

Is it that Bevel has ceased teasing? Or is it that my perception of Bevel has shifted?

Pip comes back from the stream with dripping hair, wringing it out over her shoulder as she walks, her teeth chattering. Her lips are vaguely blue, and if I were still her lover, I would go over and wrap her in my arms, chafe them to get the blood flowing, and kiss the life back into her mouth. Instead, I stand, sweep my pack into my arms, tighten my sword belt buckle, and make my silent way past her and toward the stream, head held high for fear of meeting her eyes and sending her a pleading look that becomes neither the Lordling of a Chipping nor the Shadow Hand.

Kin says something about my sword as I go, but I don't care to hear it. It is probably lewd, at any rate. I wash perfunctorily, especially since I decided I didn't need a shave yesterday, and I am barely on my way back to camp when the two naked forms of Kintyre and Bevel go whizzing by, laughing uproariously and splashing affectionately.

The jealousy of yesterday curdles into a loathing that resembles the hatred I'd felt toward Kintyre and Bevel's past visits to Turn Hall. How *dare* they play, and feel joy, and be in love when I—the good son, the wise son—suffer in misery!

Pip preoccupies herself with packing up her back and coddling Karl.

When I am dressed—and wrapped once again in my scarf and the spare cloak, leaving the Shadow Cloak for Pip—I make my way over to the horses to similarly spoil Dauntless. He is a very grateful recipient of my attentions and currycomb, his mane damp from the perpetual mist and his skin bunching and shivering, communicating quite clearly how ready he is to be clear of here. Kintyre and Bevel rode no horses, but the ghost of Stormbearer, Kintyre's lost steed, seems to linger around the camp. I never got the full story of the horse's glorious last hours, but I remember very keenly the way Kintyre and I had climbed the paddock fence as children to watch Stormbearer's late mother grunt, and pace, and squat, and finally push the shaky dark foal out. Dauntless had come of the same dam several years later, though of a more pedestrian breed of stud.

A sharp sadness breaks against my ribs like a cresting wave, and I swallow hard. *Poor, loyal Stormbearer.*

I turn to Pip to share this anecdote with her, to expand her understanding of the world of the Writer. "Pip—" I begin, but she raises a hand without turning her face to me.

"Not yet," is all she says. Then she presses her forehead against Karl's wide cheek, and I am struck, for the first time, with jealousy for a horse.

Between Pip's reluctance to speak and the delighted laughter of my brother and his lover, I am left grinding my teeth and swallowing back both a sour expression and a sour taste. I spend the remainder of the time packing Bevel and Kintyre's gear, leaving out the garments that smell the least offensive. I don't even know if they brought towels or anything to cover their modesty to the riverbank, and have to clamp down on the reflexive urge to yell down to the water and reprimand my brother for his lack of forethought, *again*.

I disassemble the fire circle, close up the tomb, and then sit on the steps investigating a block of wood that I found amid the jumble of my brother's things. After a cursory glance, I realize that it is the beginnings of a wood carving stamp. Bevel's scrolls are adorned with such illustrations, and it occurs for me that, for the first time, they are the product of Kintyre Turn, and not, as I'd thought, the Bynnbakker scribe-house that manufactures copies of Bevel's stories.

When Kintyre and Bevel return, flushed with the cold and laughter, wrapped only in their cloaks and leaving very little to my imagination, Kintyre makes an annoyed sound. "Oh look, Forssy's packed for us. Just like him to be so boss—"

Bevel grabs Kintyre by the ponytail and stops his insult with a kiss, which I, not that anyone asks me, think savors too much of a reward and too little of a reproach. All the same, Bevel dons the clothing I left out for him. Kintyre accepts all but the shirt and goes back into his pack for one that is visibly no different to me than the one I laid out. This is Kintyre being contrary just to be contrary, and I open my mouth to harangue him about it, but Pip clears her throat pointedly and *looks* at me. I've become quite intimate with that look these last few weeks and snap my mouth shut. It is more reflex than conscious choice, and I reflect with only the slightest resentment that I have been well trained.

Pip obviously wants me to consider my words before I speak, and I cast my mind back to decipher what it is that I was about to say that would have caused strife. It would have been nothing that I have not said to Kintyre before, and—oh. Yes. Last night's eavesdropped conversation. Kintyre resents my "bossy" ways, and I was just about to . . . well. That's uncomfortable.

Rather than saying anything at all, I shoot Pip a return look which I hope conveys my gratitude and hoist my pack up to buckle it onto Dauntless's saddle. Kintyre and Bevel, with many years of practice, are ready to go before Pip and I, despite their later start. With Kintyre and Bevel on foot, we tie their packs to Karl and Dauntless and take to walking with them.

We emerge from the Valley around noon, the mist behind us and the sun burning away the lingering dampness from our hair and clothing. The horses perk up, heads high and steps dancing, and it seems that they are as pleased to be away from the depressive atmosphere of the tombs as we are.

A quick stop to consult the Excel and my map, and for Bevel to distribute venison jerky with a thoughtless ease that makes me think this is his "we're taking a rest" habit, and we are headed down the road to the narrow strip of Stoat Forest that marches up to meet the foothills of the Cinch Mountains.

The conversation between us as we ride remains stilted and mostly absent. Pip spends much of the time chewing her bottom lip, thinking. What I wouldn't give for a Deal-Maker spirit of my own, so I could bargain to know her thoughts. Though, knowing Deal-Makers, the price would be something so high, something so precious, that someone such as I could never hope to pay it. Pip's lip itself has grown chapped, red with sores and last night's scab, and I want to kiss them away, kiss her to keep her from harming herself further. But every time I touch her, even accidentally, she flinches so violently that Karl snorts and dances away.

We pass into the cool darkness of the trees a few hours before sunset. There is a debate between Kintyre and Bevel about whether it is better to turn back and camp on the forest's edge, where the sightlines are clearer, or whether it is better to do so in the shelter of the forest. Normally, I would be angry with Kintyre for presuming to speak for me, to make decisions for me, but right now, I do not have the capacity to care. I am tired, footsore, and heart-weary. Or maybe just plain weary.

All I want right now is some wine, my bedroll, and Pip to curl and cuddle against me. As we're out of wine, and the latter is out of the question, I will have to content myself with just the bedroll. If only our companions could decide where it should go.

The forest path is narrow, and the sunlight slants amber and gold through the leaves. We walk in single file with me at the head and Kintyre at the tail, Pip and Bevel between us. Which, in retrospect, was a foolish thing to do.

When the rogue steps out from between the trees and blocks my way, I can only stop in my tracks, sigh, and pinch the bridge of my nose. His sword is up, the blade pocked with rust, and he has the hood of his dagged-hem leather cowl pulled theatrically low over his brow. There seems to be an overabundance of buckles on his high boots and a tangle of belts slung across his narrow hips, and I wonder how he stalks through the forest without getting caught in the brambles with every step. Obviously, he's learned how to walk softly enough that all the metal on his clothing doesn't click and give him away.

All in all, he's the most clichéd portrait of a bandit I have ever had the misfortune to meet.

Usually, King Carvel's rangers deal with such brigands, keeping the roads clear for travelers. Whoever is meant to be patrolling Stoat Forest just earned himself a very severe demotion.

The rogue says nothing, just stands there looking threatening, and, from the back of the line, I hear Kintyre and Bevel's nattering cut off and the soft, unmistakable metallic hiss of Foesmiter being unsheathed.

"Forssy?" Kin asks from behind me.

"A thief, I assume," I answer back.

The man before me twitches, his sword wavering.

A sort of choked howl breaks across the still air of the forest, and I realize that it is Bevel laughing, and trying not to. "A thief!" he chortles. "Really? Let me see!"

He crashes through the underbrush to stand beside me, and now the rogue's posture goes tense. He takes a step back, sword tip flicking between me and Bevel.

"Your money, or your lives," the rogue intones, and his voice is low, deliberately low and gravelly, and he sounds like a boy playacting at being a man.

This sends Bevel into another fit of poorly contained hysterics, and he has his hand clapped over his mouth, his face going red behind it. "Come on, boy!" he giggles. "This is something you want to do, here? Now?"

The rogue wavers.

"I must point out something very pertinent," I say, flicking back the edge of my cloak so the unmistakable hilt of Smoke—the Shadow Hand's sword—is visible. The rogue makes a choking noise that, unlike Bevel's, has nothing to do with him laughing. "And, of course, this man beside me is Sir Bevel Dom."

The rogue actually stumbles backward this time, his hood sliding back to reveal a face dark with scruff and dirt, and pale with realization.

"I—I . . ." he says.

"Let us pass, young man, and we will all completely forget that this ever happened," I say, voice carefully modulated to remain soft and calm. Behind me, Dauntless whickers and noses my shoulder, bored.

Instead of taking me up on the offer, the idiot raises his sword at Bevel.

"No," I say. "That is not the wise choice."

"Your money, or your lives," the rogue demands again.

"Listen," Pip pipes up, and I turn my head slightly to see that she's got herself half up a tree beside the path in order to see what's going on, Karl's reins wrapped loosely around a nearby limb. "Whatever you're stealing for—to feed your family, or to buy medicine for your ailing mother, or to pay off ruffians threatening to burn your village's crops—trust me when I say that this is not a fight you want to have. You will not win it. Why not let us help you instead?"

"Miss Piper," Kintyre says. "A side-quest?"

"We have seventeen days," Pip replies. "Surely there's time to roust some ruffians, right?"

The rogue draws himself up, insulted. "There aren't any—" he begins indignantly, voice squeaking. "I mean, my life is none of your concern! You should be more worried about yours!"

"Oh, by the Great Writer," Kintyre groans, and the slam of Foesmiter back into its sheath rings out. The unnatural hush of the forest has begun to give way to the joyfully noisy business of birds calling out to their offspring and mates, the musical avian equivalent of: "time to come in and wash behind your ears, now!"

The rogue, evidently done waiting for us to cut the strings of our coin purses for him, makes a move toward Bevel. Almost faster than I can see, Bevel's got the lad on his back in the underbrush, the tip of his sword gently dimpling the soft underside of the rogue's chin.

"*Now* we have a problem," Bevel says, and his voice is low, dark, and filled with the kind of steel that I've only ever glimpsed in him once or twice before. Pip's earlier assessment of Bevel Dom as an unreliable narrator sparks in my memory, and I can see where, perhaps, Bevel is of far greater help and a much bigger threat to their enemies than he chooses to share in his tales. I wonder if this is modesty, or a deliberate ploy on the part of Bevel to make those foes who might read his words underestimate him when they meet.

Contrary to what I would expect, the boy-rogue just grins up at the grim granite of Bevel's glower, his mouth spreading wide and eyes crinkling in cattish amusement. "I'll say!" he crows, and there is a crash in the underbrush.

"The bags!" Pip shouts, leaning down from the tree, knuckles white around her stabilizing branch.

Karl, startled by the way his burden suddenly drops to the ground with a *whump* and a crunch, rears and stomps the path.

"Peace, beast!" Kintyre bellows, startling Karl even more. The horse backs into him, and Kintyre has a job of keeping Karl from trampling him, trying to calm him from behind.

"Forsyth!" Pip shouts. "There's a . . . thief? Oh my *god*! It's a—hey! *Oof!*" Pip goes flying back into the trunk of a tree, and I duck under Dauntless—who is finding all the excitement only minorly irritating, if the twitch of his ears is anything to tell by—and rush to her side.

"I'm fine!" she snaps. "The bags!"

A flash of red, bright and sharp, catches my eye. Scales glint in the shards of sunlight that pierce the veil of the trees, a low, sibilant hiss filling the air. Another rending tear, and the crash and crunch of our gear being scattered along the path, and then a triumphant roar that sounds like a hundred eggs being cracked into a hundred spitting frying pans.

Dragon!

There is the whip crack of leather wings, and then Pip is down the tree and off like a shot, after the creature.

"Pip! Are you mad?" I howl after her, reaching out to try to pull her to a halt. My fingers brush her back, but I can gain no grip.

"The Chalice!" Kintyre shouts from somewhere behind us. "Bev, the blasted creature took the Chalice!"

And now, looking ahead, I can see the vitally important cup clenched in one of the dragon's forepaws. The denseness of the forest and it's awkward three-legged gait have slowed the creature down enough for me to see that it is small still—no taller than Dauntless, no longer than fifteen lengths at most. It is still quite young, probably not even out of its first century yet.

I reach for Pip again, fearful that the dragonet will spit fire back over its shoulder at us, but Pip is faster than me. Pip's jogs have conditioned her to running, and she speeds, now, after the horrible little lizard, as she once did after Lordling Gyre.

There is a crash and a howl behind me, the frightened whinny of Karl, and then Kintyre is shouting: "To one side, Brother!" I flatten myself against the brush, and Kintyre speeds past me, Foesmiter flashing. I follow at his heels.

"How fortuitous to meet you in my forest!" the drakeling hisses, rounding suddenly in the middle of what appears to be a close clearing. "I've waited an age to have you between my claws, Kintyre Turn! Murderer!"

A trap! We've been led solidly and stupidly right into a trap. *Now*, the drakeling has room to maneuver, and it rears back and slashes at Kintyre. Pip skids to a halt on the edge of the clearing, and I fetch up behind her. She grabs my hand, but I do not know if it is out of fear, or awe, or to keep me from charging into the area with Kintyre.

I am swift with Smoke, but my sword does not have the heft and strength of Foesmiter. To go in there would mean a broken blade for me, and potentially my death or that of my brother if he is distracted in defending me. No, I am smart enough to know when I am outmatched.

Pip strains forward, shouting. "Stop! Both of you, please, stop!"

"Murderer, murderer!" the drakeling snarls, as each of its strikes are turned back.

"Forsyth!" Bevel shouts from behind me, and it is just enough warning for me to shove Pip and I to the side to avoid the wide arc of the rogue lad's sword. There is blood on his chin and fury in his face as he slashes at us, clumsy in his anger.

"You leave her be!" he snarls. "You've done enough!"

"You're the one hacking at *me*," I snarl back. "Stand down or I shall—"

I needn't finish telling him what I shall do because, in an instant, Bevel has the boy flat on his face in the dirt, the tip of his sword pressing into the soft flesh at the back of his neck. He is sitting on the boy's waist, his hands pinned to his sides at the wrist by Bevel's knees.

"Let's try this again," Bevel says.

The drakeling makes a moaning hiss, like a geyser, at the sight of the boy-rogue so pinned, and brings its paw down hard on Kintyre's shoulder. It is enough to knock Foesmiter from his grip and flatten my brother under it.

"Kintyre!" I shout, knowing it's ridiculous to do so but unable to refrain all the same.

"*Stop! Stop! Everyone stop!*" Pip bellows.

I don't know if it is the power of a thrice-given command or just the volume of her voice that makes everyone freeze in place, but it works. Beneath the dragon's hand, Kintyre coughs, and the drakeling arches it's paw just enough to keep him pinned in place beneath its claws but allowing him to breathe. Bevel makes the same courtesy for the rogue, leaning up enough for the boy to get his face out of the dirt and hack up dust.

As soon as he gets his breath back, Kintyre begins to yell invectives, which the drakeling volleys back with fervor. Kintyre wriggles around until he gets his hand on Foesmiter and raises it to slash at the drakeling's arm, but Pip snarls, "Don't you dare, Kintyre Turn!" and he pauses like a guilty child.

"Don't hit it! For fuck's sake, *talk to it!*" Pip orders. "Both of you! Enough of this phallic weapon waving! Pretend for five fucking seconds that you are civilized, sentient creatures and *talk!*"

The drakeling's lips pucker in a strange way, and I realize that this is the serpentine version of a moue of confusion. "I *am* talking," it says.

"I mean, to each other." Pip sighs, arms thrown upward in exasperation. "*With* each other."

The drakeling looks to Kintyre, and there is a moment that should not be as comical as it seems to me right then as they both shrug. I clap a palm over my mouth and try to keep my shoulders from shaking. It must be the hysteria.

"Let Kintyre go," Bevel shouts, when nobody else seems keen to end the silence. "And give us the Chalice. Or . . ." He whispers his sword against the boy's scalp and a soft pile of dark hair flutters to the ground.

"No, no!" the drakeling says, clearly torn between the Chalice in one hand, Kintyre under its other claws, and Bevel's sword at the boy's neck. "He's mine! He's mine! You can't hurt him!"

A delicate sound, like coins clinking together, catches my ears, and I try to figure out if we're being ambushed by someone else. Keeping the drakeling in my periphery, I search the shadows, but there are no tell-tale glints, no rustling foliage. The glade is still and silent, save for us.

"I will," Bevel says, voice like gravel. "I will if you don't hand Kintyre the Chalice and let him go."

Another soft, metallic plinking sound breaks across the air, and I blink as reality tilts ever so slightly, one more veil of mystery about how the world works cut from its mooring and fluttering away. Realization creeps in to take its place.

"Dragons don't hoard gold," I say quietly. "They *weep* it."

"Weep gold?" Pip echoes, and follows my line of sight to the small pile of gold shards that is collecting beside Kintyre's head. They fall as liquid, and then, somewhere between the drakeling's cheek and the ground, turn hard and sharp.

"Don't look!" the drakeling shouts, mortified. "Don't look!"

Bevel makes a noise that sounds very much like a strangling fox. "So, dragon hoards of stolen gold, crushed and fragmented as the dragon claws through isn't . . . shredded coins and bars and jewelry, it's . . ."

"Tears," Pip whispers. "Dragons literally sleep on a hoard of their own tears."

Kintyre takes in the height of the pile before him, bottom lip between his teeth as he clearly compares it to the hoards he has seen in the past. "Dragons must be extremely lonely creatures," he says at last.

It is like a punch right under my ribs, and I can't help the gasp.

"Let me up," the rogue lad cries, and squirms. "Please!"

Bevel, struck with the same sudden weariness as the rest of us, releases the boy and sheathes his sword.

"Sweeting," the boy croons to the drakeling, scrambling to his feet and plastering himself along the dragonet's neck. "Let him up, come on. I told you this was a bad idea, didn't I? Come on, now, my sweet."

"But . . . but . . ." the dragonet sniffles. "*Mother*."

"Oh my god . . ." Pip whispers. "Drebbin."

"What?" Kintyre thunders, pushing at the drakeling's paw, but its claws are too embedded in the turf for him to budge them. "That foul old dragon that I—"

"Silence!" the drakeling roars into his face, and Kintyre goes still and meek again, stunned, as we all are, by the raw anger, the terrible pain that one word carries. "She was my mother, and you *killed her!*"

"She was eating innocents!"

"She was not!" the rogue lad snarls, snapping a finger in Kintyre's face. "She was recruiting egg-sitters! We volunteered! All of us!"

"But . . . the magistrate said . . ." Bevel stops, then scratches the back of his neck, baffled.

The lad turns his sharp finger to Bevel. "Do you think the magistrate would let people know that he was such a tyrant that the youths of Drebbinshire would prefer the freedom of being a dragon's minder over being chained to the whiskey still?"

"Chained?" I ask, just to be clear. There's business enough for the Shadow Hand when this adventure is sorted, if it's true.

"Chained!" the lad snarls. "But you never thought to *ask*, did you? The great Kintyre Turn, hero and *fool!*"

"I'm sorry," Kintyre blurts, and every pair of eyes swings his way just in time to see him flush red with shame. "For what it's worth, and I know it's not worth much, I *am* sorry about your mother."

Pip makes the same strangled-fox sound Bevel made earlier. Bevel is watching both rogue and drakeling warily, clearly wishing he hadn't sheathed his sword just yet, fingers wrapped white and hard around his pommel.

"I made a mistake," Kintyre says. "I struck first and asked no questions, and I am learning . . . I am *learning* that bulling one's way through is not always the . . . the wise way." Here, he tilts his head back in the dirt and meets

Pip's eyes. His glance is so thankful, so pleading, that it takes everything in my power not to turn away, jealous of their momentary communication, their connection.

With agonizing slowness, the drakeling lifts its paw. Instead of scrambling out from under it, Kintyre waits until the dragonet has left him enough room to sit up. He does so, then stands and immediately reaches out to touch the drakeling's snout. It is a soft, kind gesture—an apology and an offer of sympathy all in one.

The rogue sobs and wraps his arms around the drakeling's neck. The drakeling drops the Chalice in order to balance itself, curls its head around to rest on the boy's heaving back, and, just like that, we are dismissed.

Our roving band of adventurers are superfluous.

Quietly, we sheathe our weapons, gather the Chalice, murmur our apologies, and go.

Dauntless is waiting patiently by the path where I left him, Karl nickering and pawing beside him. Pip unties his reins and buries her head in his mane, murmuring soothing nothings to him in order to disguise the way her own eyes have grown red around edges, glassy with unshed tears. The tense but jovial mood of the morning is gone.

"We need to make camp," Bevel says softly, as he and Kintyre look to repacking the bags and securing them to the horses. "It's too late to go back to the forest's edge, now."

"What about the clearing?" Pip asks, still not looking up.

"The dragon—" Kintyre begins, but then stops himself, mouth twisting in disgust. It is aimed mostly at himself, I'm sure.

"Probably gone," Pip says. "I'd take off if I was them, too."

With little nods and total silence, we make our way back to the clearing in the last of the amber, slanted sunset. As Pip predicted, it is abandoned. Fascinated by my new discovery, I let the others take responsibility for setting up the fire and preparing to make dinner, and focus instead on the small pile of tears the drakeling left behind. I have been taking notes on our adventures since we left Lysse, for my own edification and not, of course, with the intent of fictionalizing them as Bevel does. So, in the dying light, I sketch what I can and make notes along the margins of the paper, and then fashion it into an envelope and sweep the shards inside, sealing it with a bit of pine tar.

"No wonder dragon-riders never seem to need payment," Bevel says as I join him by the fire, plopping down onto my bedroll. Pip and Kintyre are collecting firewood together and talking in tones hushed enough that it makes me think they are talking about me. "What other precious metals do you suppose the rest of their bodily fluids crystallize into?"

"Ugh," is my only reply, along with an artfully scrunched nose, so he knows how very little I think of his bawdy humor and curiosity.

Bevel laughs and holds his hands up. "All right, you prude. I withdraw the question."

"I'm not a—" I protest, but his laugher amplifies into guffaws, and I snap my teeth down on the rest of it.

"Apologies," he chuckles as he at last runs out of air. I grumble an acceptance and put away the pouch of gold while he makes culinary magic in a use-blackened frying pan and stew pot that looks well scrubbed and cared for.

As he stirs, I think on the rogue and his dragon.

"Do you suppose they were a Pair?" I ask. "In the sense of a Binding?"

Bevel shrugs. "I've heard of a woman Paired with a faun, so possibly. Not that strange, as long as everyone is happy with it. It doesn't even have to be a romantic Pairing. Maybe it's like it is in the army for them—shield Pairs."

"Maybe," I murmur, and look away, hoping the shadows conceal that I am doing my best *not* to seek out Pip's shape in the darkness.

"Oh, Forssy," Bevel says, and it is filled with such *pity* that I want to scream.

"Do not," I caution him. "I will not talk about it. No more talk of women, or love, or *Pairs*, please, I beg you."

"Do you think you're not *capable* of a Pairing? Is that it? Or is it that that you think don't *deserve* one? That you don't deserve a wife, and happiness?" Bevel asks me, softly. Before I can answer, he says, "You know, I asked Kin the same Writer-be-damned thing. Do you know what he said?" He coughs once, tucking his chin against his chest and puffing up his shoulders in an approximation of my brother. "The things I've seen, Bev. The places I've been. The deeds that I've *done*. It lives inside me, a shadow in my soul. An evil stain that I can't scrub away, that looks out through my eyes when I am at my angriest, my most hateful. Who would want that beside them, in bed? Who would want to wake in the morning to *that*?" He releases his stance and a puff of self-deprecating laughter. "My beautiful idiot," Bevel says, with a long sigh. "I'm no blushing maiden or in-experienced farm boy. I think he forgot that I was there with him. That those things live inside of me, too."

"They live in me and Pip, as well," I say, too embar-rassed to want to hear him actually say it out loud. "But Pip's darkness . . . Pip's pain—" I sigh and cannot go on.

Bevel just nods, smiling softly. "You will sort this out."

I am not as certain as Bevel, and I have no other reply to give, so I take the tuber he offers from his bag, and the paring knife, and let my brother's lover teach me how to prepare fried gilly-root for dinner. Later, Pip says it reminds her of her grandmother's cooking, and says nothing else for the rest of the night, wrapped small and alone in her bedroll, refusing all offers of comfort.

✍

The ride to the mountains which shelter the Eyrie takes another day. Unfortunately, having heard my conversa-tion with his lover the night before, Kintyre decides that, by daylight, it is his turn to impart romantic advice to me. I do not *want* his advice, especially since it's taken him the better part of two decades to actually come to terms with his own inclinations, but it seems that I cannot avoid it. So, I linger at the rear of our troupe with Dauntless, pulling the gear from his back and loosening the saddle so that I may remove it. It will be an arduous trek up the dry riverbed course, and we'll have to leave our horses behind. I won't leave them saddled and chafing, to boot.

"Give it time," Kintyre says softly from where he is knelt beside me in the scrub, checking over our water supply.

"I don't know what you're talking about," I lie.

"Women always need to think about things," Kintyre says, full of blustery confidence, as if he's imparting some great secret. "You'll see, she'll give you a goodbye tumble if nothing else."

I resist the urge to tell him off, tell him what he got wrong, that he has to change his attitude, change his outlook—all the things I usually do, and all the things my eavesdropping has revealed he despises. Instead, I take a deep breath and say, "I don't think she will. But thank you for trying to cheer me up."

Kintyre blinks at me, deflating a little, clearly wrong-footed by the lack of the verbal assault he expected to receive from me.

"You don't think so?"

"No," I say, and turn back to the task of relieving Dauntless of his saddle.

"But she loves you," Kintyre insists. "They always come around if they love you." He looks at Bevel—I can see it from the corner of my eye—and his gaze is soft, introspective. His eyes are the same soft blue as our mother's. "Even if it takes a long time, even if it's someone like me. Love them enough, and they'll get it. They'll come around."

"I don't think P-Pip lo-love-loves me," I admit, and bite my own tongue for the sin of stumbling over that. *That word, of all things!*

Kintyre's gaze sharpens and swings back around to gauge my expression. "Doesn't she?"

"Y-you n-never saw us in the middle of th-things," I say. "Don't make judgments based on what you think ought to ha-happen between a man and a maid on a quest."

Kintyre grins and reaches up to rub Dauntless's nose. My horse whickers and allows it, and I have to quash down the urge to call the beast a traitor.

"I did see the way she looked at you in Turn Hall," Kintyre says. "I am not entirely blind."

"No, you were entirely drunk," I hiss. "And trying to get your hand up her skirt!"

"And why do you think it didn't work?" he asks. "Because she already preferred *you*. She wanted *you*."

"We're not an either-or!" I snap, keeping my voice down so Bevel and Pip cannot hear us fighting. They would both scold us. "You know, women are allowed to be platonic. They don't *have* to be in love with one of us!"

"I know that!" Kintyre bristles back. "I'm not an idiot."

"Then why would you say that she was too in love with me back then to look at you! That doesn't make sense!"

"It does if it's true!" His voice rings back at us from the foothills. There is little vegetation and cover here, and sound carries too easily. Kintyre is not being careful.

"Shh!" I hiss. "By the Writer, Kintyre, have some discretion!"

"And there we go!" he snarls. "I wondered when you would start telling me what to do!"

I open my mouth to retort, to say something vicious about him being a big dumb animal who needs orders, but at the last minute, I snap my teeth closed on the words. No. One of us needs to try to repair our relationship.

Instead, I shake my head and haul off the saddle, setting it on the ground and turning my attention to the blanket, the bridle, and a currycomb.

"She did," Kintyre says. He takes the comb from me and works the tangles out of Dauntless's mane sulkily. He winds the hair into braids like the ones that he used to give Stormbearer. I always thought it looked a bit silly on a hero's horse, but now I can see the advantage—no briars. "I'm not lying."

"I know you're not lying," I reply. "I just don't know how to make you see that it wasn't Pip who was looking at me like that. That lust, that flirting, that wasn't her. That was Bootknife, and through him, the Viceroy."

Kintyre frowns. "Why would they pick you, then?"

I pause, comb hovering above Dauntless's flank. He pushes into my hand, and I begin brushing again, needing the repetitive motion while my mind is processing, tumbling over itself, trying to figure out what it was in

Kintyre's question that has filled me so suddenly with such a cold, tight dread. I cannot figure it out.

Finally, I ask: "What do you mean?"

"I just . . . I'm not as clever as you, but it seems to me that if the Viceroy wants me dead, then why would he have Pip turn me down when Bevel and I offered? Wouldn't it be a better plan for her to go with us, than go with you?" He shakes his head and mumbles, "It's probably just something I don't understand, I know, but it just seems to me that the Viceroy must be up to something."

"Or . . ." I say softly, and lick my lips to buy myself a few moments of contemplation. "Or it was Pip's own will that prevailed. She told me they were more passive at first—that she didn't even realize they were in her head, making her act, until later. What if . . . wh-hat if-f-f . . ."

"What if she was of her own mind that night?" Kintyre finishes for me, because the thought of it has my tongue too tied up to complete the sentence.

I nod.

Kintyre shrugs. "Then maybe you have a chance of winning her back."

"But su-su-surely sh-she doesn't-t lo-lo-love me anymore," I say softly. "N-not af-af-after all tha-that."

"You only have a few days left to figure it out," Kintyre says. "So don't waste them."

He leaves me to Dauntless, to my thoughts, to the ache in my chest that feels like my heart has suddenly become swollen, inflamed, and more tender than the cut on my cheek.

And I have several hours to prod at both. The climb is as difficult and hot as I predicted. There is no shelter from the summer sun save for the occasional boulder, and the angle of the incline is steep. Our packs, even reduced to essentials, weigh on us greater and greater as each hour passes. Pip's hair has now grown long enough for her to tie it back. This leaves the skin of her neck vulnerable, and she slathers on some of the healing ointment to keep away a burn. The scent of lemon and menthol mingles with the smell of Pip, sweating with exertion and glistening with ointment, and it is too much, I cannot walk behind her, not with such a tender, intimate part of her so exposed. My favorite little leaf remains unkissed.

I speed up when the riverbed widens enough for us to walk two abreast and ask her how she is faring.

"I'm fine. You don't have to coddle me," she says.

"I'm not. I genuinely want to know."

"Well, now you do," she huffs.

"Pip, please—"

"Please, what?" she asks. She stops and turns to me, hands on her hips. "What do you want me to say, Forsyth?"

"I don't know!" I admit. "Something. Anything! Talk to me *at all*."

"About what? How I *feel*? How hurt and betrayed I am? How I'm dealing with the fact I have now joined the one-quarter of all women who have been raped?"

I flinch at the ugly word, and she laughs, but it too is ugly and low.

"Please," I say again.

"And what are you begging for?"

"I don't know. I just . . . I *miss* you, Pip."

"I'm right here." She spreads her arms, mocking.

"No, you're not. You are silent, and you don't let me touch you, and you don't talk to me. We don't laugh together anymore. I miss *you*."

She turns away, guilt and what I can only hope is loneliness on her own face before she slams down on her expression, pinching off her feelings.

"Pip, please," I say. "It wasn't my fault."

She scoffs. "So, what, you want me to stop punishing you by denying you and pretend things are back the way they were before?"

"No, never," I say. "I would never want you to pretend. But I want you to let me apologize for my part in it, however unknowingly and unwillingly I participated."

"You have."

"Then let me repeat it until you believe me. I never wanted to hurt you. And all people have done to you since you arrived is hurt you. Tied up and laughed at you when you tried to hurt them back."

Her gaze sharpens in my direction. "How do you know that?"

"You said—"

"No, I never did. Not once. I never told anyone I tried to hurt the Viceroy back. So, how did you . . ." Her eyes fall on the Chalice, hung upside down from the strap of my pack. A small dark spot of saltwater has collected on the dry clay of the riverbed under our feet, the earth sucking it up thirstily.

She rolls her eyes and throws up her hands. "Of course! Men! I wouldn't tell you, and so you just *had* to pry into it!"

"Pip! Wait, I just wanted to—"

"Oh, *you* wanted to," she sneers. "No. Don't bother to think about what I wanted. What I requested! Pay no mind to *me*, I'm just a *woman*!"

"That's unfair!" I yelp. "I would have done the same for *anyone* I care about."

"Break your promise and pry in where you don't belong, you mean?"

"Checked up on them in case something worse had happened. Prepared! Researched! *Surely* you have to appreciate that!" I bellow.

Above us on the slope, I can hear that Bevel and Kintyre have turned back. They are coming toward us, and I am rapidly running out of the privacy I need with her.

"Pip." I reach forward, grab her by the elbows and clamp my fingers down, refusing to allow her to flinch away this time.

"Let go!"

"No, not until you *listen* to me," I say, pulling her toward me, angling my lips against her ear. "I love you. Right now, I love you, despite everything, because of everything. You are strong, and you are brave, and you are clever, and I love you, no matter what you've been through and what has been done to you. To *us*."

Pip stops struggling, stops pushing against my chest with her fists, and sags, eyes on the ground.

"And I suspect there is a part of you that loves me back," I press on. "Kintyre figured it out—if the Viceroy had been in control back at the dinner at Turn Hall, he would have made you go with him. But he didn't, because your will was stronger, and you chose me. You chose *me* that night."

"But not like that. It was just to . . . you know, just to be near you. Maybe dance, if I could have."

"And that was enough, don't you see? That was you. The real you. It was *you* who nearly kissed me in the stairwell. So please, *please*, Pip; search inside yourself and find the place where you care for me. Please, let me help you. Let me care for you, let me protect you, and let me help you get well again."

"There's nothing you can do!" she spits, and tries to wrench her arms out of my grip.

I won't let go; I refuse. Call this my heroic task, but I *will not* let Pip think she is alone in this.

"Then let me just *be beside you*," I plead. And then I lean back, duck my chin, and slot my mouth over hers. It is not an elegant kiss, and it is not slow or sweet or playful, any of the things that Pip and I both prefer. Her lips are rough and taste like scabs, but the press and slide of flesh to moist flesh far outweighs the bitterness of the taste. This kiss is *meaningful.* It must signify, must stand in for all the things that I cannot seem to force my tongue to say as words, so I must curl it around the feelings and use it to press them onto her. I must kiss her until she understands.

When I pull back for a breath, intending to tilt my head the other way, to brush my nose along her cheek, to murmur against her lips, to inhale her air, she jerks back. My grip has loosened with the kiss, turning to a caress, and she breaks it easily.

My eyes have closed—I don't know when that happened; I don't remember consciously choosing that—so I ratchet the lids back up with aroused difficulty. They snap open the rest of the way when I take in Pip's expression.

Her face is puce with fury, her whole body shaking, and her brown eyes are wide and wet. "Don't," Pip thunders. "Don't you *dare* force your desires on me. Don't you *dare* kiss me without my permission *ever again.*"

She runs up the hill so quickly that Bevel and Kintyre are startled apart. She darts between them, running around a river bend and out of sight.

"Forssy," Kintyre sighs. "Now what did you do?"

"I don't know!" I say, feeling impotent in my own inability to help Pip, to make her understand, to make myself understand what she needs. I run my hands through my hair, pulling at it, furious and frustrated and tired, Writer, so damn tired.

✍

We reach the apex of the mountain several hours after nightfall. Pip has neither spoken nor looked at me all day. We set up camp swiftly, deciding to forgo a fire in favor of just crawling into our bedrolls. The wind is colder at this altitude, and swifter, but we have found a bald crag in which to huddle, and the warmth of four bodies is enough to keep us comfortable for one night.

In the morning, we explore the roof of the world as best we are able with a spyglass. The Cinch Mountains as a whole form a massive round caldera around the acid-green remains of a volcano that blew off its top long before human memory. The caldera is formed of five distinct mountain ranges. We are in the Eyrie, home to many of the great legendary birds. The Rookery, that small part of the Eyrie which resembles a writing desk, is small and hard to spot, but we don't want to begin scrambling across mountain peaks if we don't know which direction we're going.

The absolute swarms of birds look at us askance, but none of them talk when Pip tries to engage them in conversation. Whether they can't, or they won't is unclear. We pass a fruitless first day pouring over Bevel's maps of this region and Pip's Excel, and, in the end, decide to stay put for the second night. We don't seem to be bothering any nests here, which is a blessing, a luck that is welcome and was unlooked for.

The second day sees us making no more progress than the first, though I have devised a grid system with which to study the other mountains through the glass, instead of wheeling it about willy nilly the way Kintyre was doing. On day three, Pip seems to have been able to coax a riddling raven close, but it is only staring at her with its glass eyes, blinking but not responding. It is possible that the creature has never heard human language before, living so high up and so far away from civilization.

Maybe it only speaks Dwarvish or Goblinese. I try both languages, but it only croaks a laugh and flies off.

Day four comes, and we are all so frustrated at our lack of progress that we are at one another's throats. Kintyre yells at Pip when she unfolds her Excel yet again, trying to decipher where we went wrong. "Adventuring is not scholar's work!" he snarls.

And Pip blows back: "Well, *one* of us around here has to do the thinking, 'cause it's sure not ever you!"

Kintyre throws his arm to the west. "We should just start *walking*. We'll come upon it!"

"That's your big plan?" I sneer. "Just waste days and days scrambling over mountain peaks in the hopes that we'll stumble upon the right one? What if it's that way, instead?" I point south. "We'll waste *weeks* going all the way around the range, and we still can't guarantee that we'll cover every chasm and peak."

"Our rations are nearly gone," Bevel adds. "We need to go back down, check on the horses, and gather more. We need more water. Kintyre, you need to hunt."

He draws his sword. "I can do well enough here."

Pip yelps. "Not the birds! You think they'll help us if we start *eating* them? Idiot!"

"They're serving no other purpose!" Kintyre bawls.

Pip runs her hands through her hair, frustrated. She's got her jerkin off, and when her arms raise and shift, I can still see the puff of ivy on the nape of her neck. The scars remained, though why that surprised me when I realized it, I don't know. I suppose I was hoping that, with Bootknife's death, they would fade. But that is silly. Scars are scars; they don't just vanish.

I can't help but touch my own scar, a thin, angry red line that arcs from my temple across the apple of my cheek.

Pip huffs a sigh of frustration. "Okay, maybe I'm thinking about this wrong. If we're not meant to find the location from the birds, then who else can tell us?"

"Why don't we just *ask*?" Bevel suggests.

"Ask who," Kintyre snaps. "There's no one here!"

"Ask *whom*," I can't help but correct.

He turns a thunderous glare on me but doesn't comment.

"There is something else here; there has to be. Come on, what else lives on mountains?"

"Goats?" Bevel suggests.

"Goblins live under them," Kintyre says, "but I saw no passages or openings."

"Dragons," I say, our encounter with what Bevel is already calling the Desolate Drakeling of Debbinshire fresh in my mind.

"No dragons here," Kintyre says. "No massive droppings or animals large enough to sustain it. There was barely anything bigger than a rabbit in that forest at the foot of the slopes."

Everyone is silent, minds churning, when Pip lifts her face to the wind and smiles. Eyes closed, her hair flying back over her shoulders, she looks content and beautiful, framed against the mountain's dark gray-and-white caps, the clear blue of the sky, and the haze of clouds.

I swallow hard and force myself to look away, to remember that Pip doesn't want me anymore. That my regard is unwelcome.

"The wind," she whispers.

"Oh!" Bevel says, latching on immediately. "Zephyrs!"

"The wind always blows you what you need. You've used it before," Pip says softly, opening her eyes and turning to face us. "As long as you have something of equal import to give it in return. So, what do we have to give?"

Nineteen

As Bevel and Kintyre go about scratching the sigil necessary for summoning a zephyr into the stone of our little campsite, Pip and I huddle in the lee of the crag to discuss what we have with us that might be worth the price of being taken to the Rookery. Pip suggests that, instead of asking to be taken there on the back of the wind, we could ask for knowledge of where the Rookery is. I manage to convince her around to my way of thinking—we have wasted four days, and could waste more traveling there. Far better to ride directly to it than risk walking and being ambushed by the Viceroy or any number of creatures on the way.

"But what have any of us got that's worth it?" she muses. "Kintyre's sword?"

"Not ours to give," I demure.

"The Shadow's Mask?"

"I dare not, not with the Words of Knowledge on it, not with the enchantment. Who knows where the wind may drop it."

"And we need the rest of the objects." Pip squirms, trying not to look as if she's keeping distance between us as she shifts on the uncomfortable ground.

"It doesn't have to be a physical thing," I say softly. "It could be a name. Or a future possibility." *Or a relationship*, I think, but dare not say aloud.

An idea is beginning to germinate in my mind, but I don't know what shape it will take just yet, so I remain silent. Before Pip and I have come to a consensus, Bevel calls us back out into the open air and directs us to stand at the cardinal points.

"You still remember this from when you were searching for the Iridium Crown of the Nightking?" Pip says, watching Bevel begin to make a series of very grave, very silly looking hand gestures.

"Shh," Kintyre admonishes, and Pip does, watching Bevel's every movement with rapt fascination.

She used to look at me like that. Bile burns against the hollow of my throat, and I swallow it back.

When Bevel finishes, he drops his hands to his sides, tilts his head back, and waits. The wind suddenly vanishes, the howl that has been hounding our ears for the last four days immediately ceasing. Silence drops over us like a blanket, and I resist the urge to scrub at my ears. Even the incessant cawing of the birds has been silenced.

Something sweet and soft suddenly perfumes the air, like the ghosts of a thousand summer-dappled meadows. It tickles my nose, and a warm breath trails like a finger across the back of my neck, over my cheek. I cannot help but lean into the sensation, and, around the circle, I see the others doing the same.

"Hello," Bevel says.

"Hello," the wind says back. Its voice is neither male nor female, but it is high and sweet as the scent it carries, an exhalation of breath that somehow, strangely, trans-lates as words. "What can I do for you?"

"We need to be taken to the Rookery, please," I say. "All four of us, if it's not too much trouble."

"Amount and distance are no trouble," the zephyr agrees. "This I can do. And in return, what do you offer?"

The four of us exchange glances across the circle, but no one seems to have any idea what to propose. Can I do it? Do I have the bravery to suggest what has been growing in my mind?

"Take my scars," Pip says suddenly. "The vines!"

If the thoughtful silence is anything go by, the zephyr seems to contemplate this. "No," it says finally. "They aren't yours to give."

Pip pounds her fist against her thigh, frustrated.

"Forsyth's stutter?" Kintyre asks, tentatively.

"Yes, I'll accept that," I agree.

"No," the zephyr says. "That is not precious to you."

Pip turns in a circle, hands jammed against her scalp. She is muttering, "Think, think, think! You're supposed to be the clever one! C'mon, Lucy, c'mon!"

Her wrists are delicate and elegant ,and I remember kissing her there, over those little bones and tender veins. I remember those fingers twined with mine. I remember the burn of her touch, the slick drag of the heel of her hand against the base of my cock. I remember kissing her nail beds, licking the moisture from her own intimacy away, chasing the flavor of ink and sex in her cuticles.

I have grown to love her so much. It is real. I love her, and I never want to be without her. I want her in my life always. I want to watch her face, to try to guess what she is thinking. I want to care for her. But more than taking care of her, I want her to let me care *for* her. I want her to *let me* . . . just, let me. For as long as she is alive. I want to keep her, mine forever, to see her everyday, to share her secrets with her, and to have the privilege to share my own. I want her, in every selfish way a child could ever want a toy, and in bigger, nobler ways that mean sacrificing everything of my own just for the privilege of waking up beside her every morning. I love her.

I love her, and it's real. It means something. It *is* real.

It is.

Isn't it?

Can my love for her be real? Can my feelings be genuine when her own are not? Does that invalidate them? Is what I feel fake because it grew through false encouragement, because the physical affection we shared was coerced, even if I didn't know it, because everything she said and did to make my feelings grow bigger, stronger, truer, were not her own words, her own actions?

Can I really love Pip when all she was, was a puppet?

And do I *want* to love her, now that she is leaving forever?

"Take it from me," I say to the zephyr, suddenly, mind made up as soon as the thought, the idea that has been chasing its way around between my ears crystallizes. "Take it. You know what I'm thinking. Take it."

The wind vanishes for the briefest of moments, and for the length of it, I fear I have offended the zephyr and it has left. And then, there is a gust of wind so strong that it blows me back. I fall, the wind clutching at me, and my back does not hit the ground. The zephyr is sucking the air from my lungs, caressing, grabbing, sliding down my throat until I am choking, choking. I burn. All over, I burn, flayed open by the wind, skin rubbed harsh and red.

I cannot scream because I do not have the air for it. I will not scream because this is what I asked for.

I try to keep my eyes open, but I cannot see past the way my own hair is whipped against my face—even my eyelashes are being tugged upon—and the grit the wind storm has swirled up. I cover my face with my hands, struggling to lift my limbs, to protect my eyes, my mouth from the dust. Nothing can keep out the wind, and I would not want it to.

And then it is over. I am lying on the ground, gasping, lungs screaming for air, limp and wrung out and *done*.

Pip slides onto her knees in the dirt beside me, her hands on my chest, as if to gauge whether my heart still beats. It does. It does. And I wish she'd stop touching me.

"What did the zephyr take?" Pip asks. "Forsyth, what did you offer?"

"Let me up," I say instead of answering, and Pip backs up just enough for me to haul myself into a sitting position. Kintyre and Bevel hover nearby, giving Pip and I space that we don't need.

"What was it?" Pip asks again, hands coming up to frame my face, and I shake them off, annoyed by the grittiness on her palms. "Forsyth."

"My love," I pant, forcing myself to breathe slowly, carefully.

Pip jerks backward, eyes suddenly wide, shaking so hard that her legs nearly dump her on the uneven ground. "What?"

"I don't love you," I say. It feels good. It feels right. It feels hot and strong, and I feel fantastic. I feel empty and buoyant. There is no worry for her, no fear, no pathetic sniffing after her, no desire for her body or her time or her opinions. I don't care. "I don't care!" I say out loud, just to hear it. "I don't love you! Ha! Ha ha! I *don't love you!*"

It doesn't even hurt when Pip's olive face turns white, and she closes her eyes slowly, painfully, like she's just been gutted.

Travel by wind is nowhere near as overwhelming as having a zephyr steal an emotion. The thing allows us time to gather up our gear, and then lifts us together; it feels like riding on an overstuffed feather pillow, gentle and sweet smelling. Within moments, we are set down again, just as gently, in a very deep, very low basin in a peak on the far side of the range. There are stairs cut into the side of a wall composed of gray-lavender stone that sparkles like fey trails in the sunlight, revealing veins of gold and crystal with each intricate swoop.

Vegetation carpets a full third of the walls, vines growing up or down, I cannot tell, but glistening with moisture and life.

"It's beautiful," Bevel says, eyes on the way shafts of sunlight highlight the glittering interior of the Rookery. Kintyre and Bevel drop their packs, draw their swords, and begin to make a circuit of, ducking behind boulders and climbing halfway up the stairs to make sure that we are safe. It leaves Pip and I alone, but that doesn't bother me in the slightest.

My eyes are for the desk itself. It's less a Desk that Never Rots and more like a naturally occurring shelf of stone that has since been smoothed by the hands and stomachs of a hundred thousand scholarly pilgrims, coming to touch and kiss the place where they say the world began, the place where the Great Writer first Wrote.

I stand in the two indents in the stone floor, where generations of feet have worn a groove. I close my eyes and run my fingertips across the silky surface. It doesn't feel special, or different, not colder or warmer or anything other than what it is—stone. Purple-gray granite scattered with crystal. But it feels *reverent*, somehow. Holy. Perhaps it is my own perception that makes it so, but isn't that what faith is, anyway? One's own perception?

"Pip, come see," I say. "The Great Writer's desk."

"Elgar Reed began writing in his shitty community-housing co-op apartment in 1978," Pip grates out. "On a beat-up old typewriter he inherited from his aunt. It's in the Smithsonian museum now. I've seen it. This is just a slab of rock."

I am inordinately pleased that my brother was not near enough to hear her say that. "Hush, Pip, we agreed to keep it secret from them."

"Don't tell me what to do!" she snarls.

I turn to her, take in the tightness of her shoulders, the way the skin around her almond-shaped eyes has gotten wrinkled and tense, her hands balled into fists. "What's the matter with you?" I ask.

"What's the . . . the *matter*?" she splutters. "Forsyth, you *gave away your love for me*. I think I'm allowed to be upset about that!"

"Why?" I ask, genuinely curious. There is nothing attractive about her anger, not the way they describe it in the epic poems. Her eyes don't glitter; her cheeks don't pink delicately. She is mottled and flushed and scared looking. Not attractive at all. "What does it matter to you? You don't love me back."

"You don't know that!"

"I do!" I thunder, taking a step toward her and enjoying the way she flinches back from me, small and surprised and, for once, *not yelling at me.* "I *asked* you, and you said *nothing.* You couldn't answer with anything but to shove me away. I think that was a pretty clear indicator of your feelings, *bao bei.*" I can't help but add a sneer.

"I just wanted space," Pip says, desperation creeping into the edges of her words. "I just wanted time to *figure it out.*"

"Why?" I ask again. "You're leaving. You're leaving *today.* Now. As soon as we get this riddle solved. So why does it matter to you whether or not you can untangle how you feel for me from the horror of what you suffered? And why does it matter if I love you back anymore?"

"I just . . . I want . . ."

"I *wanted,*" I challenge. "I have needs too, Lucy Piper, and you can be a bully! I was suffering too, you know!"

"I-I . . ." She licks her lips, seemingly unable to figure out the words with which to respond.

"I was suffering, and you pushed me away. You told me I had no right to overwrite your desires with my own, but you never, not once, acknowledged *my right to desire.* You are so *full* of self-righteous ire that you never once saw how much my love for you hurt me, too." I spread my hands, and my grin. "Well, now it's gone. And when you go, it won't hurt me."

"It will hurt me!"

"That is not my problem," I say calmly.

"I don't want to leave with you hating me."

"I don't hate you," I correct her coldly. "I just don't love you."

Pip walks right up to me, throws her arms around my neck, and, decisive and sure, pulls herself up onto her toes and slots her mouth against mine. The kiss is uncomfortable, with her weight hanging off me, her tongue cool and slightly slimy against my lips. I twist my head away, breaking contact.

"Why aren't you kissing back?" She pulls away, eyes searching mine for something I know with cold certainty she will never find there again.

"You are allowed to kiss me with no permission given, but I am not accorded the same respect, I see?" I ask, and can't help but sneer: "Is it because I am a *man*?"

"Forsyth!" Pip gasps, shocked by the keen cruelty of my rebuff. "I . . . I didn't . . ."

"And now you see? You shoved me away, but all I wanted was to be able to communicate with you in a way where our words would not get in the way of the message. But you rebuffed me, and now, we are through."

Pip's breathing hitches, and she clutches her hands at the base of her throat, startled. "I thought . . . I mean . . ."

"You told me never to touch you." I spread my arms. "I am complying."

"I said never without permission! God, Forsyth. I wanted . . . of course I wanted you! I still—I . . . I just didn't know how to . . . to give it to you without it being tainted. I was scared that you . . . that all you'd see in me was Bootknife, that you would be searching for double meanings in everything I said, searching my eyes for green at every turn."

"You never need fear that now."

Pip screams in frustration, slapping her palms against my chest, angry. It stings. It is *irritating*.

"Don't *do this*!" she wails. "Forsyth, don't do this to me! You were the *one good part* of this whole miserable fucking world! *You were it*! Don't take that away from me, *please*."

I feel sorry for her. I would be lying if I said I didn't. It is a misery to see another person miserable. But I can't give her what she wants. I am not capable.

Kindly, gently, I disentangle her limbs from me, hold her by the wrists at arm's length.

"I'm sorry something so good has to end this way," I say gently. "But it is over, and you need to accept that. Please."

Pip's face crumbles, and she coughs, choking on her sadness.

Applause, slow and mocking, fills the space where Pip's protest might have been. We both jerk our heads toward the staircase, startled.

Descending it, clad in skin-tight black and gold, arrogance embroidered into every thread of his elaborate, opulent jacket, is the Viceroy.

I whip my head around, searching for Kintyre, but he is absent.

"Your brother is chasing Shades," the Viceroy oozes. He flicks his wrist lazily, and a shadowy copy of himself turns and runs up the stairs before flickering into nonexistence at the rim of the cavern.

I draw Smoke and push Pip behind me, then circle around the desk, keeping it between the Viceroy and us. For once, she goes when I push her. Her fingers clutch at the elbow of my travel robe, face pressed into the cloth between my shoulder blades. She is hiding. And she is shaking. Terrified. I hope that she has enough sense to let me go if I need to lunge at our enemy.

"Why are you here?" I ask.

"Oh, Shadow Hand, what a good opinion you have of yourself. It is not for you." He hops down the last few steps, demonstrative and gleeful, his beautiful face twisted with mischief. "I seem to have misplaced my second-in-command. I thought, well, now would be the perfect time to replace him with Bevel. Bootknife was so *jealous* of my feelings for my little knight."

"You don't love Bevel," I say, but it is a question.

"No, but I *want* him," the Viceroy replies. He takes a few careful steps toward us, keeping the desk between his body and my sword. "You see the way he trots after that oaf, Kintyre? You see how loyal and good to him he is, and see what little thanks he gets? I would treat him better. I would earn his loyalty and appreciate him. Ah, you feel the same—you don't like the way your brother treats his companion."

"I didn't used to," I correct. "If you're here for Bevel, why are they out chasing Shades?"

"Because I thought I'd like the privacy to check in on my other little project." He tilts sideways, theatrical, making as if to peer around my back. "And how is my little mousey-mole? Have you enjoyed your adventure?"

"Fuck you," Pip says from behind my back, but it is muffled by fabric and fear.

The Viceroy laughs. "Such a temper! But I see you're talking to me again. That's a good sign."

Pip presses her forehead tighter into my back and her arms come around my waist. She is doing everything she can to remain upright, to stand up to the literal source of her nightmares, and for that, I have to respect her. She has neither fainted nor fled.

"Hm, or not," the Viceroy muses when she says nothing more. "No worries, once I've killed the Shadow Hand and taken his Mask, you'll come with me and Bevel. You'll have no other choice."

"Kin-Kintyre?" Pip asks.

"His death is mine to deliver, but not collect. Just to be on the safe side, you understand. I can't let either Turn live," the Viceroy says conversationally. "It is always wise to end the entire line. No pesky revenge vendettas from over-inflated relatives to worry about then." He raises a hand consolingly. "Don't take it personal, Lordling Turn. I'm sure Sheriff Pointe will make an excellent lordling to Lysse Chipping in your place, and I do find him ever so much easier to intimidate than you. He has much more than you to lose, you see."

"Don't you dare touch that child!" I snarl.

The Viceroy stomps a foot against the loose gravel of the basin floor. "I'll do as I like! You won't be in any position to issue demands, Sha-sha-shadow H-h-hand," he mocks.

I know he is trying to infuriate me, trying to break through my guard and force me to make mistakes. I have read about this tactic enough in Bevel's scrolls, heard about it from Pip and Kintyre both. It works on my brother, reliably. I will not let it work on me.

He lifts his left hand, and it is encircled with cold blue light. It makes his fish-pale eyes glimmer gold and the cavern around us dance with sparks. "Step away from her," he commands.

"No."

"I don't want to harm my pet," the Viceroy warns. "But I will. If you step away from her, I will end you gently, swiftly, and I promise she will be unharmed."

"Until the next time I don't do as I'm told!" Pip snarls.

He smiles gently, benevolently, but his golden eyes remain dead and flat. "That is a lesson for you to learn, pet. I'm sure you will. Eventually."

Pip lets go of me, breaking her hold and loosening her arms just enough that I am free to move, but so the Viceroy cannot see that she has released me. I take this for encouragement and, without a sound or a cry of warning, lunge. My stomach drives up against the edge of the desk, but Smoke more than reaches across it, and I manage to score a slice against the Viceroy's breast. A red line wells up where I have parted the fabric of his jacket, but it's not enough, it is not deep enough.

With a cry of rage, he lets fly the ball of light in his fist. I duck, smacking my arm against the side of the desk on the way down; numbness radiates across the limb. The light crackles over my head, and the scent of singed hair suddenly fills the air. I have no time for my own vanity, however, and switch Smoke to my other hand so I can cut at the Viceroy's knees under the desk.

"Aren't you full of yourself, Forsyth Turn!" he crows. "You think *you* can stop *me*? Fat, stupid, old, stuttering lordling!" He dances out of reach, and I am forced to scoot backward enough to rise. His attention is on Pip, his right hand out and glowing green, tracking elaborate runes into the air.

I dodge around the desk, and he skips back a step, laughing. "The isolated and useless younger son of a drunkard and a throw-away woman. Insolent and meaningless, until he is needed to play his part, speak his words on the world's stage, and then vanish, melt back into the shadows like the rest of us puppets, eh?" he howled. "Aren't you *sick* of it, Forsyth Turn? Aren't you sick to *death* of existing at the behest of another? The way you are the supporting character in your own life, doesn't it just *kill you*? Doesn't it just . . ." He grins, slow and sly. "Make you want to *kill*?"

"Stop it!" Pip snarls.

But it does, and I lunge, and he slaps his left hand against the side of my head, hand cupped, making my ear ring. A spell blasts against my skin, harsh and burning, throwing me against the cavern wall. I just barely get my feet under me again.

"I'll kill him, I will!" the Viceroy hisses. "First you, then Kintyre, then little Miss Pip here will tell me how to get to her world, and I'll kill that self-important Elgar Reed for putting me through twenty years of *hell*! For making me lose *every time*!" he bellows. "I should have won! I should be king! I should own the *whole damned world*!"

His right hand glows a more intense green, and I realize, suddenly, what that means. I whip a look at Pip, and groan. *Dear Writer, no!* She is back under his spell! Pip herself is tense, holding her arms tightly at her sides, her head bowed and her jaw clenched, teeth bared. "I won't, I won't!" she is snarling, neck a mass of jutting tendons and eyes screwed shut.

"Obey!" the Viceroy snarls, and I take advantage of his distraction to try to bring my sword down on his arm.

He must have been expecting it, after Bootknife, for he swings himself wide and out of range. He raises both hands, each shining a different color, and Pip screams.

I risk a look over my shoulder at her and my heart stutters in my chest, horror crawling up my throat. She is hovering above the ground, toes brushing the loose gravel, arms straight out. Through the sleeves of her jerkin, I can see the green glow of the vine scars writhing, sliding over her neck and across her cheeks. Her head is thrown back, and the green glow is coming from inside her throat, too, illuminating her mouth. Green light radiates from her eyes, wide and lined with tears.

"Stop it!" I shout over the sound of her agony.

"Surrender to your death, and I will," the Viceroy replies, all calm. His left hand is ready, red filling the cracks between his fingers this time, prepared for the moment I lay down my sword.

"If I surrender, you will hurt her again, anyway."

"True," the Viceroy says. "But only because she screams so prettily." He twists his right hand, and Pip shrieks in demonstration, high and piercing and so filled with agony that I wince, my own throat tightening in sympathy. "Surrender, and I will stop."

What can I do? He is using Pip as a shield, for all that she is not between us. But he has been fighting me as he would fight Kintyre, all magic and threats, no finesse. Could I . . . ? Would he . . . ?

I take a clumsy, two-handed grip on Smoke, as my brother would do on his own great battle sword. The Viceroy tenses and rocks onto the balls of his feet. Smoke is too delicate a blade for bashing about, but I lift it as if it were heavier, more substantial, as if it would make me slower.

The Viceroy laughs and dances out of the way when I swing the sword down, all fleetness of foot but no skill, and he makes Pip scream again. I chase him again, thrusting clumsily, and he dodges. A third time, and I am sure of it. The Viceroy has fought heroes with swords before, but none with any skill. None like the Shadow Hand. None like *me*.

As rapidly as possible, as soon as I am steady enough after my third lunge, I spin on the ball of my foot, correct my grip on Smoke, and flick the blade at one of his wrists. I score a gouge in the left one, and he shrieks. It is not deep enough to sever the appendage, but blood begins to pour from the wound, and I feel confident—as the light in his fist flickers—that the blood loss will kill him in a matter of hours should the wound remain unattended.

I don't have hours, however, and neither does Pip. The Viceroy drops his left hand to his side, features twisted into the only human emotion I've ever seen him really feel—rage. I execute a needlessly flashy lunge, hoping the swiftness of the motion and the complicated arm gesture will distract him as easily as it ever distracted Pointe, and side step him. He thinks I have missed and takes a step back, right into the path of my point. It sinks in just above his right kidney, and he screams again.

Blast, I had been aiming for a lung.

The Viceroy wrenches himself off my blade and gestures with his green hand. Pip drops to the floor and curls herself upright, eyes narrowed and shining and focused on me. Another gesture, and I feel my stomach sink. Pip throws herself at me, arms wide for a grapple, and I just barely manage to duck under her. She is fast, and she has stamina. I am taller, but she is quicker. The Viceroy lands a blow against the back of my head, and I stagger forward and reel to the side in time to avoid Pip again.

Two on one, and one of my opponents is someone I would prefer not to harm.

Blast, shit, and fuck!

Pip steps forward, I step back, the Viceroy steps up, and we are waltzing. The three of us are dancing and ducking, limbs flying, spells sizzling, and my blade flashing. I am getting tired. I have never had such an extended bout, and never without breaks before. Adrenaline has given me what boost it can, but I feel myself flagging. My cuts are slower, my sword drooping, and I am making stupid, amateur mistakes that not even Pointe would make.

I stumble backward and land hard against the desk. My hip drives into the edge, and I swallow my yelp of pain. I pant, gasping, grasping for air, lungs and forearms and biceps burning. The Viceroy and Pip have me at an impasse.

"Surrender," the Viceroy hisses, glee crawling across his mouth but avoiding his eyes.

"How about no?" someone behind us says, and something fast and hard slams into the side of the Viceroy's head. He is on the ground before I can blink, head bleeding profusely from his temple.

"That's for all the times you threatened to pull out my eyes, you creepy twat!" Bevel snarls down at him, fingers flexing on the branch that he'd used like a club. The end of it is splintered and splattered with gore, and he tosses it away from him.

I look over to Pip, but she has fainted also, and is hanging limply from Kintyre's arms.

"Good fighting," my brother says to me. "Never seen anyone get close enough to score any hits, not with his magic."

"Do you concede that all of my 'flighty' style is worth something now?" I pant, unable to suppress my smile of triumph.

"Perhaps," Kintyre allows, but he is smiling too.

In his arms, Pip stirs. He sets her on her feet just as her eyes open and she lifts her hands to her head. "Ow. Christ. Forsyth?"

"I'm here," I say, and reach out for her. Instead of just taking my hand, as I thought she might, she curls herself against my body, tucking her shoulder under my arm and her cheek against my heartbeat. Her face is wet with sweat and tears, her eyes screwed shut, her breathing harsh.

I shoot a startled look at Bevel and Kintyre over her hair. Kintyre looks satisfied, but Bevel has such a look of pity in his dark eyes that I cannot help the feeling of guilt that curls in my gut.

I want to comfort Pip, but I can't. I don't love her. Not anymore.

"Pip," I say softly.

She straightens stiffly, pulls herself away. Her eyes are brown when she opens them.

"Are you well?" Bevel asks.

"Well enough." Her mouth is pink and red and white, not glowing, not green.

Kintyre kicks the Viceroy's shoulder, and the monster's head lolls, his eyelids fluttering. "He's alive."

The blood still pumps from his wrist, slowly, sluggishly, but continuously. An hour longer, and the Viceroy won't be alive anymore.

"Shoulda hit him harder," Pip says.

"I can finish the job easy enough," Bevel says and draws his sword. For all that Kintyre is the one the Viceroy has sought to destroy all these years, Bevel is the one he has tortured most. It feels right that Bevel should end him.

"Wait," Pip says softly. "Wait. No. Don't kill him. I have a better idea."

Kintyre and Bevel truss the Viceroy with vines pulled from the cavern wall. Pip laughs mirthlessly with the appropriateness of the rope. We do not treat any of his injuries—he is still slowly bleeding to death—but we don't need him to live. We just need him to be alive *for now*.

When he is secured, we prop him back against the desk, sitting, with his legs bound together before him. Bevel stands guard over him, eyes refusing to leave his frame, determined that the Viceroy will not escape this time, no matter that he is certainly in no condition to do so. The Viceroy's face is gray and slack, his head lolling, the bruise around his temple already a nasty black. I would lay even money down that his skull is fractured. With any luck, perhaps even his brain is bleeding. I can only hope.

"Are you sure you're ready?" Kintyre asks as Pip pulls both of our sacks over to the desk.

"I don't have anything to stay for," Pip says quietly, without looking up at either of us.

There is a small, soft surge of possibility in my gut, like my body remembers loving her, but my mind has forgotten, and won't be reminded. I feel like I should *want* to reach out, to protest, to fold her in my arms and kiss her into staying. To apologize for our fight, to soothe, to make it up to her with my lips and my hips. But I just stand there, frozen between conflicting yearnings, between instinct and intelligence, what I feel and what I know.

When I fail to protest, Pip begins to unpack the spoils of our quest.

Carefully, deliberately, Pip lays the objects on the desk, in order of our finding them. First, the sheet of paper with the Deal-Maker spirit's sigil, then the quill, the cup, the parchment, and the knife.

"Now what?" I ask.

Pip shakes her head. "I'm not certain. Your prophecy didn't really say what to do next. Just to get everything together."

"Perhaps we were meant to collect the Deal-Maker spirit, as well," I say.

"How do you collect a Deal-Maker spirit?" Pip asks.

"You don't," says a woman behind us.

We both turn, even as I hear Bevel and Kintyre draw their swords. There is a woman standing behind us, dressed as a serving girl with a scarf over her hair, obscuring her face. She wears Turn-russet livery.

"You're the Deal-Maker spirit that brought me here," Pip says softly, face slack with wonder. "I remember you."

"Yes," the spirit replies, and there's something about her voice, something about the way she says it that itches against my memory. There's also a bit of a sneer.

"Are you summoned?" I ask. "May we deal with you?"

"I am summoned," she allows, and then raises her head so that her face is visible. "I am summoned, and you may deal with me, Master Turn."

Beside me, Pip gasps in recognition and confusion. "You?"

"Ne-neris?" I stutter.

"Well, I had to keep an eye on my investment, didn't I?" Neris replies, with a smile like knives.

Twenty

ho is she?" Kintyre asks.

Pip rolls her eyes. "Exposition time. Of course. This is Neris. She was my lady's maid in Turn Hall."

"Your maid is a Deal-Maker spirit?" Kintyre says, eyebrows wriggling up into an expression of confusion that must be identical to the one I am wearing.

"But you're Cook's daughter," I say.

"Cook has no daughter," Neris replies, spreading her hands. "I made her think she did so you would welcome me to your household. Which is the first thing you said to me, if you'll recall, Master Turn. You bid me well come, and to stay. And that was all I needed."

"What did you do?" Pip asks. "What did you do to me, while I was . . . ?"

"Nothing," Neris admits. "And do not forget, I cannot lie. I did nothing to you, Miss Piper."

"And you did nothing for me, either."

Neris pouts. "Was I not an excellent lady's maid? I enjoyed it."

"I meant Bootknife. The Viceroy." Pip's voice is shaking, but her hands are steady, her stance solid even though I know her back must still be a riot of pain from the Viceroy's spells.

"Why would I?" Neris asks. "That would be interfering with the deal I struck with the Viceroy."

"What did you exchange?" I ask, eyes narrowed, trying to decipher Neris's appearance, use her gestures to guess at what she's thinking, but she is a blank slate. She is unreadable. Because she is not real. Her body is not *her*, and it leaves me answerless and frustrated.

"Ah, ah," she scolds. "That is my secret to hold."

"It must have been something spectacular," Bevel says, "to summon down a Reader."

Pip and I both goggle at him.

"What?" he says, shrugging. "Did you think it was a secret? From us? Please, I'm not an idiot, for all that I'm in love with one."

Kintyre shoots him a look that is part lust, part fondness, part exasperation, and wholly inappropriate right now.

"It was Kintyre's soul, wasn't it? Or his life? Something like that?" Pip blurts, suddenly. Neris makes a face, which means Pip has guessed correctly. "I thought so. Something was strange about the way the Viceroy talked about Kintyre's death. Said it wasn't his to collect."

"So, why have you waited?" Kintyre growls.

"I cannot kill," Neris sneers. "I can only take your death when it happens. But it has been *promised* to me. And I will keep it forever. I will make you relive it a hundred times, and then a hundred times again, just to savor the sensation."

Kintyre lifts his sword, but Bevel stays him. "You can't actually hurt her. Save your strength."

Neris laughs.

"No, hold on, that's wonky," Pip says. "The Viceroy can't bargain with something that isn't his, that's not how the rules of this world work."

Neris's expression clouds, her fists clench, and, from between her teeth, she hisses, "No, he should not have."

"But you were forced to accept it," I jump in. "Why?"

Neris shakes her head.

"Tell us the truth," Pip demands. "You *have* to."

"I can choose not to speak!" Neris snarls.

"Tell us, and maybe we can break it," Pip says. She has her hands out before her, pleading, and I can see the marks on her wrists from where she first came to my world and cut them. Small, white pebble scars. I know how they feel against my tongue, even though I didn't know what they were at the time. That same conflicted yearning pulls at my insides, and I squash it back down. Now is *not* the time.

Neris's whole body slumps, liquid, and, for a moment, I fear she will splash down against the ground and vanish. She wavers like a water spout instead, and then rises back up. "Blood," she says. "He obtained the blood of a Deal-Maker and used it in the spell. She was my sister."

"I'm sorry," Pip whispers. "I bet you want revenge."

"Yes."

"Is that something we can trade in?" Pip asks. She gestures to where the Viceroy is bound and gagged at the foot of the desk. "Can I give you him, even though he's not mine to give?"

"I am still bound by the blood," Neris says, and her voice has become sharp and horrific. "I must take that which is offered."

"Then I offer the Viceroy," Pip says.

Neris makes a high keening sound of animal joy. "I *accept*." It is a low hiss. She reaches out and touches the top of his head, covetous and cruel. The Viceroy stirs, eyes fluttering open.

Within seconds, he understands his position, and he tries to scream. But Neris's hand is on his throat, and no sound escapes.

"Will you hurt him?" Bevel asks, shifting, uncertainty flicking across his features.

"Oooh, yessssss," Neris hisses.

Bevel nods, firmly, once. Decided. "Good."

The Viceroy begins to buck and writhe, but he cannot wriggle away; he soon tires, the blood loss too much. Neris waves her hand over his face, and he slumps, sinks into the ground as if he was made of liquid, and vanishes.

Forever, I hope viciously.

Then, Neris straightens. "And what do you want in return?"

Pip is about to speak, but then she stops, hesitating. Before she can change her mind, I say, "Send Pip home. To her own world. Restore her to her place as a Reader."

Neris considers, and then slowly, just once, shakes her head. "No. The payment is not great enough."

"But it's a whole person!" Kintyre protests. "Surely, one person for another is enough!"

"One person for one person, agreed," Neris says. "But I never received payment for the first exchange." She licks her lips at Kintyre, who balks and takes a step back, hand tightening on his hilt.

"That's hardly our fault," Pip says. "So renege! Send me back."

"No," Neris says. "I will accept the Viceroy as payment for bringing you here, and I will swap that only for Kintyre's death."

"That's not fair!" I explode, but the look of relief in Bevel's eyes stays the rest of what I was going to say.

Kintyre lets go and reaches toward his lover, and Bevel clings to him with deliberate desperation.

"No, it is fair. We accept," Pip breaks in, eyes also on their clasped hands. "Kintyre's death remains his own."

"Agreed," Neris says, and shakes Pip's hand.

Pip stares at it after the spirit withdraws, fascinated, obviously, with the texture of Neris's skin. Had Neris ever touched me in Turn Hall? I can't recall. I want to experience it, too, but I daren't reach out, in case I accidentally accept a deal as well. Neris is staring at me, smug, challenging.

"Now, about sending Pip home," I say.

Neris smiles and shrugs. "I must expend a great deal to do so. I'm not certain there is anything at all which you could offer me that would make up for that."

Pip bites her lip, thinking hard. Even Kintyre and Bevel look like they are considering it. I see Kintyre's eyes flick to his hand, still twined with Bevel's, and Bevel shakes his head viciously.

Don't you dare, I say with my expression, when Kintyre levels a look at me.

Make him understand, his eyes say back.

I won't let you do it, either, I reply. *You're happy.*

I am. He relents, and Bevel presses closer, resting his forehead on my brother's bicep, relieved.

Pip sucks in a great deep breath and tilts her head back, eyes on the small circle of blue sky visible at the top of the chasm.

"Everything," Pip says. "I offer everything. My whole time here. My memory of all of it, my scars, any physical, mental, or emotional proof that I ever existed in this place. I give up the one thing that every scholar, every fan-girl has ever wanted—I will give you my adventure."

It feels like a betrayal in the worst way. It feels like someone has reached into my guts with a hot iron and scrambled them all around. It feels like a punch in the face, and a punch in the sternum, driving all the air from my lungs, the oxygen from my blood, the joy from my heart.

"Pip," I gasp, and it sounds like a drowning man begging for water, and I don't care, I don't, because I *am*.

I don't love her anymore, but that doesn't mean I want her to *forget* me. To forget any of us! All of this!

"Pip, no!" Bevel says, and the pain on his face seems to reflect the one that is shooting across the underside of my skin. "You can't mean that!"

"What else is there? A person for a person, an experience for an experience!"

"I want that!" Neris snarls. "Yes, yes. Give that to me. I accept, oh, I accept! Give it to me, your time here. Give me everything that you were, everything that you *felt*!" Her eyes have become slits; her pupils elongate, and there is a tongue flicking between her teeth, black and long, licking her chops, her mouth watering for Pip's life here, for her love, for her suffering, for her joys, and . . . no. No, this creature cannot have it. Everything that I felt is tied in with everything Pip felt, and this monster *cannot take that away*.

"Give it to me, I accept, give it to me!" Neris howls.

"No," I shout over her squeals of excitement.

"It's not yours to give!" Pip shouts back at me. "Or to deny!"

"But it is my life, and she can't have that. I don't want her to see how much I loved you!"

"You gave it up!" Pip shrieks. "You decided it was too hard, and you *gave it up*!"

"I gave it up because it was making you *miserable*!" I snarl back. "I gave it up to make it easier *on you*! I gave up my love for you because I *love you*, you fool!"

Pip rocks back on her heels, eyes wide.

"No, no," Neris hisses, fingers grasping and long, clawed and ready to rip into Pip's adventures, Pip's memories, to rend and to tear and to desecrate, and I *will not have it*.

Before anyone else can make a move, I turn on my heel and snatch the sigil paper off the desk. "Spirit, we are done deal-making!" I snarl, and rend the paper in two, breaking the sigil.

"No!" Pip screams. "Forsyth, *no!*"

She lunges for Neris's hand, even as the spirit wails, writhing and melting, sinking into the ground. Pip tries to follow her down, but Bevel grabs hold of her shoulders, hauls her off her feet and back, hugging around her waist. Pip kicks futilely at the air, her heels drumming against his shins, but he doesn't let go.

"No, no, no!" Pip screams, wails, sobs.

And when Neris is completely gone—not even a wet patch on the pebbles to show where she was—Bevel releases Pip. She whirls around and socks him in the jaw. His head snaps sideways, eyes wide with surprise, and Pip dances backward, shaking out her fist and swearing.

"You son of a bitch!" she screams. "How dare you, all of you!"

"You have no idea what you were about to do!" I shout.

"I was *going to go home*!"

"No, you weren't!" Kintyre snarls. He starts toward her, hands up as if trying to calm a skittering horse, and Pip stumbles back out of his reach. He stops. "It was a trick!"

"What are you talking about?" Pip snarls. "She has to tell the truth!"

"But she can still twist things!" I snarl back. My whole body is one great big ball of tension, unused energy, fear zinging along every nerve, leaving me nauseous and hurt. "She would have taken everything. Not just what you experienced. She would have erased you *entirely* from this world."

Bevel sucks in a shaking breath. "Me and Kintyre?"

"Yes, that would never have happened!" I say, pointing at them.

"Forssy's new self-confidence," Kintyre says.

"Yes, that too," I say. "And the death of Bootknife and the Viceroy."

Pip opens her mouth to challenge us, and then snaps it closed. For a long second, she glares hatefully at each of us in turn, but then I see it, the moment it happens in her brown eyes, the exact second when she *gets it*.

"Oh my god," she breathes, realization rolling up her face like a cloud of steam. "That's how Reed works. You're right. That's what he would have done. If I'd agreed, it would have all gone back to the way it was. Cosmic reset. A retcon! 'And then they woke up!' God, that's *just* his style," Pip whispers. She sucks her lips inward, biting on them, torn and hurting and surprised, too shocked to really process what she's saying, I think.

"How would that have been bad, though? I mucked up everything in this world. Surely a reset—"

"No," Kintyre interrupts. "No, I don't want to. I don't want to go back to that man who . . . doesn't love Bevel. And isn't kind to his brother. Who sees no merit in emotional attachments. I don't want to, and you can't make me."

Kintyre's proclamation is so sincere that Pip is startled into tears. Her chin wobbles. "I nearly ruined everything."

"But you didn't," I say softly. "It's fine."

"It's not *fine!*" Pip says. "I nearly ruined *everything.* How can you all just stand there and forgive me?"

"We're heroes." Bevel shrugs. "It's what we do."

"Oh, god," Pip whispers, covering her face with her hands. "Oh, god, I'm sorry. I'm so sorry."

"It's okay, Pip," I say, and gather her carefully into my embrace, petting her hair with one hand, the other cupped gently over the vulnerable flesh at the nape of her neck. "It's okay."

✍

It is too late in the day to climb out and make it back to the base of the mountains, so we make camp against a wall of the Rookery, each of us wanting to be as far away from the desk and the red-stained stones around it as possible. There is a bit of forest around the lip of the chasm, which explains where Bevel got the branch he brained the Viceroy with. It is from there that Kintyre returns with an armload of firewood and a brace of birds for eating. I don't look too closely at what kind they are before they are defeathered.

Pip is curled up once again under the Shadow's Cloak, small and thoughtful. She isn't as miserable this time, but she doesn't seem happy, either. I sit down near her, in case she needs me, and she scoots over, wrapping both of her arms around one of mine, resting her head against my shoulder. She is warm, and it is comfortable, so I don't shake her off. Besides, I think we could both use the comfort of human touch just now.

Bevel and Kintyre busy themselves with dinner preparations, whispering to one another and stealing impertinent kisses when they think we're not looking. Pip sighs, and it's not one of longing, but I can't tell what kind it is, either.

"I'm sorry," Pip says.

"You don't have to keep apologizing," I say.

"No, I mean . . . for what you said earlier. About . . ." She fidgets. "About being an emotional bully."

"Oh."

"I just . . . I thought I knew everything about these books, about how Reed writes, about his . . . *failings*. And I thought, I can fix this! I can bludgeon fairness into this world! Only, I didn't realize I was bludgeoning you, too."

"I wouldn't call it *bludgeoning*, per se."

Pip chuckles a little, low and not entirely genuine. "But I wasn't kind. I wasn't . . . I didn't treat you like a person. I treated you all the same, when I should have listened, and watched, treated you like a human being in and of yourself. Instead of as an extension of Reed's issues."

I turn my face down to meet her gaze. "I did learn from you. Things I wouldn't have considered otherwise."

"But I was an asshole about it. That's what I'm apologizing for."

"I learned from you," I repeat. "And I will never regret that. No more than Kintyre will ever regret it, or Bevel. It just . . . it broke my heart that your pain was so great that you missed what I was trying to say."

"If I had the chance, I would do better. I can," Pip says. "I can do it better."

"But we don't have the chance."

She grimaces. "Who knows? I might be stuck here forever now."

"I don't love you," I say again, but it seems rather more like a knee-jerk denial this time.

Pip looks startled that I would even say it, and, immediately, the hurt flits across her expression, then is gathered up and tucked away behind a cracking mask of indifference.

"I know that," she says, and it is just this side of too polite, too cool to be truly indifferent. Something that had started swelling in my chest, at her concern, heats and grows. I try to tamp it back down, but it won't go. "But we seemed to work, you can't deny that. I mean, we're the same. You loved me, and I . . . could learn to love you on my own. Maybe even do, a little." She grimaces again. "This isn't fair. Him using me like a prize in a cereal box like that. It's just so the way Elgar Reed uses women. I would have liked to . . . to have decided if I loved you on my own merit."

I say nothing. I don't want to push, but if Pip goes away now, if she leaves me now, I will spend the rest of my life wondering if we could have been something, something just our own, without the Viceroy, something . . . *marvelous*.

But then, another, uncharitable part of me immediately thinks, *Well, do not expect an invitation back to Turn Hall!* Which is unfair, because, though I may no longer care for Pip as a lover, she is yet my friend, and I will not see her abandoned. It is just me feeling a bit mean and ill-used, her apology dredging up the feelings of inadequacy and anger that the original offense created.

Another, smaller part of me, some breath of smoky ember buried under the ash of my disappointments and weariness, flares a little closer to true heat. For Pip *has* apologized, and she *is* my friend, and with more time together . . . with more *time* . . .

We could both do better. If we had the chance. But better at . . . ? At what, precisely, are we both so cautiously aiming that we daren't name the target? Our arrows are knocked, our strings pulled tight, but what is the intent?

I am silent in my contemplation, and for apparently long enough to discomfit Pip. She pokes my side gently to regain my attention and asks: "So, what do we do now?"

I think about the long descent into the Stoat Forest, of the remaining twelve days, of how long it will take us to make it home, and to my library. "Go back down, go back to Turn Hall, I guess, and start researching again," I say. "Or back to Kingskeep to beg a preservationist from the king and return to the Lost Library?"

Bevel and Kintyre, each carrying two trenchers of roasted bird and some sort of wild leaf salad, come to sit beside us against the wall. They hand a platter to each of us. Obviously, they have been eavesdropping and are choosing now, once the emotional mire of our conversation has been rerouted to the more practical course of planning, to join us.

"Do you really want to go back?" Bevel asks Pip as he juggles the hot meat between his fingers. "You don't have to. And with Bootknife and the Viceroy gone . . . I mean, the king will probably give you a title and some money. You could set yourself up here. Stay."

I say nothing, because, if I say anything, I have decided that it will be begging for her to agree. Pip, like Pointe, has grown to be one of my best friends. I do not wish to be parted from her, even knowing how selfish a wish that is. Pip has family back home—a grandmother, parents, a little dog—and she misses them. She will be missed.

But she will be missed here, too.

"Will you take a title and wealth for murdering two men?" Pip asks Bevel, eyes narrowed, thoughtful.

"Reckon I might," he says, licking grease from his fingers. "I grew up with nothing, and for those two, I *regret* nothing. I consider it a service, and, frankly, I'm sort of ready to, well . . . stop."

He looks up at Kintyre and squeezes his hand. Kintyre continues licking supper from between his teeth and shrugs, seeming to ignore Bevel's hand in his, except for where he curls his fingers around Bevel's. "Already got a title, don't I?" he says. "Could always use the wealth, though."

"The living is still quite well off, despite how much of my whiskey you drink when you're home," I point out.

"Then I'll give it to your free school," Kintyre says.

For a moment, all I can do is blink in surprise. "I . . . I thought, perhaps, that you . . . would have forgotten," I admit.

"Why would I?" he asks. Kintyre seems genuinely confused.

Bevel grins and pats Kintyre's thigh, amused. "You're all they talk about to me when I'm in town. Forssy this, Forssy that; 'Oh, Kintyre's brother, the lordling.' 'And did you hear what Master Turn did for that old poor widow? What a thoughtful soul!'"

Kintyre snorts, and bumps his lover with his shoulder. "Shaming, sometimes, to think all I do for Lysse is slay monsters."

Your people love you, Pip had told me once. I think I might finally believe her.

"As if slaying monsters is such a small service," I point out.

"It's one anyone with the right tools could do." Kintyre touches the hilt of Foesmiter in demonstration.

Bevel elbows Kintyre gently. "Sure, we take some evil out of the world, but, Forsyth, you fill it with good."

I do not know what to say to that, and my tongue flutters against my teeth, useless. I simply nod my thanks, feeling the blush creeping up my ears, and focus on my dinner.

When our trenchers are empty and Bevel has collected them up, we lay out our bedrolls. Kintyre and Bevel share, of course, and as Pip lays out her own bedroll and blankets, she gestures for me to lay mine directly beside her.

"It's cold up here in the mountains," she says, and I accept the excuse for the invitation it is.

Neither of us wants to admit that we are lonely, that we are missing one another, that we are trembling with the effort of holding our arrows back.

✍

We sleep wrapped around each other, content to just have another person in our arms; just us and the world. Bevel and Kintyre do the same, and it feels strangely wonderful to wake up in mirrored positions of contentment. Kintyre flashes a genuine smile at me over Bevel's shoulder—the kind I never thought I'd receive from my brother—when he catches Pip and me whispering to one another in the dawn.

For once, I do not covet what he has with Bevel, for I have it for myself, and I understand, suddenly, how much better it is to be happy for my brother than it is to be jealous of him.

Oh. No. Wait.

I sit up slowly, carefully untangling myself from Pip so as not to wake her, and run a hand through my dirty hair.

No. No, that's wrong. I do not love Pip.

The target at which yesterday's contemplations were aiming suddenly becomes clear. The topic that Pip and I are both avoiding, the thing for which we are shooting but dare not loose our bolts too soon toward, is *love*.

By the Writer.

Pip and I are falling in love.

Again?

No, for the first time. For she was not herself last time, and did not pick me; and the woman I thought she was was a ploy, so it was not the real Pip for whom I held my deep affection. But here, this, right now, this is Lucy Piper and Forsyth Turn, with no barriers between us but ourselves. A new love is growing. It is fresh, and new, and mine again.

I reach out, slow, bold, and brush the back of my fingers across the soft swell of her cheek, recalling the daring with which I had fallen asleep in her bed that first night, the way she had looked in the dawn's sunlight, the scent of her hair on the pillow. The arrow trembles.

My heart begins to rattle against my rib cage, and suddenly, my tongue is jumping in my mouth, my breath stoppered up behind my larynx. *Oh, Writer, it feels. . . .* It is a river at high swell, rushing over me, a river of warmth and golden light, and I cannot breathe, I cannot *breathe*.

My harsh pants must wake Pip, for she makes a soft little moaning sound, and it is intimate, Writer, so *sweet*, for I remember it so fondly from other mornings. My heart surges, the bullseye comes closer, and I feel like I should be shouting a warning to the world, that I should be pushing Pip away or gathering her close, or screaming, or *something*, but all I can do is stay still, frozen, powerless and happily so, as she stretches and turns a little so her face is to the sky.

Her eyes are closed, and I'm somehow at the edge of a cliff I didn't even know was there, toes already out over open air—and I am going to fall. The moment she opens them, I will fall, the arrow will fly, and I will be lost again. And found.

Pip turns her face up, automatic and comfortable. She reaches her arms up, curls them around my shoulders, finds my neck, and pulls my head down before I realize what is about to happen. She pecks a short, distracted kiss on my lips.

I dare not move. I dare not *breathe*. The edge of the cliff crumbles out from under me. The string of the bow fights me.

Pip's eyes slit contentedly, like the Library Lion while receiving scratches, and then blow wide with shock as she realizes what she has just done. What *habit* has made her do.

"Oh," she breathes. "I . . ."

"Pip."

"I'm sorry," she says, and tries to squirm away, but I'll not let her.

No, I will not be a coward about this, and I will not let her be a coward either. I roll just enough to pin

Pip beneath me, watching her face for any sign that she wants to be let up. She twines her arms around my neck instead, pulling me down on top of her so that we are touching from nose to knee cap.

I lean down, slow enough to give her time to protest, and cover her mouth with mine. It is warm, slick, and I kiss first her bottom lip, then her upper. Her tongue dances out to lick, and I open, obliging, *welcoming*. And it is like waking up after an eternity of being asleep.

Something fizzes against my mouth, and I swipe my tongue into hers, warm and wonderful and perfect. She moans against me, reaches up and tangles her fingers in the hair at the base of my neck. I am in desperate need of a haircut. There is something warm against my palms, and I realize that I have lifted my own hands, am cradling her face, pulling her closer. Pip rises to her knees, presses her breasts against my arm, half crawls into my lap in an effort to consume me with her kiss.

We part for breath, and stare in wonder at one another.

The arrow flies, swift and sure, and twangs into the bullseye.

Oh, I think. *Oh, well then. That was . . . quick.*

Pip breaks first, giggling, and I follow after her, letting her settle into my lap. I lay my hands over her bottom, and she lays her cheek against my collarbone.

"Do you believe in love at first sight?" I whisper into her ear. "*Bao bei?*"

Pip laughs, just a little, a soft, sweet sound that puffs against the bottom of my ear and makes me shiver. I tighten my arms around her shoulders, and she nuzzles closer.

"At first sight?"

"Or True Love's Kiss, then?"

"Yes," Pip says. "Yes. All of it. Now, I do. And you?" Her eyes are anxious, searching, darting across my face, as if trying to seek out any answers I would hide in the wrinkles beside my eyes or the hairs of the sparse beard that I have not had the opportunity to shave in a week. "You said you loved me. That you gave up your love *because* you loved me."

"That is a contradiction, an impossibility," I point out, and I cannot wait for her answer, for her kisses call to me like a siren I am helpless to disobey. I cannot seem to separate my mouth from her skin.

When I move down to press my mouth to her neck, to that little place under her ear that makes her gasp and squirm, the place where I like to leave my mark, Pip throws back her head and gasps: "Impossibility or not, you're the one who—*Christ!*—who said it. God, don't stop." She writhes and presses up against me, hands scrabbling to hold on, curling into my hair, into my collar, along my back, gripping, grasping, holding on for dear life. "Oh, Forsyth. Do you only love me because this is how these stories work? I am the female protagonist; I am the trophy. I am the quest within the quest, and you only want me—wanted me—because you were supposed to?"

"No," I smear against her throat, kissing down to the '*v*' that the laces of her shirt leaves bare between her collarbones. "No, never, Pip. Never. I want you, only you, Lucy Piper. Writer, Pip. I lo—"

On the other side of the growing fire, Kintyre and Bevel whistle and hoot and applaud, surprising me so badly that the rest of what I was going to say splutters and takes off like a startled pack of grouse.

I jerk back, falling into the wall of the Rookery, and Pip topples to the side, surprised at first, and then filled with unrestrained, joy-filled, full-belly giggles.

We break camp after that, and pack up. It is slow going because Pip and I must stop to touch, to reaffirm, to kiss and smile and giggle as much as possible, to be certain that the other one hasn't wandered too far away. Bevel takes our dawdling as permission to do some dawdling and canoodling of his own, and twines himself around my brother, leaning up for kisses when he can reach them, kisses which Kintyre suffers gamely and with much eye-rolling.

Pip takes charge of the desk, packing away the objects. She picks up the cup and turns it around and around, watching the salt water slosh along the rim.

"What I don't understand," she says out loud, "is why *these* objects? Why the desk, and the cup, and all that?"

"Deal-Maker spirits are vain," Kintyre says.

"She probably saw herself as some sort of Writer," Bevel elaborates. "Wanted the set-up."

"But it's . . . it's nearly too perfect," Pip says. "And we never really *used* any of it."

"We never do," Bevel says, coming over to stand beside her and fiddle with the knife. "It's always just a pretty tableau."

"Still . . ." Pip says. "It's a bit convenient, isn't it? I mean, a desk, a quill, a parchment . . . a cup of water—that's like ink—and a knife to sharpen the quill. It's as if . . . as if . . ."

Time seems to slow to a molasses crawl, and then, suddenly, with the shattering tinkle of epiphany, the answer is *there*. I figure it out the same time she does, and we exchange an identical look of wonder and triumph.

"I got it!" Pip says. "I got it! Dear lord, I got it!"

I drop our bedding, where we were rolling it up, and rush to her side. "If you . . . if you just *write*," I say. "Then it may happen!"

"I could. I could just . . . write that a way home for me opens."

"And it ought to!" I crow.

We throw ourselves at one another, thrilled by our mutual cleverness and kissing through the happiness. It is Bevel who ruins it. His voice is like the knell of a gong through the Rookery, deep and somber: "So, you are leaving, then?"

Pip and I part, slowly, as if we are connected by spider webs of toffee, mouth to mouth, eyes to eyes. Heart to heart.

"I . . . I guess I am," she says. She looks up at me, confused, surprised, and then sad, so *sad*.

"You don't have to," Kintyre protests. "You can *stay*."

I can see her hesitating, see her weighing it in her mind, balancing the life she could have here, with me, with us, at Turn Hall, in Hain, against the life that she had before, the one I know almost nothing about, but the one where she is a respected scholar and a beloved daughter. And I see it, the moment the balance tips out of my favor.

Forsyth Turn . . . still not *good enough*. She must see the pain of it in the way I squeeze my own eyes shut, my eyelashes clumping with moisture that I will not allow to fall. She must see the way it crushes me. The way the arrow and the target both turned to powdery ash. The way the fall from the cliff ceases to be a comfortable dance in the air and becomes a terrifying plummet.

She reaches up and cups my cheek in her palm. "Oh, *bao bei*," she whispers. "I don't belong here."

Bevel makes a noise of protest, low in his throat. "You could."

"No," I say softly. I open my eyes and find myself looking into a mirror. We both know that she wants to stay. But we also both acknowledge that she cannot. "It's too dangerous, isn't it, Pip?"

She nods. "I know too much. I know *everything*. I could ruin it all."

Bevel and Kintyre twine their fingers again and say nothing. They are proof, proof that all it would take is the right words at the right time . . . or the wrong words, at the wrong time.

"And you have a family," I say. "Mother, Father. Grandparents?"

"Just *wai po*, Mu—Mum's mum. She was crying at my graduation, she was so proud."

"You have to go," I say softly.

"I have to go," she agrees.

It feels like there are magnets in my lips. I can't not kiss her, and once we connect, I cannot stop kissing her. Bevel and Kintyre don't interrupt, and Pip allows it because . . . because this is it.

This is our goodbye.

I knew this was coming. I knew it all along.

It does not make it hurt any less.

We finally part, and, Writer, how it aches. But it is a good ache, a happy ache, because it means I got my love back. That I love Lucy Piper, and I will for the rest of my life. And I would rather love her and miss her, than never have loved her at all.

Pip turns to the Desk that Never Rots. She picks up the Blade that Never Fails. She shaves the barest curl of silver off the point of the Quill that Never Dulls. She dips the raw quill in the Cup that Never Runs Dry. She shakes off the excess salt water and writes on the Parchment that Never Fills.

She writes:

And then the girl used the Writer's tools, and with them, wrote the Words that opened the portal back to her own world.

The flash of light is exactly like the one from the scrying mirror—dazzlingly white and oblong, hovering in the air to the left of the desk. There is no wind from it, no sucking force, no breeze. Just the soundless impression of shattering. And then, it just . . . *exists*.

Light glimmers around the Rookery, turning everything silver-lined and bright.

Pip sets down the quill and takes a step toward it. Then she turns, startlingly fast, and slams herself against me—knees, chest, lips, nose.

"Thank you," she says between increasingly desperate kisses that I am helpless to rebuff.

"I have so very much enjoyed being your hero, Lucy Piper," I admit, breathing the words back into her mouth.

"And I hated every second of being a damsel in distress, Forsyth Turn," she sobs back. "But I loved having an adventure with you."

I run my hands across her temples, smoothing back the wild lay of her hair and wiping the tears from her cheeks with my thumbs. "Shh, no, Pip," I say softly. "You were never just a damsel. You rescued me. We rescued each other. You were my partner. You were my Bevel. You were more, to me. You were my hero, too."

She surges up and wraps her arms around my neck, as if, in not touching me, I will suddenly dissipate into smoke. I allow it, cling back, my long arms around her back, the tips of my fingers pressed to the bottom of her breasts, because I fear the same of her.

"*Bao bei*! I'm going to miss you so much!" she cries.

I turn my head so my nose is resting along the delicate shell of her ear. "And I you, my darling woman."

Through the strands of Pip's hair, standing behind her, I can see that Bevel is dabbing at his eyes with the cuff of his shirt. I turn my head the other way in an effort to keep the burn in my own eyes from growing in sympathy, only to have my gaze land on Kintyre. He is weeping unashamedly, the tears rolling in fat gobs down his rugged cheeks. It seems as though heroes do, in fact, cry.

I am powerfully affected by his blatant display, and my own resolve crumbles. I bury my face in Pip's neck and weep.

"I don't want you to go," I say, smearing the words into her skin, wishing they could leave a mark there, a tattoo, for her to see in the mirror every morning. *Here is the spot where Forsyth Turn told me he didn't want me to go, and still I went. But I was loved, the spot proves it, and I am missed.*

"I've gotta," she whispers back, laying her own invocation into my skin.

"I know. It doesn't make my want for you to remain lessen any." I sniffle into her hair.

"Oh, by the Writer's balls! This is stupid!" Kintyre blurts.

Pip and I both jerk apart from one another, and I turn to face my brother, affronted. *I thought we were beyond this!*

But before I can chastise him, he makes a shoving motion toward the split of light that hovers in the sky. When I only blink at him, he rolls his eyes and makes an exasperated hand gesture. "Go with her, you dumb mule!"

"I can't—" I begin, but I do not know how to finish that sentence. *I can't go with her. Can I?* Or is it that I fear it? "What about Turn Hall, and Lysse Chipping?"

Kintyre mops at his face and hooks his thumbs into his belt. "Reckon it's about time I stepped up and did my duty as the eldest, eh?"

"Oh, sleeping in a bed!" Bevel moans, and the sound is nearly sexual. He claps a hand over his mouth, blushing furiously, and then lowers it to grin sheepishly at us. "I'll make sure he does it right. Go on, Forsyth. We'll even return all the objects to where they belong for you, like you promised you would." Pip makes a sound somewhere between a hiccup of laughter and another wet sob. "Be kind to the Library Lion. He's lonely."

"Maybe he'll like Turnshire," Kintyre says.

"No! Think of the fur!" I protest, but my brother only laughs at me.

"You'll have to appoint a new Shadow Hand," Bevel says, voice soft, as if he fears bringing up administration logistics and interrupting our emotional moment.

"Sheriff Pointe?" Pip suggests.

"He'd be rubbish. He's too kind," I admit. "It must be someone sneaky, but moral."

Bevel coughs deliberately and bounces on his toes, grinning like butter wouldn't melt in his mouth. "Beds are all well and good, but Turnshire's boring," he points out, idly.

"I see," I chuckle and nod. Because, yes, of course. That is the most sensible option, but, honestly, the Writer help King Carvel. Bevel is a stubborn bastard, and is also probably the first Shadow Hand of low birth Hain has ever seen. He will be *perfect*.

Bevel just grins impishly. I hand the Shadow's Mask to Bevel, and he secrets it away in his Turn-russet jerkin. I cannot take it with me and strip Hain of all its power and knowledge. I lean forward and whisper the Words of Acceptance into his ear, and I can feel his smile stretching into something flattered and genuine.

Then I pull back to study Pip's face, and she is smiling, even as she cries. She wipes her nose on her sleeve, and then cranes her neck up for a hot, salt-flavored kiss. We take our time over it, tongues curling around one another, lips slick with wanting and acceptance. We part slowly, with a dozen lingering touches mouth to mouth, less like kisses and more a mutual drawing out of breath, connecting each to the other.

"Okay," I say. "Okay. I'll go."

"It'll be weird," she says.

"Weirder for me than this world was for you?"

"Maybe." She steps toward the light, one hand curled in my belt to drag me along with her. I dig in my heels, though, uncertain. Pip nods to herself and lets me go, then takes another step back. Even though we are not touching now, I am dragged forward by the movement. How I fear having her out of the reach of my arms. "Don't be scared, don't be scared, don't be scared," she says. Three times.

"I'm not," I say. And not because she said it three times, either.

"So, *bao bei*?" Pip asks, holding out her hand for me to take. Her eyes are bright and so very brown in the late summer sun. Her lips are wet, and her smile wide. "What do you say, Forsyth Turn? Think it's about time you had your own Happily Ever After?"

There is no hesitation in my reply.

I take her hand. And then, we step through.

Twenty-one

 am decided that, as much as I dislike quest-ing, and horseback riding, and heroic pursuits, airplanes are by *far* the worst form of travel that mankind has ever inflicted upon itself.

True, it is a great wonder to be able to fly as a bird, or a fairy, or a dragon might, and higher up in the air than any of the three. But the wonder is quite polluted by the airports themselves, by the lines, the security checks, the screaming children, the ignorant fellow passengers, the terrible food, and the indignity of cramped seats and aisles. Just the serving woman's hand upon my headrest each time she walks by is enough to jostle me closer and closer to annoyance with each subsequent pass.

All the modern conveniences, as Pip would say; and yet, none of the courtesy. Nobody is careful of one another's personal space. It is as if concern for one another evaporates the moment the liminal space of the terminal is breached.

The indignities don't end when our wheels touch the tarmac, either. Pip says I must not be so very upper-class and old-fashioned, but I really do wish there was a set of servants available to fetch our luggage from the carousels for us. Such a battle of shoulders and toes!

One of the things I like most in Pip's world is the way that people *are* expected to do things for themselves, rather than relying on laborers and footmen to do the fetching and carrying, rather than relying on cooks and serving women to do the domestic chores; but it is also sometimes the thing I like least. I enjoy being independent, being free to do as I like when the desire or need strikes. But I do very much miss just ringing a bell and having a meal brought to me in the library without having to rise from my chair or my book. Pip calls me lazy when I sit in my home office and bemoan the lack of servants, and adorably hopeless when I ruin her cookware by trying to do it myself.

Contradictory woman. I find it more endearing than I should allow.

But even the gently reared must work for their suppers in Pip's world, and, to that end, Pip has procured for me a daytime position stacking the shelves of the university at which she studied and to which she has returned to teach. Two mouths eat the food we buy, two bodies live in the condominium apartment that soars above the city in which we live, two people require clothing and money for transportation, and so, two pairs of hands must work to procure the currency required.

We are not too badly off, however. The condominium is purchased, not rented, because we made a very good trade on the golden dragonet tears I had been carrying in my purse when I crossed into Pip's world.

And working at the library gives me something to do with my long days while Pip is in her office, preparing the coursework for her students. I steal the books sometimes, for everything within this world is recorded, every action set down for posterity, and I want there to be no electronic record of my self-imposed syllabus. No . . . trail.

I am still trapped within the patterns of the Shadow Hand. For years, I left no path through paperwork and government for anyone to follow—I cannot make myself give up that habit now. I always replace the books, of course, the next day. Or the day after. Whenever I am done reading them. They are books on government and finance, commerce and agriculture, books on the history of the world, on the wars, on the politics, on the religions. Oh, so many religions. And so many of the wars *because* of how people interpret a single god's edicts.

I once told Pip I'd felt abandoned by Elgar Reed. Now, I feel lucky for it.

Once I have found our shared suitcase and plonked our travel bag on top of it, Pip leads me through the throngs of weary travelers to the outside. We get to bypass the security line, this time, because we are traveling within the same nation. I have no passport—the set of documents that are required to cross borders. Pip and I have signed a marriage license in order to begin the process of building a legal identity for me, but it is too new to allow me to have the passport of a "naturalized citizen" just yet. (Her parents were displeased with our lack of ceremony, done as it was in haste and at the city hall, but her *wai po* patted my cheek and called me, in her language, a "good boy." I had felt such a pang of warmth and welcome that it had made me weep. I miss Mother Mouth terribly.)

All these rules and regulations, and so much tracking of and accounting for citizens, it is a wonder that I have not been found out as having no past, no papers. It is a wonder that I am not already in jail for daring to sneak into existence.

When we reach the outdoors, the air tastes of dust and fuel fumes. I search for any whiff of greenery and find none. There is a shuttle to the hotel, which is nowhere near as dignified as it sounds. It is a very large bus crammed with people and the added joy of large suitcases, which makes it doubly claustrophobic and difficult to navigate.

Triply so when Pip's generous stomach must be taken into account.

Lust makes us do irrational things; Pip and I had been making love in my world for near on a month without prophylactics or medicines of prevention. I had no thought for such things, and Pip says they fell straight out of her head when we were together in my world.

So, when Pip first showed me the little blue cross on the white plastic stick seven months ago, it had been with an eye-roll directed at herself. "The heroines in the stories never get knocked up on quests," she had said.

"And so, it never occurred to you that you would?" I had asked. "Pip, I thought you smarter than that. We were having *sex*. An excessive amount of it. That *is* how one gets a baby into a woman."

"Shut up," she'd said, with a soft punch to my shoulder and a snarling grin. "We're not naming it after your brother."

"No," I'd agreed, kissing my favorite spot, the little scarred leaf at the back of her neck. "Certainly not."

"What's Sheriff Pointe's first name?"

"Rupin."

She'd made a face and said nothing else.

On the shuttle bus, people stare at my pregnant wife as if they are blaming me for her discomfort. They are, in a basely biological way, correct. Perhaps in a cultural way, as well.

Because, if we were home, she would be in her confinement by now. She would be in our bed, feet up and comfortable, being waited upon. I would be fetching dinner from Cook myself, feeding her with my fingers as she lay back in our marital bed, hair an ebony fan on the pillows, face aglow with our child. Pip despises laziness, thinks it's preposterous the way women about to give birth are coddled in my world, but I miss it. Women creating life are to be celebrated, pampered. Here, women are expected to work until their feet tire out and they can no longer stand, the weight of their soon-to-be-children sending them groaning to the floor.

It's barbaric.

Is it so wrong to want to cosset my wife? To keep her comfortable? To make the experience of bearing my child a pleasurable one?

At home, creating a child is magic, and is treated as such.

Here, they seem to think that creating a child is an inconvenience. And treat it as such.

For the journey, Pip and I had enough foresight to amalgamate our luggage into one wheeled case. We are only going to be away from home for six days, there is no need for a lot of clothing, and so there is relatively little space I need to carve out for my family on the bus. All the same, I wish there was a more pleasant way to go to the hotel. The sedate pace and the gentle civility of a coach and four would be ideal. Though, perhaps one fitted with an automobile's shock absorbers.

"You off to the con?" a woman seated beside Pip asks. She has a case nearly the same size as she is pinched between her knees and is holding an oversized paper mask delicately in her hands.

"Yeah," Pip says. "How did you . . . ?"

The woman jerks her chin up at me. "Great costume," she says. "Is it a sort of modern variant? Turn-russet jacket and everything, I love it. His hair is just perfect."

"Oh," I say, patting at my thinning fringe, and then running my palms down the chest of my coat. It is cashmere, and very finely tailored, and it was the first luxury I bought for myself with my first paycheck. It is Turn-russet, as I'd wanted to wrap myself in familiarity. My silk scarf is Sheil-purple. "Yes? I do thank you."

The woman makes a sort of short, high-pitched squealing sound. "And the accent!"

"*Bao bei*," Pip murmurs, and takes my hand. "Don't worry."

"About what?" I ask.

"There might be a lot of people who . . . I didn't think about that. Damn."

"About what? Pip?"

"I'll . . . I'll explain later. Right now, I can't . . . never mind."

"Can I get a pic?" the woman asks, pointing her cellular phone at me already. I nod my assent, and the machine clicks and whirrs, and then her fingers are flying over the keypad. "I'm so posting this. Have you got a handle?"

I look at my other hand, wound around the grip of my suitcase. "Yes?"

"No," Pip answers. "He doesn't tweet." I feel my mouth twist into a frown. I want to ask, but now is not the time. "I'll tell you later, *bao bei*," Pip murmurs, clearly agreeing.

When we arrive at our inn, I allow myself a few short seconds of gawking. For reasons that I can't explain, I had expected our lodgings to be rather like the taverna where Pip and I faced down the Schrödingers: reeking of grease and tallow, floor of packed dirt and rushes, walls stained with soot and stale splashes of old beer. Of course it is a towering, glittering sculpture of glass and chrome instead, rather like our condominium.

All the buildings stretch to the stars in this world, businesses and homes alike. Why should the inns be any different?

We make our way to a line of people awaiting their turn to approach a counter. I wave Pip toward the seats of a nearby lounge, but she shakes her head. "I've been sitting too much today. Swollen ankles or no swollen ankles, I am *standing*."

"As you wish," I concede, and it earns me the blinding grin I was looking for. She turns her face up to mine, and I obligingly lower my own for a kiss. It is soft, gentle, and, above all else, breathtakingly comfortable. The easy familiarity of it, the gift of having someone that I can kiss and it can be *routine*, is one in which I will never stop reveling.

Around us, a clamor of life rushes through the lobby; people of all walks clutching bags and talking animatedly with one another, embracing friends and shaking hands with new acquaintances, making exclamations over revealed identities, smiling and laughing and just happy to be here.

Pip surveys the spectacle with pride and joy in every line of her body. "My people, my tribe," she says. "Welcome to the madhouse, Syth."

I grin at the diminutive. It sounds a bit like *Seth*, which is a name of her world, and much less unwieldy for the people around us to use. We use it around her family, her colleagues at the university, our neighbors. My full name, my *real* name, is a secret treasure for Pip and Pip alone.

When we reach the counter, Pip tells the woman standing behind a computer terminal her full name and our reservation confirmation number. When the woman asks for the credit card we made the booking with, Pip looks to me expectantly.

Ah, yes, we are trying to build my credit rating and a paper trail. I fumble my wallet out of my back pocket and stare a bit dumbly at the contents, slightly overwhelmed by the plethora of shiny plastic squares that seem to stand in for *everything* here. The length of the flight and the noise around me has me a bit dazed, and I blink at the rainbow of squares dumbly.

"This one," Pip murmurs gently, gesturing subtly at the black card.

The woman behind the counter continues to smile a thin, milk-water smile and judges us with her gaze. I can tell that she very much wants to be an actress by the way she does her makeup, the way she stands, the way she gestures in a measured, theatrical way, by the cut of her hair and the style of her earrings—all of these give her away. But she will never achieve her dream because, for all that she has copied the poise and the style of the glittering stars of the fashion magazines, she is too abysmal at disguising her true feelings to project another's.

She finds the lobby full of geeks disdainful.

I sign the slip of paper she offers to us, and Pip takes the key cards; and then we are heading for the elevator doors. Even if there were servants to help with the luggage and to escort us upstairs, there are too many guests arriving at once. It is simply faster to attend to finding our rooms alone.

The first thing Pip does when we get inside our rented lodging is to make a bee-line to the bathroom.

"Your kid is napping on my bladder," she moans.

"Perhaps he has the right idea," I say back, voice raised to carry through the closed door. The room is dominated by a very large bed and an overabundance of beige. There is a set of drawers and a massive television, a small desk with a chair, a pair of armchairs set before the floor-to-ceiling window. We are very high up, and I abandon the suitcase in the closet to stare down at the people and cars crawling along the roads spread out below me like a map.

"No sleeping," Pip says.

"Do we have any plans? You haven't told me a thing about why we're here."

"No plans. Not until after dinner."

"Then I don't see why I can't nap. I'm tired."

"We crossed three time zones," Pip calls back out of the bathroom. "It's only three o'clock here, though. You can't sleep yet."

"Why not?" I ask, and the words come out a bit more petulant than I wanted.

"It'll throw your internal clock out of sync. Just stay up until our regular bedtime."

"That's seven hours away, Pip!"

She chuckles. "So have some coffee, you whiner." The toilet flushes.

I scan the room, shedding my overcoat as I go, and find a very small coffeemaker sitting on top of an equally small fridge. It is less than half the size of the machine at our house, but it looks like it operates the same.

I pull out the basket and flip open the lid, but there, I falter. There is no can of beans, no grinder, no paper filters, nor faucet to produce water for the machine anywhere in the room. The fridge has no freezer, which is where Pip stores our unground beans, and there are no cupboards stocked with cups and saucers and spoons. There are only metallic sachets that have pictures of flowers on the side. I read the words slowly, still having to take my time with Pip's alphabet, and they declare themselves coffee. But when I rip open the packages, I only find outsized tea bags.

I cast about for cups and only find paper cylinders of the sort we get at the local take-away shop, and the closest thing to cream I can unearth is a white powder in plastic squares.

"There is no coffee!" I shout to Pip, kicking the fridge in my frustration.

What I do not admit out loud is: *And if there is, I don't know how to make it.*

It is *infuriating*, this being *unable*. I was once master of my world, and now I cannot even decipher how to produce a simple cup of coffee from some stupid little machine! How I *loathe* feeling so *stupid*!

"Of course there is," Pip says, coming out of the washroom with a towel between her hands. "Here, give me the pot, I'll fill it."

"From the *bathing room*?" I ask, horrified.

"From the sink," Pip says. "Put that filter in the basket."

"It's *tea*," I protest.

"It's coffee. It's just in a bag, like tea. Same principle, different beverage." She turns her back to me to fill the carafe as soon as I put it in her hands. Good, because I do not want her to see how I shake.

Of course. Dumb old Forsyth. How could I not have reasoned that the tea-bag marked *coffee* would in fact contain coffee? I bite my lower lip hard enough that it stings, though I don't taste blood.

I forget that there is mirror above the sink, and Pip looks up and catches my expression in the reflection. She puts down the carafe, steps out into the room, and wraps herself into my embrace. I lean my cheek against the top of her head, spread my fingers along her back, and inhale.

"Sorry," she says. "I didn't realize how rough this was going to be on you."

"I'm f-f-fine," I say.

"You're lying," she replies. "You're not fine."

I nod slowly.

"Too much new in one day?"

It's our code for talking about the differences between our cultures, technologies, the pace of life, and the speed of information in Pip's world. I nod again.

"Culture shock sucks, eh?" Pip says.

I nod a third time.

"Listen, I'll make the coffee. You lie down and close your eyes for a bit, okay?"

"You said I shouldn't sleep," I say.

"A small nap won't throw you too far off."

"No," I say. "I'd rather stay awake and sleep well tonight. I will unpack the case."

Pip smiles and offers up a kiss, which I gladly, desperately take, needing to breathe her in, to taste her, to surround my senses and ground myself with the known. Then, we move on to our appointed tasks. The gurgle of the coffee machine is familiar, and the room takes on the scent of mornings at home. I am so sharply, swiftly reminded of the two of us dancing around one another in the kitchen with beautiful, domestic familiarity that I feel the tension slide out of my shoulders.

Once our clothing and coats are hung in the closet and tucked into the drawers, Pip and I each take a seat in one of the armchairs by the window and gaze out at the city spread beneath us. To the south, a very tall, gray tower needles toward the sky, and I wonder what its purpose is. Does this city's mayor or sheriff rule from this seat, or is it some monument to a past leader? Perhaps we will have time to visit it. Pip hands me a paper cup of coffee and puts her swollen ankles up on my knees. I obligingly rub the instep of one of her feet with my free hand.

Pip groans, and her eyes slip closed even as her hands tighten around her own coffee.

"Oh god, I love you, Forsyth Piper," she moans. I like it when she says my name like that, the way it is written on our marriage license.

"And I you, Lucy Piper," I reply. I take a sip of the coffee when I deem it cool enough and do my level best not to spit it back out immediately. I swallow and gag. "But I do not love this. This is disgusting," I say, staring at the flecks of white that have yet to dissolve into my drink.

Pip eyes me sideways and sips at her own cup. Then her nose wrinkles, and her mouth screws up in one corner. "Blech, you're right," Pip agrees. "Fuck the budget, let's phone up room service and get some proper coffee and cream. A snack, too; your kid is starving. Oh, do they have deep fried mozzarella sticks?"

"The inn provides a kitchen?" I ask.

"Yeah."

"Then why did we not take advantage of this service before?"

"It's expensive. And despite the mortgage, we're not wealthy, *bao bei*."

I used to be wealthy. But things here cost so *much*.

"We could be, if I could find better work."

Pip grunts. "We've been over this. You need to be patient. We need to build up a paperwork background for you before anyone will consider having you on as a securities manager or accountant. People are paranoid."

"What about being Shadow Hand? Can I not work for your queen?" I ask.

"She lives on the other side of the ocean," Pip says.

"You could move with me."

"We don't have the paperwork for that. Visas and things. They cost money, Syth." I make an indignant sound. "And when we get there, what would you have to recommend you? I doubt Liz has need for a spymaster— or, another one, at least—and Charles and Wills even less so. Prince William might have even read your books, and then what? They'll think you're a kook. They'll never let you near Kate and Georgie and Charlotte."

It is truth, but it still stings like a slap to the face. "I have services to offer. I hate being *stagnant*."

"I know, *bao bei*," she whispers, and leans forward, generous belly pressed to her thighs so she can bus a chaste, soothing kiss to my lips when I meet her halfway. "I know you do. But Queen Elizabeth the Second of the United Kingdoms of England, Wales, Scotland, and Northern Ireland and the Commonwealth does not need a Shadow Hand. She has MI5."

"And James Bond."

Pip chuckles. "Nope, he's fictional too. Books, as well as the films we've watched."

"But if Double-Oh Seven showed up on the doorstep to her castle, she would employ *him*, I am certain."

Pip looks at me with such sadness in her eyes, such pity, that I am forced to look away.

"Tell me how to phone up room service," I say, rising to my feet and going to the telephone on the desk, desperate for a change in subject and mood. "I believe I have room for one more new thing today."

☞

I lay down for a small nap while we wait for the food to be delivered to our door. Well, I close my eyes, at least. But with Pip pacing circuits around the room, reading through a plastic bag of documents that she acquired down in the lobby, my attention, if not my gaze, is on my wife.

Wife.

I had dreamed many times in Lysse that I would find a wife in the abstract, that I could attract a lovely, kind companion and helpmeet of my own. And when Pip and I began our affair, there had of course been fantasies of being able to keep her forever. But in her world, partners don't have to be wed to be together, or to have children. Many couples simply cohabitate with no legal documents to bind them. When I learned this, I decided that proposing marriage to Pip would be unwelcome. She was of a world where it was the choice to remain together that was important, the romantic gesture, and not the actual binding.

Such a surprise, then, when Pip had come in to breakfast one morning, very shortly after I arrived in her world, when we were still in her old apartment, and said, "Yes, I accept."

"Accept what?" I'd asked, attention on the newspaper spread out in front of me, practicing my reading.

"I'll marry you."

I had looked up so sharply that I had nearly bit my own tongue. "I . . . w-when d-did I . . . ?"

"On the road," Pip had said. "You wanted me to laugh the shadows out of Turn Hall. I asked if you were proposing to me, and you blushed and didn't answer. So, I'll answer instead. Yes, I'll marry you."

I had folded up the newspaper carefully to buy myself a few moments in which to organize my thoughts and calm my tongue. Then, I had looked up and reached out, taken Pip's hands between mine, threaded our fingers together and kissed each soft, small knuckle.

"You don't have to simply because you think my morals dictate it," I had said slowly. Pip had thrown back her head and laughed.

"I want to," she said. "Besides, I was thinking about how to get your legal paperwork started. You have to exist somewhere. A marriage at city hall just needs some photo ID, and I'm sure I can find someone to make you a fake driver's license. My undergrads do it all the time. And then, if there is something official on file, we can build you up. Get you a social insurance number, get you some legal work, you know."

I had tried not to let the ball of icy disappointment that had been crystallizing in my gut show on my face. "So, it is a marriage of legalities?"

"Well," Pip had said, "I'm twenty-five, and you're twenty-seven, and I think calling you my *boyfriend* is just a bit juvenile, don't you think? I much prefer the term *husband*."

The icy ball shattered under a swift warm glow of relief. "I rather do like the term *wife*."

Pip grinned. "Strange how something so blatantly economic and patriarchal can make me so gooshy."

"You believe, as many of your compatriots do, that marriage is not necessary for a couple to declare their love?"

Pip had used her grip on my hands to pull them toward her mouth, kissing each of my wrists. "Marriage was originally a business contract, in which an object called daughter was exchanged with another man and changed into an object called wife."

"But surely that's not still the case."

"No, now wives and husbands are meant to be equals in the relationship, to both have a choice. Marriage is now a declaration before friends, family, and the government that the relationship we have is one that we have decided to declare as permanent, and binding. And that whatever personal arrangement we have within the framework of a legal marriage—whether we're poly, or swingers, or have decided to be solo monogamous—is ours alone, and one we are happy with."

I had grimaced. "That is not very romantic."

"Sure it is," Pip had said, grinning cheekily. "There's nothing more romantic in this world than being willing to do all that damn paperwork."

I can't help the chuckle that now escapes as I recall that morning. It is traditional for couples to exchange tokens of intent in Hain when an alliance is formed. The Pairing gift is an important and symbolic. Rulers exchange property, soldiers exchange knives or swords, knights may swap pennants or horses, and farmers offer tools or Words. With lovers, it is less dictated by tradition. If the couple is male, they will sometimes exchange garments, or tools or weapons appropriate to their trades. Bevel and Kintyre, it seems, bought each other clothing in the colors of House Turn. Between women lovers, I am of the understanding that the tokens are usually more sentimental—blank books for turning into diaries, or small decorative combs for the hair.

In Pip's world, the proposer usually gives the propose-ee a ring. I don't know why a ring, instead of any other piece of jewelry, but I do know that it is a tradition. I have seen it enough on the television.

Though I couldn't afford it immediately, I did eventually procure a ring for Pip. And she one for me. Bands of matching silver reside on both our hands, and I brush the pad of my thumb over the smooth, warm metal now.

The soft moment is ruined by a subtle knock on the door. I rise and allow the serving boy to enter with the wheeled cart. He lays out a coffee service and a covered platter on the narrow desk, and then retreats as far as the door. He looks at me expectantly.

Unsure of what he wants, I say, "Thank you, that will be all," and he rolls his eyes. The rudeness of the gesture startles me.

Pip heaves herself toward her purse, fishes out two silver-and-gold coins and presses them into the boy's hand. He smiles, nods, thanks us, and closes the door.

"You must pay them to go away?" I ask.

"You tip them for the service."

"Does the inn not pay them?"

Pip chuckles. "Yes, but not a lot. If you tip really well, they'll pay extra attention to you."

"So, we are paying extra for a level of service that we should receive anyway, and the inn does not pay them a fair wage in order to make them servile to our whims? Ridiculous."

Pip shrugs. "I never said everything in this world makes sense."

We resume our seats in the armchairs and our perusal of the city, this time with proper, decent coffee. Pip has a plate of French fries balancing on her stomach, and they nearly topple when the baby stretches and kicks it. We both can't help but laugh.

Twenty-two

When it is time for dinner, Pip showers and changes into fresh denim trousers and a soft, floaty green shirt that covers her scars but leaves her impressive bosom on tasteful display. I exchange my t-shirt for a waistcoat in Turn-russet, which matches my trousers, and a button-down in cream. I leave the top two buttons open, and even now, eight months later, having no neck cloth feels indecent. So does leaving my bottom visible in the trousers, with no house-robe to cover it.

531

"So posh," Pip murmurs, running her hands over my chest and down the lapels of my waistcoat. "You sure do clean up nice, *bao bei*. Put me to shame."

"Not at all," I demur, and hold open the door for her.

We go down to eat in the hotel restaurant, and it is a buzzing field of fans and friends indulging in the ability to take a meal together. The room is filled with the soft, far-storm grumble of accents that are slowly becoming more familiar to me. Some are new, though, and I try to turn my ear toward them without appearing that I am eavesdropping.

"American accents," Pip says, knowing me and my body language well enough to guess what has caught my interest. "Not deep south, so I'd guess maybe mid-coast? And that one is pure Texas."

I turn my head the other way.

"Indian, I think, but I'm not sure," Pip offers. "Possibly not. And that's Chinese."

"That I knew. It is like *wai po* when she attempts English," I say.

"Yes."

"Why is your mother's accent not as noticeable?"

"She trained herself out of it. And I grew up here."

"Of course." I smile at the gift Pip has offered me—a room full of people to catalog and learn about—and sit back as the waitress pours us glasses of water. She inquires over beverages, and Pip requests ginger ale (which has no alcohol, despite its name), and I ask for whatever red wine they have the most of. Then I sit forward, ignoring the menu for a moment, and say: "This is a gathering of geeks. But beyond that, I know nothing of why we're here."

"It's a surprise," Pip says.

I twist my mouth into a bit of a frown.

"I know you're not keen on surprises, *bao bei*, but trust me on this one?"

"Of course." The wine arrives, and I take a sip to cover my dissatisfaction. It mingles unpleasantly with my tiredness and the stresses of the day, the "too much new."

We order our meals (such a variety of choices!) and almost immediately, the woman from the bus approaches our table.

"Hi again," she says.

"Hi," Pip replies, ever polite.

"My friend wanted to see Forsyth," the woman explains, gesturing to a man hovering behind her shoulder. "He didn't believe me when I said I'd seen the best Forsyth Turn ever on the bus."

I startle so hard that the wine glass nearly topples. I manage to catch myself quickly and put it down on the table. Pip rises, but I wave her back. There is only a small red spot on my trousers, and I reach for the table salt quickly to absorb it.

"Sorry," the woman bleats.

"No, all is well," I say. "But may I ask, how did you know who I am?"

The woman grins. "The Turn-russet? The accent? You're really good. The scar, though . . ."

I raise my fingers to the thin puff of white that runs across my cheekbone. It is nothing so as horrific as the scars that Bootknife left on Pip, but it is a daily reminder of that villain's hand in our lives.

"Bootknife," I murmur. "We dueled when he tried to steal the Shadow's Mask."

The woman claps her hands and squeals in delight. "Of course! That's really smart! I love fanon back story! Listen, can my friend get a picture with you? Real quick, I know you're eating."

Pip sits back, hands folded over her generous stomach like a smiling Buddha statue, amused.

"I do not know why, but very well," I acquiesce. Something is beginning to wriggle at the back of my mind, a puzzle squirming into existence, its disparate pieces beginning to coalesce. I do not know what picture these pieces will make, but it is early, yet.

I stand, and the young man hovering behind the woman comes forward. He slings an awkward arm over my shoulder and smiles at the camera. I fold my hands in front of me, loathe to touch someone I have not even been introduced to, and smile as well.

The photo flash attracts the attention of others, and quickly, there is a small crowd of cameras popping at me.

"Camera tribbles!" Pip laughs, and I plaster an expression of desperate pleasantness on my face as person after person asks me to stand with them for a picture. Only, I cannot understand *why*.

Comprehension slides abruptly closer the moment a pair of young women dressed in foam armor and Sheil-purple robes sidle up to take a photo with me. They are attempting to imitate my brother and his lover, as far as

I can tell. One girl wears a long flaxen wig, and the other has contact lenses in to make her eyes the same dark sapphire shade as Bevel's.

Understanding strikes like lightning.

These people do not *know* I am Forsyth Turn. They think I am like them, a fan who is *approximating* Forsyth Turn by looking and speaking and dressing—albeit in clothing of the current fashion—like Forsyth Turn.

And then all rational thought flees because someone has their hand on my arse. Fingers squeeze, and I yelp, startled.

"Hey!" Pip snaps, surging to her feet with a speed that her pregnancy defies. "Hands off, kid."

The young woman dressed as Kintyre grins wickedly, shrugs in half-hearted apology, and waggles her dyed eyebrows at me. Ugh, my brother's seduction face, and it is being aimed at *me*. My stomach rolls over entirely, and the wine burns at the back of my throat.

"No," I say. "Stop that."

"What?" the woman asks, falsely nonchalant. "I'm Kintyre Turn; I can flirt with the pretty ones."

"If you are Kintyre, then I am your brother," I protest. "Please stop."

The young lady dressed as Bevel giggles. "Turncest is hot."

"Turn . . . what?"

"Fan fiction," Pip clarifies, pushing her way between the lecherous young ladies and me. The crowd of cameras, embarrassed by their fellow fans' behavior, has vanished. "Literary fantasies. And there's nothing wrong with it on paper, or on a screen," she says to me, and then turns her attention and her masterful scowl to the interlopers. "But when a human being's body is involved, you *ask*, and you don't *assume*."

"But it's my character. It's just cosplay—"the Kintyre protests, her breezy entitlement melting under the glare that Pip had cowed the Viceroy with.

"Costumes are not consent," Pip snaps. "And Cons are not spaces filled with people who exist solely to please you. Learn that, grow the hell up, or get out. I'm not going to call Con security, because you seem to genuinely not understand that what you've done is not only unwelcome but completely inappropriate, but so help me if I catch you using your costume as an excuse to violate other people again. I will have the Stormtroopers on your ass *so fast*."

The girl's eyes go wide, and her friend tugs her away. They flee the restaurant to a smattering of applause aimed at Pip. She waves to her adoring audience and turns back to me.

"You okay?"

"I'm okay," I say. "A lesser man might be humiliated by his wife riding to his rescue, but all I can think is how attractive you are when you are defending my honor. And what's yours."

"Fuck," my wife sighs as she sits, but grins, as I hoped she would. "Did she pinch you hard?"

"There may be a bruise," I admit. "It's possible you will have to kiss it better."

Pip snorts into her ginger ale.

After dinner, we take a stroll through the hall of vendors to help settle our digestion, and my nerves. Pip likes the stretch, and moans, as she always does, about missing her morning runs. She has threatened to strap the infant to her back and take it running with her once it is old enough, and I, having seen how her speed saved our quest and lives more than once while on our adventure, have no reason to dissuade her.

Now that I know what I am seeing, I catch sight of a great many folks masquerading as people from my world. There are others, of course, from films and television programs that Pip has shared with me, but there is by far a greater number of "Turnies." It is both flattering and disconcerting, and, in some cases, when the costumer particularly resembles someone I know and love, vertigo-inducing. Pip wraps her hand around my elbow and steers me through the crowd when my knees lock up, or my breath is punched from my chest.

I am very quickly becoming overwhelmed perusing the costumes.

"Are you okay?"

"I'm coping." I say it with the most sincere tone I am able to conjure, but it must not be very convincing. My whole body feels strung as tight as a longbow string, and I can barely open my mouth enough to force the words between my teeth, the way my jaw clenches.

Pip narrows her brown eyes at me and puffs out her cheeks. "Right, no, it's okay. Let's go back to the room."

"Yes, thank you." I sigh in relief, and just like that, it seems the string is cut.

We take a shortcut through something called "Artist's Alley," and I am determined to simply keep my head down and save the gallery of creations for tomorrow, when I am better able to appreciate the talent on display. I cannot help but come to a halt, however, when I catch sight of a particularly well-painted scene of Kintyre and Bevel with their mouths locked. With a shaking hand, I reach out and lift the piece of paper—the print—from the table and show it to Pip.

"It's good," she concedes, her own tone filled with a little awe. "Looks exactly like them."

"From where did you model their faces?" I ask the artist, a young woman with a rainbow of hair, who stands behind the vendor's table looking pleased and eager.

"No one in particular," she says. "I mean, not actors or anything."

Nausea pulls at my stomach, my dinner sitting ill, but the woman's answer is honest. She is not lying, I know that well enough. The body language and tells that I was taught and which I employed as Shadow Hand have not changed between worlds. This woman merely used her imagination and did not cross between, as I did.

She is no Deal-Maker. And yet, everything around me is uncanny, horribly familiar, and awfully not at all like home. A burning pull rises up behind my eyes, and I pinch them shut, rub at them for a moment with my free hand, hoping to encourage the mounting tension to dissipate. When I open my eyes again, I tilt the picture in my hand so I can get a better look at the lip-lock. "It seems as if I really was the last one to know," I say, forced-jovial and trying to win back our light mood from dinner.

I swallow bile hard.

Pip chuckles, but it too is thin and sick-sounding. "Well, next to them," she says, and takes the portrait from my hand, placing it back on the table.

✍

"I wish them to stop *photographing* me!" I say as I close the door to our hotel room behind us. We have been stopped three times between the hall and our room, and I am not-so-slowly losing patience.

"Change your clothes," Pip says. "Did you bring anything that's not Turnish?"

I manage to assemble an outfit of dark denim trousers, and I am broad enough of shoulder but thin enough in the waist that one of Pip's t-shirts fits me fine. It is dark blue, and perhaps there is too much material at the stomach to be really flattering, but I manage to hide that by wrapping my purple silk scarf around my throat a few times and letting the ends dangle to the front.

I feel horrifically underdressed with no waistcoat, but when I look in the mirror, I am satisfied. Pip offers me a hairbrush, and I use it to push around the limp, gingery strands until they sit in a slightly different configuration. It feels strange on my head, and I have to consciously avoid brushing the part back to hide my high forehead.

"This is so frustrating," I say. "To avoid being thought that I am in a costume, I must put on what essentially amounts to a costume."

"Sorry," Pip says. "It never occurred to me that you might be recognized here."

"Why am I?" I ask. "Why are we here, Pip? What for?"

"It's a surprise," she starts again, but I have had enough.

The stresses of the day, compounded by my unhappiness over the handsy Kintyre woman and the lack of sleep have pushed me to the edge of my patience.

"No!" I snap, cutting her off. "Tell me!"

"Just . . . one hour, okay? Just give me one hour."

"*Now*, Pip."

"Forsyth, please."

"Now! Why are we *here*?" I shout. I don't want to be shouting at my wife. I don't want to be standing in this tiny room, in this extravagant inn that smells faintly of other people's feet, shouting at my wife. But I cannot seem to help myself.

"For this!" Pip says, and slams open the drawer of the bedside table. She pulls out a packet of papers and tosses them in the general direction of my head. A magazine flutters open, disrupting the trajectory of the papers, and they scatter around my feet and across my shoulders like the feathers of a fatally wounded bird.

Pip flops down onto the edge of the obscenely large bed and fumes, arms crossed under her breasts, resting on her belly, and the expression on her face makes it clear that she will say nothing else until I've picked up all the papers and examined them.

FantaCon 29, the glossy magazine's title says, and the image painted on the cover fills me with an abrupt shock of homesickness so acute that I actually feel my legs give out from under me. I am somehow sitting at the foot of the bed, on the floor, my back against the mattress and my legs akimbo.

It is Lysse. My Lysse. It is the view of the Chipping from the rise that marks the boundary between Law Manor and the Turn estate. I know this view well, for this is the very route Dauntless and I would take when we returned from one of Mrs. Pointe's excellent afternoon teas.

In the low of the land, I can see my trout pond, throwing up glittering reflections of the over-warm sunlight. A fairy hovers in a sunbeam there, a rainbow glitter that will surely be food for the fishes if she doesn't stop admiring her own reflection quite soon. To the side is the small covey forest, and yes, a small dash of red against the canvas marks my fox and her kits, slinking from shadow to shadow, making their way to the low stone wall that separates my gardens from my tenant's fields. The wheat beyond the wall is high, just starting to turn brown with an oncoming autumn. The forest's rich verdigris is dappled with a few flecks of red and orange. The rolling hills are green and grand, and they lead the eye to the centerpiece of the painting—Turn Hall.

The stones are red, bedecked in the green ivy that Father had hated but that I had allowed to run rampant across the sills and stones, softening the harsh scowl of the dark house after his death. The path up to the back door—for it is toward the rear of the house we are look-ing—is wide and clear. Cook's wooden garden shoes are small, light brown specks on the doorstep, and a pair of Turn-russet curtains are hanging out of the window of my second-floor bedroom, fluttering in the painted breeze.

And central to this beautiful, painfully accurate vision of my home are two men on horses, their backs to me as they make their weary way to the Hall. One is blond, broad of shoulder and thigh, wearing a Sheil-pur-ple jerkin and Foesmiter on his hip. The other is smaller, shorter and slimmer but no less muscular, with short sandy hair and an eager air. He is dressed in a short-robe of Dom-amethyst.

My brother Kintyre and his lover, Bevel.

But they are not lovers here, not in this picture. Not yet. This is early. They are neither of them wearing the colors they adopted when they finally admitted their af-fection for one another, and I can see the glitter of the Blade that Never Fails in its holster at the small of my brother's back.

A man clad in black, with a silver mask, waits upon the heroes' arrival in the shadows at the lee of the house, and I know that this Shadow Hand is Lewko Pointe the Elder, and not me. He wears Smoke on his right hip, and I wore the sword on my left.

Without my knowing it, my hand touches my left leg, palm against the raised texture of my denim trousers, fingers splayed and searching for the sharp leather edge of my holster—and failing to find it.

I wear no sword in Pip's world. It is illegal, she says, to wear any sharpened blade in public.

"Syth?" Pip says softly, and I turn my cheek into the hand she has laid on my head, petting through my hair and down to my neck.

"I'm okay," I croak. "I just . . . I'm okay."

"You're a terrible liar." She heaves herself to her feet and fetches a tiny bottle of water out of the very small fridge. The pricing guide on the door of the unit declares that the bottle is extremely expensive for water. Everything in this hotel room is hilariously disproportionate, and I stifle the frenetic giggle that threatens to burst across my tongue.

I crack the cap on the bottle and sip slowly, washing the hysteria back down into my gullet. Pip sits on the edge of the bed again and pets my hair.

"You'll make it fall out more," I grumble, and she laughs, just like I hoped she would.

"It's a beautiful painting," I whisper, running the fingers of my free hand over the glossy curve of the herb garden under the kitchen window. "Can we get a copy? A big one? I want to hang it in our condo."

"Sure," Pip says, sounding surprised. "If you want."

"Why wouldn't I want to? It's my *home*," I say.

"I just thought that you might . . . not want the reminder."

I chew on that for a moment. "It would not make me regret my decision, if that is what you fear," I hazard. Pip blows out a breath, and I realize I was right, that I have hit perhaps a little closer to the center of the target than she expected. "And I should like our child to know Turn Hall, even if it is only from a painting. It would be his inheritance if we were there, as Kintyre and Bevel cannot procreate."

"They could adopt," Pip points out. "And it might be a she, you know."

I turn my head and kiss the swell of her belly. "Of course. *Her* inheritance."

Pip runs her hands across her middle, into my hair, and back out again, over and over, soothing. "I think we can get posters of the calendar art. They did a great series of landscapes like this. We could have them printed on canvas, put them up in your office?"

"In the living room," I amend. "Where everyone can see."

"Okay."

We sit like that for a long while, the three of us, quiet and softly happy. And then I ask the question that has been nagging at me: "What is FantaCon 29?"

Pip sighs and retrieves the magazine from where I set it down on the bed beside her leg. She flips through until she finds a particular page, and then folds back the cover and hands it to me:

GUEST OF HONOR—ELGAR REED
"THE TALES OF KINTYRE TURN"

Underneath, there is a picture of the man, and I cannot contain my gasp of shock. A low twisting of horror curls through my guts. All of my hard earned ease shatters. There is a brief biography of the man, and a list of his published works, and then a schedule of where he will be and when to allow, I assume, his fans to mob him.

"Wh-why are we h-here, Pi-Pi-Pip?" I ask, and the chill of horror in my voice is so predominant that I jerk away from our child, fearful of freezing him or her with my breath.

"I thought, maybe, you might want to meet him."

"*Why?*" I explode, surging to my feet, borne on a wave of such sudden and incandescent fury that I shock both of us. But I cannot rein it back. "Wh-why do you th-think I would ever want to meet such a selfish, h-h-horrible man!"

Pip draws back from me, hands over her stomach as if to cover the child's ears, her eyes wide with surprise. "Horrible?" she echoes.

"He m-made the Viceroy. He thought up *Bootknife*!"

Pip flinches again, gets that look in her eyes that sometimes appears when she remembers that there are scars on her back and where they came from. Like she is looking at something that the rest of us can never see, and that is right over my shoulder. I resist the urge to whirl about to check, wringing the magazine between my hands as if it was Bootknife's neck instead.

"All writers create villains, Syth," Pip says, but her voice is small and shaky. "They have to."

"And the Drebbin Dragon? And the sylph at the Salt Crystal Caverns? The Library Lion? All the suffering of the creatures of the world simply because they are not human? All the poverty, the wars, the starving small children in the Chippings run by resentful, neglectful lordlings? What of *that*?"

"I . . . I wasn't looking for an existential battle here, *bao bei*," Pip protests.

"Then what *were* you looking for?" I snap. "What is the *point* of this?"

"Closure, maybe?" Pip suggests, but her expression is drawn and wary now. Not of me, never of me; she has nothing to fear from me. But perhaps she fears what my temper will drive me to think, or say, or do. In truth, I'm not certain how I will next react either.

My mind is a white rush of rage and fear, and I can feel my heart thundering against my larynx. I swallow hard, and it tastes of bile and anger and cowardice.

"I thought you'd like a chance to talk to him. To look at him?"

"If I wanted that, I could have looked him up on the internet! I didn't on *purpose*, and I'm glad I didn't," I shout, snapping my finger with absolute violence against the pages of the magazine. The sharp pop makes Pip startle, her eyes going wide. "All I see when I look at him is my F-F-*Father*!"

Pip's gaze swings down to the magazine, disbelieving, *stunned*. The photo is in grays instead of color, so I cannot determine the shade of his hair or his beard, but his jowls and the puffy bags under his eyes are identical, as is the bullish expression in his gaze. The shape of his eyebrows matches my own, and his nose is Kintyre's.

Elgar Reed and I are very clearly family.

"Really?" Pip breathes, lips pursed with academic curiosity. "The resemblance is that—"

"Do n-*not* turn this into *yet another* intellectual puzz-zzle for you to p-p-pick at!" I snap, and she clicks her mouth shut, swallowing the rest of whatever it is she was going to say.

"Sorry," she says instead.

I want to shout more, so instead, I put down the magazine, go into the washroom, and splash cold water on my face until my breathing has returned to normal and the urge to vomit has passed.

When I come out, collar damp but my ire cooled, Pip is lying on her side on the bed, face buried in the pillow. I feel a pang of guilt for yelling at her, and for ruining her surprise. My feelings on the man should not negate the hard work Pip clearly did to arrange this for me.

She didn't know that I wouldn't want it.

I crawl up onto the bed behind her, careful of my shoes, and curl myself around her back, my arm over her swollen belly, and kiss the little leaf. She shudders and makes a sound that takes me a moment to identify as a sob. I lift my other arm from under my own head and brush her hair off her cheek. Pip has been crying.

I crane up, kiss her cheek and taste salt water.

"Thank you," I say.

"For pissing you off?"

"For arranging this surprise for me."

"But you don't want to meet him."

"You didn't know that."

"I should have asked," she says, miserable.

"That is quite against the spirit of a surprise," I remind her. "Oh, no, please, don't cry more."

She hiccups. "I'm not upset, it's just . . . stupid hormones."

"I think you are upset," I say gently. "I ruined it. And you expected me to be happy."

She flops over onto her back, trapping my leg underneath her hips. I kiss her nose.

"I will gird myself and meet him," I say. "In fact, I think it better that I am forewarned. I do not think I would have been able to contain my shock and disdain if I'd met him in person without warning."

"Does he really look like your father?"

"Nearly identical."

"That's creepy as hell."

"Hmm," I agree.

"If you still want to meet him, I have to clean up my face." Pip sighs. "Help me up."

I do, and when she waddles to the bathroom, I retrieve the magazine and inspect Reed's scheduled appearances. "There is nothing here," I say. "He is nowhere this evening where we *can* meet him."

Pip dries her face on a towel and meets my eyes in the mirror.

"You've secured us a private audience," I say, and it's not a question. Pip nods anyway and begins to repair her eye makeup.

I sit down hard on the foot of the bed.

"We don't have to go if you don't want," Pip says. "I can cancel."

"No," I say, and reach out to grasp her hand. My grip must be tight, because she winces slightly. "No. I can do it. I can do it if you're with me."

✍

My palms are damp as I lift the pint glass of beer, and I feel a cursory flit of fear that it will end up on the floor before I can deliver it to the table. The waitress takes pity on me when I stretch a desperate smile into the corner of my mouth, and pulls out a rubber-matted tray. I let her take the other two drinks as well—a pint of apple juice and my own glass of wine.

I am too overcome with nerves to even point out where we are sitting. Pip saves me the trouble, raising her hand and waving to the waitress, then pointing to the low round table between the three bucket chairs she has pulled together for us. I take my time carefully placing my credit card back into its spot in my wallet, then tuck that into the back pocket of my jeans. It still feels odd to have my posterior so exposed, but the way Pip licks her lips and slides her fingers into the belt loops when we walk side by side is a generous compensation for my humility. I follow the waitress, letting her cut a swath through the crowded lounge and following in her wake like a rowboat, eyes on my feet rather than on the man who has just now joined our table.

Pip has not risen to meet him, allowing him to bend down to shake her hand. But she is well beyond the ability to stand or sit comfortably and unaided anymore.

He is just settling into his seat, reaching out to shake Pip's hand and undoing the button of his very well-worn blazer with the other. The man himself is twice my age, portly without being fat, and sort of carelessly dressed—wrinkled and comfortable, as I have found to be the result of all plane travel, no matter how carefully I pack my case—though the blazer is quality, if not new. His hair is limp from travel, and of a style that clearly means he hasn't had the time to get it cut recently and is quite due. It is brown, shot through with white, and with a slight ginger sheen that makes it almost the exact same shade as my own.

I repress the shudder that comes of that comparison.

His unmemorable eyes are on the waitress and the approaching beverages, rather than the man who is following them, for which I am thankful. It gives me a moment to study him and to gird myself for our meeting.

He is relaxed, confident; he knows the people around him recognize him, know who he is, and his body language is projecting welcome. I wonder how long it will be before we are interrupted by autograph seekers.

"Thanks for going up to the bar, *bao bei*," Pip says to me as the waitress hands her the apple juice, and I smile involuntarily, recalling that first night when she had tried scrumpy. And what had happened next. Ducking my head and concentrating very hard on *not blushing*, I drop into my own seat as the waitress places the beer and wine down on the table.

The newcomer flips lank brown hair out of his face and picks up the beer—the brand Pip's research proved he prefers—and raises it to us. "Cheers," he says, still mostly to Pip, and we duly toast. "So, Lucy, can I call you Lucy? How did the dissertation go? I was really happy to get your letter about it. Imagine, someone doing a PhD on *The Tales of Kintyre Turn*!"

Pip dodges both the question and the heavy-handed invitation for praise. "I'm happy you had the time to meet me, around all of this." She gestures at the hotel lounge full of science fiction and fantasy authors and their entourages, all just-arrived for the convention.

"Oh, well, you know," he says. "Who am I to turn down a pretty girl when she offers to buy me a beer?"

Pip flashes him one of those beautiful, blindingly sweet smiles that means she'd rather be breaking his nose with her fist than talking to him. Something warm and wonderful flips over in my tummy when I realize that I can tell the difference now, that I can parse what that expression means. Pip hates to be called a "girl." And Pip is feeling *defensive* on my behalf.

She is ready to cut this short and have us leave the moment I grow uncomfortable, and I love her, oh, how I love her.

And, yes, I can definitely see from where Kintyre inherited it. It is a very good thing I had been warned about his behavior in advance by reading Pip's thesis, else I might be disappointed. And equally lucky that Pip has told me that not everyone of his profession behaves as he does. Many she had met were far more grateful for their luck, for the support of those whose money went toward their royalties, who were just happy to be able to create worlds and make a living on it with no arrogance present. A good thing, too, or I might have been completely put off of her world altogether.

Our guest takes a sip of his beer, not even acknowledging me, and continues to—I can only call it as it is—*leer* at Pip. Of course, I find her beautiful like this—I would find her beautiful no matter how she looked—but there's something indecent about leering at a woman eight-and-a-half-months pregnant like she's some sort of . . . pork chop.

"And the dissertation?" he pushes.

"Top marks," she replies, unable to sidestep the topic, as she had hoped she might. "The oral defense was a bit of a bitch. That's what happens when your paper's on something that every geek on the internet has an opinion about, and you make the defense public."

"Stupid questions?" He grimaces in sympathy. "Or the kind where they point out every mistake you made in the minutia of things that nobody but they were keeping track of?"

Pip's smile gets wider and less genuine, and I grin into my own glass, amused by how poorly our guest is able to read her facial expressions and body language.

"Oh, no, none of that," Pip says. "None of the stereotypical nerd rage stuff. It was a really great group, all really smart, and, you know, together. Just, it went on for*ever*. It was only two hours, but when your whole degree is on the line . . ."

"Yeah, but my fans—" our guest begins.

"Are not automatically all losers for being fantasy geeks," I cut in, just to see him splutter. I quite like this colloquialism—*loser*. It encompasses so much, is a lovely shorthand for how I felt my whole childhood. And perhaps I am feeling vindictive. "And many of them, in fact, are very well adjusted, intelligent, and eloquent young people like Pip. Lucy. You mustn't speak of them so, not when they admire you so completely."

It is not fair to take out my hatred of my father on Elgar Reed, to push my own discomfort and anger upon him, but I cannot help it. I want to see him *squirm*. I want him to account for himself, for what he created, for what he did. Which is also not fair, because he did not think he was beating up a real little boy, or verbally abusing a real woman. He was just writing a story.

I want to see him suffer for something he didn't know he'd done. And for a brief flash of a moment, I suddenly understand why the Viceroy hated Reed so much, why he resented him enough to try to find a way into this world and kill him. The man in front of me is personally responsible for every single moment of suffering I have ever endured, and I want to give it back to him tenfold.

But then, I must pause. Because he is also responsible for every moment of joy. Were it not for Elgar Reed, I would not have Pip, nor our child.

I am not grateful to my creator. But I can be forgiving. I can *try*.

Reed turns his face to me, expression frozen between shock and insult, and really looks at me for the first time. At first, his glare is dismissive, but then it seems to catch like warm toffee on my features, the way I dangle my glass of wine between my fingers, my wrist on my knee, the scar on my cheek. And I am not even wearing russet.

"What's that accent?" he asks, his words suddenly tight and small, his expression a war between disbelief and hope and horror, each chasing the other back and forth like children at play upon his face.

"My own," I reply, laying it on thicker, just for the fun of it. "Everyone in Lysse Chipping shares it."

"Ah, right, sorry," Pip says, with a grin that says she is anything but. "How remiss of me. Allow me to introduce my husband. This is—"

"Forsyth Turn," the man chokes out, eyes bugging outward. "I'd know you anywhere. I *do* know you. You're Forsyth Turn. But you can't be . . . !"

"I a-assure you, I c-can, and I a-a-am," I say softly, wishing that my nervousness at this confession would vanish and allow the sentence to come out more smoothly.

He rises unsteadily to his feet, clearly torn between running away and staying to hear more, mouth working, but no sound coming out. He shoots a look around the room, as if to confirm that he is still in the correct reality and that it hasn't imploded or lost gravity or turned purple.

"You stuttered," he whispers. "Oh my god, you *stuttered.*"

"A-as I of-of-often do-o when I-I'm ner-nervous o-or sur-surprised," I say, forcing the sentence out, no longer ashamed by the impediment but still annoyed at the way it delays my speech, the way it forces my words to flow at a slower pace than my mind. "A-as we-ell you kno-know."

"But I never wrote that in! It was in my character notes, but I *never* . . . what's the name of your horse?" he asks quickly, hands spasming as if he has no idea what to do with them—grab a pen, or grab his beer, or grab me.

"Dau-dauntless," I answer, willing to take his test.

"Your mother's name?"

"Al-Alis."

"The Shadow Hand before you?"

"Lewko Pointe, whose gran-grandson is named for h-him, inc-inciden-dentaly."

He gasps, loud and full of amazement.

Pip reaches out and puts a possessive, comforting hand on my knee. It is still slightly chilly from her recent grip on the cider glass, and the disparity in temperature sends goose bumps running up my spine.

"He's the real thing," she says.

"You're not just a really good cosplayer," he says, and it is part denial and part hope, I think. "God, you . . . there's things I never put in the books. Things that got cut by my editor . . . but you have it all right. You . . . you're *you*."

"P-Please, do sit, Mr. Reed," I say softly, reaching out to lay a gentle hand on his wrist. He jolts his arm back, startled by my touch, perhaps even a bit scared, and then surges back and wraps my own hand between both of his. Pip leans back out of our way, giving us our moment. Giving us this.

"You're real," he whimpers, all his swaggering self-importance deflated.

"I am real," I agree. "Sit. P-please."

He falls into his chair like a toy dropped by a child, mouth an open cavern of disbelief, legs akimbo. He does not release my hand.

"It's a pl-pleasure to meet you, Mr. Reed," I say softly. It isn't a lie, not now. Because I can see that this scares him as much as it scares me.

We can be frightened together.

Reed releases me to scrub both of his hands through his hair. "Who. *How?*"

I smile, take a sip of wine to wet my throat, and lay a hand on his calf. It feels like closing a circle.

"Let me tell you a story," I say.

Acknowledgements

Once again, massive thanks go first and foremost to Stephanie Lalonde. She named pretty much everyone in this novel; I kept texting her inane directions like, "Now I need a name for the protagonist! He's a spy-master, and he's a nice guy, but he's eccentric! Go!" It is the mark of a good friend that she met each text with what I envisioned was a smiling sigh and answered.

Writers make stories, but editors make novels. To that end, I have to thank my beta readers: Devon Taylor-Black, Liana Kerzner, Jason Meyer, Ashley Kung, Ruthanne Reid, Brienne E. Wright, Kimbr, Leah Petersen, Alex James, and Sunny Hope.

I repeatedly called this novel my "love letter to the Strong Female Characters in my life," and I need to thank them all for teaching me not only what it means to have a voice of one's own in geekdom, where women are quite often shouted down, but to also defend my right to speak with it. And so, a big thanks to: Devon and the Scarborough Museum Youth Team, Liana K., Ruby Pixel, Brandy Dawly, Dr. Jennifer Brayton, Kenickie Street, Random Nexus, Sunny Hope, Adrienne Kress, and Lesley Livingston. There are also awesome men in my life who are strong characters and who also deserve celebration: Alex James (and The Monster), Jason Leaver, Mark Askwith, Teddy Wilson, and Ajay Fry (no relation).

The Toronto nerd community is fantastic, and I have to make a point of thanking everyone who has supported me for doing so, including but not limited to the members of the Toronto Steampunk Society, the Toronto Nerd Mafia, Nerds with Guitars, the cast, producers, hosts, crew and overall wizards behind the scenes at the SPACE Channel, and the organizers and volunteers of Ad Astra, Polaris, TCon, FanExpo, GenreCon, SO Sci-fi, FutureCon, Geek Trivia, Nerd Nite, Star Trek Day, and every other fandom-celebrating events in the area.

To my Aunt Brenda, who loves my work more than anyone I know, and who lets me hide in her bunkhouse every summer to compose another new inanity whilst drinking all her tea.

To my agent, Laurie McLean, who—dear gods—is a bigger fangirl than I could ever be, and with a marketing background to boot. I love her to bits. Her "I love it!" flail is so adorable it should be illegal. Laurie, I'm so very glad that I'm not the "one who got away" anymore.

Thank you to Kisa, Ashley, and Summer of REUTS Publications, who have made this whole process painless and fun. I'm still flattered beyond belief that you ran up to my agent and said, "That book you were talking about! We want it!" I cannot imagine more wonderful, entertaining, kind, and effervescent women. I am lucky beyond measure to have such fantastically feminist fangirls working on my feminist fan book.

As ever, a big thank you to my parents, who are so supportive it's sometimes insane, and to my two big little brothers, who never quite know how to take their little big sister's flights of fancy, but whom I hope are proud of me and what I've accomplished anyway.

Lastly—most importantly and most profoundly—I must thank the brave, honest, intelligent people who have published the struggles with harassment and misogyny both in real life and at SF/F events, in SF/F literature, and in the writing community. I especially must thank The Mary Sue, Jim C. Hines, and Seannen McGuire for their blog posts on the topics. Your words affected me deeply, and any time I needed to remember why Pip says the things she says, why she needs to say the things she says, I would read the words of people who believe that SF/F can involve fantasy realms and futures where people of all races, creeds, genders, sexual orientations, and cultures can be represented and included—respectfully—and think, "This is how I can do my part to affect change." This book wouldn't exist if it wasn't for your books, your blog posts, your articles, your cries for equality, inclusion, and diversity. Thank you.

About the Author.

J.M. is a voice actor, SF/F author, professionally trained music theatre performer, not-so-trained but nonetheless enthusiastic screenwriter and webseries-ist, and a fanthropologist and pop culture scholar. She's appeared in podcasts, documentaries, radio programs, and on television to discuss all things geeky through the lens of academia. J.M. lives near Toronto, loves tea, scarves, and Doctor Who (all of which may or may not be related), and her epic dream is to one day sing a duet with John Barrowman.

Her debut novel Triptych was nominated for two Lambda Literary Awards, nominated for the CBC Bookie Award, was named one of Publishers Weekly's Best Books of 2011, was on The Advocate's Best Overlooked Books of 2011 list, received an honorable mention at the London Book Festival in Science Fiction, and won the San Francisco Book Festival for Science Fiction.

www.jmfrey.net | @scifrey

CPSIA information can be obtained
at www.ICGtesting.com
Printed in the USA
BVHW032139090819
555487BV00005B/477/P